#00
DITTMAR

THE PROSPECTOR'S SECRET –

Treasures of the Pimeria Alta

Book I

A Novel by

Paul Hathaway

H-5 Publications Nogales, Arizona

This edition was prepared for printing by
Ghost River Images
5350 East Fourth Street
Tucson, Arizona 85711
www.ghostriverimages.com

Cover illustration by Mark Dittmar

ISBN 978-0-9840669-0-2

Library of Congress Control Number: 2009910955

Printed in the United States of America
Second Printing: June, 2010
10 9 8 7 6 5 4 3 2

Table of Contents

Acknowledgements:

The author thanks family members and friends like international traveler Sigrid Maitrejean for their comments. Mark Dittmar did the "old prospector" pencil art work on the cover. Also, the author extends a special thanks to Michael and Tama White, who edited the manuscript and put it in final form for printing.

Author's Note

This book is a novel and work of fiction. Its settings are in England and North America during the mid and late 1800s.

Dedication

This book is dedicated to my older brother Gilbert Harrison Hathaway (1937-1958), who died as a result of a tragic accident on the family ranch in Southern Arizona.

Chapter 1

Harshaw

It was December 1, 1887. The weather had been pleasant during the fall months in the Patagonia Mountains near the Mexican border, but now I cast a wary eye skyward at the darkening clouds blowing in from the west as I rode my mule, Bartholomew, along the steep mountain trails. I had an anxious and unsettled feeling in my gut, also a strong hankering for a drink.

The day had dawned fine for my monthly trip to the small mining town of Harshaw, even with the cold winter storm moving in. But shortly after we left camp and started our climb on the steep ancient Spanish trail out of the *La Escondida* Basin, my dog Cuca scampered ahead and picked a fight with a pack of *chulos* (coatimundis). By the time Bartholomew and I caught up with her, the damage had been done. She was waiting by the trail, bleeding profusely. I could see the last three chulos of the pack rushing through the oak and manzanita brush to escape.

Cuca should have known better, because two months earlier she had been cut up by the razor sharp teeth of a single chulo, thinking she could easily dominate the comical looking, raccoon-like creature. Luckily, that time I had been close enough to fire a shot and frighten away the chulo before he butchered my poor dog.

This incident soured my mood and delayed my ride to Harshaw by almost an hour. I tried to comfort my dog and stop the bleeding, but to no avail. I even thought of humanely putting her down because of her wounds, but before I could act, she died. Cursing the chulos, I buried Cuca in the only soft dirt I could find in a steep mountain ravine. After piling a few heavy rocks on her grave so other wild animals wouldn't dig her up, I climbed back on my mule and was again on my way.

Bartholomew was getting old, but was doing the best he could. Mr. Peck said the jack mule was 14, but I thought 20 was more like it. Bartholomew couldn't lope very fast, but he was strong, could trot along at a good clip all day, and had an easy gait. Anyway, I had liked to talk to him and Cuca as we traveled along. This helped me to sort out my thoughts and ideas. Bartholomew would respond with an occasional flick of his long ears. He was a good old mule and a friend, but losing Cuca to the chulos bothered me. I hoped it wasn't a bad omen of things to come.

I had bought my mule along with my saddle and gear from Mr. Peck in Nogales in August, just after getting off the train from Mexico. Mr. Peck owned a local livery stable and said he would give me a better deal for the old mule and gear if I also took the dog. The two animals were inseparable friends and he didn't have the heart to split them up.

Mr. Peck, a talkative gent, had gone on to explain that he had bought Bartholomew from an old Jewish trader out of Prescott. He said that the old fellow came into town on the mule, accompanied by the dog and leading some pack burros loaded with trading goods. After selling Peck his animals, the old trader took his wares into Mexico on the train, hoping to again multiply his lucre.

Mr. Peck jokingly said he didn't know who was worth more–the mule or the dog. However, for two gold double eagles ($40) he would sell me both, along with a well-used Mexican saddle with gear–and even throw in a burro. That way I would get a good deal and he could sleep at night. I laughed and bought the critters, saddle and the gear. My free burro died a week later.

During my ride up the steep trail toward the Guajolote Flat, I went

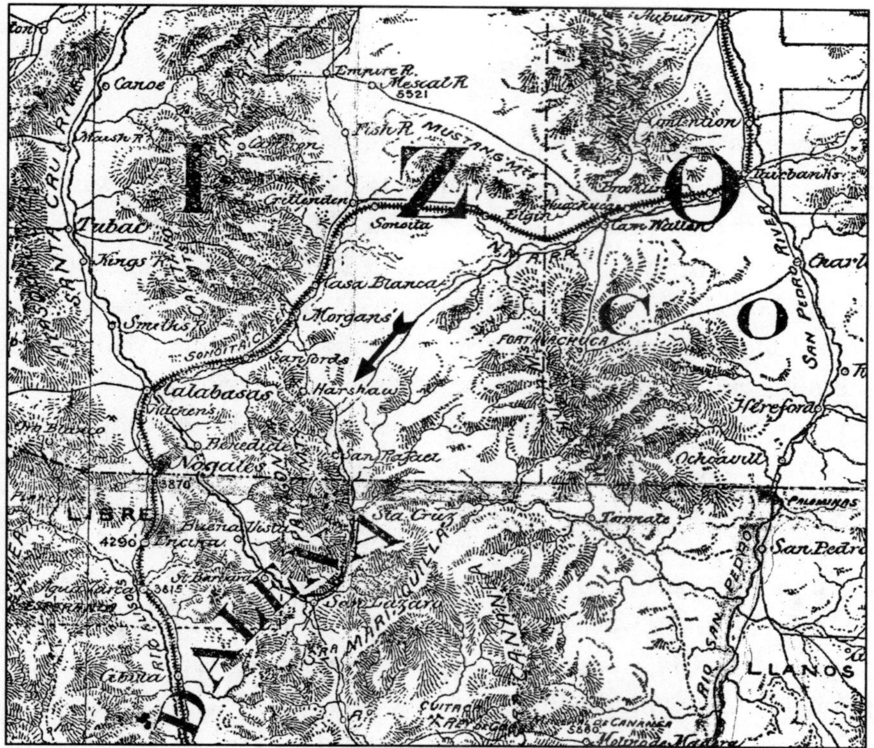

Figure 1 Map of Harshaw in 1887

over the important things I needed to do in Harshaw. First, I must get to Mr. Watkins' Assay Office in time to sell my modest *monthly workings of gold dust* and then go to Molly's Café for flapjacks. I needed to check my mail at Mr. Farrell's store too. And, oh yes, I needed to buy a few camping supplies to last me until Christmas when I would be returning to town.

But who was I kidding? Having a thorn in the flesh–a penchant for alcohol–the thing I wanted *most* in Harshaw was a drink! I had been fighting to control my problem for years, and camping in these mountains alone for the last few months had made things worse.

I liked most of the people in Harshaw, but no surprise; there were also some I didn't. The feelings were mutual. In the short time I'd been in the Arizona Territory, I had earned the reputation for being that crazy old prospector from the mountains. I was sure Deputy Kruger now headed the list of people who disliked me. But a bigger problem was that Kruger also wanted me dead.

As Bartholomew and I finally reached Guajolote Flat, the storm blowing in was dropping temperatures fast. The cold weather was even bothering a tough old fart like me. I figured I had been living in Mexico too long and my body had not yet adjusted to the colder winters north of the border. I couldn't wait to get to Molly's warm café and have some sourdough flapjacks flooded with warm ocotillo honey and a big, steaming cup of black coffee. That, and some good conversation would go a long ways toward soothing my innards and soul after camping out alone for over three weeks.

I liked Molly, but thought that if she would lose about sixty pounds and twenty years, she would look a lot better. Anyway, she had always been nice to me since I had arrived in these parts. She'd even helped me a couple times when I fell off the wagon and made a fool of myself. Woe unto *Jenkins,* whose name I used to represent my alcohol problem. Would I ever get him under control?

Trotting along on my mule, I also looked forward to getting out of the cold and having a nice evening meal with my new friends, Preacher Sullivan and Padre de la Riva. But I still had a little missionary work to do before I could settle in for the evening. The last time I'd been in town, I did not leave on the best of terms.

Bartholomew stumbled looking back for his missing friend Cuca and broke my concentration. With a curse, I jerked him up. Afterwards, trying to forget about my dog and the cold, I toted up the interesting and awkward situations I had experienced in the bustling little mining town of Harshaw since coming into the territory the summer before.

After arriving in Nogales by train in August *to prospect* in the Patagonia Mountains, I learned that Harshaw would be a handy place to sell the *gold from my pannings* and buy supplies. A few Apaches were still wandering about, but they were quickly being gathered up by the U.S. Cavalry and put on military–controlled reservations, so I figured they should not be a big problem.

After setting up my prospecting camp in the Patagonia Mountains, I'd ridden Bartholomew to Harshaw for the first time in late August to check the place out and buy my next supply of camping and prospecting goods. I liked the quaint, territorial mining town tucked away in the high desert mountains and decided to use it as my supply base. It would have worked out fine if I could have controlled my drinking, but I couldn't.

The second time I visited Harshaw was in mid September. It was then I first met Preacher Sullivan when he came to my aid outside the Durazno Bar. In fact, he probably saved my life. Because of my stupidity and drunkenness, I'd been beat up and robbed by three low-life, *gringo* drifters who were passing through town.

I had spent the afternoon playing cards and drinking too much beer at the bar. Most of the time I played poker with several local men, then, the last hour, one of the *gringos* joined our game. After winning a little money and talking too much, I quit. Tucking my little poker stake money and winnings into my saddlebags, I threw them over my shoulder and left to go eat supper at Molly's.

It was after sundown when I walked outside and was heading around the side of the building to the privy when they jumped me. There were three of them. One of the drifters struck a glancing blow to my head with his pistol barrel, then stepped back as I fell. This gave room in the narrow dark alleyway for one of his smelly cohorts to come at me with a knife.

I stumbled forward, falling onto a pile of lumber stacked along the side of the building. Grabbing a handy board, I came up swinging and managed to knock the knife from the second fellow's hand. But then all three pulled me down and ripped away my saddlebags. The saddlebags contained my .44 caliber Colt revolver, a small bag of gold dust and a few dollars in silver coins–including my sparse poker winnings.

Luckily for me, the big Irish preacher man happened to be walking home from his leather shop when he heard the commotion in the alley. He shouted, disrupting the thieves, and then knocked one of them down with a powerful blow to the bastard's shoulder. The three startled thieves quickly gathered themselves, ran down the street with my saddlebags and slipped behind another building, where a fourth buddy was holding their horses. They all jumped on their critters and tore the hell out of town, then up a nearby canyon into the mountains. Deputy Sheriff Kruger was out of town in Sonora at the time, so they got away.

What impressed me was what Preacher Sullivan did afterwards. First he helped me up and dusted me off. I was not thinking straight, from the blow on the head and from the several quarts of beer I had consumed. And I had pissed in my pants from the excitement and effort of trying to keep from getting killed by my attackers.

After Sullivan saw that I was not seriously injured and was just a drunken old prospector who had been robbed and wet his pants, he could have left me and gone on home, but he didn't. In the aftermath of my traumatic experience I nervously mumbled something about wanting to go to Molly's for supper, but now I had no money.

The big preacher quietly looked me over for a moment and then took me back to his leather shop, which was a few buildings down from the bar. Inside his small shop, he poured water from a blue porcelain pitcher into a wash basin sitting on the entrance table. He then tossed me a cloth and told me to wipe the blood off my face. As I did so, he handed me a cup of warm leftover coffee from the grimy pot on his wood stove.

Next, the big Irishman produced a metal tanning tub and a bar of homemade lye and tallow soap. After pouring a half-bucket of water into the tub, the preacher told me to take off my wet trousers and wash them. Silently, I complied. I also took off and washed out my undergarment. Finally I poured another bucket of water the Preacher had left for me into the tub and carefully rinsed off the rest of my body. It was the closest thing I'd had to a bath for several months, except for cleaning up in the canyon water near my camp.

I sobered up very quickly as I stood there naked, taking care of my humiliating situation and sipping the half cup of sludge from the coffee pot. The September weather was warm, but I was shaking. Thankfully the preacher man had disappeared into the adjacent workshop and busied himself finishing a harness repair job while waiting for me.

After wringing out my shorts and trousers as best I could, I put my shorts back on and temporarily hung my trousers over a chair in the little, two-roomed leather shop. Then the preacher stuck his head through the door and held up a pair of ladies' white buckskin shotgun chaps with fancy fringe trimming on the legs and offered them to me.

"Maybe you could wear these with your green shorts," he said with a grin. "I made them for one of Cano's working girls over at his bar."

I had to respond to his joke.

"I might get more attention if I wore your fancy chaps without my green shorts," I responded dryly.

The big man nearly doubled over with a loud husky laugh. I knew at that moment that this man was going to be my friend.

Still humbled from my experience, I went with the preacher man over to Molly's Café in my wet pants and we had supper. Nobody except Molly noticed my wet pants and the preacher paid for the meal. That night Molly let me sleep on a cot on the back porch of her café. The next morning she let me pay for breakfast by cutting some stove wood and doing some other chores. She was a kind lady and left me with a little honor.

Preacher Sullivan paid for my monthly stash of supplies then I headed back into the Patagonia Mountains. As far as this hardworking, poor preacher man knew, he would never see me again. But he did.

Between September and November of '86, I made more visits to Harshaw to sell my meager gold workings and buy supplies. Drinking continued to complicate my life. It complicated my life and earned me a reputation.

During my October trip to Harshaw, I met Deputy Sherriff Kruger for the first time. He would never forget me, nor me him.

Sheriff Johnson of Pima County had an office in town manned by his deputy, a big German hooligan by the name of Bruno K. Kruger. Kruger liked to go by the name Big Buck. Most of the time Kruger was gone, theoretically chasing bad guys and bandits–which he seldom caught. His excuse was that they had disappeared into Sonora and were beyond his legal jurisdiction. The local word had it Kruger was spending time with some Mexican girls in a Santa Cruz bar.

Deputy Kruger was a political hack of county Sheriff Johnson in Tucson. The locals put up with the worthless bully because his mere appearance was intimidating to most troublemakers, and he was usually smart enough to only put the bite on strangers. I became one of his victims when I rode into town, because he viewed me as a harmless newcomer.

This episode had occurred during the first week in October when I rode into town on my mule, with my dog following, to buy supplies, have a few drinks and visit. The next day, I woke up in Deputy Kruger's jail. It was a stone storage room on the edge of the town with a high hole in the front wall for light and air. The Spartan room had no furniture, a dirt floor and a folding canvas cot. There was also a shit bucket in the corner of the room that smelled like it had never been cleaned.

After waking up in Deputy Kruger's dark, smelly jail, I took stock of my situation and what must have happened. My boots were missing in which I had hidden two gold double eagle coins. I was steaming, because I suspected Kruger had robbed me. Luckily, I had left my Sharps rifle, new saddlebags containing some money and my new Colt revolver with Pete Ashburn at his livery stable.

After Kruger let me out of his jail that morning, I demanded my money. He laughed and said he didn't know what I was talking about. He handed me back my boots, but the coins were gone. He said he put a drunken Mexican in the room with me during the night. If I was missing anything, the Mexican took it. I knew there was no Mexican and that the whole thing was a lie.

Sick and still fuming, I quietly picked up my rifle and saddlebags from Ashburn's livery stable, then ate and bought my monthly supplies. By early afternoon I had Bartholomew packed and was ready to leave town. I asked around, inquiring where I could find Deputy Kruger and heard he was at the Nugget Saloon playing poker.

I tied Bartholomew to the hitching post outside the Nugget Saloon and walked inside with my Sharps rifle in hand and Peacemaker (revolver) tucked into my belt. Sure enough, Kruger was there playing poker, laughing and drinking with two other men.

His smiled quickly turned to alarm when I approached him with my rifle in hand. He spilled his beer while attempting to stand and go for his pistol. I sprang in front of him, my cocked Sharps 50 rifle barrel shoved into his face. He froze in an awkward position half standing and holding the handle of his still-holstered pistol.

"One more move, you thieving bastard, and I will splatter your little brain all over that wall," I growled.

The shocked patrons and bartender scrambled for safety, then watched.

"Last night you stole $40 from me," I said coldly. "The *next* time you try that, I'll kill you."

Hearing these words, Kruger struggled to stand and pull out his pistol. I fired my mammoth rifle near the side of his head. The flash and roar was deafening inside the dark saloon.

The concussion knocked him down onto all fours and his Colt pistol bounced onto the wood floor in front of him. My ears were ringing and gun smoke filled the room. As I had intended, my rifle bullet had come within a few inches of Kruger's head before it knocked a fist-sized hole through the side wall of the saloon.

Through the gun smoke, I could see Kruger sitting on his fat *arse* on the barroom floor frantically slapping his head and face and screaming curses at me as he tried to put out the smoldering fire in his curly, dark hair and beard.

I jerked out my Peacemaker and leveled it at him while setting my rifle down on the card table. I grabbed up and dumped a half-filled beer mug on the smoking Deputy's head, then shouted at him.

"If this happens again, I'll kill you, you fat bastard!"

The wet bully stopped cursing and just sat there on the barroom floor, glaring at me and holding his ear. He looked like a singed bear that had jumped into the river to escape a forest fire. He smelled like burnt hair and beer.

Thinking that this was not a place to linger, I grabbed my rifle and Kruger's small poker stake of about $12 to compensate for my stolen gold double eagles and left the bar. Outside, I puckered when I saw that Bartholomew was missing. The mule had broken one of his reins and was waiting with Cuca for me about 100 feet down the street, near some other horses tied in front of the hardware store. Undoubtedly my mule had broken away from the hitching post when he heard the loud gun blast inside the saloon.

Snatching the piece of the broken rein from the hitching post, I trotted over to Bartholomew. After quickly splicing the broken rein together with a knot, I mounted the trusty old critter and got the hell out of there. For the next half hour, I kept looking over my shoulder as I loped Bartholomew toward my camp in the mountains. Twice I had to stop to tie down the bouncing supplies that were tied in a gunnysack on the back of my saddle. I expected the angry German deputy or one of his friends to retaliate for my actions, but no one came. *At least not then.*

And now I was headed back to Harshaw along that same dark, mountain trail. The cold wind was kicking up worse than ever and dark storm clouds were gathering. It looked like snow. The dead oak leaves blowing across the trail made a quiet, rustling noise. The sound of Bartholomew's hooves striking the earth were soothing and hypnotic. He occasionally looked back for his missing friend as we moved along.

I ignored it, wondering if I could spend the night in Pete Ashburn's livery stable barn because of my last bad experience. Ashburn had kicked me out in November after I came in drunk and damned near burned his place down. At the time, I didn't accept responsibility for the accident even though it was totally my fault. As usual, I was drunk when the incident occurred.

After a serious night of drinking at John Brickwood's Durazno Bar, I'd stumbled into the barn storage room where Ashburn gave me permission to sleep. I vaguely remembered fumbling around to light the glass kerosene lamp. After finally getting it lit, I set the lamp on the box next to the metal cot where I was going to sleep. Somehow, I knocked over the lamp and it broke on the hard dirt floor.

The burning kerosene puddle and the flames flowed under the storage room's thin wood walls into a manger half filled with dry grass hay. The hay caught fire. If it was not for Shorty Welch, a cowboy also trying to sleep in the storage room that night, the whole place would have gone up in flames.

The next morning, Ashburn had some sharp words for me and told me not to come back. My pathetic defense was "that fellow Jenkins took over again." I also suggested he keep a metal lantern in the barn. I carefully explained that a metal lantern would not break–not even if a horse kicked it or if it accidentally fell over. In addition, I tried to explain that I was not feeling well when I went to bed, so the incident was not totally my fault.

The day after the little row with Ashburn, I managed to stay sober and bought my next month's supply of goods for my remote camp in the Patagonia Mountains. I also bought Pete Ashburn a replacement metal kerosene lantern for his barn. To make further amends, I gave Molly the money for a meal for Pete and his wife, Nancy, and asked Molly to include one of her famous peach pies.

On my way out of town, I dropped the lantern off at Ashburn's livery stables. Pete was out, so I'd left the new metal lantern along with an apologetic note on the old table he used as his desk.

I sure hoped that had mended the rift, because tonight, with the storm coming in, I would need a dry place to sleep. As Bartholomew and I continued on, I could smell wisps of sweet juniper smoke from a fire burning inside the nearby Martinez stone house. Juan Martinez was a miner who worked for Jack Chapman at the Humboldt Mine. He had a nice little Yaqui Indian wife and eight children, three of them big enough to work. I envied Martinez, because at least he had a wife and family to come home to at night.

Martinez reminded me of another *faux pas* I had made after having a few drinks under my belt. During one of my many visits to the Durazno Bar, I told Chapman to sell his mining claim while he was still getting a little color. Mr. Chapman had been quietly minding his own business, sitting at a table reading a newspaper and drinking a beer, when I came up to him and offered my sage advice.

Chapman disagreed with me. Chapman said he was sure the lead deposit vein with a trace of silver in it would expand and its silver content would increase. I volunteered that, from my experience, and looking at the mineral outcroppings on the surrounding hillsides, the vein Chapman was following would run out. I again told Chapman to sell his claim before his minerals ran out and use the money to do something else. Chapman didn't appreciate my advice. A bit insulted, I told him my advice was free, so he shouldn't complain.

I leaned over Bartholomew's shoulder. "Idiot," I said, referring to myself.

The things I did when I was drinking.

I finally dropped down from the higher mountain trails onto the Mowry Road. Harshaw was now less than two miles away but the cold weather made my ride seem longer. As Bartholomew trotted along at a good clip, I stood up in the stirrups of my Mexican saddle and twisted to relieve my aching back. A troubled conscience and the damned chulos killing my dog Cuca had caused me to sit tense in the saddle during most of the ride over the mountains.

Bartholomew's pace increased slightly and his ears pointed forward. The jack mule sensed we were getting close to town. We passed two Mexican woodcutters leading six heavily-loaded pack burros carrying dry oak wood for the Hermosa Company's stamp mill steam engine in Harshaw. Several dogs barked behind the trees in the distance.

I knew I must get help to continue with my plan. However, because of my drinking and sometimes bizarre behavior, this might be hard to do. This bothered me, but I also considered it could have its advantages. My unpredictable behavior might allow me to make my next moves without too much notice. I weighed the option of using my two clergyman friends to help me. Was it possible to have two men of the cloth succumb to greed? We would see.

Approaching Harshaw, I could smell more chimney smoke coming from several adobe houses at the mouth of Hermosa Canyon. It had to be after four o'clock, with the cold storm clouds thickening. I could almost taste Molly's flapjacks.

Smiling ruefully to myself, I thought how my perspectives had changed over the years. It was hard to imagine how such a small pleasure as having flapjacks at Molly's could now seem so important to me. I also shivered to think how little it would take for me to bypass Molly's flapjacks and go directly to the Durazno or Cano's Bar for the evening. I could get some basic grub for supper at either bar, but more importantly, a drink. It was destructive thinking and I would not surrender to it or Jenkins–at least not tonight.

Harshaw was a bustling little mining town of about 800 souls in the high desert mountains of the Arizona Territory near the Mexican border. It had three bars, two hardware stores, an assay office, school, livery stable, leather shop and a doctor's office. It also had a weekly newspaper. The doctor's office was usually open late in morning, when the old Civil War gent was sober. To my surprise I had found I knew the old doctor. He was a character from my past life.

The town had a water tank filled by a small spring which ran part of the year and was located further up the Hermosa Canyon. When the spring dried up, the Company would pump water into the town water tank from one of three hand-dug wells at the edge of Hermosa Canyon above the town privies. However, two of the three wells were below the stamp mill where they used quicksilver (mercury) to recover the gold from the ore.

On earlier visits I told Mr. Best and several other merchants in town they should always use the spring or upper well to avoid any chance of having quicksilver in their water. He chuckled at my suggestion, saying perhaps the heavy quicksilver in the water was the reason they were gaining the additional weight they didn't need. After their sick joke and indifferent attitude toward a suggestion coming from me, the crazy old prospector, I kept my mouth shut and quietly filled my canteens from the upper well after the spring water gave out.

However, the water situation still bothered me, because I remembered my father telling me a story about a mountain village in South America. There the Spaniards mysteriously killed off about a third of a small mining village's women and children over the course of several years before they realized they had contaminated their water with mercury. It would be a shame if the same thing happened here with these folks and their families. Later I explained the situation to my friends–Molly,

Sullivan and de la Riva. I hoped they could do something about it.

Anyway, I had several things to do that cold December afternoon in Harshaw–and the most important one was to *stay out of the bars*. While riding up the main street on Bartholomew, I saw Pete Ashburn step out of Robert Best's hardware store. He was walking away from me, toward his livery stable on the other side of the canyon.

The storm clouds had darkened and the cold wind was kicking up dust in the street. A few big rain drops began spotting the dry ground as I called out to Ashburn with my hoarse gravelly voice.

"Good afternoon, Mr. Ashburn. Care to join me at Molly's for supper?"

Surprised, Pete Ashburn turned and looked down the street at me, partially covering his eyes to block the blowing dust. I was surprised at my own anxiety as I awaited his answer.

"Good afternoon, *Mr. McAllister*. No thank you, I had a late lunch at home. Maybe tomorrow–if your offer still stands," Pete Ashburn responded, smiling.

"Sure it does. I'm hoping to be in town several days. Can I work something out with you to corral Bartholomew and maybe use one of the extra cots in your barn? And I'm sorry about what happened last time. It won't happen again," I said.

"Sure Jack, if you promise not to burn the place down. You gave me a pretty good scare," he responded and then continued. "After you unsaddle, put Bartholomew in the pen with the other mules. If you don't mind, throw them about four good pitches of hay. That will save me some time. I've got to get back and finish work at my butcher shop."

"Thanks, I will. And Pete–can I leave my Sharps rifle in your office again? I don't like carrying it around town."

"Sure, Jack. When will you be leaving?"

"Probably Sunday afternoon or Monday morning, depending on the weather. Will I see you and the Mrs. at Preacher Sullivan's service on Sunday?" I asked, trying to further ease the tensions between Ashburn and me.

"Yes, you know he's not having his services in Cano's Bar anymore?

He's having it over at the schoolhouse. My wife and some of the other ladies complained about going to church in a bar," Pete Ashburn said, laughing.

"Good! I didn't like it either–the temptation is too great. For me, it's like being a cook in a pastry shop! Have you ever seen a *thin* cook? I don't think the preacher would appreciate it if I broke open a bottle for a quick snort during his sermon."

Pete shook his head with a pained laugh, then casually waved as he turned and continued through the blowing dust toward his livery stable. His unspoken message was that things had improved between us, but he still didn't totally trust me.

It was late Thursday afternoon and I still had to get over to Watkins' Assay Office before he closed. I needed to sell him my color and get some spending money for supplies and the weekend.

I trotted Bartholomew over to the livery stables, following Pete, and quickly pulled off my saddle after removing my rifle and saddlebags. After scratching Bartholomew's big ears, I put him in the pen with the three other mules. They were happy to see him, but Bartholomew seemed uncomfortable without his friend Cuca.

By that time Pete had gone, so I left my rifle in his unlocked office and tossed the mules their grass hay. Then I left for Watkins' Assay Office with my pistol and small leather pouch of gold dust tucked safely inside my saddlebags.

On the way to Watkins' office, a young Mexican boy came scampering down the opposite side of the street with his dog. I called out in Spanish and asked if he wanted to earn a dime. Thrilled, the little fellow ran over to me. After learning his name was Beto Jimenez, I asked the boy to take a message to Padre Lorenzo de la Riva and Preacher Michael Sullivan, inviting them to have supper with me at Molly's.

I had the boy repeat my instructions in Spanish, then English, which he did perfectly. After grasping my outstretched coin, the little chap tore off to do his chore but stumbled, dropping his precious dime in the dusty street. After frantically scratching in the dirt for a couple of seconds, he recovered his coin and then disappeared down the street. I laughed and continued on towards Watkins' office.

Mr. Samuel Watkins was the closest thing Harshaw had to an enlightened soul. He was an educated man and a certified U.S. Government assayer. He also wrote articles for the town's only small weekly newspaper, *The Arizona Bullion*. The man was friendly, curious and also maintained tight control over the filing and recording of mining claims in the Harshaw Mining District. He was the type of man I normally would have enjoyed striking up a friendship with, but because of my prospecting situation in the Patagonia Mountains, I kept him at an arm's length.

Mr. Watkins' adobe office building was on the north side of the street in Hermosa Canyon, up from the livery stable. The upper side of the narrow canyon street was tightly packed with mostly wooden buildings with sweet smelling juniper smoke pumping out of their stovepipe chimneys. I thought the whole town could burn to the ground if any of the buildings caught fire and the wind was right. Then I figured, oh well, it was not my town or problem and I had already given too much unsolicited advice, so I walked on.

Mr. Watkins was alone inside his office. Wearing spectacles, he sat at his roll-top desk writing in a ledger. He looked up at me when I entered and smiled.

"Well if it's not *Mr. Jack McAllister*. How are you, Jack? Haven't seen you here abouts in a few weeks. Got some color for me?" he asked with a big smile.

"*Shore do,* Sam. It's got to do me for another month. The government raise the price of gold yet?" I asked jokingly.

"No, still \$20 per ounce. Any nuggets this time?"

"A few, but mainly dust. But it's good quality dust."

"Yes, Jack. Your color is always good. Not like some of the others. Some of them want the full price even if they have sand or pyrites mixed in with it. I can't afford to do that. Couldn't stay in business that way. My processing fee is still 10%, you know, Jack," Mr. Watkins commented.

"Fair enough, Sam. Fair enough."

He had two sets of gold weighing scales, one was his basic work scales which hung on an open stand on his work table and the other was a more precise Deiz counter balance scale he used for his U.S.

government-certified assaying work. He kept his better set of scales out of the dust under a beautiful wood-and-glass case on a separate work table. That evening he said he would use his good scales, since I was one of his best customers.

Amused, I watched the man start the same little ritual he used each time he bought a customer's gold. Basically, his ritual was to describe each step of the process he used to weigh and calculate the value of his customer's gold. It was a way to visit and at the same time keep track of the transaction.

I gave him the small leather pouch containing my color. He poured the gold dust and small nuggets into the weighing tray and placed it back on the scales, describing his every move. He guessed at the weight of my gold, selected the appropriate brass counter weights and set them on the scales to see if it would balance. He was close, but a little over the weight of my gold, which disappointed me.

After trading around some counter balancing weights, he made his final adjustments with the counter balance caliper on his scales. All of this was not new to me because as a student at the University of Edinburgh, I was paid to run the mining engineering laboratory for a semester, all those years ago. That lab had many more sophisticated weighing and testing instruments in it. I smiled and said nothing.

I noted that Mr. Watkins' measuring technique was basically sound and honest, except for two things. He rounded the transaction off in his favor, and he used $20 instead of $20.67 per troy ounce as the official price of gold in the U.S. But he left no dust in the measuring tray by playing the oily tray game, or used filed counter balance weights nor forget to properly balance the scales. Instead of rounding things off and judging the price, I thought he should charge a little extra for his services and call it even. But it was not a big deal, and I liked the man because he provided a valuable service in this remote territorial town.

"That measurement should be good to the nearest penny, and I will give it to you if there's a question," Sam said, still smiling.

"Good enough for me," I conceded.

After his little ritual of careful and professional measurements, Sam scratched some numbers on a torn piece of scratch paper with a pencil.

He smiled then looked over his wire rim glasses at me.

"Hmmm.... Looks like a little over three troy ounces, Jack. That would be $68 dollars less 10%, or er.... It comes to exactly $61.20. Sound right to you?"

"Sam, it sounds fine. Would you like to join us at Molly's for flapjacks?" I asked.

Sam laughed as he opened the door of his heavy steel safe.

"Jack, flapjacks sound good to me for breakfast. If I see you down at Molly's tomorrow morning, I will buy you flapjacks."

Sam took a metal box with folding wire handles from his open safe. Inside the box were stacks of paper money, each tied with old string, and rows of $10 and $20 gold coins.

He asked me how I wanted the money–paper or coins? I chose coins because I always liked the look and feel of gold. He then carefully removed six 10-dollar eagle gold coins and meticulously slid the other coins over to fill the vacant slot. He then pulled out a silver dollar and two dimes from a canvas bag in the bottom of the box and handed me the money. I thanked him.

"Sam, I would be careful in this town with your money. I would hate to have some *desperado* come in here and try to rob you," I told him.

"Thanks for the concern, Jack. I sometimes worry about it myself. Two years ago I convinced Sheriff Johnson to set up his local office just up the street. His new deputy, Ty Sorrells, is there a lot of the time, especially if he has clients in the rock house. It makes me feel a lot better," Sam explained.

"New deputy?"

Then with a smile Sam Watkins responded. "Yes. Didn't you hear? Big Buck Kruger left for Tucson over two weeks ago. He had trouble with a bleeding eardrum and couldn't walk straight after some crazy drunk tried to take off his head with a shotgun. He said he had headaches and was dizzy all the time, so he went to Tucson. Sorrells was hired as his replacement. I was glad to see him go. I think Sorrells will be a lot better."

Surprised, I thought, *it wasn't a shotgun, it was a Sharps 50 rifle. And it wasn't just a crazy drunk, it was me. And if I had wanted to take off his head, I would have done it!*

I responded by just saying. "Oh."

Then I changed the subject and again cautioned him.

"Well anyway, be careful. There are a lot of tough *hombres* around here."

Sam smiled, nodding as he poured my gold dust into a one-quart Kerr fruit jar half filled with other gold dust he had purchased. He handed me back my empty leather pouch after carefully tightening the lid on his jar.

Sam cleared his throat as he started to prepare my receipt. "*Hrummp*... Jack, it seems like you are consistently doing pretty good at your prospecting and panning. You even bring in some nuggets with your dust. Are you going to file a claim on your diggings? You know I can help you with that."

I knew this question would be posed by someone here in town, even though I had been careful not to raise suspicions. Sam was fishing and I was not going to bite or bait his line.

"No, Sam. In Mexico, I got pretty good at spotting small concentration points in canyon bottoms where I could pan. So far these mountains have been fair to me, but if I don't find some better color pretty soon, I'll be moving on to Colorado," I replied, lying and with a little smile on my face.

I changed the subject. "Sam, my offer is still good for supper. Want to join us?"

Looking disappointed at not getting the information he wanted from me, Sam smiled stiffly and shook his head as he shut and locked his safe, preparing to close his office for the evening.

"No, Jack. Thanks anyway."

After joking about who would buy flapjacks at Molly's in the morning, we shook hands and I departed.

It was almost dark and the cold rain began to fall in earnest as I walked down Harshaw's main street toward Molly's Café. Buttoning my coat and adjusting my hat, I quickened my step and took refuge from the rain under the porch roof of Mr. Best's closed store. It was across the street from Molly's Café, a good spot where I could see when Padre

Lorenzo or Preacher Mike arrived to meet me for dinner.

As the rain fell, I sat and quietly rolled out and lit a cigarette, all the while watching the evening's activities. Tired miners and mill workers began streaming down the road into Harshaw from the Hermosa Mine and the Company's ore stamp mill. The mill's steam whistle had blown about fifteen minutes earlier. The clanking and rock crunching noise of its heavy machinery was silent for the day. It brought back memories from long ago.

About half of the town's merchants kept their businesses open so they would not miss the evening trade from weary workmen. As darkness fell over the town, lights from candles and kerosene lamps began to appear throughout the little mining town. It reminded me of a Swiss alpine village Christmas card scene. All it lacked was snow–and we might have that by morning.

The miners hurrying by me in the rain still wore their muddy work boots and dirty canvas trousers held up with leather suspenders. They also wore heavy canvas jackets, soiled caps and battered hats. Some of the tired men joined their wives and children who excitedly waited for them under store-front porches. Immediately, the men relaxed and lit cigarettes as they laughed and talked to their excited families. It was a pleasant sight to watch.

The personality of the little mining town changed as darkness fell. It took on a happy ambiance as tired workers met their families to buy supplies at the local meat market and dry goods stores before heading home. Others headed to the bars for a drink and quick card game before going home.

With Big Buck Kruger gone, it was all I could do to keep from acquiescing to Jenkins and joining them, now that I had some money in my pocket. But I prevailed. Taking a long drag from my cigarette, I patiently waited for Mike Sullivan and Lorenzo de la Riva to meet me at Molly's Cafe.

Chapter 2

Molly, the Preacher Man and the Mysterious Padre

Sitting under the dark Best Hardware Store porch, I lit my second rolled cigarette, holding it for a moment while thinking about my predicament. This interesting country had been my temporary home since August, but that would soon change. The Spaniards had long called this land the *Pimeria Alta* or upper Pima Indian region.

But the times had changed. First the Spaniards took the land from the Pima Indians. Then the Apaches took effective control of the land away from the Spaniards and Mexicans. After wars and land purchases, the American cavalry were now permanently removing the Apaches as a threat to the settlers.

Padre Lorenzo de la Riva was a very well-educated and knowledgeable man and knew a lot about the history of this area. He told me the Pima Indians previously called these mountains the *Chihuahuitas.* Later the Spaniards and the Mexicans called them the Santa Cruz Mountains. Now most locals called them the Patagonia Mountains–named after Sylvester Mowry's old Spanish silver mine, *La Mina de Patagonia*. The clear message to me was this country was rapidly becoming tamed and settled, I could not wait much longer.

The cold rain fell harder and I began to shiver in my damp clothes. I was almost sorry I hadn't stayed another two days at my camp in *La*

Escondida Basin where I could wait out this storm in my snug old mine tunnel. At least I had made peace with Pete Ashburn and could sleep in his dry livery stable barn tonight. Perhaps I could borrow some extra blankets from Molly to keep my worn out, old body warm.

Finally I saw Padre de la Riva walking quickly up the street through the rain and shadows before ducking into Molly's café. I flicked my cigarette into the wet darkness, then crossed the street to join the Padre in Molly's brightly lit restaurant.

Inside, Padre Lorenzo de la Riva sat alone at a table, talking to Mr. and Mrs. Moreno and another couple at the next table. Mr. Moreno and his crew handled the hard rock drilling and blasting for some of the local mines.

Molly saw me enter as she came out of the kitchen carrying three plates of steaming steaks with potatoes and gravy. She gave me her usual big smile, greeting me loudly as I sat down.

"Good evening, Jack. I was wondering when you would get back into town. Flapjacks?" She said jokingly.

"Sure, but first let's see what my partners in crime want," I responded, happy at the attention Molly gave me before she disappeared back into the kitchen.

Preacher Michael Sullivan came through the door dripping wet and still wearing his leather work apron. The big man grinned then came over and greeted us. Sullivan spoke as he took off his wet hat, jacket and work apron, hanging them on the back of his chair before sitting.

"I'm sure hungry. I've been chopping wood for the last hour."

"I thought Farrell's men supplied your wood," I responded.

"Yes, they do. I bought four cords of oak from Farrell. He had his woodcutters drop it off for me in October. I had a pretty good woodpile before this cold spell hit, then gave most of the smaller stuff to Widow Sanders for her cook stove and to keep them warm. She and her little girl, Christy, are having it pretty rough. Some other people in our church are helping her too."

Padre Lorenzo leaned forward. "Who is she?"

"Her name is Doris, Dick Sanders' widow. Sanders is the man who started hauling ore to Crittenden for the mines in August and was killed in October."

"How did it happen?" I asked.

"On one of his trips, the back wheel on his ore wagon hit a rock and broke. The wagon fell on him when he tried to fix it. He was alone and they found him dead about an hour after it happened. They say he would have lived if someone had been there to help him. Apparently his mule team moved while he was trying to fix the wheel. He bled to death, trapped under the broken wheel and the wagon," the big preacher soberly explained.

"I thought the Mexicans did most of the mule skinning," I commented.

"Well, most of the hauling rigs and teams are owned by Americans, except Yourgules. He's a Greek. Most of them hire Mexicans as mule skinners and swampers to run their rigs. They have a lot of money tied up in their wagons and teams. They can't afford to lose a loaded wagon and trailer with their mule team on a slope because of an inexperienced driver." Sullivan tapped on the table thoughtfully, then continued as we waited for Molly.

"Yes, the best mule skinners are Mexicans. They are naturally better with the animals and always work in pairs. But there are several small haulers, like Sanders, who cut corners and work alone. Even so, the lone haulers usually hire temporary help, inexperienced boys and Mexicans when they have a heavy load. They make more money that way if they can get the ore moved to Crittenden in time for the train. But it's not safe, as Sanders sadly found out…," Sullivan hesitated.

"What are you saying, Sanders should have had help?" I asked.

"Certainly, he should have! What's bothering me is that I helped him twice when he first started hauling to Crittenden. And on the day he was killed, he asked me to help him again. But I had four broken sets of harnesses to repair by the next day, so I told him I couldn't go. If I had gone, he would be alive today. But I had to get those darned things repaired by the next day. I'm the only one around here who repairs those heavy harnesses, you know," the Preacher said remorsefully, still trying to justify his fateful decision.

Padre Lorenzo and I were silent for a few moments before I responded.

"Mike, you can't blame yourself for what happened. He should have *hired* someone else to help him."

The Padre agreed with my remark, then I changed the subject.

"I am familiar with how they haul ore in Mexico. They usually haul small loads of ore in two-wheeled carts pulled by oxen or burros. They also use pack trains of burros with a special wooden ore bucket or bags tied to each side of the pack saddle. Not very sophisticated, but it works," I commented. "I've seen a few of those big ore wagons and teams around here and they are impressive. Are they hard to work?" I asked.

The preacher seemed relieved to get past his moment of guilt and began explaining this part of the local mining business as Padre de la Riva and I listened.

"Well, it's pretty straightforward. If you are getting into the business, you start with a $600 heavy ore wagon–$850 if it has a small trailer. The best ore wagons are built in Colorado or back east. Then add another $600 for a good team of eight mules with a full set of harness riggings and you build from there. If you want to haul more ore, you get a full-sized wagon trailer and more mules. The largest haulers have ore wagons with two full sized trailers. These rigs can haul over 20 tons of ore on flat ground and use teams of 18 to 20 mules."

"The big rigs are very dangerous on our hilly, mountainous roads. They use the driver or muleskinner and two or sometimes three swampers or helpers to control the teams and work the brakes on dangerous slopes. The rigs are usually set up so the driver or skinner sits in the left seat of the lead wagon to work the brakes. This also gives him more room to work the long jerk lines and "black snake," a long driver's whip, to control the mules. The swampers ride the wagons on the flats if the mules are pulling steady, then walk the slopes to control the trailer brakes with ropes and keep the mule teams pulling evenly. It's quite a sight to watch a good mule skinning team working to get one of those huge wagons with their trailers up and down some of our dangerous roads."

"So what happens if they get into trouble on a slope?" I asked.

The big Irish man continued enthusiastically. "Well, if they haven't lost control of the situation, they lock the brakes and stop everything. They put logs or rocks under the wheels so the wagons don't roll or topple. Then they unhook the mule team and the trailer wagons from the master wagon and slowly recover by working each wagon and trailer individually by temporarily putting together a smaller team of mules. They move the wagons to a flat, safe place, then reassemble them. Sometimes they even unload the ore or freight from the wagons, if they think they might lose it."

The Padre and I stopped questioning the preacher about the fascinating local ore freighting business when a busy Molly charged over from tending other customers and poured us some hot, steaming coffee.

Sweating profusely, she commented with a wink and a smile. "Well, isn't this an interesting hand to draw to? I hope you *gentlemen* don't get into any religious arguments tonight and break up my little café."

"Don't worry about me, Molly. Catholics are well-mannered and civilized. Worry about those infidels," Padre de da Riva said, winking at Molly and pointing toward Sullivan and me.

"Anyway, I'm a hungry infidel," I responded. "Gentlemen, what's your pleasure?"

Molly cut in. "Jack, I know what you want. I have some fresh mountain honey that Francisco brought down from the Guajolote Flat last week for me. The good desert ocotillo honey is all gone. How about you gentlemen?"

I interrupted. "Gentlemen, it's my treat. I found *Maximilian's* treasure last week."

"Maximilian's treasure, huh? That sounds like a Porterhouse steak to me. Molly, that's what I'll have with plenty of potatoes and gravy," Preacher Sullivan said with a smile.

The padre spoke. "*Hombre Misterio*, our generous mystery man, I don't mean to be impolite, but eating decadent sweet food for supper is against my religion. The *Papa* (Pope) says it's the sure sign of a heretic, so I think I will have one of those steaks too. But instead of potatoes, give me frijoles and tortillas, if you have them."

We all laughed as Molly topped off our coffee cups and charged off toward the kitchen, where she had a cook and several other people busily working.

Preacher Michael looked me in the eye. "Jack, we haven't seen you in town for a few weeks. In fact it's been almost three weeks. It was November the 13th when you left here ...ah, not feeling too good."

"You mean *hung over*, don't you?" I asked.

"Well, you weren't feeling too good," the preacher responded, still trying to be tactful.

"So what is Mrs. Sanders going to do?" de la Riva interrupted, changing the subject again.

Sullivan answered, "Well, she is planning on going back home to Kansas in the spring. That's where she came from. She's been taking in washing to pay for their train tickets."

"How old is her little girl?" de la Riva asked.

"She's nine, and I understand she is the best little speller in the whole school. She's a smart little lady."

"Is your church helping her?" de la Riva inquired, apparently genuinely interested in Mrs. Sander's plight.

It was now black as coal outside, except for a few remaining lamplights in the buildings along main street. All tables in Molly's warm little cafe were filled as Preacher Michael Sullivan again responded.

"Yes, Padre, thanks for asking. Like most people around here, Dick Sanders had nothing and was working payday to payday. And he owed for his mules and the wagon. He was hoping to expand his little freight business to include merchants here in town and over at Washington Camp. Obviously, he didn't get very far with his dream."

I sat listening to the conversation between Sullivan and de la Riva as Molly brought over a tray and plopped down our plates filled with steaming food. We then focused on our meals as Molly returned with a refill of hot coffee, some warm tortillas and a big jar of fresh, warm honey with a few dead bees floating in it. She then handed me a knotted oak branch carved into a scoop for the honey. It all looked like *ambrosia* to me. I had been dreaming about eating these flapjacks for a month. The Preacher and Padre were delighted too.

Conversation temporarily stopped as we hungrily addressed our meals. A good percentage of the town's businessmen, with their wives, were enjoying supper in the small restaurant that cold December evening. Molly had a fancy glass kerosene lamp on each table, along with about a dozen large, red candles in holders with copper reflectors mounted to the walls. She also had some red and green ribbons hanging in the four windows and a crude handmade evergreen wreath with mistletoe above the door, giving the place a distinctly Christmas flavor.

After recently coming out of Mexico, I felt Molly's place had a friendly, American feel about it. The customers inside were getting their second wind, happily socializing while enjoying the hearty food. I enjoyed the camaraderie and conversation after my long lonely weeks of camping alone in the beautiful Patagonia Mountains.

But other things were on my mind, and time was not on my side. They say that with age comes wisdom. That may be true, but, pushing sixty, I was finding old age was not all it was cracked up to be. I thought they should add stomach problems, constipation and sleeplessness–not to mention the body and mind slowing down–to the wisdom thing. Adding my growing love for the bottle to this list gave me an additional challenge. I needed some trustworthy people to help me follow through with my plan.

The café door opened, letting in a cold gust of wind. With the cold wind came a wet and tired looking Dr. Dorsey Harrison wearing his old felt hat, overcoat and muffler. Inside, he slowly surveyed the room for an empty table. The old doctor looked ill and unsteady as he eyed the crowded room. Seeing no empty tables, he turned to leave.

Our table had an empty chair, so I invited the doctor to join us. He looked down at us disapprovingly as if we did not fit into his evening plans. Finally he nodded and sat down heavily in our extra chair.

This should be interesting, I thought. Dr. Dorsey Harrison and I had crossed paths years before during the Civil War, under strange circumstances. I didn't think he recognized me, since I was now old, skinny, with a heavy, unkempt beard and long, thinning gray hair.

Dorsey was the only practicing doctor in Harshaw, and I had seen him from a distance several times during the last few months. I was not sure I wanted to renew my acquaintance with him. We both had dramatically different lives back then. Besides, I wasn't anxious to open the door to conversations about my life since, in Mexico, especially with this man. Perhaps he would not recognize me. I would soon find out.

"Good evening, Doctor, my name is Jack McAllister. This is Padre Lorenzo de la Riva, and Reverend Michael Sullivan," I said in an attempt to be friendly.

"Good evening," Dr. Harrison said curtly looking like he was still scrutinizing us or not feeling well–perhaps both.

For the time being, I was sure the good doctor did not recognize me from years gone by. Molly came over and poured the doctor some coffee before taking his order. He leaned forward, stared at Molly's slate board menu on the wall and chose pot roast for supper. Preacher Sullivan had finished his steak and decided to join me in having flapjacks when I placed my second order with Molly. Laughing, the preacher man called it his dessert.

With the glum doctor present at our table, the conversation temporarily dried up. Feeling rakish, I decided to have a little fun badgering the grumpy old doctor.

"Doctor, Bartholomew and I got into town this afternoon. Coming off the mountain, we about froze our asses off. Is this normal weather for this time of the year?"

The doctor glanced at me, annoyed at being drawn into a conversation he really didn't want.

"Bartholomew?" He asked, obviously aggravated.

The padre continued to slowly enjoy his steak while the preacher waited for our next helping of flapjacks. Both listened, amused at where this conversation might be leading. Both knew me well enough to know I enjoyed stirring the pot a bit when I was sober, and more so when I had been drinking.

"Bartholomew–oh, he's a half-ass friend of mine," I replied, not explaining that my answer was a quite accurate description of a mule.

The doctor looked puzzled, then shook his head and said nothing. Instead, he took a sip of Molly's coffee after loading it with sugar.

Padre de la Riva changed the subject a third time when he saw the doctor was annoyed by my lame humor.

"Doctor, thank you for tending to the sick little Soto baby. I understand from her mother she is doing much better."

The Doctor glanced at him and nodded. "Are you going to pay for her medicine?"

At that moment, Molly arrived with our next batch of flapjacks and thankfully interrupted the uncomfortable conversation. The doctor looked at our flapjacks and again shook his head, saying nothing. Shortly afterwards, Molly brought the doctor his pot roast with her normal generous serving of mashed potatoes, gravy and biscuits. Several minutes later, after taking a few bites of his hot meal and having some more coffee, the old doctor seemed to cheer up.

"Gentlemen, I don't mean to be so antisocial. Thank you for letting me join you. I'm a little tired and don't feel so good this evening. This pot roast should do the trick. It's just what the doctor ordered," he joked, trying to lighten up the mood at our table.

As we ate, I again spoke, but this time trying not to annoy the good doctor.

"Doctor, I am relatively new to this country. I am staying in the mountains over in Soldier's Basin. I came out of Mexico in August, so I'm not used to cold weather. Is this weather normal? Do you get much snow here?"

The doctor looked at me intently as he took a bite of his pot roast then buttered his biscuit. I suspected something was stirring in his mind about me. He responded civilly.

"Well, Jack, I think we are all relative newcomers here. This town didn't even exist fifteen years ago. I came into the area a little over a year ago from California. This is only my second winter here, and it's cold for me. These gentlemen can probably answer your questions better than me."

Preacher Sullivan responded, "I've only been here for two years and, yes, it does get cold in December and January. We got about a foot of snow here in town last March the 10th."

The doctor was obviously feeling better with some food in his belly. He settled back into his chair then asked, "Padre, how about you? How long have you been in the area?"

"Well, I was born 41 years ago in the little pueblo of Santa Cruz,

70 kilometers south of here. My grandmother was a Pima Indian, so I guess my family has been here, oh, maybe 1000 years. My grandfather was Spanish, and they've only been in this area since 1711, about 177 years." The padre meticulously continued to eat small bites of steak and beans wrapped in pieces of tortilla.

I winked as the three of us *gringos* glanced at each other and smiled. There was no doubt about who was the old-timer here.

The doctor asked the padre another question which got a decidedly defensive and cool response. "Padre, how long have you been in the Church? Were you educated in Mexico?"

"Oh, about five years. I was educated in Spain, at the University of Cordova."

The padre offered no more details and Dr. Harrison didn't push it further. I was positive the mysterious Padre had a past he was not revealing. But he had helped me and was my friend.

My first dealings with him occurred several months earlier while having another episode with the bottle. I had stopped by Cano's bar for a drink after I had Bartholomew packed and was ready to leave town for my camp in the Patagonia Mountains. After a couple of drinks, I fell asleep! Several drifters began looking me over and also starting going through my things packed on Bartholomew, tied outside the bar.

Cano stopped the two thieving drifters and sent a boy down to fetch the padre. De la Riva came to the bar and, with some help, got me and Bartholomew to his one room adobe behind the Catholic Church. There he put me on a cot and let me sleep it off. He also unsaddled Bartholomew and had the boy take my mule to the livery stables. Early the next morning I left town, again embarrassed at my antics.

The happy chatter in Molly's little café increased as the patrons relaxed after enjoying their excellent meals. Nobody was in a hurry to leave and go out into the cold, wet December night, especially me. Molly kept the place toasty warm with her kitchen stove almost glowing and a fancy potbelly stove fired up in the dining area. An old, crippled Mexican fellow, Francisco, kept the hot fires stoked with split logs of oak wood.

We finished our meal and remained seated, drinking coffee. The doctor was becoming much more cordial and wanted to visit. Now I was sure he remembered me.

"Jack McAllister? Your voice is familiar. Seems like I've heard it somewhere in the past. Were you in the Civil War?" The doctor asked with a slight smirk on his face.

Of course, how could he forget? Twenty-four years had passed swiftly since those Civil War years which were indelibly etched in my mind. But he had almost as much to hide as I did.

I dismissed his question with a passive comment, so as to waylay further discussion. "Yes, Dr. Harrison. Perhaps we've met somewhere. Those were hectic times I would just as soon forget."

"Indeed!" The Doctor responded, his smile fading.

Now that Dr. Harrison remembered me, we both steered our conversations away from our past. However, I knew we would soon talk privately later about our war experiences. We had shared some extremely dangerous and interesting times, though, not always dancing to the same tune.

With a full belly, the doctor came alive, especially after he recognized me. Carrying the conversation at our table, he focused on Preacher Sullivan.

"Reverend Sullivan, not to be too inquisitive, but I thought most Irishmen were Catholics. You are not?"

Padre de la Riva cut in. "That's a good question. Where did you go astray?"

Sullivan chuckled. "Doctor, call me Mike. I have a hard time thinking I deserve the title Reverend, or Pastor, or even Preacher. Anyway, you are right. I was brought up in a Catholic home in a Pennsylvania coal mining town. It's a long story, but I consider myself a Christian, as does the Padre here. There are a few doctrinal issues we may not totally agree on, but we shouldn't let that knock the wheels off our wagon."

I probed further. "Well, Mike, it's cold outside, Molly has a big pot of hot coffee on the stove, and I'm not in a big hurry to go spend the night in Ashburn's barn. So please tell your story, if you don't mind,"

The gentle preacher man responded, "Gentlemen, I don't like to talk about myself. Why don't we talk about something more interesting?"

"No, no. Please tell us about how you became a preacher," the doctor pressed him earnestly.

The preacher, still embarrassed, began hesitantly. "Well, it is an interesting story…. To begin with, I'm not an educated man like you gentlemen. I only have a third grade education. And worse than that, I'm a reformed drunk. Once in a while I've been known to fall off the wagon. I'm lucky it hasn't happened to me here in Harshaw. It would be terrible for my few church members to see their preacher laying drunk in the alley behind Mr. Farrell's office."

The three of us glanced at each other, then I made a comment. "I'm impressed, Mike. You are several steps in front of me. I haven't reformed yet, and I don't know if I ever can."

"Jack, if I can, then anyone can. But it's hard. I'm going to have to deal with my problem every day of my life. Anyway, that's another story," Mike Sullivan explained.

After a few moments of silence Preacher Mike sighed, deciding to tell his story.

"My father was killed in a coal mine accident in Pennsylvania when I was a boy. We were a big family. There were eight children and I was the second from the youngest. I have a younger sister."

"I was eight when the mine accident killed my father and six other miners. There was a cave-in. It took three days for them to get the bodies out. Most of the miners were crushed so bad you couldn't recognize them. My dad was one of them," the big man explained, wiping a tear from his eye.

"You had older brothers and sisters?" I asked.

"Yes, I had four older brothers and two older sisters. Two of my oldest brothers were already working in other mines. One of my older sisters was married at the time," he replied.

"My dad insisted we kids go to school as long as we could, but most of us lost interest when we were old enough to work. After my father died, I did odd jobs around the little town, like sweeping out the school and a local bar on weekends. I was in my third year of school when I got a job in a local leather shop. I worked part-time and helped the man who owned the shop. He made saddles, reins, harnesses and did repair work–things like that. It didn't pay very much, but I felt pretty good when I gave my mother four dollars after my first two weeks of work. Thinking back on it, it probably didn't even pay for my food at home, but she was proud of me," Mike said, smiling at the memory.

"So what made you become a preacher?" Padre de la Riva asked curiously.

"Well, that's the most interesting part of the story. If I told you the whole story of my life, we would be here till breakfast," he said, chuckling now.

"My whole family, at least the boys and my dad were heavy drinkers. Good Irishmen, I guess. I started early too. When I would sweep out the bar on Saturday mornings, I would steal little drinks from any of the open beer kegs or bottles lying around. By the time I was 13, I was a good sized lad with a good sized taste for booze."

"At fourteen, I got a full-time job in the mine with the help of my older brother, Charles. I still worked part time for Mr. Weaver, the man with the leather shop. My mother wanted me to do something else, so I would not ruin my lungs. After a few years working there, I agreed with her, so I left the mines and Pennsylvania."

The big preacher rested his hands on the table, linking his thick fingers. "Well, Padre, you asked me how or why I became a preacher. I will tell you. I was an oiler and fireman–basically a stoker on the railroad–for ten years after I left the mines. I would shovel coal into the boiler furnace of a locomotive steam engine. It was hard work, but it paid well, and I got to travel around quite a bit. I liked the job. I got married during that time and we had two little girls and a boy. My family lived in Chicago, and I traveled out of there with my railroad job."

"On April 19, 1877, me and my engineer, Cliff Worthington, were on a run between Springfield and Kansas City. It was early in the morning and it had stormed during the night. It was foggy, we were behind schedule and the conductor was pushing him to make up time. Anyway, he was looking out into the fog in front of us as I shoveled coal into the firebox of the boiler. Then I heard him shout, '*Oh, shit! Another train!*'

"He grabbed the brake handle and hauled back on it, trying to stop the train while at the same time pulling on the whistle rope. I barely had time to stop shoveling and help him when we hit. I remember the impact and a lot of loud metal crashing, then crunching noises as the trains hit and went off the tracks. Then everything went blank." Mike Sullivan paused to take a sip of coffee.

He was silent for a few moments as we anxiously waited for the rest of the story.

"So, did the train wreck kill you?" I asked sarcastically.

"Well, that's an interesting question. Frankly, I'm not sure what happened right after the crash," the big preacher answered.

After a few moments of silence the padre said, "Tell us what you *think* happened."

Obviously a little emotional, Sullivan took a deep breath and continued.

"Well, gentlemen, I haven't told many people what happened next. And I hesitate to tell you, because you'll probably think I'm crazy. Maybe getting hit on the head made me go out of my mind. I don't know."

The three of us listening glanced at each other, then the doctor said, "No, Mike, I'm sure you weren't crazy. During the war I saw a lot of strange things happen to hurt men. Some of them died from simple injuries and, inexplicably, other survived under hellaciously bad odds. And many spoke of strange experiences."

Mike remained silent for a few more moments, looking down at his coffee cup, then continued with his story.

"Well, the next thing that happened changed my life. I can't explain it, other than to believe God had a hand in it." He hesitated again, as if about going on with the story.

The padre was hooked on Sullivan's story, just like the rest of us, and said, "Mike, go on. Tell us about your experience."

The big preacher carefully looked at each of us and then continued.

"I said I went blank. Well, I did, but when I woke up the first time, I was not in the middle of the smoking train wreck. I was walking down a trail in the mountains near our home in Pennsylvania. I was fully grown and wearing my only nice suit, but I was also barefooted. It was summertime. The flowers were blooming and the birds singing. The sounds and colors seemed exaggerated and beautiful. I seemed to know where I was going, and I could see a person waiting for me on the trail.

"As I approached the person, I could see it was my mother. The trail divided into two paths behind where she stood. I knew both my father and mother were dead, but I was not afraid. I was about to hug Mother and ask her about Father, but she held up her hand and said '*No, not yet, son!*' She then turned and looked at a man I had not noticed standing behind her on the second path."

Mike paused for a few moments then continued.

"It was as though I could communicate with the man without speaking. He knew my thoughts and I knew his. The man called me Michael and said I had a choice. He said my work was not finished, but I could end it here if I chose, or I could go back and do more. To end it, I could continue down the second path with my mother.

"I told the man I was far from a perfect person and I had few talents. I sensed he was telling me that so far my life had counted for little, but I had the opportunity to do more. I was embarrassed.

"I asked the man if I could take a look down the first path. He agreed, and said I could go to the first bend and no farther. I did. Then I came back and told him I would like to go back and try to make a difference. He smiled and said he would see me later. As I started to return, I looked and my mother was gone. I then awoke, for the second time."

Mike Sullivan took the last gulp of his coffee and stared down at his powerful and callused hands holding the cup. We waited for him to finish his fascinating story, but he said nothing.

Finally, the padre broke the silence. "Mike what did you see when you looked down the first path? Did you see the future?"

With reddened eyes, Mike looked up at the padre and nodded slightly, but said nothing.

Most of the people in the little café had finished their meals and were drinking coffee or hot chocolate. None of them heard the preacher's story except us.

Doctor Harrison asked the next question. "Mike, you said you then gained consciousness. Where were you when you woke up? Were you still in the train wreck?"

The preacher blinked several times, like he was coming out of a trance, and responded, "Well, Doctor, when I woke up the second time, I was looking at a pleasant, and rather large middle-aged lady with streaks of grey in her hair. She was trying to feed me warm noodle soup with a spoon, but apparently I was not cooperating, and most of it was spilling on my chest. It was hot! That's probably what woke me up.

"I learned I had been unconscious for two and a half days. My head felt like someone had taken a sledgehammer and whacked me with it. My ears were ringing. My left collarbone and four ribs were broken. In addition to some bad burns on my neck and back, my left wrist and left leg were also broken. For some reason, most of the damage was done on my left side. But the most serious injury was a puncture wound I received when my shovel broke during the wreck and a sharp splinter from it went into my lower belly. That was on my right side!"

"Mike, sounds like you were lucky to be alive. Was anybody killed in the wreck?" I asked.

Mike looked at me for a moment like I asked a dumb question, and it was. "Yes, there were 17 people killed in the accident. Both train engineers and the other fireman were killed. Both trains were carrying passengers and freight. The conductor and two passengers in our train were killed. The rest killed were passengers on the other train.

"I was not found until after dark on the night of the accident. They did not have the necessary railroad jacks to lift our heavy steam engine and look for Cliff and me during the daylight hours of the first day. They didn't hurry, because they thought we were both dead anyway. Our steam engine wound up on its side halfway down the hill from where we went off the tracks."

"I was buried in tools, spilled coal and dirt. The rescue workers walked right by me a number of times without seeing me. Cliff and the other train's engineer and fireman were thrown out of the locomotive cabs and were lying lower on the hill in the wreckage. When the steam engine boilers blew, the hot water rushed down the hill and cooked them. They never had a chance. Some people said I was lucky, but I know better."

The doctor, padre and I were quiet as the preacher, still with watery eyes, finished his story. He remained quiet for a few moments, then bowed his head and appeared to say a silent prayer. What happened next was also interesting. Preacher Mike started to quietly sing *Silent Night* in his deep baritone voice.

The people in the Molly's Café looked over at us from their tables, pleasantly surprised, then they all joined in, including Harrison, de la Riva and me. Molly came out of the kitchen to see what was happening. She then came over and put her hand on the preacher's shoulder and sang with us. When the singing ended, everyone applauded. The emotional preacher quietly got up from our table and disappeared into the cold December night. It was an appropriate finale to his story and the evening. People then began to leave the little restaurant.

After the padre agreed to meet me for breakfast at seven-thirty the next day, I borrowed a couple of blankets from Molly and started to walk toward Ashburn's livery stable and barn. The rain had turned to sleet and snow.

A lot of sad memories followed me as I traveled alone down the main street of Harshaw. Cano's bar was on the way and was still open. I stopped and stood outside the bar, aching for a drink. But then I remembered the preacher's story. No, if Sullivan could do it, so could I. Then I walked on. It was a small victory, because I had defeated Jenkins one more time, at least for tonight.

At the livery stables, I checked in on Bartholomew. He was standing alone in a corner of the muddy corral without his friend Cuca curled up nearby. The other three mules were huddled together under a small roofed shelter in the corral to keep warm. Bartholomew's ears twitched when he saw me.

I went into the barn and set my blanket down on a cot. After lighting Pete Ashburn's new metal lamp, I grabbed a handful of hay for Bartholomew. Standing in the blowing snow, I watched as my loyal, old mule gratefully ate his little morsel of hay. I then led Bartholomew toward the dry barn.

Seeing that an animal like my mule, Bartholomew, could hurt from losing a friend tugged at my heart. I could relate to him, because I also had lost my dearest friend years ago. I too would be spending the night alone in a place far away from home. In fact, I no longer had a real home.

Chapter 3

Sleeping in Ashburn's Barn

After tucking my cold, wet mule into a stall inside Pete Ashburn's barn and giving him some extra hay, I shuffled around to get myself settled for the night. Even though I'd spent an enjoyable evening at Molly's with my new friends, filling my neglected belly, I was working hard at not becoming sad or depressed. The sound of rain imbedded with sleet beating down on the barn's metal roof was soothing. I knew the rain was turning to snow. Knowing I would have a snug, dry place to spend the cold night, a shiver of relief shot through me.

I was alone in the barn, no drifters or cowboys about, so I could relax. It was just me and the animals–four horses, three mules plus Bartholomew, two milk cows, a calf and the chickens, the noisy damned chickens. I was sober and had the necessities–a lamp, cot, blankets and a roof over my head, simple but important pleasures. Had I been drinking, this was a night I might easily have done something foolish like falling asleep in an open shed in town, catching pneumonia or freezing to death.

But being sober had its problems too. With a clear mind came a restless conscience and too many memories. *Why had I lived so long?*

Using the metal kerosene lamp, I found Ashburn's office key. It was hanging on a brass chain in its normal place behind the impressive mountain lion skull mounted on a wall inside the barn. I unlocked

Ashburn's office and gathered up my Sharps 50 rifle and saddlebags, then secured the messy room and returned the key.

In the barn's unlocked storage room, Pete had three metal cots arranged in a row against a wooden wall. These he made available to drifters and cowboys for 50¢ a night. I chose the private cot next to the warmer inside wall. It was separated from the other two cots by a small pile of heavy rock salt Pete used for the animals. The rock salt was covered by a torn canvas.

A large dusty wooden crate sat near the middle of the room that visiting cowboys and drifters used as a table on which to eat and play cards. Around the table were four empty horseshoe kegs on end, used as chairs. The tops of three kegs had stenciled on them in black paint - *#1 Horseshoes manufactured by the Shuller Iron Works Chicago, Ill.* The fourth wooden keg showed it once contained #OO horseshoes.

The grey paint was peeling and wearing off the top of the heavy crate table. Carved into it were the initials and dates of long departed travelers who had passed through this small, remote mining town. The tabletop also had old melted candle wax and cigarette burns on its edges. A well-used, grimy deck of cards sat on the table along with a Prince Albert tobacco can containing matches. Also, there was a small, worn New Testament with half of its front cover page missing. An interesting collection of items, I thought. I guessed Ashburn's good Christian wife, Nancy, left the New Testament there in hopes an occasional lost soul or drifter would read through it. She was a good lady.

I set the lamp on the table next to the tobacco can. Then I carefully stood my rifle against the wall near my cot and hung my saddle bags and wet coat on nearby nails. The arrangement and smells were already starting to feel like home–at least the closest thing I had had to a home in many months.

I picked up the Prince Albert tobacco can and momentarily stared at the image of the Royal Consort on it. It brought back many memories from long ago. After a few moments of reminiscing, I shook my head and set the tobacco can down, then went on about my business of settling in for the night.

After laying out my borrowed blankets on the cot, I sat on it and took off my boots. Next I removed my Colt 44 pistol from my saddle bag, then stuck it into one of my empty boots where I could quickly find and retrieve it during the night if need be. Next I put my pocket money into my other empty boot. As an almost useless gesture, I tossed my half empty Bull Durham tobacco sack on the table to share a smoke with any fool who might come stumbling in during this miserable and stormy night. Finally, I blew out the kerosene lamp and laid down on the cot.

Staring blankly into the darkness, I could hear a horse rustling in a nearby stall. He kicked up a little dust, which I could smell through the crude, rough lumber walls of the storage room. Several chickens clucked restlessly, roosting on the rafters above, trying to get themselves comfortable for the night.

Then I felt a drip of water! It hit me on the top of my balding head and felt like a cold stabbing icicle. Obviously Pete had some leaks in his metal roof and I had parked myself directly under one of them.

Grumbling, I got up and slid my cot over several feet, again settled down and covered up. Nevertheless, I was content to have a place to spend the night. I liked the muffled blanket effect created by the wet falling snow outside. Even the acidic smell of the wet manure and animal urine coming from outside the barn didn't bother me. Spartan as it was, this was actually a step up for me compared to some of my previous visits to Harshaw.

As I lay there, my thoughts drifted to how my little wild animal and critter friends who would visit me at my camp up in the mountain basin were doing. This sudden winter storm invading their normally dry desert home would certainly present them with a challenge. I amused myself by fantasizing about how many of these little friends would accept an invitation from me to spend the night here in Ashburn's cozy, dry barn.

Then again, perhaps I had it wrong. Perhaps the naughty little critters simply moved into my comfortable old mining tunnel where I was camping as soon as I had left. The little imps were probably doing just fine eating my scant food supplies and sleeping on my makeshift bed. After enjoying my short fantasy, I tugged my mind back to reality.

Still wide awake from all of Molly's coffee, I got up and lit the lantern, then went outside and took a piss. It was still snowing. Back in my cozy cot, I listened to an occasional drip from the leaking barn roof and began taking stock in my situation. It was not encouraging.

Here I was, 57 years old and sleeping alone in a barn in the middle of the Arizona Territory, a far cry from my earlier life. It was Thursday night, December the 1st, 1887. I had no real friends–at least not here. I was viewed by the locals as a destitute, old drunken prospector who was also a little crazy. In reality, most of it was true. But also part of it was a charade–one that I wanted to put on.

Yes, I was in fact old, or at least getting old, and yes–I was a drunk, thanks to *Jenkins*. No, that was a lame excuse. I couldn't blame *Jenkins* any more. Like Preacher Sullivan, I had to take charge of my life, especially if I was to succeed in my *final adventure.*

Also, a prospector? No–I really was not a prospector either, even though I was trained in that field and had done a lot of prospecting during my earlier life. A better description of me would be a *mining engineer and businessman* who was now looking to take care of some old unfinished business and have a little fun and adventure along the way.

And destitute or broke? No, far from it, especially considering the stash I had hidden away in the cavernous *La Escondida Basin* in the Patagonia Mountains, where I had been camping. I also had interests elsewhere.

But at this stage in my life, power and wealth were no longer my passions. How easy this was to say, I thought–especially if a person had not attained them. However, I was now doing exactly what I wanted to do and living an exciting lie. But because of my drinking problem, things were starting to get out of control.

Thinking back to past times, it seemed I had lived four distinct lives during my nearly sixty years of wandering this earth. My first life was growing up with my folks and traveling in Latin America, then going to Scotland for my formal education. Next came my exciting life in Mexico during the 50's, before the wars. Then came the two wars–Mexico's war with France and the hectic American Civil War. Those years brought me both adventure and heartache. Since then, my life seemed interesting but anticlimactic–except for what I was now doing. This adventure once again made my juices flow.

Recently I had come out of Mexico to fulfill a long overdue task and complete this chapter in my life. It should be exciting, but it would not end well if I did not stop my destructive antics and drinking. Somehow this too didn't bother me greatly, because most of what I held precious in life was now gone–just bittersweet memories.

I was born on January 3, 1830, in Havana, Cuba. A lot of Negro slave trading was taking place there, according to my folks. My father was a talented and ambitious Scottish engineer, John Kenneth McIntyre, and my mother was a southern belle from Savannah, Georgia, the daughter of a wealthy plantation owner.

My mother's name was Elizabeth May Taylor. Her family called her Lizzie May, but my father called her Beth. She must have loved my father dearly to leave her rich surroundings in the South and travel with him all though Mexico, Central and South America. She said he was an exciting man and offered her a life of adventure–and so he did. It must have been in the blood, because I unwittingly followed, to some extent, in his footsteps.

My folks named me John Taylor McIntyre. McAllister was an alias I used several times during and after the Civil War. It fit me well with my green eyes, light complexion and impetuous Pict or Scottish personality.

Along with a first-rate mining engineering education I received in Scotland, my folks gave me the opportunity to learn much during our life and travels in the Americas. Our family was on the move often, and my father made sure I learned basic survival skills along with receiving a more traditional formal education. Some of Father's family members in Scotland were gunsmiths, so he always had an excellent small collection of the latest and best firearms. He took pride in teaching me how to shoot and properly maintain both pistols and rifles. Father's teaching influenced the future direction of my life.

Whenever possible, my folks sent me to local schools and there I was able to prefect my Spanish and basic math skills. Additionally, my father would hire a teacher for the workers' children at the company mining camps when local schools were not available. Other children were welcome, but many times their families or the Catholic priests would not allow them to attend.

When I was old enough, my father took me with him and his Indian guides on many trips to investigate new mining sites. This gave me the opportunity to perfect my riding, hunting, swimming and other skills. Also, playing and competing with the local kids, many of them Indian, taught me much and gave me many lifelong friends.

In spite of his deftness with firearms, my father was killed in a duel while setting up a company office in Boston. It happened in the spring of 1849 while I was away at the University in Edinburgh. It would have been bad enough if it had been a fair duel–but it wasn't. Father was dealing with a coward and a bully.

Mother said the initial confrontation between Father and this man, *Bolton Chapman,* occurred at a fine restaurant in Boston. A drunken Bolton Chapman was sitting at a nearby table and made some inappropriate remarks about her to his friends and laughed. Father went to his table and quietly told him to keep his loutish comments to himself and was immediately called out–challenged to a duel.

The next day during the duel, Chapman fired prematurely and mortally wounded my father in the neck. According to the rules and conditions of formal dueling, Father's second should have shot the offending Chapman, but my father had no one to serve as his second.

However, three years later, with the help of my close friend Will Springer, who did serve as my second, I fortunately closed the book on the whole affair. Chapman was the second person I sent to the next world. That would change.

During the summer of 1852 I went to work for the same English company that had employed my father, The New Wales Equipment and Mining Company, Ltd. Just before my graduation in Edinburgh, I received a letter posted from London from my father's old boss, Mr. Walter M. Kearny.

Mr. Kearny was once a close friend of my father and had known me well since I was a boy. He knew I had a valuable education, a knowledge of the Americas, and most important of all, could speak perfect Spanish and several Indian dialects. Also I spoke some Portuguese. He made me what I considered at the time a very generous employment offer and I accepted it.

Being of an American mother and a British father, I had dual citizenship. However, British citizenship carried the most recognition and prestige throughout the world, so I used it.

During my time at the university, I was fascinated with and studied steam power and explosives. Both disciplines had direct military and mining applications. One of my professors suggested I consider a career in the Royal Navy because of my interests. Even though I considered it, my free spirit was not conducive to a structured military life so I took a separate path. Even so, my career choice placed me in situations where I worked closely with the military during the wars. That's when I met Dr. Dorsey Harrison.

Because of my interests in explosives, I spent one summer working in British Royal Navy ordnance development depots in Manchester and Liverpool. Professor Orley Simmons, a genius in the ordnance field, took a liking to me and mentored me while I was there. He even offered me employment there after I graduated.

Several interesting ideas the Brits were researching during my tenure at the Royal Naval development depots were steam-powered ordnance catapults and rifling or spiral grooving for large navel gun barrels. At the time they seemed more interested in the steam powered ordnance launchers than refining rifling techniques for the large naval guns. Later rifling groove technology matured dramatically under the direction of English and American Union military engineers during the American Civil War. It ultimately changed the nature of naval warfare.

While I was at the University of Edinburgh, my cousin Todd introduced me to a sweet young thing who lived nearby in Queensferry. Her name was Mary McKinney. We had many a pleasant picnics, walks and visits along the beautiful Firth of Forth shores during the two short summers I knew her. However, Mary was not like my mother. This sweet Scottish lass let me know very clearly that she wanted to stay by her family and not leave Scotland, so I didn't try to pursue a relationship with her any further.

After I left Scotland and went back to America, I received several letters from Mary indicating she had changed her mind and would like to see the world. I surmised that she probably took another look at her options in Scotland and didn't like them, even though she was a beautiful girl. My pride hurt, I did not reply and the letters stopped. I heard later from Cousin Todd that she married a local teaching professor and stayed in Scotland and raised three daughters.

Slavery was a subject I didn't think too much about when I was growing up–only that it was around and my folks argued about it. I saw it up close when we came through ports in the Caribbean and when we visited my mother's family in Georgia.

At about ten years old, I thought it would be wonderful if I owned one of my father's rich company mines in South America and had 1000 slaves working it for me. I would buy one of the biggest ships in the world and have my slaves sail me anywhere I wanted to go and there buy anything I desired. I laughed and thought later, thank goodness for unfulfilled dreams. In reality, my slaves would probably have sailed me as their ten-year-old spoiled brat master out of sight of the first port and then thrown me off the ship!

However, as I grew up my thoughts about slavery changed. I think my mother's did too when she witnessed some of the sobering Negro slave trading conditions at several island ports we visited in the Caribbean. She argued less with my father after those experiences.

Then came the summer of '51 when I visited my mother's family plantation home in Savannah after my father's death. I had the summer off from my university studies in Scotland and no summer job, even though I could have easily found one. Also, Mother sent me some of the money she made from her little textile mill in Savannah, urging me to come visit them for the summer. So I did. It turned out to be an important milestone in my life.

Cousin Howard Taylor had been a boyhood friend and was the only son of my Uncle William Howard Taylor II, my mother's older brother. We called him Uncle Will. When I first remembered Uncle Will, my grandfather had already died of pneumonia and Uncle Will was running the huge Taylor Plantation and all its business operations. He had attended Oxford University in England, but had not graduated because of my grandfather's death.

Uncle Will was the intellectual type and had an impressive library at the Taylor plantation. I think he enjoyed reading and studying more than running his family businesses. Thankfully, his son Howard was almost the opposite. He enjoyed the outdoors, politics and working on the plantation, so they made a good pair.

The second evening after I arrived in Georgia, we enjoyed a splendid formal meal in the plantation mansion dining room. The meal was served by house servants and came complete with Waterford crystal wine glasses, china from Asia and silver utensils and candle holders from England and Germany. After the meal, Howard suggested we go out and do something for the remainder of evening. It was an evening I would not soon forget.

"Jack, why don't we pick up Kenny, then go into town and play some games of billiards at the Queen of Hearts Club? Or would you just like to go over to Kenny's place and visit?" Howard asked.

"Queen of Hearts Club? Is that what it sounds like?" I responded.

"Yes, it is. It's a gentlemen's club for members and their guests. Our family has had a membership there since our grandfather, "Will The First," got it going over twenty-five years ago. He helped establish it. Would you like to see it?"

"Our grandfather? I thought you were talking about a *bordello,*" I responded, this time a bit incredulous.

"Jack, don't be so crass. Of course it's not a bordello. I told you, it's a gentlemen's club. But there are some very attractive French girls there. Members and their guests play billiards, cards and other board games. But, if you are interested in the opposite sex, those arrangements can be made too. But it's expensive."

"Sounds interesting, how often do you go there?" I asked.

"Well, not too often. Usually only a few times a month. It's an older crowd thing, you know. But sometimes a number of us young bucks go over and spend the evening and have a few drinks. It's fun if you have some friends with you," Howard explained.

Then he continued. "Sometimes, if you are nice to some of the French girls and buy them some drinks, they will be nice back–and it won't cost you a thing. They get tired of those old guys. Oh, and I don't think Father is going out tonight," he said.

"Are you saying your father goes over there?" I asked, again surprised.

"Certainly. He goes over there every Friday night and plays cards with some of the neighbors. They limit their games to a $1000 a night. And if someone loses heavily, they try to arrange it so he can win it back the next time. It's more of a social thing. They talk politics and learn what's going on in the world."

"Sure, let's go. It sounds like an interesting place. Do I need any money?" I asked cautiously, since I had very little.

"No, you're my guest. We will pick up Kenny at his place on the way into town. I told him we might be coming over."

"When do you want to go? Do we need to dress differently?"

"Old Sandy has the open, double seater carriage ready for us out back. And yes, let's take these dinner clothes off and get into something more comfortable. I'll see you out back in ten minutes." Howard then turned and headed to his room upstairs.

A few minutes later, Howard and I climbed into the waiting buggy. With a light tap of his whip, Howard urged his magnificent sorrel horse, Montigo, into a fast pace, and we were off towards The Fields of Shannon Plantation, to pick up Kenny Kerns.

The evening was warm and humid. As we traveled through the moss covered trees along the muddy roadway, I joked with Howard.

"Howard, I guess Kenny is a good friend of yours. Are you and he going to be running your plantations pretty soon?"

"Well, Papa's already training me to do it. He wanted me to go to Oxford like he did, but I'm not the intellectual type. I wanted to stay here close to my horses and hunting. And I like the farming. I'm getting pretty good at it."

"I thought you went to school somewhere up north. Where was it, Boston?" I asked.

"Yes, but only for a year. Kenny and I both went. He's like me. We both wanted to come home and help run our family businesses. His father has put him in charge of shipping and the management of their darkies. And when I say shipping, I don't just mean moving their tobacco and cotton crops out of Georgia. I mean they are really going into the business in a big way. They're working with a large Dutch shipping company and are buying an interest in their operations."

Then Howard laughed. "Life's too short and there was too much happening down here. Both Kenny and I knew what we wanted to do here and wasting our time going to school in Boston didn't fit into our plans. So we came home. Besides, the girls are prettier down here."

I leaned back into the carriage seat, enjoying the view. "If you and Kenny are going to be big plantation operators, don't you need some more training, in bookkeeping, banking, contracts, things like that?"

"Oh, sure. Papa and Mr. Kerns hired a Jew and a Dutchman to teach us. You met Mr. and Mrs. Hesselink this evening at dinner. He and his wife are living in one of our guest cottages, and the old man is teaching me how to set up production ledgers and billing accounts for our farm products. He's good, even though he's hard to understand and has bad breath," Howard said with a chuckle, as he skillfully guided our open carriage toward the Kerns' plantation.

"That sounds like a wise move. Where's the Jew? What is he doing?" I asked.

"Mr. Neil Keillman? Oh, he's living over at the Kerns place for a year, then they are going to switch. Mr. Keillman works for Lloyds of London, but Papa made a deal with them to have him come over and help us with our accounts and money. Keillman and Hesselink are helping Kenny and me put together modern accounting procedures and books for our farm operations. Kenny and I, or JK, as he now likes to be called, are spending a lot of time making sure we understand everything, and our tutoring is working. This is a lot more practical than sending Kenny, JK, that is, and me to some fancy university in Boston or Europe, wasting our family money. We all are very happy with the arrangement."

He continued with satisfaction. "When we are finished with Mr. Keillman and Hesselink, we will probably hire some local accountants to keep track of the books then, JK and I will continue to run the businesses."

I was impressed. It sounded like the Taylor and Kerns families were going to get even richer. Then I remembered Howard's earlier statement, as we could see the Fields of Shannon Plantation lights in front of us.

"You mentioned also going over to JK's and visiting. What's going on over there?" I asked.

Howard glanced at me with a coy smile. "Well, I told you. He's got a lot going on over there. I mentioned the French girls at the club are expensive. *JK's girls aren't.*"

"What do you mean? He has his own club–his own bordello?" I asked wondering where this conversation was going.

"No. No. But he manages his family's darkies," Howard said sounding a bit embarrassed.

"You mean you and he go down and *screw* his darkies?" I asked bluntly.

"Howard, don't act so innocent. You're a man of the world–you know what goes on. Anyway, he has some quadroons and other girls who are very attractive."

"Quadroons? What are quadroons?" I asked, acting innocently, but also fascinated at where this conversation was going.

We were arriving at the Kerns' plantation so Howard was anxious to close the embarrassing box he had opened. "You know, *quadroon, octoroons,* darkies with white blood in them. Some of them are dramatically beautiful. I'll show you some this summer."

Yes, I was a young and not so innocent man of the world, but this was a new door Howard was opening for me, and I wasn't sure I liked what I was starting to see beyond it.

The Fields of Shannon Plantation was bigger and even more magnificent than the Taylor Plantation. Howard and I waited briefly under the portico of the red brick mansion as one of their house servants held Howard's high-strung horse, who was agitated and anxious to go.

JK quickly came out the front door with his attractive sister, *Melanie Ellen,* on his arm. Howard introduced us, and we spoke for a couple of minutes, then Howard and JK hurriedly jumped in the open carriage and called laughingly for me to follow.

Embarrassed at our bad manners, I tried to politely excuse myself from Melanie Ellen, then hopped into the back seat of the carriage, and we were off. Looking back, I wished I could have stayed and visited with Melanie Ellen.

A half-hour later we arrived at the Queen of Hearts Club in Savannah. A young black man in a uniform held our horse and carriage as we dismounted, then he took Montigo and the carriage around back to the carriage house and stables. The club was on the edge of town and had a log cypress fence around the property, manicured trees, grass and several small ponds inside the grounds. The building was a small but fancier version of the classical colonial-style plantation. It was two-story and made of red brick, as were several smaller buildings out back and the carriage house and stables. It reeked of money and class.

Inside was as Howard had described it. An older distinguished-looking black doorman in a sharp uniform greeted us. He escorted us into the parlor, where a very attractive French lady in an abbreviated uniform offered to get us drinks, which we accepted. There were newspapers set out on one of the tables in the parlor. One wall was lined with bookcases holding some of the classics and other interesting books in it. The dim light in the room made it hard to read their titles.

The wood floors throughout the club were waxed and covered with expensive-looking, foreign rugs with elaborate Moorish designs. The parlor had four wall-mounted crystal lamps, along with an enormous, black, iron lamp with four arms. It sat on a heavy oak table in the middle of the room. I had never seen anything quite like this place, even in England and Scotland.

A strong, sweet smell of tobacco smoke was flowing from one of the rooms off the parlor, where five older gentlemen were visiting. The billiards room was empty, so we went in and started playing. The attractive French lady brought in our drinks, placing them on the table. Howard and JK joked with her for several minutes before she left and she seemed to enjoy it.

Howard's earlier conversation about how the Kern's family managed their slaves interested me. I tried to broach the subject again as we began to play billiards, but took care not to embarrass the two men.

"Howard, what happens around here on your off time or on Sundays?" I asked.

"Oh, after church, we sometimes go down to the river and go boating and have a picnic. Or sometimes we have horse races with the neighbors.

There is always something going on. Why? Did you have something particular in mind?" Howard asked with a smile.

"No. Only that Sundays are special days for me at the university. It is the one day we usually have free to get away from our studies and socialize a bit," I said, and then continued. "And Sundays are usually the time we can go to Church and hopefully visit with some of the local girls afterwards."

"You want to socialize with the local girls? I think Melanie Ellen kind of likes you," JK responded, winking at Howard.

The conversation was not going in the direction I had intended, so I didn't push it further and redirected my comments.

"I was just wondering what normally happened during the week. I think I will be here until August and want to make myself useful. Are there any projects you are working on that I can help with?" I asked.

Howard responded as he hit his billiard ball into the middle pocket. "Sure, Jack. We're preparing a new field to plant an orchard next winter. We are also retiring several of our rice fields and shifting more to cotton. I'm going to be laying it out and also going to check on our other tobacco and cotton fields. If you are interested, I would like your ideas and suggestions on our operation."

Then JK chimed in with a twinkle in his eye. "And Jack, if Howard doesn't keep you busy enough, I can show you our shipping business. I'm in the process of trying to consolidate the whole Savannah area's textile, cotton and tobacco production, so we can ship it out of our central docks and warehouses down at the river. From there we can take it north and to Europe. We're building wharfs and industrial booms and cranes to lift the products directly onto cargo ships. Would you be interested in seeing it? And maybe Melanie Ellen too?"

"How can I refuse? Yes, I would be interested in both of your offers. Especially, the last one," I said jokingly.

We all laughed as we drank our liqueur and lit up our cigars. It had started out to be an enjoyable evening as I visited with my cousin and new friend. I was beginning to think that this affluent lifestyle could be intoxicating, but a little later things changed.

Howard, JK and I continued to play billiards, flirt with the French lady when she brought us drinks, and discussed their ambitious plans. The evening was relatively young when a man from another room in the club came in and asked to join our game. Howard and JK accepted his offer. That's when I first met *Mr. Randolph P. Jenkins*, one of the most despicable men I had ever had the misfortune to run into in my life.

After Jenkins introduced himself, he took off his coat and cravat to play a game with us.

Mr. Jenkins was an aristocratic looking man, a tall, slender, well-dressed man in his late thirties. He stood over six feet and sported a manicured, reddish and prematurely graying beard and wavy, dark blond hair. He carried a carved gentleman's walking stick with a heavy gold handle shaped like a cobra's head. It could easily be used as a club, and I guessed it held a hidden sword which could be shoved into an adversary's gizzard in a flash. He sounded educated, with a deep resonating voice and a pleasant German or Austrian accent. He had the demeanor of a smooth European, and quickly let us know he spoke five languages. On the surface, the man was friendly, had a quick wit and a very disarming style about him, but I didn't like him.

Before we started our new game, Howard casually asked Mr. Jenkins what he did for a living. Smiling, he said he was a *purveyor of labor*.

"You sell darkies," JK suggested immediately as we chalked our queue sticks for the game.

"Yes, I do," responded Mr. Jenkins.

Marie, the pretty French lady, came in with drinks again, including one for Mr. Jenkins. He reached into his vest pocket and pulled out a $10 gold coin and set it on her tray. She thanked him and, as she started to leave, he deftly placed his hand on her bottom and gave it a hard squeeze. Her smile abruptly vanished as she disappeared through the door. Jenkins laughed and said he needed to get something for his generous gratuity.

Immediately Mr. Jenkins suggested we partner up and said he would partner with me.

"Gentlemen, please call me Dolpho. Why don't we make things interesting and put $20 on the game?" He pulled a gold double eagle from his vest pocket and placed it on the edge of the table.

I was embarrassed because I had no money with me, nor could I afford to gamble. Most of my father's limited fortune was now gone–paying for family expenses and my education in Scotland. However, Howard quickly accepted and put our *two* gold coins on the edge of the table. JK put his down also.

Even though Howard and JK were good players, Dolpho Jenkins and I easily won the game. My extracurricular talents and skills were paying off. We continued to play, and Dolpho and I kept winning. At least I could pay back Howard with our winnings, I thought.

As the evening wore on, the conversation with Mr. Jenkins got very interesting. JK carried most of it with the slave trader.

As we played, Mr. Jenkins volunteered that he had just culminated deals with the plantation owners in the other room for $22,000. He said he was going to Atlanta in the morning, then would be heading back to Havana in about twelve days. He said he expected to have over $150,000 in cash or contracts for slaves before he returned to Cuba. I couldn't believe the numbers the man was casually throwing around.

"Mr. Jenkins, I mean Dolpho, not to be too inquisitive, but could you tell us a little bit about your business?" JK asked.

"Certainly, I would be happy to. What do you want to know?" He sunk another ball into the side pocket.

"Well, what do your customers usually want when they come to you, and how do you fill their orders?"

"Most of my big customers are plantation owners like you gentlemen. They mainly want field workers. They want docile, young bucks that work hard, don't eat too much and don't run away," he said, laughing.

Howard then asked, "So are they the only ones you sell?"

"No, of course not. We sell domestics or house servants, both male and female, and even eunuchs, if you want them. We also specialize in finding singers, dancers, fighters, teachers, preachers, whores, faggots–whatever you want or need. We are the second biggest supplier of black flesh in the Caribbean. The Jamaican Trading Company is our name. We trade you top quality black workers for your gold," Jenkins said with a well-practiced ring to his words.

"How do you find such a wide range of ah, ah, servants?" JK asked.

"We don't find them, we buy them, or make them."

"How do you do that?" I asked.

Jenkins responded, "Well, it's not easy, that's why they are so expensive. If we don't have what you want, we place orders with our African suppliers. Special men, women, size, personality types, whatever you want. The local African chiefs who supply us know the different tribes, their personality traits and what they are good at. He does the first cut at satisfying our needs. If we still can't find what we want, we get them from our breeding and training farms in the Caribbean."

Howard then asked, "African suppliers? I thought it was against the law to bring slaves in from Africa."

"It is, and most of that has stopped. The United States Congress in its grand wisdom passed a law in 1808 banning the import of slaves from Africa. That was after England and most of Europe had already outlawed it."

"But there is still some smuggling from Africa?" I asked.

"Nobody is enforcing the law. It's maritime law out there in the ocean. No country has sovereignty to enforce their laws in the open sea."

"Could a British Man of War stop a British cargo ship on the open sea?" I asked.

"Sure they could, but they don't. Besides, the clippers or cargo ship captains have a lot of flags in their closets. If they are carrying contraband, they aren't going to be daffy enough to be flying the flag of a naval ship that can stop them." he said, a bit patronizingly.

I couldn't believe what I was hearing. I had been exposed to many things growing up and certainly did not have an innocent view of the world. But I also had a Christian perspective on how things ought to be, instilled in me by my mother, the daughter of a plantation owner, and by my Scottish father. This man and to a lesser degree, Howard and JK, were talking about *blacks* like they were chattel, cattle or livestock, without a conscience or soul. I was beginning to see why my father was so incensed against the practice.

Finally, I could not contain my pent-up anger and thoughts any longer. Working hard to control my emotions, I asked, "Mr. Jenkins, I keep listening to you talk about the darkies, blacks, Negros, whatever you want to call them, as if they are not human. The way you breed, sort and sell them, it all seems like they are just livestock or chattel, to be bought, sold and used for the benefit of a few rich people. Don't you believe they were created by God and, as such, are owed some dignity and respect?"

I got surprised looks from all three men, especially Howard, who then smiled.

"Gentlemen, it looks like we have an *abolitionist* amongst us," Mr. Jenkins said with a rather menacing smile.

"Certainly, son, they are God's creation. But God created some animals and also some humans superior to others. The blacks are superior at duties whites cannot do well–hard work in the hot fields, heavy lifting and the like. Whites are superior at duties the blacks cannot do–intellectual things like managing businesses, governing countries, starting wars and the like."

He continued, "If you look in the Bible, slavery has been with us forever, from the time Abraham had his concubine Hagar to the time the Jews were captured and put into slavery in Babylon. In fact, God made the Jews the smartest race in the world. They were His chosen people. But they still weren't smart enough to keep King Nebuchadnezzar from making slaves out of them. Even God allowed it. Son, slavery has been with us forever," Jenkins concluded with a condescending smile.

"Mr. Jenkins, I'm not an abolitionist and I'm not your son. I just think if we consider ourselves a Christian society, we should treat these people that God created with a little dignity and respect. Even the Babylonians did that," I said, not hiding my disgust for the man.

Mr. Jenkins eyes grew hard as he looked at me with his cold, forced smile, like that of a menacing snake. I knew I had made an enemy for life, but that was fine with me. He had made one too. *Our paths would cross in the future.*

"Well, Jack, it's our company's policy to treat all of our Negroes with respect. We treat them well, we feed them well, and we work hard to place them well," Jenkins said, with a disdainful twist to his lip.

My comments had the same dampening effect on our billiards game, as one of my professors would jokingly say, like somebody tossing a turd into the party punchbowl.

Our game ended abruptly, and Jenkins said he had to leave. He put on his coat, threw his cravat over his shoulder and shook hands with Howard and JK, but not me. He then left quickly.

Howard sat down on a chair with his hands over his face, practically in tears from trying not to laugh until Jenkins was gone. JK was more stoic.

"My God, Jack, I thought Jenkins was going to shit in his pants when you came out with that!" Howard finally said, bursting out laughing.

JK did not seem so entertained by my actions. "Yeah, I thought so too. The problem is, I might have to deal with that gentleman in the future."

"Hey, I didn't mean to complicate your lives, but I just didn't like the bastard," I said half-apologetically.

It was late when Howard and I dropped JK off at his place and headed back to the Taylor plantation. I was concerned I had offended Howard, but he just laughed it off. On the way back, he made some comments that warmed me up a bit.

"Jack, Father likes you and asked my advice about having you join us in our business operations when you finish the university. I told him, 'no way,' we certainly didn't want a hot-headed Scotsman and troublemaker like you here in Georgia," Howard said smiling. "Seriously, Jack, he did ask me. I told him I had been thinking about the same thing, and I couldn't think of a person I would rather work with."

For a moment I was silent, thinking about the possibilities. My mother had come back to the plantation after my father was killed and had been welcomed. But being the proud, intelligent person she was, she worked with her brother to start up a small textile factory in Savannah and pay her own way. Considering all this, the possibilities of Howard's offer sounded very promising.

"Howard, that's a real compliment. Are you sure you would want an abolitionist around?" I said jokingly.

Howard laughed, "Aw hell, Jack, you would be great. Think about it. While you're here this summer, I'll show you around. In fact, several of my projects could use the ideas of a real engineer. You game?"

"Certainly! It sounds like you and JK have some great ideas. His idea of improving the shipping of your farm products sounds like it could change the future down here. It would be quite an engineering challenge too," I replied.

"Sure, JK and I have been talking. We know we are barely touching the potential of what could be produced here. Once we show you around, maybe you could give us some of your ideas on what we could do. And maybe Melanie Ellen could give you some ideas too," Howard said, elbowing me in the side.

"Perhaps so," I quietly responded smiling into the darkness.

On this visit, I had arrived at the Taylor Plantation on a Wednesday, the 28th of May, 1851. By the next Monday, Howard and I had spent two full days on horseback, riding over their plantation and inspecting the projects he had in progress and those he was planning. Howard was a good and interesting young man. He was very intelligent and had the nose for recognizing opportunities, plus the gumption to accomplish them.

Howard was also a natural politician. He could read a situation and could deal with almost everyone he came across.

Mother told me that in years past, Uncle Will jealously controlled the family's books and money. But his health was failing, and he was proud of Howard and wanted to turn his duties over to his only son as quickly as he could. Because of the close friendship between Howard and JK Kerns, JK's father and Uncle Will made the decision to hire consultants to help train the boys to take over their large empires. I was complimented by the fact that Howard valued my opinion.

Early on during my summer visit, Howard explained the Taylor family's different businesses and projects. These included the farming; clearing new land for fields; transitioning existing fields from rice to cotton; construction of buildings, waterways and roads; and sales and shipping of their products. These products included rice, cotton, tobacco, leather, lard, and some lumber.

The newest Taylor family endeavor was Mother's textile factory in Savannah, in which she owned the biggest share. This raised the eyebrows of some of the more proper plantation ladies. A refined Southern lady's place was not to cross the line and do man's work. I thought they were jealous, and Howard believed so too.

Hesselink and Keillman had refined the family's management system by setting up accounting procedures to directly track the income of each of the plantation businesses individually. The consultants also had introduced simple and efficient procedures to determine the viability and payoffs of investments in new plantation projects. If the new projects or crops were not up and showing strong signs of being profitable within two years, the consultants recommended dropping them and going on to something else.

Howard said the Kerns family was doing something similar in their operations and, together, the two families were far ahead of the other local plantations in their management style and thinking.

I was impressed. These were things I had not learned in my engineering studies. Taking note, I hoped I could apply them in my future career.

The Taylor family was operating their plantation extremely well and knew where they wanted to go in the future. They also had the money to make it happen. They not only had the money, they managed it carefully and also knew how to enjoy it–maybe too much. My only concern was that they kept their money close to home, physically on the plantation and in Savannah and Charleston banks. Trying not to be too inquisitive, I tactfully suggested to Howard that the family might want to consider converting some of their money into British sterling currency and keep it in English banks. He seemed a bit cool to the idea, but said he would discuss it with Uncle Will.

Additionally, the Taylor family was enthralled with and enjoyed politics, always politics. This was their guiding beacon. Howard was a natural at it, and I expected it would serve him well.

Howard was athletic and an active outdoorsman. He was an excellent horseman and enjoyed horseracing and hunting when he had the time to do it. By the end of the summer the outside daily operations of the Taylor Plantation had almost totally transitioned from Uncle Will to Howard. Begrudgingly, Howard spent the necessary time with Hesselink and Keillman to do the inside planning and bookwork for their businesses and projects, except for the management of their money. Uncle Will kept control of that.

JK shared many of the same interests and characteristics with Howard. However, JK was a quiet person with calculating and methodical tendencies. Also he was more of a businessman and less of a politician than Howard. But, together, the two young men were close friends and made a formidable team.

The summer went by rapidly. Much of my time was spent working with Howard on his projects and with JK, reviewing his fascinating plans to make Savannah a first-class export location for southern agricultural products. But soon the most important time to me would be those pleasant evenings and Sundays I spent with Melanie Ellen. Except for JK, her family readily accepted me as a qualified suitor, albeit, I lacked money and political connections.

Howard Taylor had a serious girl in Atlanta. It seemed they were destined to be betrothed in the near future. Her name was Virginia Anne Davis, the daughter of a wealthy banker and ex-Governor of Georgia. The young lady was niece of the Mexican War hero and Senator from Mississippi, a certain Colonel Jeff Davis.

Besides my becoming engaged to Melanie Ellen, three other things happened during the summer of '51 that cemented themselves into my memory and changed many lives. The first incident began to hatch itself early during my visit at the Taylor Plantation.

It was my second week in Georgia. This particular morning, Howard and I were on horseback going through his usual daily routine of overseeing projects on the large Taylor Plantation. We were viewing the northwest part of the plantation when Howard gave me my first challenge. We stopped our horses on top of a hill and Howard pointed to a beautiful, wooded valley with a stream flowing through it.

"Jack, there's where I want to build a lake."

"Are you serious? A lake? What would you …." I responded, not quite finishing my last question as I began to look more carefully at the small valley below.

After a quick evaluation of the idea and location, I could see the merit of having a lake, but I wanted to hear his ideas first.

Howard went on to describe his vision. He said he wanted to dam the major stream below and create a lake for irrigation and recreation. He then gave me some of his ideas on how they would use it. Howard asked me for my thoughts on how it could be constructed and how much it would cost. I knew Howard well enough by then to understand he was serious about his dream. Listening to him describe the project again stimulated my interests in explosives.

For the next hour, we rode around looking at the land and discussing different ideas and options. After lunch, I rode back to Howard's proposed lake site alone and spent the afternoon re-evaluating the project. In the evening, we discussed it.

At the dinner table, I started the dialogue. "Howard, I like your lake idea. I even have a name for it–Taylor Lake. You wanted some ideas, so I went back and spent the afternoon looking over the land and location. Several thoughts–I suggest you move your dam site downstream a bit, a little below where the Little Blue meets with Lambert's Creek. You have an excellent site there with rock on both sides to anchor your dam. You also have an additional source of good rock to make the dam."

"That's interesting–why did you pick that site?" Uncle Will asked.

"Well, for several reasons," I replied, "First, besides the rock, there is more water flowing at that point and it would almost double your lake's shoreline and increase its volume. Also, it's high enough you not only could create a diversion for the irrigation to most of your fields, you could also put in a small mill site and run a water wheel."

Howard's face lit up. "That's an outstanding idea, Jack. When can you start?"

Uncle Will also responded. "Jack, that *is* a good idea. But wouldn't the water cover a lot of trees?"

"Yes it would. I suggest, if you are serious about the lake, you move your logging operation over there for a while and harvest those trees next so they are not lost. It's pretty much an open area, but there is some good timber there."

Our family members and the two guests sitting at the dinner table smiled and nodded at each other approvingly. Mother was beaming and Howard seemed delighted with the idea.

"However, there's only one problem," I commented.

"What's that?" Uncle Will asked with a frown.

"Well, it's not a small project. It's going to take some considerable time and money to build," I answered.

Howard glanced at Uncle Will, who was now starting to take a large bite of hot apple pie dripping with whipped cream. "Jack, don't worry about it. My father is good at taking care of those details, if he chooses."

Uncle Will hesitated for an instant, glancing at Howard, then me. With a slight smirk, he finished his bite of pie.

Howard winked at me and we continued with our meal.

Debating whether I should open another door after the first success, I decided to do it.

"Howard, you and Uncle Will might be interested in something I studied about in Scotland and England."

Curious, Howard turned toward me. "What is it?"

"Explosives–especially black powder. You could use it in your construction projects, like moving rocks and taking out stumps in new fields. And it's not that hard to make."

Howard's and Uncle Will's eyes widened as they looked at each other.

"Jack, you think we could make explosives here?" Uncle Will asked seriously.

"Certainly. I know all the ingredients to make the basic product. You wouldn't have to start off with anything too sophisticated. You just want it to work," I replied putting down my fork.

"I understand the French are working on something more powerful than black powder. But I also understand it's much more complicated and dangerous to make. No, I think making a black power plant here is doable and is something you could use. Besides, if you add that to Howard's list of projects, you could have another money-making family business."

Again the family members smiled and nodded at the idea. Then the conversation stopped at the table as everyone finished their desserts. I was concerned because I had pretty much dominated the conversation during dinner.

Finally, Uncle Will spoke. "Jack, you have given us a lot to think about. I need to talk to Howard, but I am excited about both of your suggestions–building Howard's lake and the idea of setting up an explosives factory here. Your suggestions may be very timely, more so than what you might realize."

Family members glanced at each other after Uncle Will's veiled comment, but said nothing as they sipped their after-dinner mint tea.

After we excused ourselves from the table, Mother took me by the hand and led me into another room.

"Son, I'm so proud of you. Your father would be too," She said giving me a motherly hug and kiss on the cheek.

She hesitated a moment before her delightful wit again manifested itself. "I was afraid we were wasting our money on that fancy education of yours."

After I about fell over laughing at Mother's comment, Uncle Will walked into the room.

"Lizzie May, looks like you and Mac may have not wasted your hard earned money sending Jack to school, after all."

Mother and I looked at each other, then joined him in laughter.

By midsummer, I had drawn up plans for the proposed Taylor Lake and also ordered material for their explosives factory. Initially, we converted one of Uncle Will's guesthouses into an experimental workshop and had Jason, the blacksmith, start putting together some wooden and metal containers to make trial explosive charges. We also bought some black powder from one of JK's Dutch merchants to experiment with.

Everything went well until early one morning, when we all awoke to a loud explosion! It shattered two windows and rattled the rafters of the Taylor mansion. We all rushed outside to find that, tragically, Jason had accidentally blown himself up while working in our temporary little black powder factory.

Howard and I had assigned Jason the job of making small, wooden and metal containers for our experimental explosive charges or bombs. Howard and I could then carefully fill the containers with black powder and finish the dangerous experimental devices by attaching fuses and sealing them.

Several times a week, Howard and I would load the experimental bombs into a wagon and take them to the new fields and use them to blow out stumps and rocks. It was exciting and great fun, until poor Jason accidently blew himself up.

Something obviously had gone wrong. As near as we could figure, poor Jason took it on himself to help us despite our warnings by filling the latest containers he made in the blacksmith shop with black powder. After some investigation of the smoking, flattened and bloody walls of our workshop, we figured the blacksmity must have absent-mindedly lit his pipe while he was working.

At the funeral we all agreed it was a sad lesson to all of us. *Don't smoke while you are making bombs!* After the funeral, poor Jason was buried in the black cemetery.

Poor Jason's unnecessary death was the *first* significant and memorable experience I carried with me from the summer of '51. The *second* resulted from discussions I had with my mother about my father's death. I asked her about how my father was killed and the details of his duel with Bolton Chapman.

Mother was concerned I would want to avenge my father's death, and she was right. However, she did give me the details of Father's murder one summer evening at the Taylor Plantation. It was getting dark as we sat on the veranda. There was a warm breeze, and we lit the wick lamp to discourage the mosquitoes. Then she told me the story.

"Son, this was the most painful experience I have gone through in my life. I don't want to go through it again with you, so promise me you will let it lie," Mother said.

I shook my head. "Mother, you know I can't promise you that. I don't know what I will do. But I need to know everything."

My mother told me that in April of 1849, she and Father had gone to Boston to set up an international office for his company. A man was coming over from England in June to run the office after it had been established. Then she and Father were planning to go to Scotland, where they would visit me and Father's family before returning to Mexico. She said the company allowed Father a generous expense account, so they were living well. Also, she explained that Father was a very good producer for the company.

She continued with her story.

"It was a Wednesday afternoon in early May when the incident happened. Johnny had spent the morning at the new office interviewing two clerks for a job. He invited me for a mid-afternoon meal at the Strafford Restaurant, a very nice place near the waterfront. He hoped it would not be crowded, and it was not, but there were several other couples at the restaurant, along with Bolton Chapman and his two friends. The three men had obviously been drinking.

"We had placed our order with the waiter and had just been served our soup. Chapman and his two loutish friends were getting louder and more vulgar as time went on, especially Chapman.

"We were sitting at a table near the three men and their language was bothering your father. An older man with his wife at a nearby table asked Chapman to *please not use bad language in front of the ladies*.

"Chapman glared at the older gentleman, then laughed menacingly. Next he pointed his finger threateningly like he was brandishing a pistol and told the man to mind his own business. I found out later that the older gentleman was Dr. Walter Best, a dentist in town.

"Things quieted down for a few minutes, and I wanted to leave and avoid an incident–but your Father wouldn't have it. Finally we were served our fish and started to eat, then Bolton Chapman started laughing and slammed down his mug of ale, spilling half of it. He took the Lord's name in vain then said something like, 'Those sons of bitches deserved everything they got!' His companions howled, thinking his comment was very funny.

"That was all your father could take. He quietly folded his napkin and placed it on the table, then got up and walked over to Chapman.

"Your father said, 'Sir, there are ladies in this room with their husbands who are trying to enjoy their meals. Please keep the conversation civil.'

"Bolton Chapman looked up surprised, and said, 'I told your old friend to tend to his own business. You do the same. Go sit down with your whore.' His friends then roared with laughter.

"Your father then slapped him across his face so hard that he fell out of his chair and his nose started to bleed. He was furious when he got up. Chapman was a big, husky man and wanted to fight your father right there on the spot, but the doctor and the other men, along with the waiter and the restaurant owner, stopped him. Chapman's two well-dressed buddies just sat there, very amused.

"Immediately Chapman said, '*I'm going to kill you, you bastard. If you aren't a coward, you will meet me tomorrow morning at*'–I couldn't understand the name of the place.

"But immediately Dr. Best said '*No. No. Not there!*'

"Then Chapman responded, '*All right, you bastard, pick any place. I'll see you there tomorrow morning!*'"

"Your father looked at Dr. Best and Best said he did not condone duels, but anyplace was better than where Chapman had suggested. Your father asked the doctor to suggest a place. The doctor did not want to do it, but finally said behind the Northern Fishery Warehouse would be better than Chapman's location. Both then agreed to meet there at ten o'clock. Chapman said he would bring the pistols. Your father agreed.

"Needless to say, that ended the meal. Dr. Best and Mr. Walters, the other man there with his wife, said Chapman was a drunken bully and they did not trust him. Both of them said they would come as witnesses to try to keep Chapman from cheating."

Mother choked up a bit and said nothing for a few moments.

"Mother, did Dr. Best agree to be Father's second?" I asked.

"No, but he and Mr. Walters did agree to be there as witnesses."

She started to continue, but I interrupted. "Mother, do you know if they had a duel adjudicator or judge?"

"No, you father had no one to be his second or to be in charge of the duel. Bolton Chapmen had his two friends and another person there. One of his friends served as Bolton's second."

Then Mother hesitated. "No. That's not right. Dr. Best did step in and try to keep the duel honest. I guess he tried to be the adjudicator.

"I understand from Dr. Best and Mr. Walters that everyone was there behind the warehouse at 10 the next morning. One of Chapman's friends presented the case with the dueling pistols to your father and he selected one. It was loaded, but you father insisted on reloading it himself, then test fired it. He reloaded the weapon again and was satisfied it would fire. Chapman reloaded his pistol also. They were about to begin the duel and that's when Dr. Best stepped in.

"Dr. Best told me he did not trust Chapman and his gang, so he insisted he would go over the rules and do the count. He said the two men agreed to stand back-to-back and pace off ten paces as he counted, then turn and fire."

My mother again choked up.

"Mother, if you don't want to talk about this anymore tonight, I understand," I told her.

"No, Son, I need to finish this. I don't want to go over it again." She took a deep breath.

"Dr. Best said he went over the rules three times.

"They both understood and agreed. Then Dr. Best had them both line up back-to-back. He then started the count, but when he got to nine, Bolton Chapman *prematurely* turned and shot just as Dr. Best said ten. He hit your father in the side of the neck, and he fell immediately–bleeding and paralyzed. He murdered your father."

Mother stroked the lace on her sleeve for a few moments before she proceeded.

"Mr. Walters said he and Dr. Best immediately cried out, '*Foul! Foul!*' But one of the other men with Chapman ran over to your father and pulled the pistol out of his hand. The man discharged the pistol into the side of the warehouse, close to where Bolton Chapman had been standing, to make it appear that your father had fired a shot. He then ran back to Chapman with the pistol and the four of them got in their carriage and hurried off."

Mother was quiet for several minutes as we listened to the crickets in the darkness and watched the small flame from the open oil wick torch. Then she pulled out an envelope.

"This is the statement both Dr. Best and Mr. Walters signed, describing the duel. They made another copy and submitted it to the Boston city constable, but Bolton Chapman had left town by then. As far as I know, nothing ever happed to Chapman because of the unfair duel. I found out later he had done such a thing before, in Lynn."

"Where is Lynn?" I asked.

"It's a little north of Boston." Her hand shook as it held out the envelope.

I took it and quietly slipped the sworn statement into my pocket. This would not be the end of the story.

The *third* significant event that summer happened while I was with JK, and it changed our relationship.

The first month of my summer I was pretty much involved with Howard and his Taylor Plantation projects, except for several evenings a week I spent with Howard and JK at the club, or visiting with Melanie Ellen and her family. I spent most of my Sunday afternoons taking Melanie Ellen in the carriage on picnics along the Savannah River, along with Lilly our chaperone and one of the Kerns' cute little pickaninny housemaids. The housemaid was about twelve years old.

The Kerns family members were much more formal than the Taylors. They lacked the spontaneous sense of humor the Taylors and I had. Melanie Ellen was the exception. She sometimes embarrassed her stodgy family by her spunky ways and impish humor.

Melanie Ellen's sister, Mary Helen, was the eldest in the family and was already married to an adjoining plantation owner's eldest son, Donald Gallagher. The Gallagher family owned the Stratford Plantation, about the size of the Taylor and Fields of Shannon Plantations combined. As there were only three children in the Kerns family–Mary Helen, JK, and Melanie Ellen–it was lucky for me there was no pressure for another arranged marriage to expand the family empire.

From the first time we met, I sensed a barrier between JK and me. Although he was friendly and kidded me about Melanie Ellen, something was not right between us. It may have been me as much as him. He seemed to be growing into the mold of the typical arrogant Southern plantation owner, who were in plentiful supply down there. Anyway, we both tried to rise above it and were pleasant to each other.

JK seemed genuinely interested in showing me his projects for expanding and improving the shipping of agricultural products out of the Savannah area. It fit well with their family plans to expand into the shipping business with the Dutch company and their sailing ships.

It was on Thursday, the 24th of July, the second week I had been spending time with JK, when the accident happened. We were down at the new wharf which was under construction on the banks of the Savannah River. JK was proudly showing me two of their warehouses being constructed and how the different rice, cotton and tobacco products were packaged and stored before being moved to the wharf for loading.

The new wharf held two large, vertical pole booms, about 40 feet high, with ropes and pulleys attached to them for loading freight. A lot of white and black men were there working on the construction project.

JK was truly delighted with the progress and was showing both me and Mr. Von Koffland, a partner in their new shipping operation, how the whole operation would work when it was finished.

As JK showed us around, we walked up onto the wharf and stood by one of the large freight booms. The boom had a heavy rope hanging from it. The boom rope happened to be hanging perfectly to tempt a person to grab it and swing from a large wooden crate across to a stack of lumber about 25 feet away. I think JK had done it before.

Well, as we stood there talking, the athletic young JK did just that. He jumped up onto the wooden crate, grabbed the loose rope hanging from the heavy boom standing high above us, then started to swing.

Then someone behind us yelled out, "No, don't do that! It's not secured!" But it was too late.

JK heard the man call out as he was already swinging thru the air toward the nearby stack of lumber. We all looked up in time to see the 40-foot boom come loose from the rope anchors which were temporarily securing it and start to fall. I made an attempt to try to grab one of the anchor ropes and hold it, but the boom was far too heavy.

Everyone watched in shock as the heavy boom holding JK dangling from the rope fell toward the muddy water of the river.

JK fell into the water first, then the huge, wooden pole boom with it ropes, pulleys and all, crashed into the water on top of him!

Everyone was stunned by the accident. I ran to the edge of the wharf and looked down into the muddy water and could not see JK or the boom. But there were several ropes still floating on the surface of the water, along with a lot of bubbles coming up out of the deep, murky river.

I kicked off my boots and ripped off my clothes and yelled at the workers to bring some ropes and ladders over to the edge of the wharf to help get JK out. I then jumped into the muddy water.

JK could not have been in the river for more than 15 or 20 seconds before I was in the water looking for him. I saw about where he had disappeared under the water and also where the boom hit and also disappeared. I hoped it had not fallen on him and killed him.

I grabbed a floating rope I hoped was the one JK had swung on, then pulled myself underwater–hopefully toward JK. It was the wrong rope! It had knots and other ropes tied to it, like one of the three anchor ropes. Surfacing immediately, I then grabbed another rope still floating on top of the water and down I went again.

This time, after quickly pulling myself down into the dark water using the second rope, I felt JK's leg and boot about seven feet below the surface. He was not struggling and seemed to be unconscious. He was tangled in one of the other anchor ropes, which was holding him down.

I looped my arms around his body and jerked him a couple of times, finally pulling his body loose from the tangle of ropes, then pushed him upwards above me. When we broke the surface into the bright sunlight, there were about a dozen workers lowering ropes and ladders from the wharf into the water next to me. There was also a black worker swimming in the water near us when we surfaced. He helped me quickly pull JK over to a ladder, and we tied a rope around his body. The workmen then hoisted JK's limp and unconscious body up to the floor of the wooden wharf and laid him down on a canvas.

I scrambled up the ladder, then got down on my knees to examine the unconscious man. He had a bloody gash on his forehead and was turning a dark reddish-blue color but his arms and legs were twitching. Fortunately, I had been there when my father saved a young Indian boy in Venezuela from drowning. I would do the same things my father had done.

First, at frantic pace, I had four men lift JK's body so that his legs were higher than his head while I squeezed his chest then held his nose and blew air into his mouth a couple of times to drain out the water in his lungs. A little dirty water and mucus came out. Then I had the men lay JK face down and knelt in front of him with his head between my knees. I then pushed down on the back of his chest and pulled back on his elbows to try to get him breathing again. He sputtered and showed some signs of life. We had repeated the process about four or five times when JK started to violently cough up a little more water and some vomit.

We stopped, then sat him up as he tried to catch his breath. His eyes opened a little, and he seemed to be coming to. The color in his face seemed to be returning to normal. However, he still looked a mess, with blood streaming down his forehead and mud with bits of moss and tiny leaves from the water in his hair and all over his clothes.

Relieved, I collapsed back into a sitting position, panting and exhausted, as the smiling young black man who had been in the water with us handed me my clothes. I then realized I was totally naked. I had lost my undergarments somewhere under the water. I quickly dressed while most of the workmen and Mr. Von Koffland hovered over JK to make sure he was recovering.

Mr. Von Koffland had his driver bring his carriage over and we helped the sick and dazed JK into it. Mr. Von Koffland then ordered one of the workmen to get JK's and my saddled horses and follow us back to JK's place. The three of us then rode in his carriage with his driver back to the Fields of Shannon Plantation.

Our unexpected mid-morning arrival at the plantation must have generated some concern. A black worker was riding my horse, leading JK's and following Mr. Von Koffland's big fancy carriage. Mr. Kerns and Melanie Ellen were both standing under the portico when we arrived. I jumped out quickly and ran over to Mr. Kerns and told him there had been an accident but that JK was all right. We all helped poor JK out of the carriage, walked him over and laid him on a wicker sofa on the open veranda.

Then Mr. Von Koffland and I stepped to one side and quietly explained to Mr. Kerns what had happened as Mrs. Kerns and Melanie Ellen huddled over JK. The poor man still looked like he was sick and felt terrible.

I thanked Mr. Von Koffland for his help, shook his hand, then went to my horse to leave. Melanie Ellen came running after me.

"Jack, my folks want you to join us for dinner tonight," she said, out of breath.

"No, Melanie Ellen, I don't think JK will be feeling too hot for a little while. Your family ought to be alone tonight," I replied.

Melanie Ellen nodded and said nothing as I gave her a little kiss on the cheek, then left on my horse. I could see Mr. Von Koffland intensely describing the incident to Mr. and Mrs. Kerns as I rode away on my borrowed horse.

I stayed away from The Fields of Shannon Plantation for several days, but heard that JK was doing fine and had totally recovered. On the Monday afternoon after the accident, JK arrived at the Taylor Plantation as Howard and I were coming back from inspecting the initial construction on the Taylor Lake dam. JK quietly pulled me to the side, then shook my hand and thanked me for saving his life. He had a different look in his eyes. He seemed to view me differently now, as if he owed me a debt which he could never pay. I did not need or want that. I hoped somehow things would eventually improve between JK and me, because someday I also hoped he would be my brother-in-law.

JK invited me over for dinner that evening, which I again declined. I asked him to tell Melanie Ellen that if she was free after church the following Sunday, I would like to take her out along the Savannah River for a picnic. He said he would.

After church that Sunday, using a borrowed small carriage from Howard, I took Melanie Ellen to the banks of the Savannah River. Mrs. Kerns did not send along a chaperone this time, which I appreciated. It looked like a summer storm was developing, so we chose to go to the edge of town, where there was a park and several colonnades where we could visit and eat our meal if it rained. And it did.

This was an important afternoon for me, because I wanted to propose marriage to Melanie. But before doing so, I wanted to make certain she could be happy living with a man who loved her dearly, but did not have the money to compete with her family. And I was not going to try. Also, if she married me, we would not be living in the South.

We sat there silently under the roof of the colonnade, eating our fried chicken and drinking some red Taylor wine made in their winery from grapes grown in their vineyard. The light thunderstorm was letting up. Without words being spoken, I got the impression Melanie knew what was on my mind and in my heart.

"What do you suppose Howard and JK will be doing ten years from now?" I asked.

"Oh, I don't think that's too hard to figure out. Both of them will be married, and Howard will probably be a congressman. JK will have doubled the size of The Fields of Shannon and will have bought out Mr. Von Koffland and his partners' shipping line. His fancy wife will be living in Paris and poor JK, here," Melanie said laughingly.

"Melanie, this has been the most pleasant summer of my life. And what has made it pleasant is that I met you. We've talked about marriage, but I have nothing to offer you, and I certainly cannot provide you anything like the life you are used to living," I said.

Melanie was quiet for a few moments, then replied. "Jack, you don't have to provide me with everything I have now. If we need anything, Father can…." then she stopped.

"'Father can help us?'" I said completing her thought and smiling.

"Well, no–I didn't mean that," she replied, embarrassed.

"I plan to graduate next year. Nothing would delight me more than to marry you and spend our lives together. But, Melanie, you come from a wealthy family, and I do not. But I do have a lot of pride, maybe too much, and if we did marry, I would want you to be happy. It would be like us starting from nothing. I would not and could not compete with the Howards and the JKs of the world. In fact, we would not even live here in the States, perhaps Mexico or Peru," I stated rather soberly.

Then I continued.

"Melanie, my mother is a good example of what could happen. She was from a wealthy family and married my father. They had an exciting and wonderful life together until he was killed. Now she is back here working with her brother, trying to maintain her pride so she does not have to depend on Uncle Will. She had little money remaining from what Father left her. Most of that went into my education. That could happen to you if we married."

Melanie had tears in her eyes. She responded after a long silence.

"Jack, ladies here are like trophies. They are supposed to be pretty, witty and wealthy, but not contribute much, except running a beautiful home using their servants. Most importantly, they should offer political connections and have children."

She looked down at her empty wine glass for several moments then continued. "Jack, when we first met, I liked you. You were different. You were from another world. You are from a world I would like to know and move to. It's the real world. If we got married, I would want to help you and be your friend, partner and lover, wherever you went," she said, now with a tear streaming down her cheek.

I gave sweet Melanie a long, tight hug as we listened to the thunder in the distance and watched the light rain fall from a new storm developing in the hot, Georgia afternoon. *I had found another gem like my Mother*.

"Are you sure you would be happy in my world, my poor world?" I asked.

"Certainly, I would."

"And if we got in trouble, where would we get help?" I asked, needling her a little bit.

"I would *not* ask my family. I would go chop wood instead," She replied rather impertinently.

I had to laugh. I had a hard time visualizing her chopping wood.

"Melanie, here's the hardest part. I don't have the money to come back here after I graduate. Would you come to England and marry me there?"

"Certainly, I'll go wherever you say," she said without hesitating.

"Thank you. I love you, little lady," I said, giving her another hug.

We sat silently, enjoying the moment, then I said. "I need to ask for your father's permission. Do you think he will give it to me?"

"Ask him and see," she replied teasing me a bit.

Then she laughed, tilting her lovely face up to the sky.

"What was so funny?" I asked.

"Jack, it might be better if you ask me first," she said with her eyes gleaming.

Embarrassed, I stammered, "Well, yes, it might be."

After I recovered my composure, I grabbed her two hands and stood up, facing her. "My dearest Miss Melanie, will you marry me, for better or worse, till death do us part?"

Tears in her eyes, she hesitated, then replied with a slight smile, "Yes, John Taylor McIntyre, I will marry you. But it better be for the better, otherwise I'll have to chop wood!"

And so that was the summer of '51. It was a defining time in my life. I was with family and friends. I was young and had the whole, exciting world with its challenges in front of me. And I met my future wife, Melanie Ellen Kerns, the love of my life. Even then, we could see the clouds of the American Civil War brewing. At the time we had no way to realize its terrible impacts on all of our lives.

A rooster crowed, startling me back to consciousness. It took a few seconds for me to realize where I was. It was dark and the morning air was cold. I could smell wet animal manure. Then I remembered–Ashburn's barn. I was in Ashburn's barn in Harshaw, Arizona Territory. What a lot of water had passed under the bridge since my summer in Georgia.

Thirty years ago, sleeping alone in a barn like a bum would never have seemed possible to me. It was just an indication of how out of control my life had been. Oh well, I was here and had plenty to do, if I could stay sober. Eighteen days, that was pretty good for me. I was going to see if I could make it nineteen. *If Preacher Sullivan could do it, so could I.*

Chapter 4

Excitement in the Patagonias

It was still dark and cold when a second damned rooster perched up in the rafters of Ashburn's barn started to crow. It must have been four thirty in the morning and trying to sleep below two crowing roosters was impossible. This was not going to work. I was sleepy, grumpy and had a bad taste in my mouth. The thought of taking my Sharps 50 rifle and blowing the birds through the roof of the barn crossed my mind. Instead, I decided to get up and take a look outside to see how much it had snowed.

After stubbing my toe on the metal cot leg, I fumbled around in the darkness trying to find the matches in my jacket pocket. Finally, I found them, but they were wet. Then I remembered the matches in the tobacco can on the table. With those, I got the lantern lit.

About then I started to think of everything Ashburn lacked in his barn. Hot coffee and a warm fire would be a great way to start the day, but the only stove was in Pete's locked office. Even though he showed me where the key was, I didn't think it would be appropriate for me to go in there and start a fire. Besides all the wood was outside and wet from the rain and snow.

It was cold, but not as cold as the night before. The snow must be creating a blanket effect and keeping the temperature under control. After getting my clothes and boots on I checked the water bucket standing on a short stubby table by the barn storage shed door. Of course, it was empty. Things were not starting off too good for me today.

Wanting to rinse out my foul tasting mouth and wash my face, I picked up the empty water bucket and, with the lantern, walked out to the edge of the barn roof trying to decide where I could find some fresh water. The horse trough was an option. But then I remembered Pete used a faucet near the horse trough to draw water. It was tied to the pipeline running from the spring up the canyon. If the pipeline wasn't frozen, I would be in luck.

Outside in the barn yard there was snow–about 4 to 6 inches, I figured. Between the deep snow and the wet horse shit below it, walking across the messy corral to the water facet was hazardous. I started to carefully slog across the muddy corral carrying the empty water bucket and the kerosene lamp, when my boot got stuck and came off in the thick, stinky ooze.

Then things got worse. Trying to balance myself on one foot while holding the empty water bucket in one hand and the lantern in the other, I looked for my wayward boot stuck in mud somewhere in the darkness. Then I lost my balance and fell backwards, sitting in the cold, smelly mess. To add insult to injury, my lamp went out. I was beginning to think my day couldn't get any worse!

After that, I went into an *I don't give a damn attitude*. Cursing, I got up and with filthy hands and a cold wet bottom. I felt around for my lost boot, the lamp and water bucket. After finding them, I stomped back to the dry barn madder than a wet hen. Inside the barn, I stubbed my muddy toes several times before I could find the matches and get the lantern going again.

Without hesitating, I took off my other boot and my socks, grabbed the muddy water bucket and lamp, then marched back out across the cold, messy corral *barefooted*. It felt like I was walking in a bed of coals! But then I figured my luck finally was changing, because the water pipeline had not frozen.

I hung the lamp on the corral fence, then broke the ice on the horse trough and washed my hands and face. Then I took off my pants and bottom part of my long Johns and washed and rung them out in the freezing water. It was stinging cold, but my anger still had me smoking.

After cleaning up the water bucket, I filled it with fresh water from the spring fed water facet, then bundled my wet clothes under my arm and stomped back through the muddy corral with the water bucket half full and me half naked! I was glad it was dark because I must have been quite a sight to behold!

By the time I got back under the roof of the dry barn, my teeth were rattling and I was shivering like a wayward, horny preacher caught in a whorehouse. No fire be damned! I opened Pete's locked office and used some kerosene and hay and a few pieces of broken lumber to start a fire in his small Franklin stove. After hanging my wet clothes on a chair and hovering around the fresh fire for several minutes, I ran back outside to the frozen wood pile and picked up an armload of healthy-sized logs for the stove.

On my way back to the barn in the dark morning, freezing air, the damned roosters started crowing again. Finally, I had a target for my anger–the roosters! Because of them, I had missed an extra hour of sleep and got myself into my current mess.

I listened to the taunting cocks as I fed several fresh, wet logs into Pete's office stove and stood there for a few minutes trying to warm up and thinking of ways I could get even. Finally, I went outside again and scooped up some snow off the corral fence and made a hard snowball. Back inside, I set the lamp on the dirt floor of the barn and tried to gauge where the crowing rooster was perched in the dark roof rafters above me.

I threw the snowball at the annoying invisible bird as hard as I could, but missed. I heard several alarmed chickens clucking up there, then immediately afterwards the second rooster crowed again, almost like he was amused with my frustration.

I thought hey, this is futile and ridiculous, fighting with two dumb birds. I should know better. Then the first roster crowed again and my anger returned.

"Damn you, I'll get you if I have to burn this place down!" I yelled at them.

Still barefooted and naked from the waist down, I walked back outside and this time made two bigger and harder snowballs, then carried them back inside, holding them in one hand and the lantern in the other.

Again I set the lantern on the dirt floor and took careful aim at the dark place underneath the barn roof where I thought the second wily rooster was lurking. This time, with a hard toss, I nailed one of the buggers. And what a commotion he made as he came flying down toward me out of the darkness, squawking excitedly, snow stuck to his chest and feathers flying.

I threw the second snowball and hit nothing, but the first one did the trick. No more crowing. So I left my clothes to dry in Pete's office and went back to my cot and put out the lamp. Success–and the revenge felt good. I smiled to myself, thinking how much my world had changed over the years for something as small as this to give me pleasure. I quickly went back to sleep, warm and content.

When I woke up again, the light was coming in the window. At first I was happy, then a little bit sad–remembering my journey during the night back to happier times.

After wrapping myself in a blanket, I went to the window and looked out. It looked like a different world out there with all the beautiful snow. It had been years since I had seen any real snow, only some dustings in the Mexican Sierra Madre Mountains three winters before.

Pete Ashburn and his dog were walking across the canyon toward me to do his chores at the barn. He was carrying an empty milk bucket. I quickly went to his office in a hurry and gathered up my drying trousers and underwear on his chair near the stove. The room was warm and there were still some coals in the Franklin stove.

Still barefooted and standing on the dirt floor, I slipped on my warm damp clothes and put the last two logs in the stove as Pete walked in.

"Oh ... good morning, Jack. It's warm in here. Thanks for making the fire. Were you comfortable here last night?" Pete asked, a little surprised.

"Yes, just fine," I lied as I stood there barefooted.

Then I continued to lie.

"I was just stoking up the stove and looking for some coffee so I could brew up a fresh pot. Do you have any?"

Pete opened a box on the floor, pulled out a can and handed it to me. He then said he needed to go on about his chores and would come back later and have coffee with me. I prepared the coffee and put the pot on the stove, then went back to the storage room to finish dressing and pick up after myself. Then I went out to help Pete with his chores.

Pete was tossing hay with a pitchfork into a horse manger, when he almost stabbed a forlorn and frazzled, wet rooster resting on the haystack.

"What the hell are you doing here?" he asked the bird.

I said nothing and watched.

Glancing at me he said, a bit bewildered. "I about stabbed my dumb rooster. He never sleeps out here. Must be sick or something."

I agreed and changed the subject.

"Can I help you? Do you have another pitchfork?"

Pete nodded and handed me his pitchfork and grabbed another one. We took hay out to the three mules in the corral, then to Bartholomew and the two horses he had in stalls in the barn. Pete brought his milk cow into the barn and started milking her. The thin, warm stream of milk steamed as it hit the side of the cold metal bucket. The cow had no calf, but was still wet (producing milk).

Peter and I visited as he milked the cow. He was concerned that the snow would affect his business, both at the livery stable and at his meat market. It was now after six in the morning and a few people were stirring around town. Now that I was back in the States, I decided it might be time for me to buy a dollar pocket watch to keep better track of time again.

A group of five boys were having fun whooping it up out in the street and throwing snowballs. I wanted to join them, but figured I'd rather go over to Molly's and have flapjacks. I offered to buy Peter breakfast, but he said he needed to take the warm, foamy milk back home where his wife and kids were waiting to eat breakfast with him.

I decided to go by the Catholic church down in the Mexican part of Harshaw and see if my friend, the padre, was ready for breakfast.

When the Padre de la Riva and I got to Molly's Café, the place was about half full, including a few Harshaw business owners, two mine owners and several cowboys. We sat down at a side table in the café, while everyone else was gathered around the middle tables talking about the massacre.

We quickly understood from the talk that an Indian attack had taken place the day before at the Becker Ranch in the San Rafael Valley. Mr. and Mrs. Becker, along with their six-year-old daughter, were killed. The Becker's older son, Jimmy, came in from riding on the ranch in the evening and found them massacred. His mother and little sister had been ruthlessly and crudely scalped.

The upset young man apparently reported that there were some things missing in their house and their two horses, along with two saddles and gear, were gone. Jimmy Becker then rode into town during the night and notified Deputy Sheriff Ty Sorrells. Sorrells got a couple of men and rode back to the ranch in the snowstorm with Jimmy to investigate. They had not returned yet.

Mr. Finley was talking as we waited for Molly and listened.

"I wonder if it was Apaches? The military captured Geronimo last year and took him down to Florida. The rest of his Apache bucks are on the reservation and I haven't heard that any of them have left or are raising hell anymore. No, I think it might be somebody else trying to blame it on the Indians."

A lot of people in the group agreed with Mr. Finley. Another person then added that he heard Jimmy Becker thought it was three white men who did it, based on what they took and the fact that they were riding shod horses. Jimmy had followed their tracks a ways toward the Patagonia Mountains before he lost them when it got dark and started to rain. He then hurried to Harshaw for help. Everyone was offering opinions while the padre and I continued to listen.

Molly was standing near the men with a coffee pot in her hand, listening to the excited talk. Finally, she broke away from the group and came over to pour us some coffee. Her large pot was almost empty and only some dark muddy looking stuff drained into my cup. She apologized.

"Sorry, gentlemen. I can't believe the terrible news! I'll bring you some fresh coffee from the pot I have brewing. Jack, I know what you want, and I'll bring you a clean cup. Padre, what would you like?"

The padre ordered steak and eggs, with tortillas and beans.

Molly started to leave when I interrupted. "Molly, I hope I don't mess you up, but the padre's order sounds good to me too."

Molly stopped dead in her tracks.

"Jack, I can't believe it! You are not having flapjacks? I have a fresh batch of batter just waiting for you in the kitchen. But don't worry, I can use it up."

I smiled and nodded.

"My goodness! This has been a strange morning," she said, a little bewildered, as she walked away.

I agreed with her.

The excited chatter went on for awhile, then slowly the people finished their meals and went out into the bright, snowy street to work. The clouds were gone and the morning sun coming over the hills from the east reflected brightly on the slowly melting snow covering the ground, buildings and trees.

Preacher Sullivan came in after the café had cleared out, leaving only the padre and me. We sat alone at a table near the window, leisurely enjoying our breakfast.

"Good morning, gentlemen. Jack, I'm shocked! You are not eating flapjacks! I wasn't going to have them either, unless you were paying."

About a half hour later, Sullivan was finishing his breakfast and the padre and I were drinking coffee, discussing the massacre. Through the window we saw three men ride up and tie their horses to Molly's hitching rail. The men were wearing yellow, muddy slickers and looked tired and hungry. Their horses were muddy and looked beat. The men were strangers in town.

"Gentlemen, looks like trouble has arrived. I'll lay you an eagle to a dollar that those are the Apaches they're looking for," I quietly said as the men loitered outside talking and looking around.

Molly heard my comment. I then told her to send old Francisco out the back to get help and she did.

Being unarmed, I asked Molly if she had a pistol or club in the back that I could hide and use in case we had trouble. She rushed into the kitchen and brought back a heavy oak branch with a knot about the size of my fist on the end. She explained that, except for her shotgun, this was the only thing she could quickly find. She smiled nervously and said it was what she used to stir the ashes through the bottom of the kitchen stove grate.

After she'd gone back into the kitchen, I joked that her club looked like a personal extremity that froze and broke off of my poor old mule Bartholomew. A nervous Sullivan gagged on his coffee, laughing at my crude joke. When we heard the doorknob rattle, I quietly slid the crooked club under my jacket and continued to visit with the padre and Sullivan.

One of the strangers walked into the café and looked around, then went back outside and said something to the other two. The three men took their rifles out of their saddle scabbards and came into the café. Inside, they chose a table near the door, took off their slickers and hats and set them on chairs near their table. They lined up the rifles against the wall behind them.

The tough men all looked like Texans and were armed with Colt revolvers. They smelled of old sweat, mud and tobacco.

The three suspected killers walked over to warm themselves at Molly's big pot belly stove and murmured amongst themselves.

I quietly told the padre and Sullivan that I was going to turn myself into a drunk again and warned them to be ready for some action. They both nodded. Molly also heard me as she stood next to us with coffee.

After warming up, the three men returned to their table and sat down. Molly took her pot of coffee over to them.

"Good morning, gentlemen. How about some hot coffee?" She said with a grin.

"That sure as hell sounds good to me, honey. How about a steak and a couple of eggs too? I hope you have some," the meanest looking one said with a husky Texas drawl.

He then continued. "Sam, what do you and Tom want?"

"Sounds good to me, Del. But I want four eggs, runny, and a big steak, and some potatoes, and biscuits," the one called Sam replied.

The third man, Tom, spoke with a crackly voice. "Give me the same thing, but I want my eggs scrambled. Sam, I can't figure you out. Runny eggs taste like snot."

Tom looked sick and was sweating.

"Coming right up, gentlemen," Molly said pleasantly.

Molly then turned to go to the kitchen when the first Texan, Del, asked her gruffly. "Lady, what is the name of this shit hole–Washington Camp?"

"No, this is Harshaw. Washington Camp is about fifteen miles south of here, near the border," Molly replied.

"Oh? Then how much further is the border?" the Texan called Del asked.

"About three or four miles south of Washington Camp."

"Good. Hurry up and get us our breakfast, lady. We're hungry," the same guy demanded.

Molly quickly disappeared into the kitchen.

Then the sick one Tom said, "Del, be nice to the lady, we want her to make us a good meal."

"Yeah, Del, be nice to her, we don't want the fat bitch to poison us," Sam said, chuckling with a mean sneer.

Luckily, Molly had already gone into the kitchen and didn't hear his ugly comment.

"Damn it, Tom, you don't look so good. Maybe we had better find a doctor and get you some medicine before we go," Sam said, in a loud voice.

"Fellows, I feel like hell. I don't think I can go much farther without getting some medicine and rest," Tom responded, hunched over and obviously hurting.

"Damn it, we need to get to Mexico. It should only be a few more hours. You can get a doctor and rest there," Del replied.

Del then took notice of us quietly drinking our coffee and chatting across the room.

"Say, *old timers*, we're headed to Mexico and need to get some money before we go. Is there a bank in this shit-house town?" Del asked, obviously half-snockered.

Sam let out a horselaugh and even Tom smiled, but then flinched from the pain.

The three of us looked at each other, then I replied with a slurred loud voice.

"No gents, there's no bank in this shit-house town. But we are fortunate, here. They call this place Harshaw, not Hard-shit. *You know, like they call Pecos–'soft-peckers.'*"

The padre and the preacher looked shocked. Del turned red and started to stand, but Sam touched his arm to calm him down. At the same time both Sam and Tom about fell out of their chairs laughing. Apparently Del was from Pecos.

"Del, let it go. We don't need any more trouble here. But you've got to admit, it was funny," Tom said with laughter in his eyes.

Del glanced at his buddies and calmed down a bit. "Listen, you crazy old fart, if you had a gun, I would drain a little of that bullshit out of you!" Del shouted angrily across the room.

I shrugged and smiled back at them. That dampened conversation in the room for awhile. Then the Texans started talking again, this time quietly, as they drank their coffee.

"What the hell are you trying to do, get us killed?" Preacher Sullivan whispered hoarsely.

The padre was hiding a smile, seemingly finding the whole exchange funny.

The three of us talked quietly for a couple of minutes, discussing our situation.

"Gentlemen, I don't think there's any doubt about it. These fellows are the ones that killed the Becker family. And I bet they'll raise more hell here before they head off to Mexico," I said under my breath.

"And Deputy Sheriff Sorrells is out of town looking for these guys. He might not be back until this afternoon," commented Padre Lorenzo de la Riva in a low voice.

"So what do we do?" Preacher Sullivan asked.

Molly came out of the kitchen with the Texans' meals and placed the food on the table in front of them. They lit up and immediately started to dig in and talk to each other excitedly.

Molly went back to the kitchen and returned with a fresh coffee pot, filling their cups.

"Lady, I've been waiting for this for a week. Tom can't cook for shit," Sam said, also obviously greased up a bit.

The other two chuckled as they shoveled down their food and gulped their coffee.

Molly came over to our table and filled our cups.

"What are we going to do?" she asked in a whisper.

"Now's the time to make our move, while they are eating," I said, "I'm going to act like I'm drunk and start to leave. When I get to the door over by that mean bastard, Del, make a big commotion in the kitchen to distract them. I think I can take care of him if I get close."

Molly and Preacher Sullivan nodded slightly.

"If we don't do something here, where they think they're safe, they sure as hell are going to rob a store or something and probably kill someone. Are you game?" I asked.

"I'll take care of the noise. And I have a double-barreled shot gun in the kitchen too. I'll be ready to use it!" Molly said, trying to maintain a normal smile.

"Jack, if you can get close to them and take that Del bastard out, toss me one of those rifles," Preacher Sullivan added.

Padre de la Riva nodded, opening the edge of his long coat, exposing a small two-shot derringer he held in the palm of his right hand. He then switched hands and started drinking his coffee with his left hand.

The Texans were eating heartily and talking not noticing our developing little cabal. We agreed to start the show in about one minute, giving Molly enough time to get back to the kitchen and get ready.

The padre and the big preacher adjusted their chairs slightly. A few moments later, we saw Molly look out from behind the kitchen door, which was ajar. She nodded.

I excused myself, speaking rather loudly and telling Preacher Sullivan I would see him down at Cano's Bar after lunch. The Texan, Del, looked up casually when I said it. Then I purposely spilled my coffee cup and spoon on the floor as I stumbled to my feet. Playing the role of a drunk came easy for me, because I was well practiced at it. The three Texan's looked up from their food and snickered.

"Worthless old drunk," Del told the others, and they again chuckled and continued with their meal.

The preacher stood up to help steady me, then stooped down and picked up my cup and spoon. Acting embarrassed, I dusted myself off, then awkwardly put on my coat and hat and headed unsteadily toward the door. The preacher remained standing, as if he was concerned I would fall again.

The three amused Texans watched me as I approached the door close to where their rifles were standing, and Del was sitting. I adjusted my hat like I was getting ready to go outside. Then crash, it sounded like a tub full of dishes hit the floor in the kitchen. The startled Texans looked toward the kitchen, and I made my move.

"What the hell was that?" Del said, still looking towards the kitchen.

Immediately, I had my oak club out and brought it down hard on Del's head. He fell to the floor. I then grabbed two of their rifles and tossed one to the preacher, who caught it on the fly with one hand.

Big Molly then appeared in the kitchen doorway with her 12 gauge, double-barreled shotgun aiming at them. The padre stood stiffly, his silly little derringer in hand and steely resolve in his eyes.

As Del hit the floor like a dead man, both Sam and Tom instinctively started for their pistols.

"You bastards will wake up in Hell if you make one more move," I said calmly, cocking a cartridge into the Henry rifle.

The two shocked Texans sat back down when they saw four guns pointing at them and their buddy lying sprawled out on the floor.

The preacher then took charge. "You bastards keep your hands on the table and don't even twitch."

He then told the padre to get their pistols.

Del laid on the floor, not moving. I thought I might have killed him, but then saw he was still breathing.

About that time, Mr. Finley and three other merchants with shotguns burst into the café dining room from the kitchen. Francisco had done his work.

I asked Big Molly for a rope. She brought me some heavy twine, which Preacher Mike Sullivan used to tie Tom. Sam cursed angrily as I tied him up, but Tom almost seemed relieved. We then rolled the bleeding Del over and tied him up while he was still unconscious.

Francisco brought a wheelbarrow to the front door and the four merchants dragged Del out and laid him in it. The husky preacher then wheeled the unconscious killer over to the iron lockup cage in Deputy Sheriff Sorrell's office. We marched Sam and Tom over behind them. Mr. Finley had two of his workers guard the locked cage with shotguns until a tired Deputy Sheriff Sorrells returned to town that afternoon.

That night on my cot in Pete Ashburn's barn, I mentally went through the day's events. After a miserable start, both the day and the events finished with a happy ending.

Tom, the sick Texan, finally confessed to Deputy Ty Sorrells that they killed the Becker family, but only after a promise of some medicine from Dr. Harrison and a warm place to sleep.

The next day was Saturday. I bought supplies to take back to my camp in the Escondida Basin. This time, I painfully left the four quarts of booze off the list of supplies I normally took back with me. But I knew I still had a ½ quart of hooch back in the old Spanish tunnel where I was staying.

Monday morning, the town's weekly newspaper, *The Arizona Bullion*, came out with a single page special edition. Its caption read *Molly's Muggers take down Texas Killers*. We were the heroes in town for several days. We were all offered drinks many times. It was terribly hard for the preacher and me to decline them.

I was proud of myself when I left Harshaw on Bartholomew Monday afternoon, wearing my mud-stained trousers. This time I visited Harshaw without getting drunk and embarrassing myself. Progress!

Chapter 5

My First Real Job

On my two and a half hour ride back to my hidden camp in the Patagonia Mountains, I had plenty of time to reminisce. Being sober helped. I mentally went over my early professional life. It had been full and exciting, with many unexpected twists and some heart-wrenching turns.

My now being here in the Arizona Territory was a direct result of what happened to me during my early career. I'd come out of Mexico in August less than six months ago. I was on a mission, an unfinished mission. What my friends in Harshaw did not know was that *I had been here before*, years ago, when this country was still under the sovereign control of the Mexican Republic.

On my first visit here, I had also come from the south. The Patagonia Mountains were then known as the Chihuahuita Mountains–named by the Pima Indians. It had been quite an experience, one I would not trade for the world.

Occasionally talking to myself like a madman, I rode up the wet trails into the mountains. Memories of the circumstances that led to my first job and the strange sequence of events that had once brought me to this part of the world poured through my mind.

After I left Georgia in the summer of '51, I was totally focused on finishing my mining engineering degree at the University of Edinburgh and finding a job. My goal was to bring Melanie Ellen Kerns to England so we could be married, then travel to wherever my new job took us. I was hoping it would be Mexico. My father's old boss, Mr. Walter M. Kearny, ultimately gave me the job I wanted, but it also complicated my life.

Mr. Kearny was the General Manager of the New Exploration and Business Division of The New Wales Equipment and Mining Company, Ltd. Before I graduated in June of 1852, Mr. Kearny sent me a telegram and asked me to meet him at his office in Manchester if I was interested in a job. He knew I would have the exact credentials their company wanted for their international project managers.

Mr. Kearny and his company had gone the extra mile with Mother and me after Father's death. They gave Mother a small bonus to help her through the difficult times and to help pay for my education. Although there were no commitments, I did hope I could work for Father's old company, or a company like it.

After my graduation in June, I met with Mr. Kearny at his office in Manchester. When we met this time, I looked at the man through different eyes, those of an adult and not a child. Albeit young and inexperienced, I could see what Father had said about Mr. Kearny. He was a good company man–careful with the company's money and not a risk taker. Nevertheless, he made me a very good job offer for employment with his company somewhere in Latin or South America. He said people at the company headquarters in London would make the final decision.

I explained to Mr. Kearny about wanting to get married first but lacked the money to do so. Mr. Kearny then sweetened the offer by saying he would advance me four months wages on my salary if I accepted the job. But then he also quickly added another qualifier. He said that most likely I would need to go to my first foreign assignment alone and get the project going before I could send for my wife. I didn't like it, but I could understand the company's logic.

Mr. Kearny said he would advance me the money immediately, but first we would need to go to the company headquarters in London. There

I would meet the big man, Sir Edward Chadwick, president of The New Wales Equipment and Mining Company, Ltd. and all of its subsidiaries. He would make the final decision on my first foreign assignment.

With a handshake, I accepted the job from Mr. Kearny. I also told him that Mexico was by far my first choice as a place to work and I would appreciate anything he could do to influence the decision.

Figure 2 Map of Northern England 1852

Then Mr. Kearny told me that he was considering me for one of two different assignments. One was in Mexico and the other was in Peru. He said the Mexico assignment was to finish opening a company mine in central Mexico, in the state of Querétaro and near the town of Querétaro. He said he could probably persuade Sir Edward to give me the Mexico assignment.

He quickly went on to explain that for the Mexico assignment I should use my British citizenship papers, because Mexican President Mariano Arista was serving at the pleasure of the past President, General Santa Ana. Having an American show up at their doorstep would not sit well because of the recent Mexican-American War. Joking, he said I would probably be shot if they suspected I was a *gringo*.

Mr. Kearny went on to explain that I would meet a Mr. Salvador Villarreal in Mexico City. There I would spend a month with Mr. Villarreal, who would introduce me to the key government officials before going on to Querétaro and opening the mining operation. He said another company engineer had already located the mine and confirmed the availability of ample silver deposits and laborers. But this engineer was pulled out because of problems and had been reassigned to a job in Peru. So my job would be to finish cleaning up, reopening and expanding what was once an old Spanish silver mine.

When I probed as to what problems the previous engineer had encountered, Mr. Kearny explained that the man did not speak Spanish well and he got himself in trouble with a local girl. But most important of all, the Mexicans did not like him. I asked no more questions.

Mr. Kearny again reiterated that he highly recommended my new wife not accompany me for at least the first three months of my assignment. Specifically, she should not come until after I made proper political connections for our company in Mexico City and then moved on to Querétaro and found a place for her to live. I understood, but was disappointed.

A major dilemma was brewing in my mind. Melanie was in Georgia; I was in England, and my first job would be in central Mexico. And most important of all, we were still apart and not yet married. Also, even with the advance, I still wouldn't have very much money. I was determined to work out the details.

The promise I'd made to Melanie the previous summer was that I would send for her so we could be married in England. It sounded like a good idea at the time, but things had changed. I wanted to wait until I met with Sir Edward Chadwick in London before making any final plans, then write to Melanie.

On Monday, June 14, 1852, Mr. Kearny and I took the early morning public stage from Manchester to London. The weather was beautiful and for most of the day there were only four passengers on the stage, so we were not too crowded. In the evening, we arrived in the town of Coventry in Warwick County. Mr. Kearny said we were about midway to London. We spent the night at a pleasant inn and had a nice meal with plenty of ale. We were off again early the next morning and arrived at the outskirts of London by late afternoon.

This time we stayed at an inn with a pub near the business district, where our main company headquarters was located. Both Mr. Kearny and I were tired, so we cleaned up and had a light dinner of soup with bread, cheese and ale. We went to bed early to prepare for the next day at the company's international headquarters.

Being in London for the first time was exciting. All my other trips to England and Scotland had been through the St. George Channel to Liverpool, bypassing London.

The next day was also a real education for me. I met Sir Edward Chadwick, the president of the company. Mr. Kearny said Sir Edward made it a policy to meet with all new company engineers scheduled to be sent on a foreign assignment.

At precisely 9:00 a.m., Mr. Kearny and I were escorted into Sir Edward Chadwick's office. Sir Edward was a short, stout man in his early fifties, well dressed, with thinning grayish-brown hair and a manicured beard. His office reminded me of a combination of the chancellor's office at the University of Edinburgh and parts of the mining museum in Newcastle. It was very nicely furnished with rich, carved wooden office furniture and three massive bookcases filled with technical mining books. Also on the walls were a selection of sketches, maps and small tools that depicted the history of mining from around the world. I could have spent an hour just looking over the interesting items he had there.

Anyway, after some polite talk about some of the places where I grew up and my interests at the university, Sir Edward spent the next four hours with Mr. Kearny and me. He lectured us on the company's policy, on how he expected to do business in other countries around the world. He spoke little of mining and almost exclusively about politics, the unique politics and dangers of doing business in foreign countries. Mr. Kearny had heard it all before, but he still listened intently.

"Mr. McIntyre, your father was one of our top producers. We were devastated to hear of his murder in Boston. He was a good man and a keen engineer. And your mother, how is your fine mother?" Sir Edward asked.

I politely answered and thanked him for his company's support after Father's death.

Then he abruptly continued. "Mr. McIntyre, do you know why The New Wales Equipment and Mining Company exists?"

Uneasy, I responded. "I assume to make money for the company owners."

"Yes, you are correct. But the challenge is, how do you go into someone else's country and ask them to allow you to extract their valuable minerals and ship them to England? Do you know how to do that?" He asked.

"No sir, not exactly. Could you explain?" I asked, knowing he was going to tell me anyway.

"Well, Mr. McIntyre, if you had a flock of a thousand sheep and I came along and said I wanted fifty of them, what would you do?"

"Well, assuming I wanted to sell them, I would try to make a deal with you. I would want you to buy them from me at a fair price–at a *good* price," I responded hesitantly groping for an answer and trying to guess at where he was going.

"Yes, Mr. McIntyre, you are correct. It's a simple concept. And when you are working in a foreign country, you must do the same thing," Sir Edward said looking at me intently. "Mr. McIntyre, may I call you John?"

"Certainly, John or Jack. My friends call me Jack," I responded.

"Thank you, Jack. Jack, this is a very simple concept. In order for us to do business with another country, we must offer them something. We must make it worth their while. Money is a good start, but there are always other things on the table which are important to the leaders of a country. It's not always money, but money is always a good second option. Do you understand what I am saying, Jack?" he said.

"Yes sir. I believe so. So we need to know what else might be on the table, what's important to these people," I replied, parroting his words and attempting to track his line of reasoning.

"Exactly, Jack. But this is something few people can do effectively, especially engineers. They may know what to do, even how to do it, but, as I said, only a few people can actually do it and do it effectively. Brains and honesty may sometimes impede you. Or simply they might not have the ability to work with other people. Our last man down there certainly couldn't."

Sir Edward then had his steward come in and serve us tea as we talked.

"Jack, this is called *politics*. Another interesting fact about dealing with countries is that you are still dealing with individual people. However, these individuals are usually not the most intelligent or honest men in that country, but they are the most dangerous and treacherous. They are also the most vulnerable. By that I mean to say, they are the most likely to be assassinated. So keep that in mind when you are dealing with them. They may not be around too long. Also, honor, with these people, is either a nonexistent or very rare commodity."

I could see where he was going. Suddenly, my training as a mining engineer from a prestigious university almost seemed secondary. His message was clear. If you did not know the right people in the country where you were working, and take care of them, your efforts were doomed to failure. I continued to listen.

"Jack, before we start a new operation in any country, especially in Central and South America, we make sure our project managers and engineers take the time to meet and hopefully make friends with the people running that country. We need to know these people and their politics, their strengths and weaknesses. We need to know if we can trust and deal with them. We need to know if they can and will deliver. They need to know the same about us.

"The rule of thumb for our managers is to recover our initial investment in one to three years. Another rule of thumb is to plan on paying their government up to 20% of our gross proceeds from the venture. It can be anything from paying off their president to building schools to bribing pain in the arse key people, whatever works. Just make sure you can recapture the money for the company in three years. We want to be profitable after that.

"And Jack, the man at the top is not always the power broker. Most times there are some very powerful men just below him, *the impresarios,* the powers behind the throne, so to speak. We also need to be able to identify and take care of them. Mexico is a good example. Santa Ana is not the president, but he sure as hell is running the place," Sir Edward explained.

Then he winked. "And, don't forget their women. Northern European women are usually thought to be more visible and controlling. But theirs can be every bit as smart and deadly. Enough said, since I can't give very much more advice there," he said, chuckling.

It was midday and Sir Edward invited Mr. Kearny and me to lunch. He said he would take us to The Banister's Pub, where we could have some privacy. We walked down the street and into the lobby of a fancy hotel where the pub was located. It was very posh.

After we ordered our meal, Sir Edward continued his almost one-sided but fascinating dialogue with me. "Jack, Walter here tells me he wants you assigned to our new operation in Querétaro, Mexico. I concur with that. Let's talk about Mexico for a bit," he said.

"Mexico did to Spain what the Yanks did to us Brits awhile back. They decided to throw the Spanish out and try their hand at forming a republic too. I personally don't think most people on this earth are either smart enough or unselfish enough to make a democratic republic operate for more than a hundred or so years. Aristotle, I think it was, said it best–*When the people learn they can vote themselves the spoils and wealth of their country, then their democratic republic will collapse*, or words to that effect. Anyway, we will see.

"However, Mexico is different than the colonies. The Spaniards accidentally did in Mexico what the Romans purposely did in their conquests. The Spanish went in and conquered the local Indian tribes and empires. Then they intermarried and bred with them, so that after several hundred years, most Mexicans now are more Indian than Spaniard.

"Also, the Spaniards are almost as arrogant as we Brits. Unless you had pure Spanish blood in your veins, you didn't have the right to own property or rule. They got their arses thrown out because of it.

"Like I said before, right now General Santa Ana is running things in Mexico, even though he is not president. He controls the military and almost everything in the country. In reality, Mexico is more like a monarchy–with him in control. He has some of his strong men under him too.

"Walter says you will be going there as a British citizen. That should keep you out of the shit going on between the Mexicans and the Yanks. Our man Villarreal, a Jewish banker, has helped us out in the past. We will send him a letter of introduction for you. He knows somebody is coming, but doesn't know who. We will also give you letters of introduction for General Santa Ana and President Arista, or whomever the hell they have in there now. These might help. But the important thing is that they know you represent our company, a very substantial international British company.

"We will also give you the authority to draw on our account at the Bank of Mexico in Mexico City, where Villarreal works. The monies will be sufficient to get the Querétaro operation going.

"However, we want you to go to Mexico City first and make your political contacts through Villarreal and assess the situation.

"If you are comfortable that our mining venture politically is not too risky, then you are authorized to spend up to twenty thousand pounds to get the operation going. After it is running, you can continue to pay up to twenty percent of the gross income to whoever needs to get it to keep our mining operation going. If you can better our production or local inducement goals after the first year, we will consider giving you a bonus."

Sir Edward paused for a few moments, looking directly at me and waiting for a response after making his bonus statement.

I nodded and said nothing.

He then finished his lecture. "You will be there no more than three years before we move you to your next assignment. Do you understand?"

I felt like a human volcano had erupted for the last few hours, showering me with his burning coals of wisdom. Sir Edward looked at me, with one eye brow raised.

"Yes sir, I understand."

"Do you have any questions?"

"Yes. Sir Edward, I am going to get married. When do you think I can take my wife to Mexico?" I immediately regretted placing the decision in his hands.

Sir Edward and Mr. Kearny smiled at my question.

"Yes, Jack, I understand, and we want you to be happy. We have found our project managers are happier with their wives and families with them, if conditions allow it. However, under the circumstances, I think it best if you go to Mexico City first and see how the political winds are blowing. If favorable, then go to Querétaro and get things started. My money says that you will be successful. I would say you should have things well enough in hand after a year to have your wife come join you."

My heart sank, but I was not surprised. I had few options, at least none as good as this, so I said nothing and nodded.

Finally, Sir Edward Chadwick said, "Jack, we usually don't give our new men this much responsibility to begin with. They usually work three to five years with one of our more senior engineers first. But your father was a top project engineer and Walter has great confidence in you.

"Don't worry. Use your good judgment. It's more important to lay the proper political foundation first. If you are not comfortable with how the political winds are blowing, we would rather abort the project and save the company's money. We can go elsewhere. It's just good business sense."

At lunch, Sir Edward said he had meetings in the afternoon with project engineers from Chile and Peru. After walking back to his office, he bade us *adieu*. He said he expected to receive a good report from me in three years, when I returned. Confidently, I told him he would. But I also wondered what might lie ahead. I knew it should be interesting.

As we were leaving, Sir Edward told Mr. Kearny that the company's box at the Palace Theater would be empty in the evening and for us to use it. Kearny accepted and thanked him.

Walter Kearny rented a carriage for the afternoon and showed me around London. In the evening, we had an excellent meal at the Fox Hound Pub then went to the Palace Theater and watched *A Lover's Quarrel* from the company's private balcony box.

That whole afternoon, while looking around London and later during the evening at the theater, I digested Sir Edward's words to me while they were fresh in my mind. The man was tough but pragmatic. I decided I could condense his advice into two ideas.

I summarized it as follows.

First, success comes at a price, a price which was more than money. Success also comes at the price of compromise, compromise which can try everything from your ethics and morals to your taste for risk and hard work.

Secondly, politics was the art of compromise, compromise which found the limits of your ethics and morals–but often went beyond.

Sir Edward had given me the criteria by which to measure the price our company was willing to pay for its success. My challenge was to determine if our company's price for success matched mine.

This was my first introduction to London, the good life and the real world of business. I decided I could easily grow to enjoy it–and did so for many years.

Chapter 6

A Change of Plans

On our way back to Manchester from London, I weighed my options, wanting to try to minimize Melanie's disappointment in my failing to send for her so we could be married in England. I knew her mother, my mother–and probably Melanie herself–would love to make our wedding a grand affair at the Fields of Shannon Plantation in Georgia that summer. But with my new job, that was not to be either, nor was a solo wedding in England. Perhaps I could suggest a wedding in Georgia the next summer. That might take some of the sting out of this change of plans. I needed to study the possibility further.

Also, on the return trip, Walter Kearny reviewed Sir Edward Chadwick's guidance to me. First of all, he said what Sir Edward told me was well-established company policy. He explained that our company had two types of mining engineers who worked overseas–exploratory and project mining engineers. The exploratory engineers quietly went into foreign lands and found the types of minerals and mines our company wanted.

Next, the project engineers went back into the country and made the political contacts and negotiated the deals. If successful, they went on to open the mining operations, which hopefully turned a profit as soon as possible. Alternatively, if the project engineers smelled failure, for whatever reason, they were to get out before the company invested a lot of money.

Mr. Kearny took a little wind out of my sails when he explained that Sir Edward's comments about sending me out as a junior engineer so early with so much responsibility was a bit of an overstatement. The fact was, the company had no one else to send, and the project was not that big or important. Even though it deflated my ego a bit, I did appreciate Mr. Kearny dealing straight with me.

By the time we reached Manchester on Saturday afternoon, I had decided on a plan. I would post a letter to Melanie and, after telling her how much I loved her, lay out my dilemma. I would explain that the conditions and constraints of my new job did not fit in with our original plans for marriage. Then I would propose we postpone our marriage for a year and have the ceremony in Georgia instead of England. Travel plans permitting, I would visit her at the end of this summer in Georgia, on my way to Mexico. Then we could make our final plans.

Mr. Kearny then complicated my newly laid plans somewhat. He explained it was company policy for all new project engineers to visit and work at the company's three manufacturing plants in Manchester and Liverpool before they left for their foreign assignments. The idea was for the outbound men to spend a week or so at the factories to learn about the company's products, so they could use or sell them in the Americas.

It looked like the soonest I would be leaving England was mid-July, depending on my required manufacturing plant visits and ship schedules leaving Liverpool. I hoped I could find one of Mr. Von Koffland's company ships scheduled out to the United States. He told me I could book my passage with them at half-fare anywhere they traveled. It would help my budget, especially if I wanted to stop in Georgia on my way to Mexico.

Before Walter Kearny and I parted on Saturday afternoon, we scheduled my plant visits. I also told him I would be stopping by Georgia to visit family on my way to Mexico. He agreed, but reminded me I would be traveling in the middle of the hurricane season in the Caribbean. It was an unnecessary caution.

That evening I checked into a local inn in Manchester. It was owned by our company, so my lodging and food expenses were paid. I was beginning to appreciate some of the benefits of my new job.

After dinner, I borrowed an extra lantern from the innkeeper and wrote the following letter, which had been forming in my mind.

Saturday night - June 19, 1852, Manchester, England

My Dearest Melanie,

This letter and evening finds me thinking of you and wanting you here with me. I love you very very much.

Since my last letter, I was offered employment with my Father's old company, the New Wales Equipment and Mining Company, Ltd. Its main office is in London. Mr. Walter Kearny has a company office here in Manchester and offered me the job. He was a friend of my father and I remembered him from when I was growing up. I also encountered him several times in the last three years when I was working summers in Glasgow.

I accepted the job. Now comes the unexpected news. My first assignment will be in central Mexico. The company wants to reopen an old silver mine there and has assigned me as the project engineer to do it. It is an important job and an exciting assignment. I can take my wife with me, but only after I make appropriate arrangements with the government officials to open the mine and determine that the project is indeed workable. I should be able to have all decisions and arrangements made by next summer. That is the bad news.

God willing, the good news is I will see you this August or September. Because of my new employment conditions, I propose we delay our wedding by one year, then have the ceremony in Georgia. This of course must meet with your approval. I should have my Mexico work situation well in hand by next summer, then return to Georgia so we can have an August wedding–if you agree. Remember the summer rain last August under the colonnade on the Savannah River?

Melanie, I know this is a disappointment to you, but it may work out even better since I hope to stop by to see you in August or September on my way to Mexico. We can finish our plans then.

Give my best to your folks and tell JK I hope to sail on one of his ships when I come to America. Also, give my love to my mother when you see her and tell Howard not to build anything valuable downstream from his new dam. He will know what I mean.

Melanie, I am excited about seeing you later this summer. Please keep yourself well and pray for us to be together permanently one year after August next.

Your loving future husband, Jack

Early Monday morning, I took the public stage down to Liverpool with my few clothes and personal items packed in a cloth travel bag. I also carried the cherry wood case with my father's .41 caliber engraved and silver-inlayed MacIntosh dueling pistols that my mother had given me the previous summer at the Taylor Plantation. The silver inlays were turning dark from inattention.

My few remaining mementos were stored at my Uncle Angus and Aunt Rachael McIntyre's place near Dundee, Scotland. Uncle Angus had retired as sea captain for a whaling company after 32 years of travel on the seas. He made little money as a sea captain, but saved enough to buy a beautiful small farm. There he and Aunt Rachael lived in a quaint rock-fortress home overlooking the Firth of Tay. They had no children and graciously extended their hospitality to me while I was working and attending the university in Scotland.

Monday afternoon, I visited the Liverpool Harbormaster's office, getting a list of the ships sailing for America. I found two ships leaving soon. One was leaving the next day and the second on Friday. The ship leaving the next day was sailing first to New York then on to Charleston, Savannah and finally to Havana before returning. Friday's ship was only sailing to Boston then to New York. I was in luck and posted my letter to Melanie with the Harbormaster. It would travel on the ship going to Charleston and Savannah. Finding a timely ship to carry Melanie's letter brightened my whole day.

Anxious to get on with it, I first chose the company plant at the edge of Liverpool for my first visit. It was a manufacturing plant where they made heavy hoist rope from hemp shipped from America. The plant employed 42 people and was not very efficient. The required visits at the company plants was like an assignment in *Purgatory.* I didn't want to be there. Instead, I wanted to see Melanie in Georgia and get on to my assignment in Mexico.

I made several suggestions to the plant manager, including putting up a plant closer to their source material in British Honduras where they could use local labor. The plant manager was not very happy with my suggestion, since it would result in closing their plant. He made the valid counterpoint that their market was mostly European. Although the plant was inefficient, their product was very good.

I stayed there only a week. The plant manager helped prompt my early departure, which was fine with me.

The other two plants were in Manchester. I visited them next. One manufactured mechanical hoist parts, drilling steel and equipment for mining. The second plant assembled the mechanical hoists and related products used for industrial and mining purposes. The hoists used rope products from the plant in Liverpool. These two company plants were run by a single manager, who had separate supervisors overseeing each plant.

I made several recommendations there also. One delayed me for an extra week–when I recommended they fire the main foreman at the assembly plant. He was a drunk and was not meeting company production schedules. However, he was the brother-in-law of the plant supervisor. They did fire the man and immediately put me temporarily in charge to replace him.

I was fortunate to find a qualified senior tradesman already working there to take over the job. He happily took over because he knew the job and was delighted to more than double his wages. The assembly plant quota was met the week I left and Mr. Walter Kearny, our mutual boss, was happy. The man fired threatened my life several times, but his brother-in-law gave him another, less important job. The threats didn't bother me because I was leaving soon.

Monday morning, on July 26, I met with my boss for last time before my departure. At his office in Manchester, he gave me three letters of introduction prepared and signed by Sir Edward Chadwick, president of our company. One letter was to General Santa Ana, the chief potentate in Mexico. Another was to President Arista, President of Mexico. The third letter was intended to be a general letter of introduction which I could keep handy in case I needed it.

I again summarized my plans to Mr. Kearny, explaining about visiting the family in Georgia in route to Mexico. This time I took care to inform him of my plans and not ask for his approval, the mistake I made with Sir Edward.

I continued. In Mexico I would meet Mr. Villarreal and make the necessary contacts with the Mexican government. Assuming success, I would go to Querétaro and get the silver mine up and going and get shipments of processed company silver headed back to England. Finally, I planned to get married in Georgia late next summer or fall and take my wife with me back to Mexico.

Walter Kearny seemed to be satisfied. His only comments were to live within the budget he gave me and, again, to take heed in traveling during the hurricane season.

With a handshake, I bid Mr. Kearny goodbye and left through the side door of his office. Thank goodness I was finally on my own. It could be years before I came face to face with anyone from our company again. I didn't care; as long as our company's money was good and continued to flow, I would do my part.

Wednesday morning, I was back in the harbor master's office in Liverpool. I found a ship sailing from Liverpool to Boston on August the 10th. From there it went to Charleston and Savannah before returning to its home port in Amsterdam. It was a clipper named *The Flying Duchess*, owned by the Rotterdam Transport Company, Mr. Von Koffman's and JK's company. What a stroke of luck! Savannah was not yet a major port in the south, so JK was making an impact by having their ships pick up products there.

While at the harbormaster's office, I met Will Springer. He was an impressive fellow, a little older and taller than me. He was looking for a ship to America and had also selected *The Flying Duchess* to book his passage. Will Springer seemed to be a likable fellow. Since we had some time on our hands, I invited him up to see my Uncle Angus and Aunt Rachael's place in Dundee, Scotland. There we could spend a few days until our ship was scheduled to depart. It was a move that probably saved my life.

On the way up to Scotland, I found out that Will Springer was a captain in the United States Army and a 1844 graduate from West Point. Additionally, I learned he was from Massachusetts.

We hit it off so well, I uncharacteristically confided in him by telling the story about how my father had been killed unfairly in a duel in Boston and that I intended to avenge his death. I was hoping to find Bolton Chapman in Boston, possibly even on this trip, since I had about a five-day layover before I sailed for Charleston.

This immediately interested Will Springer. He asked me how good a marksman I was with a dueling pistol and I unpretentiously said "excellent". I explained that at every opportunity I had been practicing shooting with my McIntyre relatives in Scotland. He said nothing.

By the time we got to Uncle Angus' farm, I found out more about my new friend. Captain Will Springer was from a politically well-connected family and had a very promising military career in front of him. He was in England on an assignment for six months as a liaison officer at the direction of Brigadier General Humphrey Styles of the U.S. Army and Vice Admiral Sir Geoffrey Sykes of the British Admiralty. A strange combination, I thought, until I found out the general and the admiral both had been assigned duty in Mexico earlier in their careers and had some common interests there.

Additionally, Captain Springer had served in Texas and Mexico during the Mexican War as a new lieutenant between 1846–7. That was where he got to know both the general and admiral who were lower ranking officers at the time. He wasn't inclined to go into much detail with me.

While at the farm, I explained my interests in explosives while at the University of Edinburgh and working summers at the British navel depots near Manchester and Liverpool. Springer opened up more and gave me a little more detail on his assignment.

Captain Will Springer said he was on assignment in England to work with key British naval and army artillery staff personnel. The British and Americans were to share information on timed, aerial, exploding ordnance which could be fired from both land and sea-based large guns.

Springer said a British naval officer was to be sent to Norfolk, Virginia the following year to continue the relationship between the countries' two military departments. There were obviously other things the captain did not want to discuss. I mused almost in jest that he must be operating in the secret world of military spies and saboteurs. *Later I found out that my initial impression had flesh.*

Chapter 7

A False Sense of Preparedness

After our arrival at the farm, Uncle Angus and Aunt Rachael liked Will immediately and welcomed him in their home. The first morning, Aunt Rachael gave us an early breakfast of oatmeal porridge with goat's milk cream and salted salmon. She also had fresh hot rolls with goat butter and honey. Afterwards, Uncle Angus proudly took us on a guided walk around the farm, where we enjoyed the early summer sun rising in the east over the North Sea. Toward the end of our walk, Will confronted me.

"Jack, you say you are a good marksman. Let's try something. You brought your father's dueling pistols. Bring them out and I want to actually see how good you are," Will said, spurring me on a bit.

I was ready for the challenge. When we got back to the large, fortress-like farmhouse, I retrieved my father's cherry wood pistol case and opened it on the porch. Uncle Angus watched, fascinated by Will's challenge.

There was a strong breeze coming up from the sea and the morning mist and broken clouds were clearing. The warm sun was drying the morning dew on the fields. As I loaded the two magnificent dueling pistols, Uncle Angus and Will set up two chalk-marked boards in front of the rock wall as targets. Then Will paced off twenty paces from the targets and established our shooting positions.

"All right, Jack, let me have one of your pistols. You say you are a good shot, shoot at the board on the left, and I will shoot at the one on the right," Will said calmly.

Easy, I thought. I've done this a hundred times before.

We both stood side by side, aimed; I fired, then he fired. Both shots were on their marks directly in the middle of the board.

"That's very good, Jack. You are a good shot," Will said, smiling.

I was trying not to smile too much as I started to reload my pistol. Uncle Angus and now Aunt Rachael were watching intently.

After Will and I reloaded our pistols, Will said.

"Now, Jack, let's try something else."

I was ready. What was he going to propose?

"Angus, we are going to need you for this–do you mind?" Will asked.

Uncle Angus was anxious to help.

"Now, Jack, get your pistol and come over here with me," Will instructed as he walked up to the wooden targets leaning against the rock wall.

"Now pretend the wooden target is your worst enemy challenging you in a duel. Turn away from your board and at Angus' count, step out ten paces, turn, shoot and kill your enemy before Angus counts to *eleven*!" Will said, smiling at me once more.

This was different, I had never done this before.

"And, by the way, I'm going to do the same thing. Don't shoot and kill me when you turn to shoot, aye?" Will cautioned, this time not smiling.

I agreed.

We both lined up backs to our wooden targets and the rock wall. Angus started his slow loud count–one, two, three,...

This felt weird, not right. I was uncomfortable. By the time he got to ten, I was a little disoriented when I turned and fired at my target. I missed terribly. I was embarrassed.

"Will, that was bad. I need a lot more practice doing that. Why didn't you shoot?" I asked.

"I did," Will replied.

Uncle Angus winked at me and pointed to Will's wooden target. It was split in half and lying on the ground. We walked over to his target and inspected it. The board was broken where Will's second round hit the wood in the chalk circle just about two inches above where his first round made its hole. Impressive. And I never heard his shot!

Will's little demonstration shook me. It showed me how unprepared I was for a duel. Then he reinforced it further.

"Jack, I don't want to hurt your feelings, but you shouldn't even consider a duel with anyone, even a drunk, until you learn a few more things. You are a good shot, but a duel is different–a lot different," Will said solemnly.

"Captain, I see that now. Can you teach me?" I asked.

Will nodded. "Yes, but it will take some time and lots of shooting. I don't recommend using these fine weapons for practicing what we need to do."

Angus immediately replied. "Gentlemen, I have four old flintlock pistols. They are in good shape and you can use them for practice. It shouldn't hurt them."

Then he continued. "Also, I have a barrel and a half of black powder and a box of flints. And we can cast all the lead rounds you want."

"Good, when do you want to start, Jack?" Will asked.

"Right now!" I exclaimed, anxious to improve my skills.

"All right, *soldier*, forget we are friends! If you want me to train you, I'm going to do it right, even if I have to *kick your ass* to straighten you out, do you understand? I don't want any shit from you, do you understand?" Will said with a hard look on his face, slipping into his normal mode of a tough military officer.

Then he smiled.

We all laughed, but I knew he was serious. This meant my life. I knew it, Uncle Angus and, most of all, Will knew it.

Starting immediately, I became Will's serious student. We practiced and practiced. When we rested, Will taught me the things to notice about location, light wind, dust, other people watching–many, many things I never imaged could be factors in a duel. He was truly a professional and if I was to survive a duel with Bolton Chapman, or any man, it would be thanks to Will. I wondered if it was providence that I had met him. I didn't know.

After the first day, I had pretty much mastered his first lesson. He then went on to the next lesson. *Quickness and accuracy.* He explained there was a tradeoff between the two. The logic was simple, but putting it into practice was not. Will explained that even an inexperienced person could kill you with a lucky shot if he turned and fired quickly. He said this was a characteristic of most inexperienced duelists. The odds were against them, but it could happen. For a day we practiced quickness and accuracy. I found my niche and tried to improve on it without shooting wild. I slowly did.

Will's next lesson was to put quickness and accuracy together with deadly pressure. This one was interesting, especially since he competed against me.

Will explained the object of this lesson was to make it as realistic as possible. The first time, he had Uncle Angus place us back to back, then each of us stepped off ten paces forward, as we would do in a duel, and marked the spot in the dirt where we would stop and turn. Then Will explained to us that after Uncle Angus lined us up back-to-back again, he would quietly place our targets at a safe distance on either side of the marked points in front of us. The objective was for each to turn, ready to fire at the call of ten, not exactly sure where our targets would be. Whoever turned and fired first accurately hitting his target, won the match.

"Uncle Angus, place Will's target a long ways away from my turning point. I don't trust Will's shooting," I joked, feeling a little anxiety at having a lead mini-ball soon flying in my direction.

Will chuckled but said nothing.

We tried it and Will won. My shot was less than a second after his, and I also hit my target. It became clear to me that this dangerous game clearly demonstrated Will's point of combining quickness and accuracy with deadly pressure. Turning, then shooting too fast and missing, or turning and taking too long to aim–both were fatal formulas. Life or death lay in what you and your opponent did in that critical one-second period. Luck also played a part. Having Will out in front of me when I turned to shoot added to the pressure, since I did not want to accidentally hit him instead of my target. The experience was exhilarating, stressful and tiring.

The first day Will won all but two bouts. On one of the bouts, my pistol misfired after Will had loaded it for me. The lesson here, he explained, was to *never trust the loading of my pistol to another*. Additionally, he explained if you ever had to duel with an unfamiliar weapon, insist on firing it at least once after you have loaded it, to make sure you have not purposely been given a faulty weapon.

Good advice. At least my Father had known that.

So we spent that week practicing the art of dueling, actually, the art of legally killing. It again shook me how little I knew. I fired over a hundred rounds a day for the next six days. Then we took a break. On the eighth day, Will had me practice with my father's dueling pistols. I had improved dramatically and was now getting much closer to being on a level with Will. He and Uncle Angus were impressed, and I was thankful.

Will and I were back in Liverpool the afternoon before our sailing. We verified with the captain of the *Flying Duchess* that our requests through the Harbormaster's office had been properly relayed to him and that we were booked on his ship. Everything was in order.

We paid the captain, and he informed us there were going to be five passengers besides him and the crew on the voyage. He also told us that his only private room was reserved for a couple, and said we young, single bucks would have to make do with the same small quarters used by the senior crew members. However, he said he did have a Dutch cook and our food would be excellent. Will and I were happy about that.

The captain also was Dutch. His name was Clause Von Voorberg. He was a friendly fellow and told us to call him Captain Vo Vo. He informed us we would be sailing precisely at 6:00 in the morning and we needed to be on board with our gear an hour beforehand. He explained that there was not room for his ship at the wharf, so he would have several members of his crew at the wharf's edge at five o'clock with a skiff to ferry us out to the ship. We understood and agreed.

The next morning was very cool and foggy as Will and I waited on the edge of the wharf with our limited travel gear. Another man arrived, carrying his bag. He introduced himself as Frank Perkins. He said he was an engineer from New Jersey, returning home. He was a little older than Will and me, and seemed like a nice fellow. Five o'clock came and the couple was still missing. The senior crewman waiting with the skiff became agitated and told the other two men to take us out to the ship and return. He would wait for the couple.

On the ship, the crewmembers were scurrying around, working busily. The captain paced nervously, carrying a leather bound ledger and apparently doing some last minute checking of cargo and passengers. He smiled and acknowledged us as we climbed on board. He was not happy when the crewman informed him the couple was still missing. He sent them back with the skiff.

Will pulled out his pocket watch and reported it was ten minutes past six when we could see the skiff returning to the ship with the missing man and his wife. The captain, although still unhappy, was relieved. It was a good thing that the skiff had returned empty to pick them up, because they had three heavy steamer trunks. The couple with the sailor and the luggage more than filled the little skiff. With a considerable effort, several crewmen attached a rope to each trunk and hoisted it onto the ship. The lady scolded the crewmen loudly, cautioning them not to damage the trunks or their contents. The embarrassed husband helped his angry, plump wife onto the ship. I thought this had the makings of an interesting trip.

With everyone on board, Captain Vo Vo had a crewman run up a black and white stripped flag. In several minutes, a small harbor steamer came along side and our crewmen threw them a heavy towrope, which they attached to their vessel.

The captain called for the crew to haul up the anchor and signaled for the harbor steamer to start pulling us out of the crowded harbor. With a sharp little jerk, empty masts with ropes fluttering, then the creaking cargo ship turned and we were moving.

Will removed his pocket watch again. The time was 7:12 a.m., about an hour after we were supposed to leave. The annoyed captain said nothing as several crewmen helped Mr. and Mrs. Hammond find their room, then moved their trunks to it. I heard Mrs. Hammond complain loudly about how small their room was and that they could only fit one of the trunks inside. The captain directed the first mate to get a canvas and cover, then secure, the remaining two trunks outside the Hammond's room. Still complaining, Mrs. Hammond finally disappeared inside with her husband.

Will, Frank and I watched from the deck and tried to keep out of the way of the crew as we were towed through the crowded harbor toward open water. We counted fourteen anchored ships, eleven sailing ships and three steamers with their powerful paddles. Additionally, another steamer was coming into the harbor under its own power in front of us. It was quite a sight.

I told Will and Frank that I was looking forward someday to my first ride on a steamer. (That someday came during the Civil War when I made eight round-trips across the Atlantic, seven in steamers.)

The harbor steamer pulled our clipper ship out several miles into Liverpool Bay, into a stiff breeze. There they released us and returned to the harbor.

The crewmembers unrolled the forward jib sails and secured them. This turned the ship in line with the wind. Soon the fore, main and mizzen mast sails were up. Finally the spankers were also up and secured. As the sails ballooned, the stately ship leaned to one side and moved smartly forward.

The captain shouted orders to the chief mate and several crewmembers to adjust the trim on the sails. After about thirty minutes of maneuvering and adjusting, Captain Von Voorberg seemed satisfied and stood quietly at the wheel, solemnly gazing forward into the choppy sea while the chief mate studied charts.

By ten o'clock we were in the open waters and the crew had made their final adjustments on the sails. We were making good progress westward into the Irish Sea, driven by a cold wind. The weather was broken, with the sun periodically peeking through the dark clouds.

Will, Frank and I put on heavier jackets after we reached open water. We attempted to help the crew a bit by rolling up ropes and securing several containers on the upper deck. The work warmed us up a bit.

By eleven o'clock, the captain and crew seemed much more relaxed and were letting the wind do her work. It was a beautiful sight, and I felt good to be on the move again. I wondered what fate had in store for me in Boston.

The captain had one of his crewmen bring us tea onto the open upper deck and he remained at the wheel, slowly turning the ship southwestward toward St. George's Channel. The tea was a nice gesture, but the cold wind made it impossible to enjoy.

The captain then broke away from the wheel, turning it over to the first mate and came over to visit with us. He invited us into his small, combination dining quarters and map room next to his cabin. It had two portholes, one toward the rear and one on the portside of the ship. He lit a sea lantern and hung it above the table. It was a welcome change from the brisk weather outside as we sat drinking hot tea and visiting in a civilized manner.

After about a half hour of visiting, the captain smiled and told us we would have dinner here at the beginning of the First Watch. Time to go. After leaving the room, I asked Will, a Yankee Army man, what time the captain meant for us to eat and he said he thought First Watch started at 8:00 p.m. At any rate, he said he wouldn't miss it even if he had to wait outside the dining room all afternoon. We laughed.

At dinner, Mr. and Mrs. Hammond were on hand and in good spirits. The captain proudly stated that his cook had already fed the crew and had a special meal for us. It was yorkshire pudding. I was not impressed.

Sitting at the swivel table, we all reintroduced ourselves and shared a little information about who we were and why we were traveling. Mrs. Hammond was not shy in letting us know they owned the fourth largest plantation in South Carolina. They had come to Europe on an extended holiday to visit and to buy furniture for their plantation mansion. They had already been to Paris and purchased $22,000 in French furniture, mirrors and chandeliers. She said they had it shipped home from Le Havre. Mr. Hammond did not seem to mind his wife bragging about their obvious wealth and lavish spending. It reaffirmed some of my feelings about the arrogance of Southerners and their lifestyles.

Frank, we found out, was Franklin J. Perkins, a steam engine engineer and designer. He worked for the American Steam Engine Company in Allentown, Pennsylvania. He had gone to England to help a British company redesign one of their steam engine pressure sensors to operate like the one he had patented. He was obviously very smart, but also a humble man. We asked him why he was not riding a steamer back to America and he said, "those damned things are dangerous–they blow up!" We all laughed.

The five passengers made a good attempt to make the best of their tight quarters and other Spartan conditions on the ship. Captain Vo Vo also made an extra effort to make us comfortable and happy. His normal good humor and jokes helped.

Will and I, along with Frank, hit it off well. We visited a lot, played chess and helped the crew where we could to stay occupied. The captain even let me take the wheel for several hours at a time, showing me some of the basics on how to straddle the wind and follow the course with the compass. I spent some time updating my diary, one of the few small books I brought with me. Most of my small book collection I had stored with Uncle Angus and Aunt Rachael in Scotland, with a request to send them to me in the Americas whenever I had a stable address and the money to pay for their shipment.

Will and I discussed Bolton Chapman and what I might do to connect up with him in Boston. Then, on the second day out, Will told me that if I was determined to have it out with this man, he would like to be present to guard my back. What a relief. I thanked him and told him I would gladly accept his offer.

Finding Chapman when we made port in Boston now became critical because conditions for me would never be better. Frank heard parts of our conversations and also became interested in my situation. After hearing the story, he said he also would delay his travel home to help me. It was now or never. If Chapman killed me, at least I had given it my best try. However, I didn't think he would. Everything seemed to be in my favor–surprise, training and friends backing me up. We would soon see.

Chapter 8

A Case of Treachery or Honor?

On August the 23rd of '52, nineteen days after we left Liverpool, the *Flying Duchess* sailed into the Boston Harbor and dropped anchor. Captain Von Voorberg was pleased with the good sailing conditions we encountered during our crossing from England.

Also, Will, Frank and I had a plan. We would check into an inn near the waterfront district and use it as our headquarters to start our search for Bolton Chapman. The three of us would go to different sections of Boston suggested by Will Springer and quietly put out feelers for Chapman. Whoever found him would notify the rest of us when we met back at the inn. The plan worked.

The afternoon we dropped anchor, we departed the ship and checked into the Neptune Hotel on Fulton Street. It was a smelly old place, but affordable. There we left our gear and put our plan into motion.

Will knew Boston well, so he gave us hand drawn maps and assigned us areas to search. We agreed that I would not confront Bolton until we were prepared. We spent the remaining hours of the afternoon visiting the places Will assigned us. I met quite a few people who had heard of Chapman, but only a few who knew him. None knew where he was, or at least they acted like they didn't know. I was concerned that word would get back to Bolton Chapman that people were looking for him, so I toned down my search.

On the way back to the Neptune Hotel, I walked by the warehouse my mother had described. Behind it, my father had been shot. I walked around the back of the building and tried to visualize where the duel had taken place. Standing there in the late evening setting sun, I hoped my blood would not soon mix with that of my father's in the soil before me. The thought angered me and strengthened my resolve to correct the wrong for the cowardly way my father was murdered. I was going to kill the bastard, come what may!

But then I remembered Captain Will Springer's almost biblical admonitions during my training at Uncle Angus' farm in Scotland. *True anger can be a deadly force of last resort, to be used best in a desperate situation. Better to be wise like a serpent, practice at what you excel and strike at the time of your choosing.* These words helped me refocus and not lose sight of my goal–*to kill Bolton Chapman at a time and place of my choosing!*

Frank was waiting at the hotel when I returned. Together, we waited about an hour for Will. When Will finally returned, he was excited. He said he'd found Bolton Chapman's freight office on Prince Street in central Boston. He posed as a potential shipping client and learned from Chapman's workers that he was returning from Marlboro in the morning. Good news.

The three of us discussed our strategy at dinner in a little pub near the waterfront. We needed to find out more about Chapman's habits and schedules. From the pieces of information we could glean, Chapman was a scrapper, bully and quite a drinker. Perhaps it would be better to challenge him at a formal eating place, rather than a pub or bar where he probably would have friends. Finding out his eating place habits would be the first order of business the next day. We made good progress the first day and also had the time to set the trap right. I was the bait and hoped I would not also wind up being the meal.

Will had good contacts in Boston. He suggested that the next day Frank and I hire a carriage and go out of town on the Waltham Road to the Chatham Woods and find a good place for the duel. Will said to pick a place easily identifiable and near the road, where carriages could pull off and tie up. Additionally, it should be level and behind trees, so as not to attract neighbors or curious spectators. He knew there were several places that would work. It was up to me to pick one.

He also suggested I practice shooting a few rounds there with my father's pistols. He said he would continue to gather additional information on Bolton Chapman.

The next day, Frank and I found a livery stable and rented a carriage as Will suggested. North of town, we found the woods and selected a location meeting Will's criteria. We spent about an hour and a half there, during which time I loaded and fired twelve rounds, practicing the techniques Will had taught me. My nerves remained steady and aim, accurate, thanks to all the training Will had given me in Scotland. Nobody came by or seemed to care about our being there.

When Frank and I got back to the hotel in the afternoon, Will was waiting for us. We went to a local pub and talked while we ate. Will suggested I drink tea.

While we ate, Will told us that Chapman lived in a fancy house in Cambridge and fortunately appeared to be a creature of habit. He usually had his carriage driver pick him up at home and take him to his freight office about nine-thirty in the morning. He had coffee with sweet bread and rolls delivered daily from the bakery down the street from his office for him and his men.

Will went on to explain that about one-thirty or two in the afternoon, Chapman had his driver take him and one of his sidekicks to either of two nice restaurants in the downtown section of Boston. There he sometimes met clients or other shady business associates. Afterwards, he would normally be back at his freight business by four. But three or four times a month, he would spend the afternoon with either his mistress or a paid whore.

His evenings were also predictable. Between six and seven he went to one of three places. One was a men's social club and the other two places were fancy bars. There he would usually stay until midnight. Finally, he would have his carriage driver deliver him home, usually in an angry and drunken state.

Will said Chapman had a wife and two children. This gave me pause for a moment. But he was still a bad *hombre,* and he had murdered my father. So without further thought, I remained determined to proceed.

With his normal, confident, military style, Will said he hired a person to follow Chapman the next morning. The hired tracker would let us know where our prey went for his midday meal. Additionally, Will suggested he and I go to the same restaurant and select a table next to Bolton and his party. Frank would stay outside just in case something unexpected happened.

Will pulled out a new model Colt revolver percussion-cap pistol and handed it to Frank. It was a beautiful weapon. I had only seen two similar weapons previously.

"Frank, hang on to this for a while. I assume you, being an inventor, can figure out how to use it," he said jokingly.

"Frank, if Jack is successful in setting up the duel tomorrow, I want you to be the duel judge and arbitrator. Keep this until after the duel. If anything goes wrong, kill the bastard that gets out of line. Make sure it's not Jack or me," Will went on without smiling.

Frank took the weapon and agreed to carry out his task diligently.

We talked some more after we finished eating. I drank tea while Frank and Will drank their ale. Will was in control of this mission, so Frank and I listened intently. Will suggested we try to create a situation at the restaurant so that Chapman would be the aggressor and challenge me. He said we did not want Chapman to suspect anything and put up his guard. Technically, it also gave me the option of picking the place and the weapons for the duel. He was sure pistols would be the weapon of choice, since Bolton was a big, heavy man. We agreed that swords would not even be considered. Besides, he said, sword duels were a thing of the past. This made me feel better.

I liked the strategy. Then we discussed how Will and I should look and how I should provoke Bolton.

Will was obviously a good-looking and well-heeled American and I had a slight Scottish brogue, which I could easily control. Because of that, Frank suggested that I play the role of an innocent and not so bright

Scottish relative just arrived in America. Perhaps I could do something annoying in the restaurant to provoke Chapman.

Frank said he even had a green and brown beret cap with a little red ribbon on it and some other clothes I could wear to help me play the part. Will and I looked at each other and laughingly agreed. The plan was on!

I had trouble sleeping that night. To keep my emotions in tow, I visualized revenge on my terms when I thought of my father's blood flowing onto the ground behind the warehouse, all because of Chapman's treachery.

The next morning, the three of us went down to a fisherman's café on the dock and ate breakfast. Then we went back to the hotel and used a small side room off the lobby to play cards and drink tea and coffee. Later we walked around the docks killing time and refining our plan a bit. Frank lent me his colorful beret and jacket so I could play my role. Periodically, both men would look at me and break out laughing. Apparently I looked and acted the part well.

About one-thirty, the three of us walked over to where Will was to meet his spotter in a side alley. We split up so as not to attract attention.

A bit after two, I saw a man step into the ally where Will waited, smoking a cigarette. Will came out after a short time and walked over to me. I thought his spotter must have ducked out the back way.

"It's the Strafford Restaurant," Will said quietly.

This was the same place Bolton Chapman and my father had their confrontation! My stomach tightened from the irony. Will took off his cap and rubbed his head before replacing it. This was the signal to Frank. Down the street, Frank turned and walked away from us.

The restaurant was not crowded. The first time I saw Bolton, he was joking and drinking ale at a table with his friend, another man of his ilk. Chapman looked as I had imagined–a loud husky man with a thick neck and powerful arms and hands. He wore expensive-looking clothes. He looked like a rich thug.

Will and I took a table next to them. They seemed annoyed we sat so close with so many other empty tables available. Bolton suggested we move. We didn't move. Instead, we ordered tea and started talking loudly about Scotland. Annoyed, both Bolton and his buddy shifted to another table closer to the window, then continued to talk and drink.

Will and I fumbled around, talking to the waiter trying to decide what to order. Bolton and his friend ordered pork roast and some more ale. Will and I finally ordered our meal. Will did a good job of playing the part of an American trying to entertain an odd newcomer from Scotland. Then I made my move.

I made a bad joke about my trip to Boston while pouring Will and me a cup of hot tea. I made another comment about wanting to see if my ship was still out in the harbor. Then I got up and walked over to the window and looked out. Bolton and his friend again were annoyed at my presence. I hollered back to Will that I thought I could still see the ship anchored in the harbor, then started back toward our table talking and holding my teacup prissily in my hand.

When I reached Bolton's table, I tripped and spilled the hot tea on the side of his neck and shoulder. The man came out of his chair like a mad fighting dog and struck me a glancing blow to the face that I managed to slightly deflect. I fell to my butt, breaking my teacup. I leaped up and indignantly faced him.

"You boorish bully! You can't do that to me! I demand an apology immediately!" I shouted.

"Leave me alone, or I'll kill you, you damned Limey," Bolton said, wiping himself off with a cloth napkin and trying to ignore me.

Will had stood up like he was alarmed and started toward us, but not too quickly.

I pushed Bolton back with my open hands against his chest. "I want an apology, immediately!" I demanded in a somewhat effeminate manner.

Bolton turned red and his friend looked up at me with his mouth open in amazement.

"You damn fag, you asshole, tomorrow you'll be dead. Pick your place!" Chapman almost hollered.

"What do you mean?" I asked.

"Get your friend to explain it to you, you asshole. I just challenged you to a duel. Are you a coward and going to refuse?" He asked, still red faced but now a little more under control.

"No! Absolutely not, I'm not going to refuse! You'll be sorry!" I exclaimed in a high, emotional voice.

I then turned to Will, who was standing near, watching.

"Will, what do we do?" I asked in the same high voice.

"Jack, you shouldn't do this. He'll kill you," Will warned me.

Two waiters and the restaurant owner and another couple in the room watched in horror.

Will lamely attempted to dissuade me from my foolish decision. I refused. He then took me to our table and sat me down, where I continued to fume. He then went back to Bolton's table and awkwardly tried to apologize. Unsuccessful, he then began to work out the details for our duel.

Will came back to our table, where the food sat uneaten. We paid and left the restaurant. Bolton and his friend stayed, and we could hear them laughing as we left the building. The first part of our trap had been set–*and under our terms.*

Again, I did not sleep well during the night. Will made sure we ate a normal meal both in the evening and for breakfast the next morning. He insisted I drink only tea or coffee.

Frank, Will and I took a rented carriage to the Chatham Woods, where the duel was scheduled at two in the afternoon, Friday, August the 27th. We arrived at one-thirty and Bolton Chapman and three of his buddies were already there. They had their carriage horses tied near the road and had a small portable table set up in the meadow where Frank and I had practiced shooting two days before. On their table, they had a beautiful set of flintlock dueling pistols in an open wooden case. The men were smirking and looking like a confident lot.

Will and I were dressed comfortably in light trousers and shirts and looked different from the day before, but I still wore my borrowed Scottish cap. We tied our carriage horses to a tree and walked over to a spot near them. Will laid the case containing my father's dueling pistols on a towel in a shady spot on the grass. I knelt down and quietly began loading both pistols as Frank and Will went over and met with Bolton and his group. I could hear them talk.

Bolton snickered and pointed to my silly looking beret and said something to one of his friends.

Acting very troubled, Will told Chapman and his friends that Frank would be the duel judge and administrator. He told them that he would be my second and that we would use the standard rules for a dueling engagement. Starting back-to-back with pistols held aiming upward in front of us, we would step off ten paces at the administrator's count, then turn and shoot. Any misfires would count as a shot, and the duel would continue. Additionally, misses by both principals would result in the pistols being reloaded and the duel continued until someone was shot or killed. They agreed.

Will said that we would use our pistols, and they would use theirs. They agreed, then Will inspected their pistols and had Bolton's second come over to inspect ours.

Finally, Will directed that each second would have the extra pistol in hand and aimed in the air during the duel in case of a misstep or foul by the other principal. If such happened, the offended principal's second would shoot and kill the offender. This rattled Bolton and his group. We had the right to set the rules, so they reluctantly agreed. They nervously looked at one another, wondering what was happening.

Will kept the pressure on and immediately turned the conduct of the duel over to Frank. Frank took charge smartly. He had Bolton and me come over and shake hands and swear to follow the rules faithfully. We did. He then said, as he held up his Colt revolver, that he would kill any principal who broke the rules. This again shook Bolton and his friends. Bolton's second started to object, but Bolton stopped him. The duel was on!

Frank lined Bolton and me up back to back and proceeded to count in a loud deliberate steady voice. One, two, three, ….

This time Bolton did not turn prematurely when Frank reached the count of ten. We both turned and fired! Both shots went off almost simultaneously. His shot clipped my left ear, and mine hit him in the middle of his chest. He fell.

Almost immediately, I heard two additional shots. Apparently, when Bolton's second saw him fall, he turned and shot at me, but accidently hit Frank instead. Frank fell. Immediately, Will shot and killed Bolton's second.

As the smoke and confusion of the situation cleared, three men lay bleeding on the grass. Bolton's second was dead and Bolton was dying. Frank had been hit in his left foot and was sitting, cursing and holding his bloody boot.

I ran over to help Frank while Will remained with his Colt raised, watching Bolton Chapman's remaining two friends. Frank told me he was all right and to tend to business.

At that time, two strangers came out from the woods and walked over to us. They introduced themselves. It was Dr. Best and Mr. Walters, the two witnesses to my father's duel! They said they got word from the restaurant owner that something was up with Bolton Chapman. They secretly followed Chapman's group out to the woods. Hiding behind some nearby bushes, they watched the whole thing. Both men excitedly told us they would prepare and sign a statement as witnesses describing what happened and stating that it was a fair duel!

Dr. Best took a look at Frank's foot while Will and I walked over to Bolton who was being cradled in a lying position by his two buddies. His friends looked at us in total shock.

Bolton looked up at me and gasped. "*Who in the hell are you?*"

"You murdered my father here in a duel three years ago. I am Jack McIntyre," I replied quietly.

With a pained look, Bolton Chapman rolled his eyes in disbelief. A minute later he was dead.

Chapter 9

On to Savannah and the Rest of My Life

Montigo paced along at a smart clip as I approached The Fields of Shannon Plantation in the late morning. From my carriage, it looked like a picture out of a fairy tale. I could see Melanie and Lilly, her little black maid, working in the flower garden. Melanie turned and looked in my direction. Pulling Montigo to a stop for a moment, I stood up in the carriage and waved to her. She recognized me and came running. The high-strung Montigo became nervous as Melanie approached.

"Jack, Jack, I thought you would be here a week ago. I was worried something had happened," Melanie exclaimed with her face glowing as she climbed into the carriage and gave me a big hug and kiss.

"Well it did! I came down from Boston in one of JK's ships, the *Flying Duchess*. We ran into the edge of a hurricane before we got to Charleston. It did some damage to the ship and Captain Vo Vo anchored there a couple of extra days to get it repaired," I explained while trying to keep the horse under control.

"Yes, JK said he was expecting *The Flying Duchess*. I was hoping you would be on it, but it hasn't arrived yet. So, how did you get here?" she asked.

Then, still out of breath, she gave me another awkward kiss on the cheek as I tried to hold the nervous carriage horse steady.

"I hitched a ride with Senator Anderson. I found out he was coming over to Savannah for a few days. I understand he is coming to the banquet your folks are having here," I responded, relaxing the reins as I let Montigo take us on toward the Kerns' mansion.

Then, frowning, Melanie reached out and touched my sore left ear and asked me what happened.

Flippantly I replied. "Oh, the war started up north and I tried to dodge a bullet."

Melanie jabbed my shoulder lightly and almost absentmindedly responded. "Oh, Jack."

Then she eagerly went on to another subject.

We approached the Kerns' mansion along the wide carriage entrance. It was lined with granite rocks and a manicured hedge. Melanie held my arm tightly and gave me another little kiss while I still focused on controlling the excited Montigo. She giggled, thinking the situation was amusing.

Samuel came out and grabbed Montigo's halter and reins. As we got out of the carriage, I asked Samuel if he could take the animal and carriage to the carriage house until I was ready to leave. He smiled and dutifully complied.

Then Melanie and I walked over to a table and bench under the shade of a large magnolia tree on their beautiful grounds. Finally, I gave her a tight hug, whirling her around as I kissed her. I had been looking forward to this moment for more than a year. She smelled great. A little sweaty from working in the rose garden perhaps, but great!

"Jack, the banquet is tonight! Senator Anderson and a lot of important people will be here. I was afraid you were going to miss it. You are coming, aren't you?" Melanie asked, animatedly.

"I don't know. Am I invited?"

"Certainly! You know you are always invited to our parties. Jack, don't tease me. That's why I was out in the flower garden with Lilly. We were pruning flowers for the tables tonight. We will pick them when its cooler this evening and put them out," Melanie explained, still excited and glowing.

"Oh, Mother's going to be disappointed. She had some new, silver place settings and other pieces coming in on *The Flying Duchess* from England. She wanted so much to use them at her party tonight."

Glancing over Melanie's shoulder, I could see Mrs. Kerns come out on the veranda, then look at us with a condescending smile.

After catching my glance, Melanie turned and called out. "Mother! Mother! Jack's here."

"Yes dear. I see that. Jack, did you come in on *The Flying Duchess*?" Mrs. Kerns asked with a sense of urgency in her voice.

"No Ma'am. But Captain Vo Vo did send a heavy box over from Charleston with me. He gave me explicit instructions to make sure you got it as soon as I arrived. It's in the back of the carriage," I responded, knowing what was on her mind.

Mrs. Kerns turned and called out harshly. "Lilly, go to the carriage house and have Samuel fetch the box in the back of the Taylors' carriage. Hurry!"

Melanie and I walked over and climbed the steps to the veranda as Mrs. Kerns, obviously with more important things on her mind, turned to go back into the library.

"Mrs. Kerns, you are looking wonderful. It's great to see you," I offered, knowing she was trying to avoid my company.

She stopped and dutifully responded. "Oh…, yes, Jack, thank you. Are you coming tonight?" she answered with an artificial smile.

"Well, yes Ma'am. If I am invited, I would be pleased to come," I responded.

"Certainly, Jack. Certainly you are invited. All of the Taylors are coming. You too, I hope," she responded awkwardly and with a touch of artificial sincerity in her voice.

Melanie was terribly embarrassed. Turning red, she avoided looking at me and spoke. "Mother, Jack says *The Flying Duchess* was damaged in a hurricane. Captain Vo Vo will not be here tonight. Jack made a special effort to get your package over here from Charleston."

Mrs. Kerns responded a little surprised then finally looked directly at me. "A hurricane? Is the ship all right? Was anybody hurt?"

"The damage was limited and no, Ma'am. No one was seriously hurt. One broken arm–a crewman. Several of the sails were torn and some of the riggings were broken. Captain Vo Vo stayed in Charleston a couple of extra days for repairs. He should be here in Savannah within the next several days," I responded.

"Oh, thank goodness for that. Jack, it's nice to have you here. How long will you be staying?" Mrs. Kerns asked.

"Mother, Jack just arrived. He doesn't know yet. But he's going to tell us all about his new assignment in Mexico, isn't that exciting?" Melanie said, trying to do damage control.

Her eyes drifted, "Oh yes, isn't it though? Yes, dear. Yes, Jack. We want to hear all about your new job. We will see you tonight," she responded, then turned and disappeared with obvious relief into their huge mansion.

Poor Melanie gave me a quick glance, then looked away, dabbing a damp eye with a kerchief. Clearly I could not live or belong in her mama's world. I hoped Melanie could live in mine.

Melanie tried to shake off the little episode with her mother and suggested we go sit in the back garden, where we could have some privacy. I readily agreed, since it would keep me out of her mother's sight and, more importantly, her out of mine. As we started to walk on the veranda toward the back of the large plantation house, Melanie suddenly changed her mind.

"Jack, I want to freshen up. Would you be a dear and wait for me in the 'Little Zebo' in Papa's park? You know where it is. I will send you out some lemonade," she told me sweetly.

Melanie's face was red from working in the flower garden. I was also sure our little episode with Mrs. Kerns bothered her. I nodded, then she gave me a little kiss and quickly disappeared inside.

In a few minutes, little Miss Lilly came to Melanie's 'Little Zebo' where I sat, waiting. Miss Lilly was beaming as she set the tray with a pitcher of lemonade, two glasses and a plate of cookies on the small table under the gazebo.

"Miss Lilly, you look wonderful. Are those for us?" I asked, teasing her a bit.

She giggled self-consciously. "Oh no, Mister Mack. They is for you and Miss Melanie Ellen. They is for white folks."

My teasing had opened an unintended door and her little comment almost broke my heart.

Feeling a sense of anger I responded. "Well, Miss Lilly, please have a cookie and sit down for a minute. Tell me what you and Miss Melanie Ellen have been doing since I left."

Poor little Miss Lilly was embarrassed and looked around to make sure nobody was looking. She did a little curtsy, then responded. "Well, Mr. Mack, I guess if you say so. I'm supposed to be getting flowers ready for tonight. Yes, Mr. Mack–if you says so. I don't want Big Osi ta sees me. But I wills eat one cookie."

The plump black girl sat down on the edge of the chair and quickly snatched a cookie. After two big bites, it was gone, and she nervously looked toward the mansion.

I was potentially getting the poor girl in trouble, so I wanted to keep our little visit short.

"Big Osi? She's in charge of the house?" I asked, knowing the answer.

"Yes sur. Big Osi, she's in charge of the house niggers. She says Miss Melanie Ellen don't work me hard enough. She says if I don't straighten up she'll send me out to the yard niggers, that's what she say," Miss Lilly responded with concern in her voice.

I then handed the girl the cookie plate. She snatched another cookie from it like she was doing something wrong and gobbled it down with a guilty smile. I grabbed the remaining few cookies on the plate and thrust them into her hand.

"Well, thank you, Miss Lilly. Thank you very much. Maybe we can visit again before I leave. Tell Osi thank you for the lemonade and cookies. They were very good."

Relieved Miss Lilly stood. "Thank you, Mr. Mack. We had a nice visit."

With that she did a little curtsy, then disappeared back toward the kitchen.

Waiting for Melanie, I reflected on my short visit with Miss Lilly and mused on how a house slave's life differed from other domestic help I had seen during my travels in the Americas and England.

Certainly the first difference between Lilly and the Indian maids we had in Mexico and other countries in South America was that our girls or women were paid and were free to go as they chose. Another difference was how the domestic help was treated. The Kerns family and a few other Southern families I had met were controlling and patronizing. They treated their house slaves like children. They used rewards–status, dress, foods and responsibilities to manage them.

Also, from my limited exposure to the South, it seemed to me that the Negro women were tough house managers and even aggressive with the black domestic staff under their charge. But I had not been around them too long and had a lot to learn.

The Taylor family was a little different. I knew from conversations with Mother and Howard that the Taylor family realized they were held hostage to the slaveholding system they grew up with. But the Taylors also knew they could do nothing to maintain or expand their wealth and power base without them.

Mother said the family had conducted a number of private conversations about the plantation going to a paid worker arrangement. But, besides being strung up by the neighbors, the Taylors knew they could never compete in the South. In fact, the whole South's economy would collapse if slavery went away. Slaves comprised about a third of the South's population and it was the working third. Mother said that was about as far as their conversations ever went.

The Indian maids we hired were usually hardworking and loyal, like Lilly, but also different. If they were Catholic, they were usually comfortable working for us. The non-Catholic Indian women sometimes seemed more remote and suspicious of us because we were foreigners and different from them. A few of them felt free to work a few days for us, then steal what they could and disappear into the hills even before they were paid.

However, Mother also said she had employed non-Christian Japotec and Mayan girls who were wonderful. She felt perfectly safe leaving me with them as a child–even for several days. Mother joked that several times she even tried to bribe the girls to take me when I misbehaved. But Mother's major point was that the girls always had a choice–to stay or to leave.

The rich Spanish aristocrats who owned the big *haciendas* and *fincas* in Latin America ran the gamut on how they treated and managed their domestic help. The places we lived, the rich Spanish families we knew, treated their help in a variety of ways. The bad examples used class ignorance, threat, punishment and money to control their help. In my mind, the South's best treatment of domestic helpers was much better than Latin America's worst, even considering the slavery issue.

Mother and Father had gotten into some heated discussions about slavery. At the time, I tried to digest both points of view.

An argument my British father used to confront my mother was citing the American Declaration of Independence. It went something like this:

"Your Declaration of Independence says that '*all men are created equal, that they are endowed by our creator with certain unalienable rights, among these are life, liberty and the pursuit of happiness*'. Beth, what parts of created equal and liberty don't you agree with?"

At first Mother would fume. But in later years she mellowed and didn't rise to the bait. But Mother's early retort would go something like this:

"Yes, God created us all equal, but not the same. Some of us are bigger, some are smarter, some have talents like being musical, some can build things–we are all different. For instance, on the *sixth day, God created women smarter than men.* But since He was tired and didn't want to change anything before resting, He said we were *all equal.* So now we must put up with your foolishness."

This usually resulted in a chuckle from my father and the subject would go dormant until the next time.

Finally, Mother used a comeback on Father, a British subject, which silenced him on the matter. It went something like this:

"Kenneth, you know where we Southerners got our visions of superiority and grandeur? It was from you Brits. Take a closer look at your grand English estates owned by your duke, earls, Royal Family and the like. They put our plantation owners to shame. And take a look at your house servants, menservants, and gardeners working generations for rich families and for a pittance in a class system. And your indentured farmers working for crop shares at starvation rates on some rich Englishman's land. And look at your colonization of India and Africa and even here in the Americas. You think you Brits were not using those lands and peoples for your own interests? When compared to you, we Southerners are pikers at snobbery, elitism, putting people in a class system and then using them. Think about it, Kenneth."

When Mother calmly finished her argument, Father nodded and became quiet. He knew it was a winner.

Then, after a few moments of silence Father quietly said with a straight face, "I'm a *Scotsman*, not an Englishman."

The last time both of them laughed and never argued the point again. But the slavery question did bother Mother, and with time her views changed very dramatically.

"Jack dear, what are you thinking?"

Melanie startled me. I was deep in thought, staring at the flowers in the garden and did not hear her slip up behind me.

"Oh, nothing. You changed clothes. You look even more beautiful. Come and give me a hug."

She smiled and obliged. And she did look beautiful in her simple day dress. But something was bothering her.

But Melanie shook it off and bounced back, putting on her normal perky and happy face.

"Didn't Lilly bring you some cookies with the lemonade?" She asked with a quizzical glance, looking down at the empty cookie plate.

"Yes, she did. And they were good," I responded without further elaboration.

"You sure must have been hungry to eat them all before I could get back," she replied, teasing me.

Then she continued. "Jack, follow me. I want to show you what we are doing to prepare for tonight's banquet."

Playfully, Melanie took me by the hand and led me to the plantation's main kitchen behind the big house. The main kitchen consisted of three brick buildings. The first building was the pantry, a large, food storage building with a basement, the second–the cookhouse, and the third–"the fat house," as Howard called it. It was a food cooling and staging building for products coming out of the cooking and baking rooms of the cookhouse and headed for the big house.

An open porch with brick floors connected the three kitchen buildings to the big house. Come rain or shine, the servants could relay the food from one building to the next without getting wet.

The day was warm. It smelled like both oak and cedar smoke was boiling out of the cookhouse chimneys as we approached. Through the open door, wonderful baking aromas were spilling out everywhere. We went in and saw Martha, Matilda and Sassy–along with Samuel and another Negro man–helping two sweating French chefs prepare the evening's banquet. Two black boys were standing in the open double doorway with hand fans, trying to urge cooler outside air into the building. It didn't look like they were having much luck.

The fat chef was scolding one of the boys in French. I couldn't understand him, neither could the boy. The chef seemed to be cursing in French and demanding that the boys move to a different positions and fan faster.

I almost laughed, but thought better of it. The cooking house did seem hot as a factory inside with its four brick and iron ovens fully stoked and operating in the middle of the warm September day. Samuel finally interceded and told the frustrated chef that he would get some more boys with fans.

Inside the cook house, Melanie and I admired the fine pastries and other food the chefs had cooling on the tables and on the counters in an adjacent building. Andre, the other French chef, smiled and proudly showed us around, explaining the menu in broken English. He selected several small pastries, put them on a plate and handed them to Melanie. She thanked him and took the plate with us.

Outside the cookhouse, we lingered as we ate our small French delights.

Then, smiling and almost mysteriously, Melanie said, "Jack, let me show you something else."

We walked about a quarter of a mile down the road, then cut behind some trees to the workers' quarters. They consisted of a row of plain frame buildings, each with a roof covered with simple clay tile. What a contrast to the rest of the plantation. But the area was clean and the buildings were whitewashed. On the near end was a larger frame building with two chimneys, smoke was coming out of them.

As we approached Melanie quietly spoke. "Jack, this has been one of my projects since you've been gone. Are you hungry?"

"Well–sure. What do you have in mind?"

"Jack, this is the workers' cookhouse. Would you like to eat lunch?"

I could hardly believe what I was hearing. "Lunch? Certainly, why not?"

The building had a long front and side porch with dirt floors. Neatly stacked on the side porch was a big supply of chopped wood. Alongside the building was a large woodpile where two black men were slowly unloading a mule-drawn cart carrying more firewood.

We quietly walked inside. Melanie spoke to the two men and three women who were working there. They smiled, then one of the ladies asked if we wanted to eat and Melanie told her we would. The lady gave us each a large metal plate and a spoon, then pointed to the food line. There were already three sweaty field workers in the line in front of us.

The men quickly stepped aside and let us move ahead and serve our selves. Without flinching, Melanie confidently walked down the food line and filled her plate and mine. Hominy, taters, black-eyed peas, sweet potatoes and corn bread were the good smelling food choices. The back eyed peas had generous pieces of pork in it.

I couldn't believe what I was seeing. Apparently the Negroes had seen Melanie do this before, because they went on about their business. But they also knew a long and rigid tradition was being broken.

Saying nothing, Melanie and I went outside the workers' cookhouse with our full plates and sat down on a log under a cedar tree. The same Negro lady, Docie, who had invited us to eat, came out smiling and carrying a tray with two tin bowls of venison soup and two metal cups of water for us.

We thanked Docie and began to eat. It tasted good.

"Melanie, what's going on here?"

"Jack, I mentioned that this has been one of my projects since you left. Well, I about got myself disowned when I started it," she said, smiling.

"I can imagine. How did you do it and what did you do?"

I've been trying to change ever since you asked me to marry you. For the first time, I've been taking a hard look at how we live here. Your mother also gave me some ideas."

"My mother?"

"Yes, since you left, I have been spending quite a bit of time with her. She's a wonderful lady. I'm learning a lot from her."

"What have you learned from her?"

"Well, she married your father and did what we are going to do. I asked her what was the hardest thing for her to adjust to–being from a grand, old Southern family?"

I continued listening while we ate our corn bread, taters and black-eyed peas.

"Well, your mother said that when she left with your father for Venezuela, they were happy as larks. Then she realized she did not know how to cook. Worse than that, she didn't know how to sew, or shop for food and supplies, or dress or manage money–practically nothing. She had stepped into a new world. Before, everything had been done for her.

"All she knew how to do was make witty conversation about topics of little or no consequence. She could do a little bit of knitting and crocheting, play the harp, grow flowers and look pretty. She said she was interested in politics and the plantation farming business, but her father and the other men generally left her out of it.

"She told me your father was very patient with her. He taught her basic cooking and house cleaning–things a man usually managed when he was doing for himself. He also hired a maid at most of the locations where they stayed. Your mother admitted she liked that a lot," Melanie said with a laugh.

She balanced her metal cup on the log and continued. "However, your mother said what she liked most of all was being involved in making the decisions affecting their lives.

"I embarrassed myself when you proposed to me down in the Savannah River park last August. You asked me–what I would do if you couldn't provide me with everything we needed. I started to say that Father would help us, but then realized that was exactly what you did not want.

"So, since then, I have talked to your mother and tried to prepare myself to be a good wife for you," she finished, getting to her feet.

I stacked my plate and bowl and rose to my feet. I silently gave her a hug for her kind words.

We stood together in the dappled shadows as I explained my little story about the last year to her.

"My plans didn't sort out exactly as I had hoped. My new job with the British company and their schedule changed everything, but now I will make enough money to take care of a wife. We won't be rich, but we certainly should be comfortable. Later, I might be able to invest or start my own business or mining operation.

"Anyway, before I accepted the job Mr. Kearny offered me, I couldn't even pay for you to come to England so we could get married. I was counting on getting a job when I graduated, but I thought it would be in England, or at least in the British Empire. Mexico, that was a bonus to me. But it's going to be a big change for you," I said reflectively.

Melanie looked at me saying nothing, then she shrugged and gave a brave smile. "Jack, it's going to work out fine. Yes, I was disappointed about not going to England to marry you this year. But maybe it's for the best. You now have a good job. And Mother and your mother are delighted they can be involved with our wedding here next year. Do you see anything happening to stop it?"

"No, I don't," I said, then hesitated before continuing. "I shouldn't say nothing could happen. I could get shot in a duel, or a hurricane could sink my ship. Who knows what God has in store for us? But right now I plan on being here next August or September for our wedding, if you agree. As a matter of fact, fall might be better, after the hurricane season dies down and it's not so hot."

"Yes, by then I will know how to cook corn bread, taters and black-eyed peas. And maybe a French pastry," she replied, laughing.

"Corn bread with icing on it would be just fine," I responded with a wink.

We both laughed heartily. She was genuine and I loved her very much.

"Miss Melanie Ellen, you're starting to act like a Scottish lass, not a Southern belle. Your family is going to disown you if you keep this up."

Then I asked, "What did you do here at the slave quarters, err… I mean workers' quarters?"

"Well, after you left and I talked to your mother several times, I decided to learn more about what went on here at our own plantation. Father was not helpful and JK actually resented it."

"Resented it?"

"Yes. So I just started going around looking at things through different eyes, starting here with our own plantation operations and businesses."

She was silent for a moment. "Then one day I walked down here and went through our workers' village, as Father calls it. It was a terrible mess."

"Why? What was wrong?"

"Well, the place was filthy and their houses were tumbling down and in shambles. They had no latrine facilities except of an open ditch. They cooked out in the open in good weather and under an open porch when the weather was bad. They had no clean or predictable sources of food and water–only what they could grow and what Father would occasionally give them."

"That bad? I would have thought your Father and JK would have looked after their investments better."

"Well, maybe it was not quite that bad. Father was careful about feeding them, including have them fish and hunt on the plantation, but still their food choices were limited. But their living conditions were bad. I was embarrassed living here so close and not paying attention to what was going on."

"Anyway, we went from that situation to this in one year. We even have a small infirmary building down at the end of workers' village row and a doctor comes out from Savannah once a month to check on our workers and their families," she said proudly.

"How did you do it if you didn't have your Father's support and JK resented it?"

"Easy. I brought Mother down here and showed her the mess. I then told her what I wanted to do. She has a way of getting things done that she wants," She laughed.

My opinion of Mrs. Kerns went up.

Chapter 10

Mr. Kerns' Strange Dream

Melanie and I walked back to the big house, visiting on the way. When we arrived, she asked Lilly to bring us some mint tea. We went back to the shade of the Little Zebo, as Melanie said she called it as a child, and continued to talk.

In a few minutes, we heard footsteps coming through the garden path towards us. It wasn't Lilly; it was Melanie's father–Mr. Kerns. He was carrying an engraved silver tray with three glasses of mint tea and a plate of fresh baked French pastries.

I stood and took the tray from Mr. Kerns and set it on the table in the gazebo. Then I stiffly shook his hand, properly greeting him before we sat. Mr. and Mrs. Kerns had always been a little distant in their dealing with me. I tactfully accepted it, because I loved their daughter and hoped someday to take her away–hopefully with their blessings.

Mr. Kerns was normally a quiet and formal man. He had always treated me with more respect than that due a poor future son-in-law. Today he was different. He seemed genuinely happy to see me and asked a lot of good questions about my new job and assignment in Mexico. He also joked with Melanie about her little project down at the workers' village row.

He described JK's projects to improve the shipping business in

Savannah and said that now, the railroad tracks were in use all the way out to Columbia and Macon. He joked that it seemed like everybody was getting into the railroad business. He described how JK was using the railroad lines in his new shipping businesses and said he was very proud of his son. He even thanked me for saving JK's life. I had never seen this side of the man and I liked it.

The conversation fell into an awkward pause, so I started to excuse myself to leave. But Mr. Kerns asked me to please stay for a few more minutes. His demeanor changed; something was on his mind.

"Melanie, I would appreciate it if you and Jack would not say anything about what I'm going to tell you."

His comment grabbed our attention.

With a somber look, Mr. Kerns took out his pipe and tapped it on the edge of the table. Nothing came out. He then packed the pipe with fresh tobacco and lit it, drawing in several puffs of smoke. It smelled sweet.

"Jack, I'm sorry we haven't had more time to get to know each other. I am excited about your new assignment and, we are looking forward to your and Melanie's marriage here next summer. The ladies will do it up in proper style, I'm sure,"

I nodded in agreement.

"Jack, I'm a Christian, but undoubtedly not as strong a Christian as I should be. I have always believed in the Bible and feel God weighs our actions and helps to plot our paths. Now I know he does, even our country's path and future," Mr. Kerns said, looking down at the pipe in his hand.

I thought that this was an odd statement and wondered where it was going.

"Melanie, something happened to me several weeks ago that I have not mentioned to anybody, not even your mother," Mr. Kerns said in a low voice and then was quiet for several moments, then he continued.

"Melanie, *I had a dream*. I don't totally understand it, but it was very clear. In fact I have had the same dream twice since."

Mr. Kerns paused again as he took a sip of his mint tea. "In the dream, I was with JK in the carriage, getting ready to go down to the Savannah River and check one of his projects, when Samuel came over and grabbed the reigns of our carriage horse. He said, 'Mr. Kerns, you need to come over to the cookhouse with me. Master JK, please go ahead, Mr. Kerns will be with you later.'

"Surprised, JK and I looked at each other, then did what he asked. I went with Samuel to the cookhouse, and JK took the carriage alone to check on his project.

"When Samuel took me into the cookhouse, the stove and oven fires were burning, but something was different. It felt cold inside, even though it was summer. There were three men standing behind the table, facing me. Suddenly, I was cold and started to shiver. Samuel turned and left the cookhouse and closed the door behind me.

"As I stood facing the three men I saw that they were young soldiers, officers. They wore crisp, new, gray uniforms. Saying nothing, the soldier on the left picked up a *golden saber* lying on the table. With a single, deliberate move he slowly swung it across the table. Immediately, like a window opening from heaven, I could see our plantation below–everything, even the smoke coming out of the chimneys from our plantation cookhouse and from Melanie's cookhouse down at the workers' village row."

We were now mesmerized by Mr. Kerns story.

"Then the young soldier looked at me and said, '*Behold,*' as he gestured toward the mysterious open window in the table."

"As I stepped closer it was as though I became a spirit. My mind took me through the open heavenly window which had opened in the table and down to the places I wanted to see.

"It was now autumn. I could see our beautiful Fields of Shannon Plantation in fine form and color. I could see the fields with their crops properly harvested and fat cattle and sheep grazing on the hills. I could also see that some of JK's projects were finished. The trains were carrying people and cotton bales from Macon to Savannah. The river was busy with ships. JK's dream was coming true. Our world here at the Fields of Shannon, that of our neighbors, and, in fact, the whole South seemed happy and bountiful.

"Then I could see a wedding taking place on our grounds. Melanie, it was yours and Jack's wedding. Then I returned to the cookhouse through the open heavenly window.

"The three soldiers were still standing there. But they looked older and tired. Their uniforms were torn and dirty. This time the soldier in the middle picked up a *bronze saber* with blood on its blade. Then he carefully waved the saber over the table ten times. When he lifted the saber, the mysterious window again appeared. The weary soldier nodded, and I again went through it and looked.

"This time, things were different. The sky was dark and there was lightning, thunder and smoke in the air. There were soldiers in gray uniforms on foot and on horses everywhere. Throughout the land there was *war, famine and the stink of pestilence.* I could see and hear the sound of cannons firing from four great navy ships in the sea. They were firing at ships in the Savannah River at the entrance to the sea. Many were burning and sinking.

"Women were crying for their lost husbands and sons. Other people looked sick, worried and sorrowful. It was a terrible time.

"I returned to the cookhouse. Now there were only two soldiers. They looked haggard and miserable. One was missing his left leg. The crippled soldier picked up an *iron saber*, rusted, chipped, and stained with dried blood and mud. This time, he quietly passed the saber over the table four times. Afraid, I again went and looked.

"This time the sun was shining, but I was shocked at what I saw. The Fields of Shannon grain and cotton fields and cattle were no more. The buildings had been burned and were in ruins. Nobody lived here anymore. Destruction reigned throughout the land. I saw an endless line of emaciated and crippled cavalry horses, four abreast, all slowly coming home without their riders to empty corrals on burned out farms and plantations. People, both whites and blacks, were living in tents and cooking in open fields and by the creeks. There were new graveyards everywhere, with gray military caps hung on small wooden crosses. It was terrible.

"I returned to the cookhouse. The soldiers were gone. There was now a single man standing behind the table. I asked, '*What does this mean? What am I supposed to do?*'

"The man answered, '*You have been granted a look into the future.*

Yours–a *proud and vain people–shall be chastened for their deeds. Hearken!'"*

Melanie and I were shocked, finally, I asked, "Mr. Kerns, what are you, or what are we supposed to do with this revelation?"

With a strained smile, he responded. "I don't know yet, son. I don't know. Oh, there is one detail I failed to mention. When I went out to see the first time, I saw something else."

"What was it?" Melanie asked with tears in her eyes.

"Well yes, I saw a wedding here at the Fields of Shannon Plantation. It was your wedding, but I also saw our graveyard. *My headstone was in it*. It was dated February 24, 1853. *I was not at your wedding*."

Melanie put her hand up to her mouth in shock, and a cold chill ran down my spine as the sad man looked at us with a painful smile. I tried to minimize the impact of his premonition by saying it was just a dream. But Mr. Kerns shook his head and said no, he had dreamt the same dream three times.

We sat quietly for a few moments, then Mr. Kerns stood and walked away. Melanie and I were speechless. Finally I told her I needed to get back to the Taylor Plantation. We walked to the carriage house and Melanie waited as I hitched up Montigo. I gave her a kiss and told her I would see her at the banquet that night. She said nothing. What was there to say?

Going back to the Taylor Plantation alone, I tried to sort out my thoughts concerning my visit with Melanie and her family. Melanie had changed a little, but it had been for the better. She was even more beautiful. She seemed to be ready to change her lifestyle and was mentally making the transition, with her taters, rabbit stew, cornbread and black-eyed peas, mainly slave food here, but staples where we would be going. Well, maybe not quite. More like *frijoles, tortillas* and *tamales*, but she was getting the idea. She seemed to genuinely love me and was ready to make the change.

Melanie's folks were something else. Her mother thought I was never going to change and she was right. She lived in the affluent style of the South and liked it. She viewed me as an interloper and foreigner. I brought nothing to the table the family wanted, like money and power.

Thank goodness Melanie was something of a rebel within the Kerns family. She was an opinionated, independent thinker. But worst of all, from her mother's perspective, she loved me. I was thankful that JK was successful and Melanie's older sister, Mary Helen, was already married into a powerful Southern dynasty. They were the Gallagher family, owners of the vast Stratford Plantation. Melanie Ellen Kerns marriage to a passing stranger ought not deal a political or financial blow to the family.

But the thing that threw me was Mr. Kerns strange prophetic dream. Yes, it did seem like the country was heading for a split, the southern states seceding from the Union. But would that mean war? Perhaps. And the part where he saw his own tombstone with the exact date and before our wedding was chilling! I did not know what to think of it and obviously neither did he.

Mr. Kerns seemed to be a different man from the person I remembered from the previous year. I hoped I could help him, but so far didn't know how. And why did he tell Melanie and me? Something was definitely happening, something at a higher plane. Many questions and no answers. *We would wait and see.*

Since my arrival, I had spent little time with Mother or Howard back at the Taylor Plantation. There was much for us to get caught up on. The Kerns' banquet was that night so most of our visiting would have to wait until afterwards, but I needed to talk with Mother for a few minutes. I found her on the veranda speaking to a businessman from Savannah. I greeted them, then went to the library and waited until the man left.

"Mother, I hear your venture is going well with the new textile operation in Savannah. Is Mr. Johnson your plant manager?" I asked as she settled into a chair across from me.

"Don't get ahead of yourself, Son. First, tell me how is Melanie? Did she remember you?"

"Well she did, after I reminded her that I proposed to her last August. Then she seemed happy to see me," I replied in the same joking way. "Yes, Mother, she's fine. And it was wonderful to see her. She was disappointed about the delay in our marriage, but she accepted it. I understand she and you have spent a little time together."

"Yes. Melanie is a wonderful girl. She reminds me of someone I knew long ago," Mother said with a faraway look in her eyes.

Then she came back. "Son, you need to bring me up to date. Tell me about the McIntyres back in Scotland–Angus and Rachael. Tell me about your last year in school and graduating. Tell me about your trip over here. I understand you got caught in a hurricane. Did anybody get hurt? And what happened to your ear?"

Mother was sitting in a wicker rocker on the open veranda and I was on a matching wicker couch facing her. I opened a bag sitting next to me.

"Well, Mother, there is a lot to tell. But first, I brought you a little gift."

Then I reached in, pulled out a small wooden box and handed it to her.

My mother was a beautiful and elegant woman. I had always liked the special surprised expression she got when something pleased her. As a child I saw it many times when I gave her one of my silly little gifts. She made me feel grand with her enthusiasm, followed by a loving hug and kiss. She had not changed.

"My goodness, Son, what is it?" she said as she carefully took the little wooden box and opened it.

Inside was a simple silver brooch with a colored stone. Quizzically, Mother smiled as she held it up.

"Son, it's beautiful! Tell me about it," she prompted with the same expression I remembered and loved.

"It's not very fancy. As you know my vast Scottish bank accounts are a bit low now, but it is something I thought you might like. Uncle Angus took me to the farm where he and Father were born, in the highlands in Perth, near Blair-Atholl. It's on the Garry River, a beautiful place. It was just a small mountain farm where Father's clan lived and grew crops. Uncle Angus said they had some cattle and sheep before they lost the place."

As I told my little story, tears glistened in Mother's eyes.

"Well, Mother, Uncle Angus showed me a little secret cave where he and Father would sometimes eat lunch or spend the night when they were watching the cattle and sheep up in the highlands. Uncle Angus said he and Uncle Roy were older than Father and were always impressed with

Father's little projects and ideas. We found a small leather pouch hidden in the cave, a pouch that Father put there with the favorite colored stones he collected in the hills by the Garry River," I explained, getting a little emotional myself.

My mother leaned forward eagerly. "Yes, Son, your Father told me many times about the cave. He even told me about the stones he hid there. He said some Scottish clan warriors, Picts they called themselves then, would hide and camp there during the time they were fighting the Romans," Mother responded with the tears swelling in her eyes.

"Well Mother, this is the only thing you have to show for your investment in my education. I made this with the prettiest stone I could find in Father's hidden pouch. Uncle Angus gave me the silver. I'm afraid a real silversmith would condemn me to being a sheepherder for the rest of my life if he saw my work. But it's strong and should last for a while."

I reached into the cloth bag and pulled out the brittle leather bag containing the rest of Father's favorite colored stones and handed it to her.

Tears ran down her cheeks and I took a deep breath to let the emotional moment pass. She said nothing.

After a few moments, Mother began to reminisce about Father's stories of his home in the highlands. The family was extremely poor after Grandfather died of pneumonia. Father was twelve years old, and he had a nine-year-old sister, Alice, who also died while they lived in the highlands.

Uncle Angus had gone to sea and Uncle Roy had become a gunsmith. Both sent money home to care for the family after they lost their farm. They also insisted Father go to school and get the best education available to him.

I debated showing Mother the last thing in the cloth bag, but I decided to do it.

"Mother, I have something I need to give back to you."

She looked questioningly at me.

I reached into the bag and pulled out the wood case containing Father's dueling pistols and handed it to her.

"I don't understand, Son. I gave these to you," she said.

"Mother, I don't need them anymore," I replied.

Her brow furrowed, "I'm not sure what you are saying. Why don't you need them anymore? They were your father's and I thought you would like to have them."

Then she looked at me again and suddenly understood. "Son, what are you saying?.... *Bolton Chapman*?"

"Yes. I don't need them anymore."

We sat there in silence for a few minutes as Mother slowly opened the cherry wood case and looked at the magnificent weapons. She closed and latched the case and handed it back to me. She then touched the sore nick in my left ear and I nodded. Nothing more was said.

Chapter 11

Politics Southern Style

Everyone at the Taylor Plantation was scrambling that afternoon. The big excitement was the banquet at the Fields of Shannon Plantation. Several important politicians and a general would be there with their wives. The important families from Savannah and several of the surrounding plantations would also be there.

I had no clothes appropriate for the affair, so Howard lent me some. He was slightly bigger than me, but his clothes would work. I was happy he decided to forgo the formal suits with top hats, since we were young bucks and were going to ride horseback to the gala affair. Formal riding outfits with spurs would be more fitting, he thought, and I agreed.

We had not seen much of each other since my arrival and Howard said riding to the Kerns banquet would give us a chance to visit. Smiling to myself, I thought I knew what was on his mind.

At five o'clock, two carriages left the Taylor Plantation for the Fields of Shannon Plantation. Mr. and Mrs. Taylor, Howard's parents, and Congressman Charles Shields and his wife who were visiting from Alabama were in the first carriage. Mother and cousins Matilda May and Constance Grace were in the second. Howard and I had our horses saddled, but tarried for a bit hoping to stay far enough behind the carriages so as not to eat their dust.

I asked Howard about his project and he gave me a few details. He said he wanted me to go with him the following week to see how his dam was progressing. He said they had ordered a water wheel and gear mechanism from Pennsylvania for the mill and should start installing it later that fall. Then he got to the subject I was expecting.

"Jack, this evening should be interesting. Congressman Charles D. Shields has been visiting us for a few days and I've been able to show him around the place. He's also a colonel and served in the Mexican War. He gave me an update on the politics in Washington," Howard said.

"Howard, if you are worried that I'm going to put on my abolitionist hat again and throw a political turd into the punchbowl, don't worry, I won't."

Howard smiled. "The thought did cross my mind."

Then I asked, "But I am interested in politics and want to know what is happening. It might be beneficial to me down in Mexico. What's the latest in Washington?"

A somewhat relieved Howard then relaxed and gave me a rundown on his favorite subject–politics.

"Jack, since you have been gone, things are not getting any better between us Southerners and the Yankees up north. When President Polk was in office, the country added almost a third to its size, with the New Mexico Territory and California. Then you add Texas. It has created some heated debates in Washington."

"So what's the issue? I would think the Mexicans would be the only ones bitching about it."

"Well, yes, they weren't too happy about it either. But that brings up another interesting point. A lot of the rich Mexicans with ranches, farms and mines on the land affected were quietly hoping the Americans would continue with their Manifest Destiny plan, but only if they, the Mexicans, could come into the United States with their property intact. Some of our congressmen said many wealthy Mexicans put out feelers, saying that their government was too unstable and corrupt and couldn't guarantee them protection for their land and property. Also they said their government was demanding more and more taxes from them. But that's another story."

"Yes. They call that a *mordida* (a little bite) in Mexico."

Dust clearing at last, Howard continued trotting our horses down the road.

"Anyway, the real issue is that the Congress is almost evenly divided between Northerners and Southerners. These new territories are potential new states and could shift the power balance in Congress to the south if they come in as slave states. It's turned into a hell of a huge issue, not only political, but also religious."

"How do you mean, religious?" I asked as we followed the two carriages in the distance.

Then we saw three more carriages coming in from another road in front of us, also headed toward the Fields of Shannon Plantation. With a sigh, we dropped back once more.

"You know, Jack. Put your abolitionist hat back on. You can argue the slavery issue from both sides. It's the same argument you got into with Randolph Jenkins–Dolpho, the slave trader. And oh, by the way, he might be there tonight. So don't assault him." Howard laughed.

"Oh, if that bastard is going to be there, I take back my promise. If I get into an argument with him, instead of politely dropping a political turd, I'll pull off my trousers and do a dump into the punchbowl!" I replied.

"Sure, Jack, and I'd like see you do that in front of Mrs. Kerns and Melanie," Howard responded with a smirk.

After a hesitation, I asked, "Do you suppose they would take me off their guest list?"

"Yes, perhaps they would," Howard responded, kicking up his horse and finishing the exchange.

At the plantation, there were a string of carriages unloading ahead of us. The Kerns had a group of Negro boys and men in crisp, red uniforms helping with the carriage horses as guests arrived. After the guests stepped out of their carriages, the yard workers would lead the horses and carriages to the side of the building and tie them there to a line of hitching posts. It looked like there must have been over thirty guest carriages at the grand affair.

It was humorous to see the ladies in their fancy clothes stepping down from the carriages, then spend five minutes unruffling themselves from their cramped ride. There was a hushed flurry of activity–brushing off, straightening and adjusting of dresses, then helping each other with their hair. They reminded me of a bunch of peacocks getting ready to strut. This was certainly not Mexico.

After Howard and I arrived and tied our horses, we went over and joined our Taylor clan along with Congressman Shields and his wife. Together we went to the receiving line at the entrance of the mansion. There, Mr. and Mrs. Kerns, JK, Melanie, her sister Mary Helen, along with Senator J. P. Anderson and a military man in a fancy uniform, stood in line to greet the arriving guests. I assumed the military man with his shinning metals was the visiting general. Howard and I followed our group in.

We were some of the last to go through the greeting line. As we started through, Senator Anderson and Congressman Shields hailed each other, talking loudly, shaking hands and slapping each other on the back. Then they paired off into a side huddle, talking and laughing, leaving the congressman's wife alone to go through the greeting line with Mother.

Mrs. Kerns was dressed like a Christmas tree. She was wearing a full, formal, green dress with hoops like most of the other rich ladies. She sported a pearl necklace, a diamond brooch and enough fancy rings to look like Queen Victoria's rich sister. But I had to admit, she did look very nice and was enjoying every minute of it.

Mr. Kerns was dressed in a white, formal suit, a shirt with lace down the front, a dark silk cravat with white polka dots and a gray expensive looking beaver top hat. He looked the part of the perfect host and stately Southern plantation owner. He smiled and nodded, giving me a knowing look as he shook my hand, saying nothing.

I had to laugh to myself when Mother went through the line in front of me. She wore an appropriately nice but modest outfit. Mrs. Kerns greeted Mother with a questioning look on her face. She reached out and touched Mother's modest silver and colored stone brooch I made for her.

"Lizzie, that's a very unusual brooch. Where did you get it?" Mrs. Kerns asked with a slightly condescending look on her face.

"Oh, it's a little thing I got from the Scottish highlands," Mother said casually, turning to me and winking.

Mrs. Kerns took a closer look at the trinket. It was as though she wondered if it was a rare piece of antique jewelry–perhaps something from the Scottish crowned jewels collection. She made a point of showing it to her husband. He smiled and complimented Mother on it.

I didn't know Mother would be wearing my little gift–and certainly didn't expect her to wear the cheap thing to a grand banquet and ball like this. Mother's class and dignity again made me proud. She wasn't in the business of trying to impress anyone and never had been.

After our family went through the reception line, Melanie came over and took me by the hand. She showed me the dining room with long tables set up with her mother's beautiful china and silver. She half jokingly said that this might be the last time we ever saw it–and she was almost right. Melanie continued to show me around the magnificent mansion set up for the festive occasion.

The Kerns family had done it up right. The banquet was indeed well planned and organized. Nothing was spared. Not only was a formal dinner to be served in the dining room, but later, pastries, drinks and fresh-cut watermelon, papayas and mangos were to be set out on tables on the veranda for the guests. People who wanted to dance had two choices–inside in the cleared great ball room, or outside on a covered dance floor specially built for this occasion.

They even had four Waterford crystal punch bowls filled with party drinks. Melanie said ice from a neighboring plantation owner's storage cave would be added to the punch bowls after dinner, when the guests were visiting and dancing. I caught Howard's eye and gestured toward the punch bowls. He was across the room talking to a cute little belle who was enjoying his company. Howard knew what I meant and laughed.

Musicians played on the veranda, where it was cooler, as the guests socialized before dinner. Melanie said her father had the musical group brought from New Orleans especially for the occasion. She said they were called the *New Orleans Deacons.* They were a mixed-blood group of musicians–French, Creole and perhaps a Spanish player. There also appeared to be a free black musician with them.

There were eight men playing violins and three playing harps. They even had a harpsichord, which the free black played beautifully. Melanie laughed, saying the musicians had been instructed by her mother to play white European music.

As Melanie and I were finishing our tour, Mrs. Kerns intercepted us and asked Melanie to show Congressman Shields and the mayor's wives the dining room, outside garden park and open tent covered dancing floor. Melanie politely obliged and left with the ladies.

Howard and JK invited me over to visit with Senator Anderson. I was impressed with how much Howard and JK had changed over the last year. Both had changed from fun-loving 21 year-old youths to 22 year-old professional men with thinning features and character lines developing in their faces. JK wore a formal suit and looked uncomfortable in it. He even had several gray hairs, which his sister Melanie enjoyed pointing out. They were now definitely future power brokers to be dealt with. I assumed I had also changed over the last year too and was pleased that Howard and JK seemed to value my company.

Senator Anderson was from South Carolina. He stood with a drink in hand, speaking to one of the lady guests when the three of us joined them. The lady glanced at us and spoke to JK. She then discretely moved on to a nearby group of ladies and continued visiting with them.

JK introduced Howard and me to the senator.

The Senator beamed. "Yes, Mr. Taylor, I am glad to make your acquaintance. I knew your cousin, Zackary Taylor, the President. He was also the famous general of our last war. He was a fine and honorable man, even if he was a Whig. At least he was *our Whig!*"

Howard replied, "Yes, I only had an occasion to visit with him three short times in the last five years. I can't say I understood his politics. It probably was because I was not paying too much attention to politics at that time."

"And you, Mr. McIntyre. You owe me a dinner in Mexico City, if I ever get there," the Senator said to me with a wink.

"Yes sir, you've got it. I will expect you this winter. The weather should be pleasant down there," I replied light-heartedly.

Howard was surprised that I knew the senator. Then he remembered I had managed to hitch a ride with him over from Charleston only a few days before, when I left the damaged ship.

Also, the senator had apparently passed the word around about my nicked ear. On our trip from Charleston, I briefly told him the story about my little problem with Bolton Chapman. It seemed to do wonders on how I was treated at the party, even by Mrs. Kerns.

The Senator tapped my cousin's shoulder, "Mr. Taylor, may I call you Howard? It's easier if we can all speak on a first name basis, don't you think? By the way my first name is *Senator,*" the Senator said with a hearty laugh.

We all joined the rotund, charismatic senator dressed in his white suit in an obligatory laugh.

"Well, Howard, JK here tells me I may see you in the Congress in a few years," the Senator continued intently looking at Howard.

"Senator, I don't know about that, but I do enjoy keeping up with politics and with goings on in Washington. Maybe I could watch it closer from there," Howard said, smiling.

At this point Congressman Shields and Brigadier General Franklin walked over and joined our group. Both held drinks, and the congressman was chewing on an unlit cigar.

Howard introduced the congressman to JK. I had already met him and his wife over at the Taylor plantation when I first arrived.

The big senator was the boss turkey of the group and led the conversation. It was interesting because the congressman had been a colonel before he retired from the Army and ran for Congress. General Franklin was still an active brigadier general in the infantry and was a West Point graduate. He also was a Southern Democrat. There seemed to be a little power play going on between the congressman and the general.

As we visited, I remembered my big boss, Sir Edward and his sage comments about politics. Taking his advice and recalling that the success of our company was tied directly to politics, I listened intently. This was a great opportunity to learn more about U.S. politics.

The senator continued, aiming his remarks at the congressman and general.

"Gentlemen, you are looking at the next generation of leaders before you. We can expect Mr. Taylor here to be in our midst in Congress within the next several years."

General Franklin picked up on it immediately. "Mr. Taylor, you have a very famous name. Were you related to General Zachary Taylor, our previous president?"

Senator Anderson answered the question for Howard. "Yes, George, he's related to him. They were cousins, isn't that right Howard?"

"Yes, Senator. And I'm also proud to say I am a Democrat," Howard replied, reddening slightly.

"Good, Mr. Taylor. Are you in the military? You look like you are a little young to have been in the Mexican War with your famous cousin."

"Yes sir General, I am in the military. I'm an officer in the Georgia Artillery Volunteers. I joined last year. And you are right, I was too young to be in the Mexican War."

"Well, Mr. Taylor, joining the Georgia Artillery Volunteers was smart. As Congressman Shields can tell you, being an officer in the Army with a distinguished military war record can be very important if you plan to have a political career. Your famous general and president cousin proved that," the general said in a rather pompous and arrogant manner.

I think the general was trying to put down the congressman a bit because he only held the rank of colonel. Also, the general seemed to be signaling that he too might be considering getting into politics.

"How about you, Mr. McIntyre, are you an officer in the military?" The general asked me pointedly.

"No sir. I work for a British mining company. I'm going to Mexico City from here to work on a project," I replied simply.

My comment sparked a glance between the senator and congressman.

The senator then commented, "Yes Charles, Mr. McIntyre here and I had a nice visit when we came over from Charleston together. He mentioned his assignment to Mexico. He might be able to help us out in the future."

The general stood blinking his eyes, being totally left out of the conversation and not knowing what they were talking about. Howard glanced at JK also, wondering about the comment.

The congressman then continued. "Gentlemen, what the Senator is referring to is that we are interested in finding a southern railroad route to the Pacific Ocean–to California. We might need some more Mexican land to do it."

"Hell, we captured half of Mexico. What more do you need?" The general asked incredulously.

The senator shook his head. "General, you and General Taylor and Colonel Shields did a fine job in the war. And I think our Senator Davis helped you fellas out a little bit too, when he switched uniforms and went down with his Mississippi Rifle Volunteers. Yes, thanks to your outstanding military work and bravery, the Union has added California and the New Mexico Territory.

"As you know, Congress is in the middle of quite a quarrel, trying to decide if the new territories are going to be admitted as slave holding states. While he was still in the Senate, Jeff Davis and the rest of us fought hard for it. We are still fighting an uphill and probably a losing battle on it."

JK then asked. "Senator, how does the idea of a southern railroad route play into this?"

But Congressman Shields answered JK's question instead. "Well, JK, that's a sensitive question. We all hope for an equitable answer to the new states having the option of coming into the Union as slave states, or at least that being the case in the land below the 36th parallel extending out to the Pacific Ocean."

"Congressman, what are you saying? If we don't get our way, we are going to secede from the Union?" the general asked bluntly.

This time Senator Anderson answered. "George, none of us want to do that. But it is an important question. If there is no other way, we as independent states must have the option to peaceably form our own country and to maintain our trade options, investments and property."

Howard spoke up, "So what you are saying, Senator, is that if this happens, the New South needs its own railroad route west to the Pacific Ocean."

"That's about the size of it, Howard. And this is where our friend Jack McIntyre here comes in," the senator replied.

I had said nothing, because the senator and I had discussed this question at length on our ride between Charleston and Savannah earlier during the week.

As we talked, I saw Dolpho Jenkins, the slave trader, come into the room and cast a glance in our direction. He tried to listen for a minute, then turned and left. He was dressed like a southern dandy and had a beautiful French-looking *lady* in tow. I was glad he disappeared.

The curious general continued his inquiry. "So what are you missing? I mean, I thought we had a direct land connection from the southern states to California."

Congressman Shields answered, "We do, but our railroad people have scouted the area. They say we should have a better route from the western part of Texas through the Mexican desert below the New Mexico Territory and on to California."

"How big a piece of land is it and how do we get it? I hope we don't have to start another war with Mexico to get it," JK commented.

"No, JK," answered the Senator, "No, we need to buy it from Mexico. It's not that big. And from what I hear, General Santa Ana is in desperate need of money. We should be sending a delegation down there soon to find out if we can negotiate with him for the land."

It was a very interesting conversation. I did not know then how much this was going to affect my future. It didn't take too long for me to find out.

Melanie caught up with me as Mrs. Kerns and several other ladies announced that dinner was ready to be served. Melanie and I, along with all of the other guests, moved to the large dining room with four long tables set with the beautiful silver, china, crystal and food. The Kerns family had borrowed some house servants from the Taylors and several other plantation owners to properly serve their guests.

The male house servants were all dressed in uniforms. Each wore a pair of smart red trousers and a white shirt with a black string tie hanging about his neck. They stood at attention against the wall facing the tables, waiting to take care of the guests. Each servant would care for six guests. They looked sharp and knew it.

After all the guests were at the tables, Mr. Kerns welcomed them and asked Reverend Woods to say a blessing over the meal. Mrs. Kerns stood, beaming. She was a happy and proud lady. This may have been the pinnacle of her social career.

The meal went off flawlessly. The French chefs came out with each of their masterpieces, describing in broken English the delicacies the guests were about to experience.

Several toasts were offered to Mr. and Mrs. Kerns for hosting such a grand affair. The banquet was in honor of the formal launching of the second phase of JK's project, formation of the *New Savannah International Shipping Company.*

JK stood, and a bit awkwardly at first, described the family projects to the guests. All knew JK was the brain behind the projects and new company. He soon became comfortable and did an excellent job of explaining how the project integrated the new railroads, docks and warehouses with the international shipping lines.

He went on to explain that the Kerns family had bought a major interest in one of the big Dutch international shipping companies–the Rotterdam International Transport Company. He explained that the project would help the local plantations and this part of Georgia become even more competitive in exporting their cotton, rice, tobacco and other agriculture products, including textiles. They would go to the northern states and to Europe. He joked that the new exporting railroad and waterfront facilities were available to competitors, but hoped the guests would use their ships.

JK got two or three toasts and a big round of applause for his visionary project. I thought it was the least any of us could do in repayment for being invited to such a grand evening.

The magnificent, four-course dinner with desserts lasted about an hour and a half. Mrs. Kerns had her family members, JK, Melanie, and her sister Mary Helen, spread out at different locations along the tables. And I'll be damned if the luck of the draw didn't place me next to Dolpho Jenkins and his fancy lady friend.

Dolpho Jenkins recognized me when we sat down next to each other.

"Well, I'll declare. I do believe I'm sitting next to our own true abolitionist," he said rather loudly, with a sneering smile.

Most people were still talking as they sat down and didn't hear his remark.

I replied not quite so loudly. "Yes, old man. One more remark like that and I will cut you another arse hole to match your mouth."

He glanced at me with a startled look and said no more. I guessed he had also heard about my nicked ear. At least he kept his comments to himself the rest of the evening.

Melanie heard both of our comments and looked at me, troubled, but said nothing. Several other people also heard the comments, but only smiled and went on with their conversations.

I found out later from Melanie that JK had invited Dolpho to their affair and that the two men had transacted some business together.

The banquet food and most of the conversations were enjoyable. Melanie was truly happy to have me visiting with her. After dinner, most guests adjourned to the empty, great ball room where the musicians were playing.

Mr. and Mrs. Kerns started the dancing to the *Emperor Waltz*, one of the few waltzes I recognized from England. I was impressed that this New Orleans group knew it. The other guests joined in after several minutes and some applause. The senator, congressman and general all took turns dancing with Mrs. Kerns to her delight.

The general danced as if he had spent more time with his horse than with the ladies. Even I could dance better than the general, and I didn't dance.

Melanie and I joined in, even though I warned her I could be dangerous on the dance floor. She smiled and promised she would cover up my mistakes. However, after several minutes on the floor she joked that perhaps she would have better luck dancing with the general.

I grinned in reply. I liked this spirited young lady.

The large room was warm with all the people inside and the lamps burning with their reflective mirrors and candles hanging from the chandeliers. Mr. Kerns directed four of the musicians to go onto the veranda and start playing for the young folks. Most of the younger couples, including Melanie and me, went outside where it was cooler. We continued our dancing on the new dance floor under a large, open tent in the adjacent garden. Fortunately, at Melanie's suggestion, the musicians started playing some more lively New Orleans music.

The whole evening was turning into an enchanting and storybook like setting. We danced to different music and waltzes. The ambiance of the music, the flaming torch lights, the attractive young couples in their fine clothes–even the fireflies flickering in the darkness–were all magical. The wine helped also. But most of all, Melanie made it perfect for me.

Melanie and I pushed back all thoughts of the next year during the wonderful evening. We both knew a lot of uncharted roads lay in my path before we would meet again to be married. But we enjoyed the moment. It was a moment I would cherish for the rest of my life.

Over the years, I often thought back to this night and place. It represented all the glory and grandeur of the South in its golden age. I later realized I had also seen the seeds of the Civil War being sown that night at The Fields of Shannon Plantation in Georgia. At the time, no one would have guessed these seeds would generate such a bloody war.

It was after midnight when Howard and I finally left the Kerns Plantation. Melanie and I had spent most of our time together, while Howard and JK did plenty of dancing with the pretty belles, but also didn't miss the opportunity to talk politics and promote their projects.

Howard and I visited while riding back to the Taylor Plantation.

"So, Jack, what do you think of our southern way of life?" he asked.

"It's hard to imagine such a life. I have been fortunate to live in the Caribbean and several other countries in the Americas, as well as England and Scotland, but you have a unique life here. Still it sounds like you are sitting on a political powder keg. You're the politician, you should know."

In the darkness, Howard was quiet for a while as he held Montigo to a good clip. We could only see the road outline through the trees in front of us as we trotted along.

"Jack, JK and I would like to talk to you."

"About what? I hope JK is not going to give me heartburn about being his future brother-in-law."

"No, I don't think so. Things are changing here for us. We are also concerned about what you just said. If we are sitting on a political powder keg, we want to know how to survive if it goes off. Will you have lunch with us on Monday? JK suggested we meet him down at his office in the new warehouse, next to the docks."

"Sure, I don't know what good I can be to you gentlemen, since I will soon be leaving and be out of the country for the next few years."

"Jack, you have seen a lot more of the world than we have. Maybe you don't realize it, but JK respects your judgment and opinions very much. So do I.

"Even though you don't like his business partner, he still respects your opinion," Howard said, apparently joking.

"Who is that, Mr. Von Koffland?" I asked.

"Well, yes, Mr. Von Koffland is one of his partners. But, I meant *Dolpho*. Dolpho Jenkins."

"You've got to be kidding! Dolpho?" I replied incredulously.

"I am joking. But JK did invite Dolpho and his lady friend to the party. JK is not fond of the guy, but he does do some business with him. I thought you should know."

"Yes, Melanie said something about JK and Dolpho. I must say I am disappointed with JK. I almost got into a fight with the old bastard this evening. Somebody sat him down next to me."

Howard laughed loudly, then responded. "Yes, I saw that. I was wondering where that would lead!"

When we arrived at the Taylor Plantation, all was dark, and everyone was asleep. Two bloodhounds came out barking to greet us until they recognized Howard and Montigo.

We unsaddled our horses and put them in their stalls. Sammie had already put hay in the stall mangers for them. We retired to the mansion, or the big house, as they liked to call it.

Monday morning, Howard and I left the Taylor mansion after breakfast and rode to the new Taylor dam and lake site. The rock dam was almost finished, and the workmen were constructing the stone and cement foundation for the bearing assembly for the small water wheel.

Howard had a German construction supervisor overseeing the project and eight white masons and carpenters. He also had fourteen blacks working to cut, haul and set the stones for the dam.

The project was following my design and looked even better than I had envisioned. They were already allowing water to flow in behind the dam for the lake, while at the same time harvesting the valuable timber upstream, so as not to lose it. It was an impressive project. I again realized the Taylor family had great wealth–to be able to do this and their other projects at the same time. Howard was very proud of the work and again thanked me for my engineering plans and help.

We arrived in Savannah a little after noon and rode down to JK's new warehouse. He was outside, talking with his white construction foreman. He called out to us and said to tie our horses and he would join us shortly.

After dismissing his foreman, JK came over and greeted us warmly. He showed us around his mostly finished warehouse. It was Warehouse #6 and the biggest of the lot. It was designed to easily hold over 1000 bales of cotton–enough to load several ships.

We walked over to JK's temporary office in Warehouse #1. Inside he had a desk, chairs, several small tables and shelves loaded with boxes filled with papers. Also on a table sat a basket with food and a large pitcher of tea. He invited us to dig in and eat. We did.

After some light conversation about his projects, JK got to what was on his mind.

"Jack, you heard Senator Anderson and Congressman Shields talking last night. What did you think?"

"About what? The railroad? The South? The politics?" I asked.

"All of it, especially about the future of the South. If you were asked to invest Queen Victoria's money for her, would you invest any here in the South?" JK asked.

I chuckled. "I have a hard enough time trying to be an engineer. I haven't even started my first project in Mexico. I don't think my investment advice is worth much."

Howard picked up the conversation. "Seriously, Jack, you have a feel for the international situation and the politics driving it. What do you think we are faced with here? Let me be more specific. If the politicians can't hold it together and the South secedes from the Union, what do you think will happen? Again, let me elaborate. JK and I, and our families, have a lot at stake here. We would like to land on our feet if it happens."

"Well, first I recommend you have a fat London bank account filled with British pounds Sterling if it happens," I said, half in jest.

Then I got more serious. "Gentlemen, I don't think you have to be a sage to make several observations."

"What are they?" JK asked intently.

"The way I understand it, if the South secedes, it can happen in one of two ways–peaceably or by war. Certainly the best way for you and the South is if it is done peacefully. You can go on with developing your land, businesses and continue building your markets and trade the way you are, perhaps forever. But if it causes war, then that's another story."

Both JK and Howard responded almost simultaneously.

"What's the other story?"

I paused and looked at both of them for a moment, then responded. "Howard, where are you getting the axle assembly for your water wheel on your new mill?"

"It's coming from a factory in Pennsylvania and the wooden wheel itself from Vermont," he replied.

"JK, where is Savannah getting the steam engines, tracks, and cars for the new Savannah railroads? And where are you getting your new steamers you are putting into service in your shipping line?" I asked.

JK stared at me for a moment, then replied, "I get your point. The railroad steam engines, rails and cars are all coming from the North, and even some of our steamers. Most of our steamers are coming from England."

I just looked at them as they glanced at each other.

Finally Howard responded. "Jack, it took you thirty seconds to put your finger on something JK and I have been talking about for months. We came to the same conclusion you did. The South cannot afford to go to war over this slavery or secession thing, otherwise we're doomed. If it comes to war, we need an industrial base that we don't have now to support us."

"Yes, that's pretty obvious," I replied.

"I think our Democratic congressmen and senators clearly understand this also. And, for that matter, so do the northern Whigs in congress," JK replied.

"So what do we do?" Howard asked.

"Don't push this thing into a war," I responded.

Then JK picked it up. "At least not for a while. Not until we are better able to defend ourselves if they call our bluff."

It was again exceedingly clear to me I was talking to two very serious young men who were in the position to impact the future of the South. They weren't the same fun-loving youths I had visited only the year before. Their minds were on the future–future of their families, fortunes, and country–the South.

Howard then asked me another question. "Jack, assuming we have no option but to go to war, what should we be doing?"

"That's a tough question. You can't start obviously stockpiling war materials. But I guess you could quietly try to develop more of an industrial base down here. Also, it would help to be on good terms with England and some other European countries if you should need them–and you will. Yes, and don't close your back door. Don't get into another fight with Mexico, especially while Melanie and I are still down there." I laughed.

They chuckled at my comment, but their minds were elsewhere. Finally, JK sprang the big question. "Jack, what would it take to keep you here?"

Puzzled I asked, "What do you mean, keep me here?"

Howard responded, "Jack, you could be a valuable person to us here. JK and I are starting some big projects. We could use your help. You're smart and we trust you. Additionally, you could be a valuable adviser to our people if we ever got into a serious pickle with the North."

I didn't respond, after being taken aback about what I had heard.

Then JK said. "I won't ask what your British company is paying you, but what if we gave you four times that amount and also gave you a chance to be a partner in some of our businesses."

I could hardly believe what I was hearing. I had not expected anything like this! The two young men, my cousin and my future brother-in-law, were dead serious in their offer and had the *palanca* or power to back it up.

"Gentlemen, you take my breath away. I did not expect this.... It's a real compliment. I think you both understand the situation I am in. I have hired on with my company and have agreed to do a project. I can hardly back away now," I explained.

"Damn it, Jack, why don't you be like us–just follow the gold?" Howard joked.

"Jack, we understand. But after you finish your first project in Mexico, might you be available?" JK asked.

"JK, I doubt if I will be finished by the time Melanie and I are married next year. It will probably take several years," I responded, not quite answering his question.

"Well, think about it," JK said.

"Your offer is a real compliment to me, but I don't think I am worth anything like that. But if I can help, in any way, while I am down working in Mexico, let me know. I will do everything I can to help out. I do have a few contacts in England," I added.

"We might take you up on that," Howard said quietly.

"Good. I will expect it," I replied.

Our lunch meeting ended on good terms. Howard and JK understood my position and, in fact, had expected my response. They also appreciated my offer to help them however I could while I was working in Mexico with the English New Wales Equipment and Mining Company.

As we were leaving JK's office, he asked, "I have been meaning to ask you, how did you get that nick on your ear?"

Howard grinned broadly.

"I got it in a duel," I said.

JK nodded. "A duel? I heard some rumors about it. Do you mind telling us about it."

"It's no secret. But I'd prefer not to make a big thing out of it. I don't even think Melanie knows about it yet. On my trip here from England, we went through Boston. I looked up Bolton Chapman, the man who murdered my father. I shot him. This is how close he got to me," I replied, touching my nicked left ear.

Then I added, "And, by the way, I suggest you fellows not try something like that without getting some professional help. I thought I was a good shot, until I met my good friend Captain Will Springer. If not for him, I would be dead right now. He taught me how to improve my chances of surviving in a duel."

"Will you show us?" Howard asked.

"Are you sure you want to open that door?"

"Sure we do. Howard is right, will you show us?" JK urged.

"All I can show you is how much I didn't know. As Captain Springer told me, you can be the world's *best* duelist and still get killed by the world's *worst*. All he needs is a lucky shot. But you can certainly improve your chances if you practice and know what you are doing. Yes, I would be happy to show you what I learned."

Before I left for Mexico, I spent an afternoon on the Taylor plantation with both Howard and JK. I gave them the basics on what not to do and how to practice. We shot my father's fancy old dueling pistols a few times. I then suggested they get someone like Captain Will Springer to work with them to improve their skills if they were serious about learning. I again cautioned them that with those skills come risks. First, they might get a reputation as a duelist, which they didn't want. Secondly, and the most serious, they might become over-confident and make challenges that could be avoided. I recommended that, if they continued, do it quietly and not let it be known they knew something about the deadly art. They understood.

Before I left Georgia, Howard gave me a set of new Colt .44 caliber revolver pistols to take with me to Mexico. I also purchased another matched set of these pistols in a beautiful cherry wood case to give as a gift. I also purchased two additional Colt Dragoon revolver pistols along with three ball casting dies and a case of percussion caps to take with me.

JK gave me a fine new Sharps .50 caliber single shot rifle with long distance elevation sights. This weapon used the new rim-fire cartridges with fulminate primers. I thought this weapon might come in handy in Mexico. I practiced with it several times before I left Georgia and liked it very much. I also developed a new appreciation for a rifle, especially for their deadly accuracy in long distance shooting.

My stay in the Savannah area lasted 18 days, from the day I arrived with Senator Anderson from Charleston on September 9th until departing on one of JK's ships to the Caribbean on September 27, 1852. Melanie had made my visit to Savannah perfect. Worries that my feelings for her were only those of an infatuated young buck for a pretty girl and that time would soon reveal cracks quickly abated. She was a deep, real person with a wonderful personality. She was indeed the person I wanted as my wife and friend, a person I wanted to share the rest of my life with.

Also, during my short stay I'd helped Howard and JK with some engineering advice on some of their projects. Being a guest at the Taylor Plantation, I had time to visit with Mother also. She was a busy lady with her textile company in Savannah, which was making a profit. This gave her a little independence from her own family.

Mother offered me some travel expense money, which I refused. I explained to her that Father's and her efforts at finding the hard-earned money to pay most of my first two years' expenses at the university in Scotland was sacrifice enough.

Since my last visit to Savannah the previous year, JK's attitude towards me had changed. JK was genuinely friendly now and took the time to show me some of his impressive projects. He didn't seem as distant as I had remembered after his accident on the wharf. He offered to help me catch a free ride to Cuba on one of his company's new steamers, which I accepted. He also asked me for some engineering advice about several of his projects, which I willingly gave. He seemed impressed.

Melanie and I agreed we would have our wedding at the Fields of Shannon Plantation in October of 1853. With my recent encounter with the hurricane, I wanted to minimize the dangers of my travels through the Caribbean on my return trip from Mexico. Melanie agreed.

We discussed Melanie's father's dream and premonition of death. We decided it was in God's hands, and we could do nothing about it. Also, her father told us to proceed with our plans. She was not happy about it, but agreed.

When Melanie finally found out about my duel with Bolton Chapman, she was hurt and angry that I had not told her. Then I reminded her I tried to tell her the first day I got back, but she had dismissed it in her excitement. Anyway, my experience apparently made an impression on her. When we would meet she would occasionally almost unconsciously, run her finger over my notched ear.

Melanie also told me she now looked at their family's life and what was going on in the South through changed and more critical eyes. She agreed with me–things were not right. She said she even talked to her father and brother about their slaves and if anything could be done about freeing them. But both agreed there was no way they could run the plantation and their businesses without them. If anything, JK was becoming more dependent on slaves as a source of labor for his many projects.

Finally Melanie told me she was becoming weary of continually hearing the talk of states' rights and the idea of secession. She was anxious to start her new life with me in Mexico as soon as possible. I agreed.

My mind then turned towards Mexico. I wondered what cards the fickle hand of fate would deal me.

Figure 3 Map of Mexico 1850

Chapter 12

Mexico City and Generalissimo Santa Ana

The stopover visit to Georgia was tonic for my soul. It removed the few concerns I had about Melanie and my relationship with her. The dear young lady left no doubt in my mind that she was ready–no, anxious to marry me and forego her rich southern lifestyle built on the backs of God's less fortunate people. Together we would venture into our new life in Mexico.

Mother told me that while I was gone, Melanie had no lack of rich suitors looking for her hand. But Melanie told them all she was spoken for. She truly was a gem, and I was not going to lose her.

On Monday, the 27th of September 1852, I boarded one of JK's new steamers to Cuba. From Havana I hoped to catch a ship to Veracruz, Mexico. But before leaving Georgia, I wrote and posted a letter to my boss, Walter Kearny, in Manchester, England. My message was simple–I was on schedule with my travels to Mexico to open up our company's new mining operation. I would write him when I reached Mexico City.

In Havana, I waited eight days before I could catch a Portuguese ship headed for Mexico. It carried tobacco plants, wheat and oat grain seed plus a small steam engine along with other equipment and tools. The captain's name was Rafael Ribeiro. He spoke Portuguese, Spanish and French, so we got along just fine. Because of growing up in Mexico,

I was able to seamlessly transition from English to Spanish and also speak some Portuguese.

After a pleasant and uneventful sailing, we arrived in Veracruz on October 14th, seventeen days after leaving Melanie in Savannah.

After stepping onto Mexican soil, I felt like I was back home. My folks and I had left Mexico eight years earlier, when I was but a youth. We went to Venezuela because of the "Texas War" with the Americans. Father told us that the political situation in Mexico was unstable and so his company sold most of its mining operations to a Dutch company before it was confiscated by the Mexican government.

But now things were different for me in Mexico. I was now a grown man and was back to accomplish a goal to open and operate a mine for my employer. With my engineering training, I found myself thinking in terms of real and practical solutions, their costs and how I might accomplish them.

I spent several days in the seaport of Veracruz, scouting the area to see where I could set up a local shipping office to support my company's mining operations in the state of Querétaro. The proposed mining site was inland some six hundred kilometers and to the northwest. I had already decided Veracruz was the best Mexican seaport from which to operate. That's probably why the Spanish had selected it some three hundred years before.

Coming from Liverpool, I found Veracruz extremely primitive in so far as warehouses and ship loading facilities were concerned, there were none. But that didn't bother me, because I knew we could easily create whatever we needed. My boss had also offered me some ideas on how our company normally did this, and I could build on those ideas.

But this all would be an empty exercise if I could not get the approval of the Mexican government for our company to operate in Mexico once more.

The trip to Mexico City was wet, but enjoyable. I hired a carriage and a driver, José Delgado, for the trip. The first night we stayed at Orizaba, after a hard day and changing horses three times. The second day on the road we got caught in a hard thunderstorm, which was a little bit late in the season according to José.

The trip to Mexico City took almost four days of hard traveling. We arrived in the middle of the afternoon after traveling through the mountains and dropping into the dry old lake bed on which Mexico City was built in the vicinity of dormant volcanoes. I wondered how many thousands of years ago the volcanoes had last erupted. The Spaniards and Mexicans were not worried about it, so I wouldn't either.

I had José take me to the old Elías Hacienda, where my folks stayed when they came to Mexico City. The owner's name was Juan Alberto Elías de Salazar. José drove our carriage through the impressive but unmanned gate in the volcanic rock security wall surrounding the hacienda.

Inside the courtyard, I stepped from the carriage and walked into the patio, then knocked on the front door of the main building. The grounds looked unkempt and run down. Many of the trees and shrubs were dead. A pretty Aztec Indian girl answered the door, and I asked for Señor Elías. The girl looked surprised, then asked me to wait outside.

A few minutes later Señora Hortencia Elías appeared and looked me over with a puzzled expression. I immediately recognized her. She was older, but still very stately and dignified. I suddenly realized it had been eight years since the lady had last seem me, and I had changed from a boy to a man in the interim.

I introduced myself to Señora Elías and told her I was *el hijo del Ingeniero y la Doña Mack* (the son of Engineer and Mrs. Mack). Then she immediately smiled and gave me an endearing *abrazo* (hug). With tears in her eyes, she said she never expected to see us again. I still viewed the gracious lady almost as an older aunt or Doña, a member of my family.

Señora Elías then explained that her husband had died two years earlier and only she, a crippled daughter and her elderly aunt were living at the large hacienda, along with their cook, the gardener Pepe, and another couple who also helped part time. The Indian girl, *Xinata* (Zeenata), also lived there.

I told Señora Elías I needed a temporary place to stay in Mexico City and asked if I could make arrangements with her. She immediately agreed and said I could use the little house in the back part of the hacienda where special guests stayed. It was also the same place my folks and I had lodged many times in the past. I was delighted and so was she.

My carriage driver was a sharp young man and appeared to be reliable. He wanted to work for me and help set up our company's operations in Mexico. I agreed to hire him full-time, on the condition I could get approval from the Mexican government for our company to do business in their country. Since José made frequent trips between Veracruz and Mexico City, I paid him and told him to check with me the next time he returned. He agreed, then returned home to Orizaba and his family.

Señora Elías' guesthouse, my temporary rented quarters, was messy and dirty. In fact, the more I looked around, the whole Elías hacienda looked in bad repair. Señora Elías, or *Doña Hortencia,* as I respectfully called her years earlier, immediately dispatched her small staff to clean the guesthouse for me. She also helped herself.

Pepe turned on a small aqueduct to provide water to their fountain and private bathing pool house. After several hours of operation the muddy water cleaned itself out nicely and left a pool of clear cool water.

After settling into the guest house with my single carpet bag and travel case full of books, maps and firearms, I took a well-needed bath in the bathing pool. Eight years before, my folks and I had enjoyed this beautiful and private estate as our base of operations in Mexico City, but the estate now seemed smaller and its obvious state of disrepair saddened me.

That evening I had a simple dinner with Doña Hortencia and her crippled daughter, Carmen, and Tia Ramona. During our casual dinner conversation Doña Hortencia complimented me on my Spanish and asked about my plans. I explained to her that the next thing for me to do was find Señor Salvador Villarreal, a banker. Doña Hortencia told me that Señor Villarreal worked for the Bank of Mexico. Apparently Walter Kearny had failed to clarify that point, or perhaps I just missed it. At least he should be easy to find.

The next day Pepe brought me a pleasant breakfast of fresh fruits, sweet breads and coffee. Later I went to the Bank of Mexico to make contact with Villarreal. There I found out Señor Villarreal was an important man who was second in command of the bank and head of the international business department. A formally dressed bank worker escorted me to Mr. Villarreal's office. Señor Villarreal glanced up from his ornate desk, appearing rather annoyed at the interruption.

"Good morning, Señor Villarreal, my name is Jack McIntyre. I work for the New Wales Equipment and Mining Company," I said, presenting him with the sealed letter of introduction from my company.

He invited me to sit down, then opened my letter and read it.

Villarreal was a portly, balding man with a mustache. His remaining hair was graying and short. He wore a dark business suit with a cravat. He looked hot and uncomfortable.

Villarreal's expression changed as he stood, removing his glasses. He then smiled broadly as he extended his hand to me.

"Good morning, Señor McIntyre, *Bienvenido* to Mexico. You are so young, I am impressed. Señor McIntyre …, Mack? Are you related to Señor Mack?"

"Yes, I am. He was my father," I replied.

I went on to briefly explain that my father was dead. I also told him that after my graduation from the University of Edinburgh as a mining engineer, my father's old boss had hired me.

Salvador Villarreal was now very friendly and complimented me on my Spanish. He then asked about my mother. We continued to visit for a few minutes before he began talking about doing company business in Mexico.

"Señor Mack, we need to introduce you to the important people before we can consider doing any business in Mexico. Your father was very good at working with the important people in the government. But that was eight years ago, before the American War," Villarreal explained.

"I thought some of our people were down here during the war," I responded.

"They were, but General Santa Ana threw them out. Even though they were British, he did not like the conditions they were offering, so he threw them out and kept their equipment," he explained.

I nodded. My boss had failed to mention that our company's departure during the war had been under such unfriendly conditions. Apparently our people simply got their arses kicked out of the country.

Villarreal went on to explain that even though President José Herrera headed the government during the war, Generalissimo Santa Ana was the *impresario,* the power behind the throne in Mexico. Nothing happened without his approval. I knew that was the situation even before I had left Mexico eight years before.

Salvador Villarreal was generous with his time and spent the entire morning with me, then took me to lunch. He told me Mexico was in serious financial straits and that I represented new foreign money and business, which Mexico desperately needed.

He took me to a Portuguese restaurant near the bank, it had a very pleasant patio complete with parrots, a fountain, and a jungle of trees and shrubs. Salvador knew almost everyone sitting at tables in the restaurant and introduced me to many of them before we sat down. It took us almost ten minutes of talking before finally getting seated at a private table. I wanted to know more about banking in Mexico, so I asked. He gave me some very interesting answers.

"Salvador, my boss, Mr. Kearny, said our company has an account here at your bank. How does it work?" I asked.

Salvador continued his friendly but business-like manner as he explained. "*Juan*, our bank, and most large banks, have several ways of doing business. I assume you have not worked with banks much in the past?"

"No, I have not."

"Then I will explain it in simple terms, if you don't mind. One way you can work with our bank is to bring in a bag of gold coins, and we can set up an account for you. We will agree to use your money for your own business and we will charge you for our services. Or, if you agree, we will lend your money to other customers and we will charge them and pay you interest for using your money," he explained.

"Yes, I understand that. But I didn't bring a bag of gold coins with me from my company–so how can I get credit or money from you to do business?"

Salvador smiled. "Juan, or Mack, what do you prefer I call you?"

"Salvador, I don't like either one, but since I can't think of anything better, please call me Jack Taylor. Taylor's my middle name," I responded.

Salvador burst out laughing. "I think you need to think of a better name than *Taylor*."

"Why is that?"

"Well, five years ago the *gringo* general, Zachary Taylor came down to Texas in the American War, then he and General Scott, with their soldiers, took away a third of our country for the Americanos. No, I don't think Taylor is a good choice. Let's call you *Victor* for now. You're English and Queen Victoria is very powerful and respected here in Mexico–especially her wonderful pound sterling. Is Victor all right with you for now?" Salvador Villarreal asked, still smiling.

"No, why don't we just go with Jack, or *Ingeniero* Mack, if you don't mind," I replied, a little embarrassed about my blunder.

"Now, let's see, where were we? Oh, you asked me about credit for your company at our bank here in Mexico. Let me see if I can explain it," Salvador replied.

As we ate our meal, Salvador explained the world of banking and finance to me in simple terms. It was all new to me.

"Jack, most of the big banks in the world have arrangements with each other. People or countries, or businesses, can have money in one bank, and if that bank recognizes and does business with another bank, we can send letters of credit instead of money or gold to the other bank where the client wants to do business. It's safer and easier to send letters of credit than money. If the letter of credit is lost, we just explain it then send another letter. That's better than losing the money, don't you think?"

"Yes, I think so. So what you are saying is that your bank, the Bank of Mexico, has credit with my company's bank, the *Bank of London*, where we have money. So our company instructs our bank to set up a credit account with you for my project, then they send you a letter of credit to do it. Is it that simple?" I asked.

"Yes Jack, you have the right idea."

"So what happens when a country goes to war with another country, or the bank is robbed by bandits, or a company defaults on its loans?" I asked.

"Well, those things happen. The bank always tries to protect its money and its customer's money. We are in the business to make money, so we protect ourselves first," Salvador answered truthfully.

Towards the end of our meal, Salvador told me he had to meet an important client in the afternoon, but he wanted to introduce me to

President Mariano Arista as soon as possible. He said the president's secretary of presidential scheduling reserved Wednesday mornings from nine to twelve for new dignitaries and important people to meet the president. He said he wanted to get me in separately and he could do it. He suggested Tuesday morning at ten and said he would confirm it with me if the President was available. I was impressed with Mr. Villarreal's *palanca* (power) as the number two man with the bank.

Salvador confirmed that I would be at Señora Elías' hacienda and also told me her deceased husband was related to General Santa Ana in some way. Salvador took care of our meal and ordered me a carriage. We departed.

I spent Saturday, Sunday and Monday riding around Mexico City in a leased carriage with a driver, Fidencio, to get thoroughly familiar with the area. Fidencio was local and was a big help teaching me more about this interesting city, one of the oldest in the Americas.

Also, Sir Edward Chadwick's words weighed heavy in my mind. *Politics comes first, otherwise the project will never happen, or, even worse–money and time will be wasted.* I did not want this to happen.

As I went about exploring the city, its history and existing businesses, I wondered how the Mexican *chingones* (power brokers) would test me–also what and how much they would want to let my company do business in Mexico. I hoped they were as desperate as Villarreal indicated, so they would go easier on me. My father had lamented that far too often the people in charge of a country put their own desires ahead of the true needs of their country. I was about to find out.

While I was out and about on Saturday, Villarreal sent word to Señora Elías that he would pick me up at her hacienda at nine o'clock on Tuesday. He said nothing else. I assumed he had successfully made an appointment with the President's Secretary of Presidential Appointments, and did not want to give out any additional information. It was prudent so I thanked La Doña and said nothing more.

At nine o'clock on Tuesday morning I was properly dressed and waiting in the hacienda patio, drinking coffee, when Salvador rolled into the courtyard in his private carriage. I hopped in and we were off.

On the way to the Presidential municipal palace and office, Salvador said, "Jack, I was able to make a private appointment for us at ten with President Arista's secretary, Hector Arias. We are in Mexico, so hopefully we will meet with the President before noon. Let me do the talking and be polite, as I'm sure you will be. He will ask you about your company and their plans. Just be brief and polite. He will probably indicate a need for something, a school, an orphanage or something else. Let me handle it. It's a polite way to get money into his pocket. It's the way we do business here."

Salvador twisted to look into my eyes. "Does this make sense?"

"Yes. I understand."

We arrived at the *Palacio Municipal*, where the President's office was located. The Mexican flag was flying, and a second plain green flag was up which Salvador told me meant that the president was in.

We were escorted by a military guard in dress uniform to the Secretary's office. Salvador greeted him, then signed us in and indicated the purpose of our visit.

To my surprise, the secretary immediately escorted us to the President's principal secretary's office, who in turn took us directly to see the President. The President got up, smiling, from his desk and greeted Salvador Villarreal, who then introduced me.

I realized then our company had chosen the right man to do business for us here in Mexico.

President Arista was a nervous-looking man of about fifty with thinning black and gray hair. He wore a simple uniform with several decorations. He was shorter than I was, almost skinny except for a small potbelly.

His office was large and empty. He had a painting on the wall of a military officer in a colorful uniform on a prancing, white horse followed by a cheering crowd of happy peasants. The important-looking soldier was holding up a sword with the flag of Mexico tied to it. It was a bit pretentious and I assumed the painting must be of General Antonio Lopez de Santa Ana.

Additionally, the President had a larger-than-life portrait of himself dressed in a glorious uniform. It was hanging on another wall.

President Arista had an ornately carved desk in the middle of the sparsely-furnished office and there were three chandeliers holding glass oil lamps in the room, one above his desk, another above a carved wooden table with chairs to the side of his desk, and the third above an empty spot in the office on the other side of his desk. Obviously the room had been used by other important people before this President.

President Arista sat us down at the table with him at the head. He then instructed his aid to call for a servant to bring us tea. It reminded me of the South.

The President asked me a few questions about my company and what we hoped to accomplish in Mexico. Salvador told him my father had also been an engineer with the same British company. The President said he had heard of my father, *Ingeniero Mack*, but never met him.

The conversation soon moved to an almost solo discussion between the President and Salvador. It was not long before the President told us that his government had a project to improve the water system to a poor part of the city and said it would be gracious of us to make a token gesture to help.

I nodded and Salvador assured him we would.

After about a half hour, the President stood up and said he had another appointment. Salvador and I also stood, thanked him for his time, and were escorted out by a military aid.

Salvador was happy with our meeting. He said we should wait about a week. Then, if I would authorize a draw of one hundred pounds sterling, he would deliver it to the President's personal aid in an envelope, indicating it was from our company and that it was for the water project.

Salvador and I ate lunch at another nice hacienda-type restaurant. I told him I wanted to pay for the meal. He smiled and said for me not to worry–either way, my company was paying for it. We continued to strategize during the meal.

"Jack, Saturday night the President is hosting a banquet for the new coordinator from France. Apparently Napoleon's nephew has just come into power and has sent over his emissary, who most likely will be his new ambassador to Mexico."

Salvador continued. "We are worried because the new Napoleon's wife is Spanish, and it's only been a little over thirty years since we declared our independence from Spain. Anyway, the President wants to properly greet and welcome the man."

Before we broke away that afternoon, Salvador said that Señor Benjamin Swartz, the head of the Bank of Mexico, would take me as his guest to the President's banquet. He said it would be a good opportunity for me to meet a lot of important people.

Finally Villarreal commented. "Jack, we need a good name for you that the Mexicans can remember. Victor is good. Mack is all right–at least it is easier for the Mexicans to say than McIntyre. The Mexicans like their nicknames. It comes from their Indian blood. I noticed the nick in your ear. How did you get it?" Salvador asked.

I hesitated, weighing the wisdom of telling him. Then I did.

"Salvador, I told you my father was murdered in an unfair duel. The man that murdered him put this notch in my ear. It was the last thing he ever did to anyone," I replied soberly.

"Did you kill him?"

"Yes."

"In a duel?"

"Yes."

"And he earmarked you with his bullet in the same duel?"

"Yes."

Salvador got a delighted look on his face and pondered for several moments then exclaimed, "Excellent! Wonderful! What a story! We can come up with an excellent nickname for you. And it will help–you are very young. Your mustache helps, but that doesn't matter anymore. You are a hero. You now have a reputation."

"What do you think of Victor Mack, *El Pistolero*? Or, maybe *El Duelista*. Or *El Asesino*," Salvador suggested smiling.

"Sounds like I have a lot of choices. I don't like any of them. I don't want to spend the rest of my life being the target of some *buqui* (young buck) who comes along and wants to make a name for himself by killing me," I replied.

"Good point. Maybe then just Jack Mack, *El Mocho* (The Chopped One)," Salvador suggested with a chuckle.

"Well, I'll have to think about it," I said.

"You may not have to worry. The Mexicans will give you a nickname whether you like it or not."

We laughed about it.

Salvador took me back to La Doña's hacienda in his carriage. On the way he told me that even after my attending the President's banquet, we could do nothing in Mexico without General Antonio Santa Ana's blessing. He also explained we could not ask for an appointment with him. If he wanted to see me, he would summon me. In the meantime, I could do no business. Only after a formal meeting with the general and receiving his blessing, which included his *mordida* or bribe, could I proceed.

Salvador had been on track so far, so I would continue to take his advice, although I didn't understand how we could see the general if we did not ask for an appointment.

The banquet for Napoleon III's minister or emissary, whatever he was, and presumably their next ambassador, was to be held Saturday, October 30, at another beautiful hacienda in a park area on the outskirts of Mexico City.

According to Villarreal, most of the beautiful old haciendas in Mexico had been built by the wealthy and powerful Spaniards before the Mexican revolution. Some of the families were either involved or astute enough to survive the Revolution and maintain their estates and properties, some with heavy payoffs.

I spent more time writing and posting letters to Melanie and several to my boss, Walter Kearny, informing him of my slow progress in Mexico City. I also sent one to Howard and another to JK, offering some ideas on several of their projects. The rest of the time I spent learning more about Mexico City and the country's intriguing history. I even looked up several of my old school chums from years before.

Another project I adopted during my idle time was working on La Doña's hacienda. I hired several workmen to overhaul and repair the hacienda's aqueducts and two fountains and get water properly flowing through them again. La Doña Elías was delighted. I also had the workmen replace some dead shrubs and six dead trees in her beautiful patio. With some plasterwork and painting, the place took on a refreshing new look. It was truly a fine-looking estate, something that would hold its own against some of the nicer plantation mansions in the South.

My gesture seemed to breathe some life into the sad widow. Señora Elías started bringing her daughter out to enjoy the patio and beautiful grounds every day. She even had a little party, where she invited some friends and family members over to enjoy the new look of the hacienda. Of course La Doña had me as the guest of honor, which I enjoyed. La Doña even had an attractive señorita relative, Maria de la Cruz, accompany me for the evening. It was pleasant, but I missed Melanie.

On Saturday evening, Mr. Benjamin Swartz's carriage driver picked me up at the Elías hacienda before sundown to attend the President's banquet. The driver then proceeded to another magnificent, walled hacienda where armed guards were posted. There they picked up Señor Swartz.

We had only met once, briefly, at the bank when Salvador introduced us. Benjamin Swartz looked and acted very formal and seemed to lack anything like a vibrant personality–much less a sense of humor.

We spoke about a few mundane things on the way to the banquet. I even tried to make a joke questioning Napoleon III's motives in sending a representative to Mexico, especially considering his wife was *Spanish*. Swartz did not react. I thought it might be another of my Taylor name *faux pas*, or was Swartz a wet blanket? I gave myself the benefit of the doubt and decided Swartz was a wet blanket.

I left it alone and was quiet for the rest of our ride to the banquet. I think Swartz was relieved. I was glad I was dealing instead with the number two man at the bank, Villarreal. I liked him and he had a personality.

At the Mexican President's banquet, I found myself comparing it to the Kerns' banquet held at the Fields of Shannon Plantation the previous month. Both affairs were held at beautiful estates. Both had music, although different kinds. Both had beautifully dressed people. Both had French and local foods. However, one difference here was that the men were over-dressed in their colorful uniforms, ribbons and all. They demanded the center of attention, much more so than the ladies.

But there were other differences too, some of them big. Here they had no black servants or slaves. The Indian and Mexican servants, however, almost acted like slaves. Most of their music and food was different. Good, but different. The *señoritas* and women seemed to be more protected and subdued, especially around strangers or foreigners. Although there were many beautiful *señoritas,* I saw nothing that looked like a flirting southern belle.

Since it was President Arista's affair, the banquet was carried out with him as the central character. All conversations stopped when he entered the room. He gave his ingratiating little wave for the guests to continue eating, visiting and dancing. His wife also attended, but she stayed in the background.

The President said a few words before the banquet dinner started. He offered several polite toasts–*first to the Mexican hero, General Santa Ana, who was not there,* and then one to the French emissary, Colonel Pierre Lafiet, and his wife.

When the evening was over, two big differences stood out in my mind showing the difference between this and the Kerns' banquet.

First and foremost, Mexico was a man's world and was dominated by a single man who was not even present–Santa Ana. The second point was that this grand banquet was put on by a country's government–*Mexico.* The Kerns' banquet was about the same size and more than equally impressive. However, it was put on by a single Southern family!

After the banquet, I rode with Mr. Swartz in his carriage back to his guarded hacienda. On our ride back, Mr. Swartz and I had less than three sentences to say–and that included me thanking him for the invitation to the banquet and the ride. After dropping Mr. Swartz off, his driver shuttled me back to the Elías Hacienda. I had a very nice visit with his driver on our way back, but I was glad the evening was over.

The next day I was depressed, because I could not get the approval from Santa Ana to proceed with our project. I had been in Mexico City for almost two weeks and had not been successful in meeting with the powerful general. I wondered how I was supposed to meet with him if we couldn't make an appointment.

Wednesday evening, I was relaxing in the Elías Hacienda patio, drinking a glass of wine and updating my diary and journal. I noted that at least my expenses were low. Doña Hortencia came over to the table where I was seated. She was carrying two glasses of wine. She set the second glass in front of me, then sat down and joined me.

Excitedly, she told me. "*Chu Chu*, Captain Vásquez came by today when you were out. He spent about an hour here."

"Is that good? What did he want?" I asked.

"Yes, that is good. He is a special aide to the general, General Santa Ana," she said, beaming.

She picked up her glass and handed me the other. "Captain Vásquez was related to my husband and he is also related to General Santa Ana."

La Doña tapped her glass to mine and laughed. As we were visiting, Pepe came up and said there was a messenger at the front gate for me.

I went over and saw a young man in a plain brown uniform. He stood holding his horse, waiting for me. After asking my name, he handed me a sealed envelope. It was addressed to Ingeniero Mack. It was from Salvador Villarreal, saying we had an appointment tomorrow with General Santa Ana at ten. Villarreal's note said he would have a carriage pick me up at eight. Success finally, I hoped!

Salvador picked me up at eight sharp at the gate to the Elías Hacienda. I learned early that Salvador did not operate on Mexican time. He was punctual, and I appreciated it.

Salvador seemed excited. He said he was surprised we were successful so soon in having an audience with the famous general and ex-President. He said he had only met with the general two other times. One meeting did not go well; in fact, it went badly.

Salvador said he could give me no advice. He said the general had a reputation for being unpredictable and sometimes ruthless. He then suggested I just be polite, answer his questions and use my own judgment.

I told Salvador I had brought a case containing a matched set of Colt Dragoon .44 caliber revolver pistols. I asked if they would be an appropriate gift for the general, even though I knew the answer. Salvador said he couldn't see how it could hurt, but he repeated that he was not able to predict the general's behavior or mood.

The general's residence was an old Spanish hacienda, which had a double rock wall around it for security. It looked like a fortress from the outside. There were six soldiers at a guardhouse at the iron gate entrance to the first security wall. We presented ourselves and were told to leave the carriage and walk with two guards to the second gate at the patio entrance to the actual hacienda. There we met three more armed guards. We waited until one of these guards summoned a person from inside the hacienda to come out and receive us. This man was dressed like a military aide in a brown uniform with a yellow, braided cord over his left shoulder and carrying a flintlock pistol.

The aide and one guard escorted Salvador and me into the patio of the hacienda. It was the classic Spanish patio with old trees, shrubs, rosebushes, vines and four large flowing fountains. There were four separate buildings that I could see inside the grounds of the hacienda. We were then escorted to a long building with a porch supported by thick adobe, Roman arches along the front. We went inside and met the general's secretary. There were also several other military officers inside seated at desks, trying to look important and busy.

Villarreal and I again signed in and stated the purpose for our visit to the general's secretary. We were seated in a large, dark room with one high window and six chairs. We waited. Swallows kept flying through the open window and several were trying to make mud nests on the wall inside the room. We waited and waited.

Finally, after waiting for more than an hour, a military aide came in and said the general was ready to see us. He took us outside across a small courtyard to another smaller building. Two armed guards snapped to attention as we came near. They saluted the aide and opened a large, wooden door and let us in. We walked down a hallway with a beautiful Moorish-tiled floor and through another door and into the general's office. He was seated at a wooden desk which was nicer than President Arista's. The old man was looking at some papers that appeared to be maps.

Without looking up, he roared at us. "Sit down."

We did. I think it unnerved poor Salvador by the sick look he had on his face. I didn't know any better, so I just waited to see what would happen next.

The general remained seated and continued looking at the papers before him.

Finally he said gruffly. "You're not a *gringo*, I hope."

I responded immediately. "No, I'm English."

"Good! I understand you killed a *gringo,*" the general said in an equally gruff voice.

Poor Salvador actually looked frightened.

"Yes, General. I killed the *gringo* who murdered my father."

"Good! Would you like some tea?" The general asked.

Salvador answered *No,* while I answered *Yes* at the same time.

The general actually chuckled at our fumbling. He picked up a small brass bell from his desk and rang it. An aide came into the room, almost running.

"Tea," the general said in a low, gravelly voice.

The aide immediately disappeared. He soon reappeared carrying a silver tray with four cups and a pot of tea. We sat silently as the aide poured the tea into three cups and set them on a low table in front of us. Frowning, the general asked the aide who the fourth cup was for? Embarrassed, the aide just shrugged. The general then waived him out of the room.

The general remained seated at his desk. The desk was on a small, raised platform in the middle of his office. The visitors' chairs and table were on the tile floor below the platform, so the seated general was able to look down on us when he spoke. I thought this was a cute little trick to help him dominate his visitors.

The general almost seemed preoccupied with the papers or maps on his desk as he spoke. His tone of voice remained harsh, but not as bad as when he first ordered us to sit.

The general asked the questions, and this time I gave the answers. Villarreal remained silent.

The general asked me if I was an engineer and what kind I was. He asked where I graduated and when. He asked about economic conditions in England and if Queen Victoria was at war with any country. I gave simple and direct answers.

The general continued with his line of direct questioning. He asked where I learned Spanish and I told him in Mexico, Venezuela and Cuba. I explained I was born in Cuba. My mother and I traveled with my father, whenever we could on his projects in the Americas, but most of our time was spent in Mexico.

The general seemed to change his tone and his questions. He asked me about surveying and if I could read maps. I told him I had studied the English surveying system of metes and bounds and surveying from established bench marks. Also, I had helped my father do some surveying field work at some of his mining locations.

Then he asked me the key question–could I read Spanish maps? I told him I had not had the opportunity to read Spanish maps, but I understood they used the international naval method of identifying locations by latitude and longitude in minutes, degrees and seconds. I also told him I had taken a very rigorous course in naval navigation and I presumed Spanish maps would be similar.

Finally, the general asked me what my company wanted to do in Mexico. I explained that we wanted to reopen some old Spanish silver mines near Querétaro, where our engineers had previously indicated there should be more silver ore. I told him we were prepared to open it up, recover our initial investment, then operate on a 20/80 basis with Mexico *after expenses.*

The general immediately said it would be on a *50/50 basis, before expenses.* I said nothing as the general looked down at me and started to smile.

As the general picked up his little brass bell and rang it twice, he said, "Gentlemen, you can go now."

A young military officer quickly entered the room as Salvador and I stood. I was a bit shocked at our sudden dismissal, then the general pointed at the cherry wood pistol case on the floor by my feet.

"What's that?" He asked, indicating the case with the wooden handle of his bell while holding the clapper so it wouldn't ring.

"Excuse me, general, it is a little present I hoped you might enjoy," I replied as I picked up the case.

The general nodded to the officer, prompting him to take it from me. The officer handed the case to the general. The general set the case in front of him on his desk and opened it slowly. His expression changed to a slight smile as he took out one of the fine Colt Dragoon pistols and admired it. He slowly cocked the pistol, then released the hammer expertly.

"Very nice," he said with a pleased smile. "I've got a whole barrel of these we took off of dead gringo officers. Samuel Colt does make very fine weapons. Thank you."

The general's smile disappeared. He nodded and waved his wrist, pointing us toward the door and saying nothing. Salvador and I quickly thanked him for his time and were escorted out by the captain.

Outside, I had a sense of disappointment, even failure as we walked back with the captain through the two sets of guards and to the carriage where Salvador's driver was waiting. The captain smiled and wished us a good day.

Salvador and I had lunch and discussed our situation.

"Jack, I told you, this is the third time I've met with the general and I cannot predict the man," he explained.

We continued to discuss our situation. Salvador said he could give me no advice or hope. I decided to wait several days before sending a letter to my boss. If we heard nothing more, my recommendation would be we minimize our expenses and pull out of Mexico. I was devastated. The job offer Howard and JK had made me the month before in Georgia was starting to look very good.

When I got back to the Elías Hacienda, I went directly to my private cottage. Sitting down at the table, I had started to write the letter to my boss when there was a knock at my door. It was Xinata, the pretty Aztec Indian girl. She said La Doña wanted to see me.

I followed Xinata over to the main building, wondering what was on La Doña's mind. Inside, sitting at the table and drinking tea with Doña Elías was the young captain I had seen that morning at the general's hacienda.

Smiling, La Doña introduced me to Captain Marco Vásquez. The captain also wore a big smile and greeted me warmly.

"Señor Mack, the general wants to see you tomorrow morning at ten in his office. I will pick you up at 8:30. Is that acceptable to you?"

"Certainly!" I responded excitedly.

I asked what the general had on his mind, but the smiling captain said he did not know and left.

My spirits were launched upward again. What did this mean?

Captain Vásquez picked me up promptly at 8:30 the next morning in a military carriage with a military driver. On the way to the general's hacienda he explained that the general wanted this to be a *secret meeting*. He wanted to see me alone, separate from the banker, Salvador Villarreal. The captain explained I was to say nothing of this meeting to anybody. I agreed.

At the general's hacienda, Captain Vásquez escorted me directly into the compound and to the general's office.

When we entered the office, the general was standing with his glasses on, stooped over a table and studying the papers on it. When we walked in, he spoke to the captain and me, this time shaking my hand. I was shocked to see the general was missing his right leg below the knee and was using a crutch to get around.

The general ordered tea. After his aide left the room, the general immediately got to the point.

"Señor Mack, I have a problem and I think you can help me," he said, still standing.

The captain remained silent.

"Yes sir, General, I hope so," I replied smartly.

"I don't want this information to go out of this room," he continued, still looking at me intently.

"Yes sir, General, I understand."

"Let me show you something," the general said.

He turned bracing himself against a chair and pointed to several maps and other papers lying on the table.

This was the first time I saw the *white vellum maps*.

"Señor Mack, I think you'll find this interesting. I did."

The general showed me two white vellum maps which were held down with paperweights. The first map was illustrated in black ink by a very fine, precise hand with small printing. It had a lot of detail–rivers, pueblos, mission churches, mountains and the like.

The second map was much more cryptic. In fact, it seemed to be a series of small separate maps and notes. Also, the second map showed very few names of places. I noticed that it had been folded and was soiled. It also had many sloppily penciled diagrams, notes and numbers scrawled on it. Somehow, the two maps seemed to be related.

He explained that the maps lying on the table before us were old. They were from a set of maps captured from the Spanish during the Revolution. The maps were intended to show where all the critical mining operations were in colonial Mexico.

Captain Marco Vásquez and I listened intently as the crusty old general continued. He said the set of maps he had laid out were intended to be used together. He explained that one was the *cerraja* (lock) map and the other the *llave* (key) map.

The old man continued with his explanation. He said the first map was the key map. It showed government roads, along with the missions, towns and military garrisons in a specific geographic area. It also showed mountains and rivers. All places shown on the map were carefully identified and named.

The second, soiled map was the locked map. It contained the specific information the Spanish wanted to *hide*.

The locked map was drawn to a different scale and only showed local vicinities with roads and trails to the Spanish mines, along with their smelter and ore reduction facilities. Most were gold and silver mines. But there were also some quicksilver (mercury), copper and other types of mines.

The general explained that the locked map was tied to the key map with a number. The general showed us a number "9" penciled in on the key map above the Cocospera Mission location. He then showed us that there was also a number "9" scribbled-in on the locked map where the Cocospera Mission's name should have been. It was used as the starting point to show where the local gold and silver mines and their related reduction facilities were located.

The general explained that we were looking at the set of maps on the table for the *Pimeria Alta* region in northern Mexico. He said these were the only complete set of maps which showed all of the Spanish active and inactive gold, silver and mercury mines in that region.

When the general finished, he was silent for a moment, then looked at the captain and me. He was letting the information sink in. I then realized that what I was looking at could be a part of the ultimate treasure map for Mexico.

Finally, the general added that he possessed the sets of Spanish maps from the Pimeria Alta region in the north, and those to the south, including central and southern Mexico. He did not have the California maps or those north of the Río Gila, above the *Pimeria Alta* region. They were lost.

Apparently the Spanish had prepared similar maps of all the territories they conquered and occupied in the Americas. The general explained that these maps were prepared by government cartographers for the Viceroy of Mexico and for the King of Spain. During the Revolution, the Mexicans caught the Spanish shorthanded militarily and in the middle of an aggressive gold and silver mining operation, he explained. The Spanish were shipping their smelted and refined cast gold and silver bars along the government roads to Mexico City and Veracruz, where they would load it on ships destined for Spain.

The old general sat down at last and let us digest his story. He took a sip of tea, as the captain and I studied the maps intently.

After I asked several questions about the maps, the general again stood. "Let me show you something interesting."

He pointed to some penciled-in changes and markings on the cryptic, locked map that showed the important mines and ore reduction locations.

"Take a look at these. Do you know what they are?" The general asked.

"No, not really. They look like some changes to the original map. Maybe some locations where they started a new mine?" I replied.

"No. The Revolution apparently caught the Spaniards unprepared. They were working hard to quickly ship all their gold and silver out of Mexico to Spain when the Revolution began. Although the Revolution took place over ten years, it created big problems for the Spanish. They had gold and silver moving about and stored throughout Mexico. They had to hide it quickly. The penciled-in location on this map represents the location where they hid one of their loads. There are *two* other locations in the *Pimeria Alta* where they hid loads, and they are shown on those other maps. Can you and Captain Vásquez find them?"

It was now abundantly clear what the general wanted. He knew of some hidden Spanish treasures he wanted to recover.

Suddenly, my earlier conversations with Howard, Senator Anderson and Congressman Shields in Georgia came to mind. The new, southern railroad to California would also go through the Pimeria Alta region. If this was the land Santa Ana was going to sell to the United States, he would want to quickly remove any treasure hidden there before he sold it.

"Ingeniero Mack, I need your help to recover these hidden Spanish shipments in the *Pimeria Alta.* They belong to Mexico. Captain Vásquez here is my nephew. I trust him. He is a good soldier, but he is not an engineer. I need a smart young man like you."

"I want the two of you to go north and recover these treasures. We have found that many of the treasures the Spanish hid in central and southern Mexico are already gone. Some of the Pimeria Alta treasures may also be gone, but we need to find out. Since the hidden shipments were from the remote, rich mines in dangerous Indian territory, they should be some of the biggest in Mexico. We need to recover them. Do you understand?"

"Yes sir, I understand very well. How can I help you?" I replied.

"I need a person I can trust to go with Captain Vásquez and recover these treasures, if they are still there. I will make it worth your while if you agree. You said your company wants to set up operations in Querétaro. The conditions yesterday your company wants are acceptable, except we will take *40% after expenses*. Those are the most favorable conditions we have offered to a foreign country. Also, there might be something additional in it for you and Captain Vásquez, if you do a good job. Are you still interested?"

But before I could answer, the general casually commented with a smile, "Of course, I could kill you after you return with the treasures, but I won't. *I am a man of honor*. You have proved you are a man of honor too."

He then pointed to my famous, notched ear.

"Yes sir, I am. I will help you," I replied, amazed at how quickly the word about my ear had gotten around.

The general, now sitting, again smiled and extended his hand. Captain Vásquez and I both shook it.

The general told us he wanted us to leave for the north in two days. He said he would give Captain Vásquez letters of introduction and orders allowing him to operate with the general's direct authority anywhere in Mexico. We were to proceed from Mexico City to the small port town of San Blas on the *Mar de Cortez* (Sea of Cortez). There we would catch a ship and sail to the small port of Guaymas, then get a military detail of 20 soldiers and proceed into the Indian territory in the Pimeria Alta to recover the hidden treasures. We would pick up wagons, horses and burros, as we needed them from the military garrisons along the way.

I asked the general to familiarize me with the area, which he did. He had a large map of Mexico on his wall. He hobbled over to the map, pointed out the different locations and related them to locations on the set of smaller, white vellum maps.

The general then gave his opinion on how the locked map with the mine locations tied in. It seemed to make sense, since the locked map did show some key rivers and Spanish missions on it. Locations of the mines were given in degrees latitude and longitude, with distances in leagues from coded numbered Spanish missions. We would need both maps and a familiarity with the area to find the hidden Spanish gold and silver.

The general said that most likely the gold and silver would be in small or round square shaped rods weighting approximately six kilos each and the silver, in about ten-kilo ingots. He said that if they were smelted, reduced and poured by a Spanish foundry, they should also be stamped with a Spanish crest and their weight. He explained that the gold could be in the form of nuggets, dust or ingots, depending if the Spaniards had time to smelt and refine it. He did not expect coins, but said it was possible, especially in their haste to remove and hide all gold and silver in Mexico during the Revolution.

Studying the pencil markings on the inked, vellum-coded map, we identified the three locations in the Pimeria Alta region where the treasures were supposedly hidden. One was located near the Cocospera Mission on the Río de Cocospera. One was farther north, in the Chihuahuitas Mountain region, and measured in distances from the San Lázaro and Guevavi Missions in the Río de Santa Maria. The third was measured from the Tubutama Mission.

General Santa Ana never brought up anything about selling land to the *gringos* for a southern railroad. But, to me his motives were quite clear. I was certain the general wanted to recover all hidden Spanish treasures in the Pimeria Alta region as soon as he possibly could, especially considering his secret railroad route negotiations with the United States.

The general rang his brass bell and his aide came into the room. The general said something to the aide, who then left. In a couple of minutes, the aide returned with a bottle of wine and three glasses. The general signaled for the captain to pour the wine for us. He then raised his glass to the captain and me.

"Success to you and Marco. Success at finding Mexico's treasures of the *Pimeria Alta. Viva Mexico!*"

Captain Vásquez and I returned the toast and emptied our glasses.

The general returned to his desk and opened a drawer. He took out my gift case containing the two pistols and handed it to his nephew, Captain Vásquez.

"Marco, this was a very fine gift from Señor Mack. You will need these more than I will. Take them with you–and don't get killed by the damned *Apacheira,*" the general said, laughing.

We returned his laughter, but my heart was not in it. The general's little joke had not struck the captain or me as funny.

The general instructed us to take the vellum maps. Also he told us to gather the other equipment and supplies we needed for our trip and to leave in two days.

General Santa Ana opened another drawer in his desk, pulled out a good-sized leather pouch and rattled it. He handed the pouch to Captain Vásquez. I assumed the bag contained gold coins for our trip. I hoped we would be bringing much more gold back with us when we returned from the north.

The general wished us well and said he expected to see us in 90 days. I hoped his predictions would come true. The general gave the captain a round, black leather container with straps containing the precious maps. After the general bid us *vayan con Dios* (go with God), we shook his hand and left.

The next day, the captain and I busily collected the firearms, powder, lead shot, percussion caps and other material we needed for our trip. I had brought some black powder and percussion caps with me from Georgia, but decided to leave them at the Elías Hacienda when the captain was able to obtain some from his military sources.

Later, I spent several hours going over the white vellum maps to make sure I understood them. I also got several other maps the government had on the northern territory of Mexico. I asked for a naval navigational sextant and got an old Portuguese device that required an accurate timepiece, which we did not have. Later, Captain Vásquez was able to get a gold pocket watch from the general. We also found a lode stone ship's compass, which might come in handy.

The specialized equipment and maps we collected would take up valuable weight and space, but we packed it anyway, thinking we might need it to find the hidden locations shown on the map. We could always leave the equipment with a military commander in the north when we were finished.

That evening, I wrote to Melanie and told her I would not be able to write to her for several months because I would be visiting a remote area of Mexico without mail service. I told her she could send mail to me in care of Doña Elías in Mexico City, as she had been doing. La Doña would hold her letters for me until I returned in four months. I was not as optimistic as the general.

I also wrote Walter Kearny and gave him a favorable report, indicating I would be out of touch for about four months. I told him that we could still have our Querétaro operation up and going by next summer. I also described the terms I had negotiated with Santa Ana and hoped he would be impressed. I was.

I asked La Doña Elías to post the letters for me and gave her money to pay for them. I also made arrangements to keep the casita and store my equipment with her while I was away. She happily agreed. She was a grand lady.

Chapter 13

The Secret Trip North to the Pimeria Alta

Our secret trek north started Sunday, November 7, 1852. The morning was dark and disagreeable when we left Mexico City. Our military driver fought one of our young, strong-willed carriage horses, jerking him around and trying to keep him under control as we climbed through the cold mountain passes west of the city. At one point, the horse managed to tangle and break a hip strap on the harness which took us about ten minutes to repair by candlelight.

I had slept badly during the night. It was because of nerves and stomach problems resulting from a bad combination of wine, fruit and empanadas I had eaten the afternoon before. To make matters worse, we had a couple of small earthquake jolts during the middle of the night. They did little damage, but put everyone in the city on edge. I hoped these were not the harbingers of things to come.

On this disagreeable morning, the Spanish treasures of the Pimeria Alta seemed very far away and elusive. But in spite of it all, I was anxious to start our adventure. *God willing, we would be successful.*

Since our meeting with General Santa Ana, Captain Marco Vásquez and I had spent most of our time scrambling to get what we needed for our trip north. We spent all Saturday afternoon checking and double-checking our maps, gear and supplies. Using General Santa Ana's *palanca*,

Marco quickly requisitioned most of what we needed, including a two-horse, civilian carriage with a military driver.

During the short time we had to prepare for the trip, I went over what the general had said, hoping it was more than just a devil's errand he was sending us on. Initially, I suspected the general's motives. But after seeing the maps and listening to his story, it all made perfect sense. Knowing of the old man's penchant for greed and that he was probably negotiating with the gringos to sell the southern railroad route land to California, cinched it in my mind.

Besides, I had little choice. I could either help General Santa Ana, or leave Mexico and fail to accomplish my company's goal, setting up a silver mining operation in Querétaro.

By late Sunday morning, after we had been on the road for a few hours, things looked better. The sun came out, it warmed up and we only had to stop once because of my stomach problem. Also, our cantankerous young horse settled down and we were making good time.

The rest of the day we traveled hard, keeping our horse team moving at a good trot. We adjusted our pace depending on the horses' wind, road conditions and terrain. Our driver was Corporal Tiburcio Contreras, from Pachuca, in the state of Hidalgo. He was 24 years old, like Captain Marco Vásquez. He was a talkative soul and excited about going this far north for the first time in his life.

I was the youngster of the group, being 22. But I had seen much more of the world than my traveling companions. Mother always told me, "Relish your youth. Remember that Alexander the Great conquered the known world by the time he was 26." Although I was not trying to follow in Alexander's footsteps, Mother's guidance helped me keep my focus and respect my elders, but also not consider them infallible or without flaws. General Santa Ana was a good case in point.

The first leg of our trip was by land to Tepic, near our departure port of San Blas on the coast of the Mar de Cortez (Sea of Cortez). There we would catch a ship. But in route to Tepic, we planned to go through Guadalajara and check with the military commanders there to collect the latest information on active garrisons and happenings up north.

The first full day and night, we traveled almost continually, stopping only to rest the horses and eat. Additionally, we changed horse teams at different military garrisons, usually about every 10 to 12 hours. Marco explained that the garrison spacing was no accident and that the Spaniards had spaced the garrisons and missions about a day's ride apart or closer for safety and convenience. We spelled Corporal Contreras behind the reins from time to time to give him some rest and change the scenery for ourselves.

Monday afternoon, we got into Morelia, where we stopped at a pleasant little *posada* (lodge) for some food and rest. Marco gave Corporal Contreras several pesos and told him to get some food and spend the night at the local military garrison. He also gave the corporal a written order for the local garrison commander, asking for a fresh team of horses in the morning.

That evening, while the captain and I were enjoying our supper of *pozole* and corn tamales with warm beer, Corporal Contreras walked into the posada with two military men, a sergeant and a lieutenant. The lieutenant and sergeant stiffened when they saw Captain Vásquez and me sitting at our table. Apparently they did not buy the corporal's explanation about what he was doing. They were also short of horses, so they challenged our corporal's word and his story.

At first I thought the situation was humorous, but soon saw the tension in the air, I kept my mouth shut. I was impressed with the way Captain Vásquez took charge, taking the soldiers outside, where he kept them at attention and chewed them out for about ten minutes. I quietly continued to eat and watched through the window.

Finally, when the captain finished his verbal lashing, he released the lieutenant and sergeant. They couldn't leave fast enough. A tired Corporal Contreras, smiling sheepishly thanked the captain then left on horseback in the direction the angry soldiers had gone.

The next morning before dawn, Corporal Contreras was waiting outside the posada with our carriage and a team of fresh horses. Captain Vásquez invited him in to eat breakfast with us. They had *menudo*. I was never very fond of *menudo,* so I had coffee and a stale *pan dulce,* trying to console my unhappy stomach. Dawn was breaking when we hit the road.

Captain Marco Vásquez and I got to know each other better after several days on the road. He was a sharp officer, slim and athletic. He was much taller than the average Mexican soldier and had brown hair and green eyes. I joked with him, saying we looked like brothers, and we did.

What I liked about Marco was his professional demeanor and friendly personality. He reminded me a bit of Captain Springer, although Will was quieter. I felt fortunate to have Marco as my travel partner, since we were going to spend the next few months together. We both were quietly sizing up the other, knowing our success and even our lives might well depend on it, especially when we reached the unfriendly Indian territory in the north.

I found out the captain was the general's wife's nephew and that he got along well with Santa Ana. He must, I thought, for the general to send him out on such an important mission. Also, he was a first cousin to Doña Elías. Her vouching for me and knowing my family was what convinced Captain Vásquez and the general to include me in this adventure.

The general's joke about killing me when we came back with the treasure crossed my mind several times, but did not concern me. What I considered a bigger risk was our coming back empty-handed. If this was the case, I could envision the frustrated general changing his mind about my company doing business in Mexico. These were things I had no control over–at least not yet. So I kept a positive outlook and quietly considered alternatives, in case they were needed.

Three days after we left Morelia, we arrived in Guadalajara and stayed there for a day. We spent time at the large military presidio of Chapala, getting information on conditions in northern Mexico. The assistant commander of the presidio was Colonel Ricardo Martinez, who had spent two years as the commander at the garrison in Hermosillo, in the middle of the Pimeria Alta territory.

Both Colonel Martinez and General Escalante, commander of the presidio, knew General Santa Ana and had served under him in the American War between 1846 and 1848. They were extremely curious about what we were up to, but backed off when Captain Vásquez showed them the orders and letters from the powerful general giving us *carte blanche* authority to move anywhere in Mexico on our special mission.

Captain Vásquez also showed me the orders and letters from Santa Ana. They implied that we were on a spy mission to the north to determine if it was feasible to set up a covert military action to take back California and parts of the other land lost during the American War. This both surprised and worried the general and colonel, that Santa Ana was considering such a bold move. Additionally, Captain Vásquez swore them to secrecy about the mission. They suspected I was an American and asked Captain Vásquez about it. When they found out I was British and spoke English like an American, it gave additional creditability to our story. I thought the ruse was an excellent ploy and it worked well, at least with these military men.

Before we left Guadalajara, the captain and I had some very interesting conversations with Colonel Martinez, who had served in the northern Mexico territory of Sonora and the Pimeria Alta. This was new country to me and the captain. For the first time, I heard Indian names like *Opata, Yaqui, Pima, and Seri.* I had heard of the Apaches before, even in England. For some reason, the *Apacheria* (the Apaches) kept coming to the top of Colonel Martinez's list and that of the other soldiers who had been assigned to the region. Obviously they were the most feared Indians in Mexico.

The colonel said we were fortunate to have Colt revolvers, giving us six shots instead of one to repel these "cunning and murderous savages." He was sure few of the Apaches had ever encountered such repeating firearms. He said, if we were good shots, this would give us a substantial advantage if they did not kill us in their first surprise attack. He went on to explain that the *Apacheria* were masters of attacks from ambush, so expect it we should. It was bound to happen.

Additionally, Colonel Martinez gave us more advice about the Indians. He said we should always travel in military groups of at least 10 to 12 soldiers, post two guards at night and camp in a defendable area. He said the Apaches would target our horses at night, scaring or stampeding them, or simply stealing them from under our noses. Also, the Apaches never attacked unless they had surprise on their side. This would eliminate or minimize their losses.

Colonel Martinez continued his lecture on the Apaches, saying they would attack and force their prey to waste their first shots uselessly in the confusion of the moment. When the victim's first shots were spent and they were attempting to reload, the Apache's major force would come in for the kill. It was an effective strategy.

This was all new to me, and the strategy seemed logical. However, his insistence on pounding it into us made clear that we were not dealing with a normal enemy. Captain Vásquez knew about these savages, but he too was rethinking our strategy as we prepared to move into this hostile country.

Colonel Martinez smiled and commented. "Gentlemen, be careful and take good soldiers with you when you get to Sonora. The *Apacheria* are *warriors from hell.* They fit well with the hot desert, cactus and rattlesnakes. Enjoy your trip and bring me back some Apache and gringo *ears* when you return."

Marco and I did not respond to his comment. He was purposely trying to scare us, to keep us alive. He gave good advice and we appreciated it.

The colonel asked if we could take two cases of Toluca wine for his friend, Colonel Trujillo, in Hermosillo. We agreed.

Almost as an afterthought, the colonel commented. "I've lost too many good men and friends who took unnecessary chances and even some who did not. Be careful and *vayan con Dios.*"

We thanked him, shook hands and left. We found out later he had lost his younger brother, a lieutenant under his command, while on a skirmish in Sonora.

Chapter 14

Old Happy–The Governor's Horse

On the morning of the 19th of November, Marco and I stood on the deck of *La Doncella Pechisima* (The Well-Endowed Maiden), anchored at Puerto de San Blas. We watched a clumsy attempt to load two fine horses onto the ship we were to take up the coast of the Sea of Cortez. The governor of Sonora had ordered the horses.

The sailing ship was an old Spanish merchant vessel captured during the Mexican Revolution over thirty years earlier. It was small, dirty and in bad repair. We had our equipment and supplies on board, including the two cases of Toluca wine for Colonel Trujillo in Hermosillo.

The sailors trying to get the two fine, Arabian horses on board were certainly not herdsmen. They had tied halters to the horses and were attempting to swim them out to the ship–about one hundred meters from the shore.

The sailors had two rowboats with four sailors in each. Each rowboat towed a frightened, swimming horse by a halter rope. Together, they were slowly moving toward the ship. The sailors obviously didn't know what they were doing, but seemed to be making up their plans as they went along.

As the swimming horses and sailors got closer to us on the ship, I could see the poor animals were getting tired and were in danger of drowning. Captain Vásquez and I attempted to help by throwing a rope to the sailors in one of the rowboats, then connecting the other end to a swinging pole boom attached to the ship, but the first mate objected. So we stood back and watched.

The nearest row boat with the sailors shouting and fumbling around let their poor, tired horse's head dip below the seawater several times. I couldn't stand it and hollered to them to hold the horse's head above the water! I then yelled to the crewmen watching from the ship to throw a net down and get it around the poor horse to keep him from drowning.

The first mate scowled at me, but the ship captain told him to do it, so they did. They also attached a net to the second horse, which was not doing much better.

Now they had two scared, panting horses in the water, scraping against the side of the ship and being supported by nets and ropes held by the sailors on deck. At least the panicky animals could rest a bit without having to swim so hard.

Now what? I had injected myself once and did not want to interfere any more. Besides, I wasn't sure of the best way to get the heavy animals onto the deck. So I shut up and watched.

The sailors fumbled around for several more minutes, each shouting out half-assed ideas on how to haul the horses on board. My unspoken ideas were not much better.

Next, the sailors on deck took the end of the rope attached to one of the swimming horses and put it through the boom pulley, planning to hoist the animal on board. So far so good. Then the sailors on board the ship tried to haul the struggling animal up to the deck. The seven sailors on the rocking ship couldn't do it. The first mate hollered to the sailors in the rowboats to come aboard and help. Three of them came up, then Marco and I joined in to help.

I was afraid the rope was going to break as we hoisted the frightened horse out of the water and into the air. But instead, the horse fell out of the loose net and almost hit the rowboat and sailors on the way down, before disappearing back into the water.

A few seconds later the terrified animal surfaced and swam toward the ship, hoping to find some footing. The sailors below quickly grabbed his halter and again wrapped the net around him, this time more securely. I suggested they also attach a rope to his tail, then use it and the halter rope to stabilize the animal as they raised him out of the water. They did not argue with me and did it.

The second time was almost successful. We hauled the animal up and swung him onto the deck and set him down. He stood shivering from fright and shock next to the first mate. As they took the net off the animal, he took a mighty leap over the side of the ship and back into the sea! This time he clipped the empty rowboat with his hind foot, breaking off some chips of wood. The captain and I groaned at the sight.

After a lot of cussing, they caught the poor horse when he surfaced again and hauled him on board a second time. This time, they were ready and tied the animal's halter to the mast and his tail to the side of the ship before they took the net off of him. He stood there on the deck shivering, panting and bleeding from scrapes. One down and one to go!

The second horse had been floating in the water for some time patiently waiting his turn. By now the sailors were experts. They had managed to do everything wrong, so all that was left was the right way to do it–or I thought.

The sailors now latched on to the rope holding the net around the second horse, tied another rope to his tail and used it and his halter rope to stabilize the animal, then hoisted him smartly on board. Marco and I again helped to pull the hoist rope. Everything seemed to go well until they got him on board.

After they put the animal down perfectly on the deck, the horse took one step back, caught his left front leg in a tangled rope, then fell forward and broke his leg at the knee. We were all shocked.

The ship captain and several of the crew huddled trying to decide what to do. Finally they made a decision. Marco and I just watched.

The chief mate and several sailors scurried down from the ship, climbed into one of the rowboats, then rowed to shore in a big hurry.

The cook came out and killed the injured horse with a mallet and, with the help of three of the crewmen, proceeded to butcher the animal. They took the stomach and guts and threw them over the side into the sea, then quickly quartered the animal. By the time they had finished butchering, we could see the sailors in the rowboat swimming *another* horse out to the ship.

This time, they quickly had the third animal on board and secured. This sorrel horse looked thin and old. I asked one of the sailors where they found the other horse so quickly.

"*We stole it*!" he replied, smiling.

Needless to say, we set sail immediately and left!

After our interesting introduction to the ship, *La Doncella Pechisima,* its captain and crew, and our hasty departure from the San Blas port, things settled down a bit. However, the second leg of our trek to the Pimeria Alta certainly was not boring.

We finally were under sail out of San Blas by late morning. The excited crew alternately joked and argued as they set the simple jib, main and spanker sails on the old ship. One sailor was assigned to work the first shift and to man the hand bilge pump to bail out the water slowly seeping into the ship. Their whole operation did not give me a warm feeling.

The crew was an undisciplined, smelly and rowdy bunch of sailors. They resembled nothing like a professional navy, much less that of the Republic of Mexico–or perhaps they did. The oldest sailor was a burly and almost toothless man of Mediterranean decent in his sixties and the youngest was a boy about fourteen. The rest of the crew looked like the ship's captain had picked them up one night from the local *cantina* (pub) and *carcel* (jail). Somehow the boy wound up in the mix. And to top it off, the old sailor took devilish delight at farting every time he walked passed Marco and me. Marco gave him the nickname of *el pedo pelmazo* (the annoying old fart), which the crew quickly adopted.

Captain Jesus Beltrán was our sea captain. Initially, his attitude toward us was strained, but he tried to be friendly. We had delayed his departure from San Blas by two days. General Santa Ana apparently sent an advanced military runner horseback to San Blas with orders to hold any Mexican Navy ship until we arrived. Apparently Captain Beltrán had gotten caught in the snare. And to add to his frustrations, while he waited for us, he got the additional task of hauling the Governor of

Sonora's horses north to the Port of Guaymas.

Despite being a bit out of sorts, Captain Beltrán made space in a small storage room off the main deck for our equipment and supplies. He gave us a table consisting of a broken door propped up by two empty whisky barrels and held together with leather straps. He even found a couple of ancient folding chairs for us. The small room and table presumably gave us a little privacy in which to study our papers and talk during the trip, or so we believed until we caught the boy listening at our door the second day out. He laughed and ran off.

We decided to sleep on mats on deck if the weather was good, which it was for most of the trip except for one night when it rained.

We found out from Captain Beltrán that the first mate forgot to get hay for the governor's horses, so we would be stopping at Teacapan, dropping anchor for the night. Marco and I got the impression the captain also had some other business there, probably a woman.

The captain gave us the option of going ashore and spending the night or staying aboard the ship. We decided to stay on board with our gear, since the crew told us there was nothing much to do or see in Teacapan. Also we worried the crew would steal our supplies. It was a miserable night.

Thank goodness the captain and his men arrived at first light with some hay and happy looks on their faces. We set sail immediately. Later in the morning, Beltrán said we would be spending the night at Mazatlán, which was only a half-day north of us. He said it was the crew's favorite port of the whole trip. I was beginning to think we had made a mistake by taking the sea route north.

By now, our ship's crew and captain had loosened up and were beginning to joke and visit with us. Frustrated, Captain Beltrán bemoaned his assignment, saying that his ancient ship, *La Doncella Pechisima,* should more aptly be named *La Bruja Estropeada* (The Crippled Witch) because of her age and problems. He commented he was lucky to keep her moving above the water with the budget he was given by the Mexican government and the headaches he had with his poorly trained sailors. He said he had made a proposal to Admiral Serrano at Acapulco to increase his budget or let him use *La Bruja* to haul freight up and down the west coast of Mexico. He proposed using the extra money for maintenance and repairs. When the Admiral refused his request, he did it anyway. It was the only way he could pay his crew and keep the ship going. Beltrán explained that the only benefit from the Admiral's refusal was now he didn't have to give him any *mordidas* for using the ship.

The crewmembers were a little more circumspect with their comments about the ship and their captain. They said their private name for the old ship was *La Puta Vieja* (The Old Whore). They explained the reason was that the captain rented the old girl out and kept the money for himself.

Saturday, at about two in the afternoon, we sailed into *El Puerto de Mazatlán*. The crewmen were excited and anxious to go ashore. Marco and I were also ready for a break.

Although we liked him, Marco and I had not decided whether we could trust Captain Beltrán. Beltrán said he would be staying onboard the ship with two sailors and would release his remaining 12 crewmen, including the cook, so they could go ashore and enjoy the evening. Obviously, we were free to do as we pleased.

Marco was relieved when I told him to go ashore with the crew while I spent another night on board with our gear and supplies. However, I proposed it with the condition that he would get us some better food to eat on board. Captain Beltrán heard our conversation and offered to lock our room and watch it so I could go ashore also, but we politely declined. I think it made our captain even more curious about our mission and the gear we so carefully protected.

Beltrán instructed his anxious first mate to have the dockworkers bring hay and water over to the ship. He also gave the cook some money and told him to stock up on supplies. I couldn't help suggesting he get some wine, cheese, fresh pan dulce and some fresh-cooked beans and tortillas. I threw in a few pesos to back up my request. Marco also suggested some fresh cooked *carnitas* (barbecued pork) to go with the order. He also added to the kitty.

Then I took Marco to the side and asked him to send some good food and wine over to the ship that night for Captain Beltrán and me.

He agreed and said he would take care of it.

After they left the ship and things were quiet, I updated my diary and journal, then went over to the Governor's horses. As I petted and talked to them I wondered what the Governor's reaction was going to be when he first saw his prized animals–one dying with pneumonia and dysentery and the second, transformed into a happy, old, Don Quixote reject. It should be interesting.

During the afternoon, several rowboats came over to the ship with food supplies, wood, water and hay for the horses. One of our sailors helped the dockworkers load it on board. The other remained below deck, either asleep or manning the bilge pump. The captain stayed in his cabin.

Being uneasy, with nothing to do, I debated about writing Melanie. I missed her terribly. Having no reliable way to get a letter posted and sent, I dismissed the idea.

About mid-afternoon, I checked the kitchen to see what the cook had left to eat. The big pot of boiled horse stew turned my stomach the moment I took the lid off and caught a whiff of the smell. The meat didn't taste that bad, but I didn't like the smell or idea of eating the poor animal. By evening I was reconsidering my situation when another rowboat arrived.

This boat had food–good food! Marcos had taken care of us. It was carefully packed into three small wooden boxes wrapped with a white linen cloth. Inside, he had tortillas, warm *frijoles* in an *olla, quesadillas*, some kind of cooked meat in another *olla*–probably *carnitas*–also *panocha* (brown sugar), *pan dulce*, and four bottles of wine! I was sure he hoped some of this would be left over so we could enjoy it the next day.

My spirits renewed, I jumped naked into the water alongside the ship for a refreshing swim, then came out to enjoy the meal with Captain Beltrán and the other two sailors. The captain carefully selected some of the food for the sailors and also gave them one of the bottles of wine so they could eat their meal separately on deck. The captain then invited me into his cabin, where we enjoyed our meal with wine as the sun set. Things were looking up.

The weather was pleasant and our trip on up the coast to Puerto de Guaymas was almost enjoyable after Marco and I learned how to fend for ourselves along the way. We would set anchor at night at small ports or fishing villages, where Captain Beltrán would spend the night and get supplies. Marco or I would go ashore and shop for fresh fruit, cooked meals and wine or alcohol–whatever we could find. We would buy extra for the crew, who very quickly were delighted to have us on board. Even the cook, Pancho Salazar, was happy, since he was getting tired of cooking jerked horse. He used some of it for bait and caught a couple of small sand sharks, then threw the rest of the horsemeat overboard. The crew cheered.

As we traveled north, Marco and I continued to study the vellum maps and other material I had managed to collect in Mexico City and Guadalajara. The extra maps I picked up were not of much help. However, Marco surprised me when he showed me three additional, smaller, maps the general had given him. These, I found, were critical and provided much more detail on each of the treasure hiding places. These maps were folded, soiled and well-worn as if they had been carried in saddlebags. They were paper maps and were prepared using a pencil, some of the writing was hard to read. However, these crude maps provided not only much more information on the three treasure locations, but also gave much more detail on what specifically was hidden there.

I was more than a little irritated that the general had not showed them to us in his office. Marco shrugged and said nothing. I decided I was still an unknown commodity at that time. Still, I was angry.

Two of the three paper maps had latitude and longitude coordinates for the hiding locations, but, after some study, I determined they were probably not accurate. We would have to use both sets of maps to find where the Spanish had hidden their treasures. Hopefully, the treasures would still be there.

Marco brought up another subject one evening after we had finished two bottles of wine. The thought had also crossed my mind more than a few times. The conversation happened when we were sitting on the ship deck while it was anchored at the small port of Topolobampo and most of the crew was ashore. The sun had disappeared below the sea to the west.

"Chu Chu, what if we recover the gold for my famous uncle and he takes it to Cuba? Is it worth it?" Marco asked.

"What are you saying, Marco?" I asked, thinking I knew where this was going.

"Well, my uncle is a famous general, and even was president of Mexico several times, but our family has found that he only does favors for people who can help him," he replied rather stoically.

"Yes, you are right. The favor he is doing for me is letting my company operate in Mexico–if he doesn't kill me first."

"Yes, and he is going to get a sizable return for the favor. Not only the Spanish gold we bring back, but also a percent of the silver your company removes from Mexico. And he will probably cheat you on that," Marco replied sarcastically.

"So what are you saying? We are crazy to be doing this for him?"

"Chu Chu, my family is not rich. My uncle hasn't helped us much, and not without heavy favors. I'm a captain, yes, partly because of his help, but now look at what he wants from me! Yes, he may give me his gold watch, and maybe several firearms, but I don't expect much more. No, I don't think he will kill you, because you are worth more to him alive and working hard taking silver out of the hills around Querétaro for him and your company. In three years, I think he will be gone from Mexico again and he'll take as much money and gold as he can carry." Marco looked out at the darkening sea.

I digested Marco's words for a short while, then replied. "Marco, sounds like you are saying we are crazy if we don't take care of ourselves in this little adventure."

"Yes, *that's exactly what I am saying*. What do you think?" the captain replied in the darkness.

"Well, it would be easy to do. And it's a good way to get killed. But we may get killed anyway, so why not?" I answered, a little surprised at how easily greed was starting to stain my thinking.

"How could we do it and not get killed, at least by the general?" Marco asked, chuckling.

"Well, the general gave us the easiest way. He said the treasures might not be there anymore. Whoever the Spanish had bury it might have come back and taken it away. That's the easiest answer–the gold was gone, taken by some of the soldiers who buried it years ago," I suggested.

"Yes, but if there is any, maybe we should take some of it back and tell him the rest was gone. That might be more believable. What do you think?"

I considered what he said and responded. "Well, we have several options. One, if the gold is gone, maybe we better not go back to Mexico City. I don't think your uncle would be very happy if we come back empty-handed."

"And the other options?"

"Well, the second option, and the most likely, is that some of the treasure is missing. Then we've got another problem. Do we have enough to take back to the general?'

"Are there any more options?" Marco asked.

"Sure, if we find lots of treasure, we could keep going north, to California, or to New Mexico Territory," I replied.

Marco was quiet for a few moments. Then he replied smiling. "The gold would let me buy a nice *rancho* in California, wouldn't it? And I bet I could even find a cute, little, *gringa* señorita to help me spend it too, couldn't I?"

He turned to me. "Chu Chu, could I trust you? You wouldn't kill me when we got into the United States with the gold, would you?" Marco grinned, his voice catching dramatically.

We both laughed. The conversation ended there, but the seed was planted and the door was open. I knew what Marco was thinking. This put another dimension into the situation, and an interesting one.

The next day, Marco and I spent most of the morning in our little room on *La Bruja,* again going over the vellum maps and the crudely prepared paper maps describing the three locations for the hidden Spanish treasure. We were getting close to Sonora and the *Pimeria Alta territory,* as the Spanish called it, so we needed to have a plan. The Spanish maps and descriptions were fascinating, and I was carefully memorizing them.

We focused first on the vellum locked map showing the mines, along with the three hiding locations. Next we studied the three crude paper maps giving more detailed information we needed to find where the Spanish ingots and gold dust were hidden. The hiding places were measured from the mission sites on the vellum map in leagues, while the crude paper maps described the locations in narrative terms and distances in terms of time on a trotting horse. The paper maps appeared to have been hastily prepared in pencil, probably by soldiers.

The first location was the Cocospera Mission. This hiding site was actually in the Cocospera mission graveyard on the hill next to the mission. Old wooden grave markers were moved from real graves to the fake graves containing the treasure. The story Marco heard was that the Spanish soldiers told the Cocospera Mission padre to have his Indian workers dig seven new graves, anticipating military casualties from the Revolution. They were to be left open until they were needed. One morning, the graves were all filled, and the Spanish military commander told the padre to bless the graves, that they were filled with soldiers killed two days before in a battle near Cocospera.

The paper map and notes indicated that treasure was buried in the graves instead. The treasure consisted of 12 burro-loads of silver and gold ingots. Seven of the burros carried loads of silver ingots with government-stamped seals and weights. Each of these burros was carrying *heavy* loads of silver brick ingots. The other five pack burros were carrying gold stick ingots.

Captain Vásquez and I figured this one would be easy to find. If we were lucky, the treasure would still be there.

The second location was measured from the Guevavi Mission in the Río de Santa Maria. The treasure was hidden in the Chihuahuita Mountains, in the cliffs at a location called *La Escondida* (The Hideout). At the tops of the cliffs, the notes said there was a pile of rocks marking the approximate location of the hidden ingots and gold dust below the cliffs. Also the notes said that at the top of the cliffs, *Sierra de las Chichies* (The Tit Mountains) could be seen to the north and the *Sierra de Guachuca* could be seen to the east.

Here the largest treasure was hidden. It consisted of 17 burro-loads of treasure–11 of gold and seven of silver ingots. Of the gold loads, four were unsmelted gold dust and nuggets. This treasure sounded exciting, but it also sounded like the hardest one to find, probably being in the middle of Apache country.

Finally, the third site was measured from the Tubutama Mission. This one was the smallest treasure, eight burros-loads, six with gold rod or *barra* casting and two with silver ingots or *lingotes*. This one sounded like it was buried in the middle of the desert at the edge of the convergence of two large dry washes. This one was described as being buried *tres píes* (three feet) below the surface in soft sandy soil and marked by three small piles of reddish colored stones, which were approximately 30 *varas* (yards) from the burial site. Standing on the middle pile of red stones, the notes stated you could see the Sierra Pitiquito peak to the west. The burial site was exactly 30 *varas* to the west of the stones and in line with the peak.

This one we thought should also be easy to find. We hoped this site would be west of the most dangerous Indian country.

We decided we should go to each site in the order we had arranged them–Cocospera Mission first, La Escondida cliffs near the Guevavi Mission next, and finally the Tubutama Mission desert location. This made a loop and headed us back toward the *Mar de Cortez,* where we would make arrangements to meet Captain Beltrán and his ship on February 15th.

Now we needed a better story about why we were out there and needed military support.

After spending the rest of the morning and afternoon trying to accurately calculate the value of the treasure, I grabbed some chow and brought it to our cabin. Marco opened a cheap bottle of wine and we discussed my problem.

Jokingly, I commented. "Hell, Marco, after going over the information we have on the treasure at each site, I think it would be easier to estimate the value of the burros rather that the treasure!"

"If that's the case, I'll take all the burros carrying gold. You and Tío (General Santa Ana) can have the burros with silver." Marco responded with a wink, as he sipped a spoonful of warm soup. "Anyway, how do you do that?"

"At this point, all we have is a tally of the burro loads of treasure, both silver and gold. But we aren't sure what the actual weights of the gold and silver were. We only know how many loads, or heavy loads were hidden."

Marco responded while emptying the remainder of the wine bottle into my tin cup. "So I guess we won't know the actual value of the treasure until we find and weigh it."

"Yes, that's true. But my father was in the mining business down here for many years. One thing I learned from him was that serious skinners (haulers) were careful how they packed their mules and burros, especially for long distance hauling."

"So what are you saying? That they were all packed with the same weight?"

"Well, yes. Burros were usually packed with the weight of a light to medium man, depending on the size and condition of the animal, and the distance they intended to travel. Mules were packed with heavier loads."

Skeptically, Marco looked at me. "Can you estimate the value of the treasure based on the burro-loads the Spaniards gave us on these maps?"

I laughed. "At this point that's about the best I can do, at least until we find something."

"I guess that's a starting point. What do you think we are dealing with, in terms of money?"

Pausing while taking a gulp of my wine for effect, I then continued. "Using my highly scientific method, we have both 20,000 gold *escudo* burros and 20,000 silver *reales* burros. Of course one gold burro is worth about 16 silver burros."

Marco shook his head in amusement, saying nothing, so I continued. "Seriously, the weight my father said serious haulers used was about 130 to 145 pounds. That's about 60 kilos."

Immediately Marco straightened up on his stool, "Based on those weights, have you figured out what the total treasure is worth, if we found the whole thing?"

Carefully, I reached in my pocket, brought out a folded piece of paper and handed it to him. Marco opened it and spread it out on our broken door table. After studying it in the dim light, he let out a low whistle.

"Damn it Chu Chu, do you think this is right?"

I responded. "With the information we have, it's a pretty good estimate, assuming it's all there."

"Four hundred thousand escudos in gold and three hundred thousand reales in silver–damn! What would that weigh?"

"If the Spanish burro count is right on loads, it would be over 2000 kilos."

"Hell, that would sink Beltrán's poor old ship," Marco responded running his fingers through his hair in disbelief.

"Yes, and that's another good reason for leaving some here for ourselves."

The voyage north took us six days. We landed in *Puerto de Guaymas* the evening of November 25th. The morning after we arrived was interesting.

An anxious Governor of Sonora's administrator was waiting at the small dock, hoping to receive his fine, Arabian horses. The animals had survived, but his only Arabian, a beautiful black with a blaze on his forehead, had progressively gotten worse. He was not eating and I was sure dying of pneumonia. The second old swayback horse was happy as a lark and excitedly waited for someone to greet him.

In the morning, the Governor's representative came over to the ship in a rowboat and boarded. He was a middle-aged gentleman with a silver-handled cane similar to that of my evil friend, Mr. Jenkins, but Jenkins' was gold and bigger.

The two horses were penned up in the front of the ship. When the administrator came aboard, he asked the first mate where the governor's horses were. The mate pointed to the lumber pen. Marco and I watched.

The distinguished man stumbled to the front of the ship and looked into the tiny, dirty pen. He looked around like he was trying to find another pen, then looked back inside again. He appeared shaken as he walked back toward us and Captain Beltrán.

"Captain, those can't be Governor Maytorena's Arabians. He paid 5000 pesos in gold for two of the finest Arabians in Mexico City. What happened to them?" the stunned man asked.

Captain Beltrán shrugged his shoulders and said, "Administrator, all I know is those are the animals they delivered to me in San Blas."

The governor's administrator and the captain talked a couple minutes about the disastrous situation, with the older man wringing his hands and rubbing his balding head.

"What am I going to tell the Governor? He will be here tomorrow to meet your ship and receive his horses. I confirmed the order myself by letter to Señor Joaquin de la Riva in Mexico City. I sent him the money. These were supposed to be his finest horses. What am I going to do?" The stressed man asked.

The captain shrugged, shaking his head.

Marco and I would have laughed, except for the pain the poor administrator was feeling.

The governor's administrator's name was Julio Moreno de Ayala. He continued to explain his predicament to Captain Beltrán, Marco and me.

"Governor Maytorena will arrive here tomorrow from Hermosillo. He was hoping you would be here with his horses. He was going to wait if you had not arrived, then take them home to his *rancho* near Hermosillo. What am I going to say? What am I going to do?" Administrator Moreno nervously explained.

As we stood there next to the smelly pen, the black Arabian horse laid down heavily.

"I don't think he's going to get up again," I said quietly.

Poor Moreno rubbed his shaking hands and fretted trying to think of a way out of his situation.

"Governor Maytorena is a powerful and dangerous man. I will lose my job, maybe worse," he explained sweating in the cool breeze blowing over the ship.

Then an idea hit me. Not knowing northern Mexico that well, except from the maps Marco and I had been studying, I asked, "Administrator Moreno, you say your boss is the Governor of Sonora. Does Sonora cover the *Pimeria Alta* region?"

The Administrator blinked at me, surprised, then answered.

"Yes. Yes it does. It covers almost all of the Pimeria Alta country.

Why? Why do you ask?"

"Is Governor Maytorena in charge of the military here in Sonora?" I asked. I knew the answer, but thought I would ask the shaken man just the same.

"Yes, well–no, not exactly. Well, yes, between him and General Pacheco. General Pacheco in Chihuahua and Colonel Trujillo in Hermosillo, they control Sonora and the Pimeria Alta, and more. Ah, yes, and also Bishop Cuevas, but what does that have to do with the horses?" He asked, a bit annoyed and bewildered.

"And you, Administrator Moreno, are his chief deputy? You run his office?" I continued to ask.

Even though annoyed and frustrated, he liked the question. "Yes, I'm the chief of his staff. I run his office. At least till now. He is going to be furious when he learns about his horses. I handled everything on the deal, the money, the purchase, everything, now this!"

I glanced at Marco, and then pulled him aside.

"Marco, this man may be able to help us, if the governor is as powerful as he says. We are a long ways from Mexico City, and your uncle, General Santa Ana. Seems like we have the opportunity here to help this poor guy. It could pay off, what do you think?"

"Well, yes. What do you have in mind?"

"Let's see if we can help him," I suggested.

We then turned and stepped back to Administrator Moreno and Captain Beltrán. They were standing looking down at the sick, fallen horse in the stinking pen.

"Administrator Moreno, Captain Vásquez and I don't know anything about the problem with your horses, but we would like to help you," I told him.

"What can you do? I am doomed. Look at them. This is a disaster!" The poor man declared.

We stared at the happy old horse nibbling playfully at the Administrator's sleeve and the dying animal for a few moments, then I made a suggestion.

"Administrator, what if there was an accident?"

"Accident? What do you mean, an accident?" the Administrator asked intently looking at me.

"Well, if there was an accident before the horses arrived, that wouldn't be your fault would it?" I replied.

Looking down at the horse laying in the manure and then at *Old Happy* playing with him, the Administrator pensively nodded.

"An accident? No I suppose not. How could I be responsible for an accident? What kind of an accident?"

"Captain Beltrán, we saw some sharks every time we set anchor for the last few days, didn't we? In fact, I think we saw two last night, right?" I asked.

The captain's brow rose. He was catching the drift of where I was going.

"Yes, we saw two little sand sharks." Then he caught himself and agreed. "And yes, we saw that big *tiburon* (shark) last night. It was a little further out. Yes, there are definitely dangerous sharks around."

"Administrator, what if there was an accident and the sharks got the horses before they got to shore. That wouldn't be your fault would it?" I asked.

The nervous administrator grasped his hands together as he replied. "Can we do it? Is it possible? How do we do it?"

"Well, it's simple. As I remembered it, the sharks attacked the horses when we put them into the water. *They ate Don Quixote's horse, poor Old Happy here, for breakfast,* and all we could recover from the black was his head. How do you remember it, Captain Beltrán?"

"Yes, that's right. We made sure we saw no sharks before we put the magnificent horses in the water, but those three big, black, ugly *tiburones* came out of nowhere and attacked them before we could get them ashore. We almost lost two of our sailors trying to fight off the damned sharks," Captain Beltrán agreed.

"Yes, I even tried to shoot them with my rifle. I think I hit one. It made more blood, and more sharks came," added Captain Vásquez, winking at me.

"You gentlemen would do that for me?" The administrator asked.

"Certainly, we don't want you to get in trouble with the Governor for something that was not your fault," replied Captain Vásquez, now signing on to the ruse.

Captain Marco Vásquez then took charge of the plan. "Captain, have your cook come out and kill the horses. Cut off the head of the black one to have something the administrator can show the Governor, then throw the rest of them into the water. Weight them down with something so they don't wash to shore."

"Can we use some of the meat?" Captain Beltrán asked.

The thought nearly made me sick.

"Yes, but make sure we have some *broken bones and black hide* to show for the shark attack," Marco instructed. "Remember–*black hide*."

I frowned, "How do we keep the crew from talking? We don't want them to spill the beans."

"Don't worry about that. I'll take care of it," Captain Beltrán replied.

The relieved administrator said nothing as he listened. A few minutes later he departed.

Then things started to go wrong.

Feeling guilty about the friendly old horse, I threw out an idea to Marco. "Marco, Old Happy has gone through hell and is still smiling. We don't have to make shark bait out of him to save the administrator. Let's quietly get him off the ship tonight, then get on with our plan."

Marco shook his head in frustration. "Chu Chu, you come up with these good ideas, then worry about killing some old buzzard bait horse. Let's just leave it alone."

But I objected. "No, Marco, it's worth it to me to get the old horse off the ship tonight. I'll even pay some of the crew to help us. How's the best way to do it?"

Frowning while scratching his head, Marco finally responded. "Damn it, Chu Chu, with our luck, we would probably get someone drowned at night trying to get your old horse off the ship. No, if you insist, I think the best way is to pay Beltrán to keep the animal on the ship for a few more days and drop him off at the next port. I hope you can spare the money to do that."

I thought for a moment and agreed. We went to our cabin, where

I retrieved five pesos from my saddlebag to convince Beltrán to spare Old Happy's life. Marco decided to rest, and laid down on his mat. As I strolled back out on deck to find Beltrán, I saw the cook standing at the front of the ship with a *bloody* butcher knife in hand and a whet stone in the other. He was looking down.

Immediately, I ran to the front of the ship and saw both the sick Arabian horse and Old Happy lying in the mire at the cook's feet with their throats slit and blood gushing from their wounds. I was sick, upset with myself for even offering up the idea.

Standing there looking at the painful sight, I tried to rationalize to myself that *no good deed goes unpunished.* But then it went from bad to worse.

Several crewmembers came over to look at the two downed horses with the cook. The ideas of butchering and eating a sick horse and Old Happy did not sit well with them either. Apparently Old Happy had also made his share of friends with the crew.

After some dialogue between the cook and Captain Beltrán, it was agree that neither horse would be butchered for food. Both would be lowered into the bay with weights the next morning to complete my suggested ruse.

And so it was. On the following beautiful October morning in the Guaymas bay, there was an ugly shark attack. Shots were fired to try to save the Governor's poor Arabian horses. Witnesses on shore heard the commotion. The only thing recovered was one of the heads from the Arabians, some broken bones and bloody, black hide. What a shame! What a tragic loss of such beautiful animals. I think it was the only known shark attack in Guaymas bay, and the administrator witnessed it all from ashore.

But, the painful lesson learned by me was to keep my mouth shut and only offer suggestions after I had carefully thought through the consequences. And perhaps most important, *expect* the unexpected.

Chapter 15

The Seeds of Wisdom or Greed?

During the last few days of our sailing north between Mazatlán and Guaymas, Marco and I continued to refine our plan to recover the Spanish treasures. It became obvious that Captain Beltrán had to be part of our plan. We even established the tentative date when he would pick us up at the tiny, Indian fishing *pueblito* of Desemboque to return us to San Blas. It would be after we made our loop through the Pimeria Alta high desert and returned to the sea with our treasure, as Marco and I now jokingly referred to it.

Over four hundred thousand *escudos* of hidden Spanish gold and silver was the prize! That certainly was more than General Santa Ana needed for Mexico, as he sanctimoniously claimed. Besides, we were the ones risking our arses to recover it–if it even existed.

We had some big problems to overcome and decisions to make. However, the biggest decision was made. If we found the hidden treasures, we were going to keep some of it for ourselves. How we did it and how much we kept were still open questions.

Our logic generally went like this: First, if we found any treasure and it was substantial, we needed to take some back to General Santa Ana. However, taking it back almost 3000 kilometers by pack burro to Mexico City was totally out of the question. We would need an army to protect it! That's what the Spaniards had used.

Going by sea was a better option. The trick would be to covertly deploy soldiers to protect us against the Apaches, then recovering the treasures at three different locations. Next, we must transport the treasures hundreds of kilometers through dangerous Indian country, back to Beltrán's ship, which should be waiting for us for our trip south.

Our dilemmas were several. After recovering the treasures, the Indians might not be our biggest problem. Our own soldiers might be. The soldiers or even bandits, after word got out that we had found Spanish gold and silver and were transporting it to Mexico City. And how could Marco and I steal some of it for ourselves and not lose everything? We were still young and inexperienced at the art of *treachery*. We could have used some of Santa Ana's advice about that.

Marco and I decided that, as in the case of the sailors loading the governor's horses onto the ship, we would have to make up some of our plans as we went along. Fate and opportunity would have to weigh into our plans. We knew *what* we wanted to do. *How* was still an open question.

It was clear we needed a plausible story when we finally reached the military garrison at Hermosillo. General Santa Ana's story was still the best. We were spies on a secret mission exploring the possibility of taking back what Mexico lost to the gringos during the American War. Not very likely, but the story did hold a little water.

Also, this story would certainly give us some secrecy and military help. To have some degree of success, we must maintain our secrecy for as long as possible. We needed the soldiers' help, but we also needed them to keep their mouths shut and not turn against us. We reasoned the best way to do that was to keep them with us in the field for the entire operation. When they returned to their garrison and homes, all bets were off. They would begin to talk. We would be in a race against potential thieves while we were trying to get our treasure to Mexico City.

Another consideration was that we knew message runners on horseback from the Pimeria Alta could beat us to Mexico City if we traveled by ship. The military did have overland mail carriers who were periodically dispatched all through the country. We could have an ambush waiting for us when we arrived in San Blas. We had no solution for this other than keeping our mission secret as long as possible, hoping for a little luck.

But first we had to make a deal with Captain Beltrán. We needed him and his ship to take us and whatever treasure we recovered back to San Blas. Using his ship and controlling his crew would be a challenge. The ship, *La Doncella Pechisima* was in bad shape, and his crew was a motley and unreliable group. But we thought the ship could make the voyage with the treasure, barring an accident or storm, if we had Captain Beltrán's support.

The same morning, after the little shark incident with the Governor's horses in the Guaymas bay, we hired Captain Beltrán and his ship. We made arrangement to have him meet us north of Guaymas near the Seri fishing village of Desemboque at the mouth of the Río Concepción on February 15th. Beltrán confirmed its location on one of my maps and I was sure we could find it. We figured this would give us over two months to travel to the three treasure sites, find them and return to the sea with the treasure, or at least part of it, if we were successful.

Marco gave Beltrán 200 pesos in gold and promised him that much more plus a bonus if he would have his ship waiting for us. He also had him promise to wait for us an additional two weeks, if we were late. That cost another 150 pesos. Everybody was happy.

Beltrán didn't ask what we were up to. He was not totally surprised by our actions, since we had asked him a number of interesting questions during our voyage north. To put us more at ease, Beltrán indicated he would not confide in his crew about our deal. He also assured us he could control them after we returned from the desert. So far so good.

After a light lunch with some wine to seal our deal with Beltrán, Marco and I unloaded our gear and supplies from the ship and stacked it on the Guaymas dock. At the dock we hired a broken-down wagon with a familiar looking scrawny horse that reminded me of Old Happy. I quickly dismissed the painful memory, and we proceeded to the outskirts of the fishing pueblo of Guaymas. There we found the small military garrison headed by a Lieutenant Lopez.

Captain Vásquez ordered the lieutenant to give us horses, a wagon and a military escort of six soldiers, showing him one of the letters from

General Santa Ana. The exhausted lieutenant almost laughed. He had just come in from a long desert scouting detail and was frustrated with the captain's ridiculous orders. He explained he only had ten horses, two burros and a mule in his corrals and grazing field. The horses and mule were tired and couldn't be used until they were rested. However, he did offer us his burros. The captain was not amused.

We decided to wait and spend the night in Guaymas, then pick up two of the lieutenant's horses with saddles the next morning after the animals were rested. We would also take the two burros for our supplies. The reality of our stark situation was starting to sink in.

On the way back to the fishing village from the garrison, Marco was frustrated. But he joked, saying he could visualize us riding into the Hermosillo garrison on two scrawny, old burros, demanding that Colonel Trujillo, in the name of General Santa Ana, give us horses, soldiers, supplies and pack animals for our spy mission north. He said we would be laughed out of the place.

He also noted that General Santa Ana's *palanca* was diminishing the further we ventured from his flagpole in Mexico City. He also lamented about the sad state of affairs the Mexican military was in. He was afraid our Santa Ana letters and threats might not go very far in Sonora.

I asked if Administrator Moreno and Governor Maytorena in Hermosillo might be options for us to consider. Marco said he wanted to keep the number of people familiar with our visit to a minimum and would prefer to deal only with the military. We would see.

That night Marco and I spent some time in Las Conchas, a little cantina where fishermen and locals gathered. The talk around the cantina was about the shocking shark attack that had killed Governor Maytorena's prize Arabians that morning. Marco and I said nothing as we sat listening, drinking our beer and eating our *chicharones* (pork rinds). He just solemnly winked at me and shook his head. Pretty soon other *tiburon* stories immerged, growing as the beer flowed. We decided our story had stuck and that Administrator Moreno should survive this painful incident without too much difficulty.

The trip across the desert from Guaymas to Hermosillo took two days. I had never experienced the desert and was glad this was the cooler time of year. The weather was still hot during the day, but cold during the clear, star-filled nights. Marco and I traveled alone and enjoyed dreaming about what we would do with *our part* of the treasure. I could already visualize the nice farm, next to Uncle Angus in Scotland, that I would buy. I wondered if Melanie would like it. I thought of her often, especially at night.

We had a growing problem on our hands regarding the credibility of our spy story, now that we were getting close to our destination. The excuse had worked with the military down south, where we needed little support. However, we were now arriving at the moment where we would need tangible support. Basically, we needed everything required to recover and safely transport the hidden gold and silver ingots from the Indian territory to the sea. Also we were finding that this remote part of Mexico had few military resources to offer.

On the first morning, traveling from Guaymas across the desert I rode my tired bay mule and led the two pack burros. Marco managed to get an exhausted but decent-looking brown horse.

Finally I brought up the subject that had been on my mind. "Marco, what ideas do you have for when we get to Hermosillo?"

"What do you mean? What ideas do we need?" Marco asked.

"On our way up here, we told our military friends we were on a secret mission for your uncle, the general, to gather military information on what Mexico might need to get back the lands she lost during the American War. That worked and shut up the military bosses down south. But think about it, if we happen to be so lucky as to find everything the Spaniards hid, we will have a hell of a problem on our hands. Especially if we keep some of it for ourselves," I responded.

"Yes, I have been thinking about it! But why is it a hell of a problem?" Marco asked, a bit perturbed, but seeming to want to feel me out.

"Marco, you know our situation as well as I do. But let's take a look at it. We have three locations where the Spaniards said they hid their treasure. First, in the graveyard at the Cocospera Mission. If their records are right, they buried 12 burro-loads of gold and silver ingots there. *Buried*–that means we've got to dig it up. At La Escondida cliffs, they said they hid 17 loads of gold rods and silver ingots. Some of it was even unsmelted gold dust and nuggets. We don't know if they buried it or hid it. But that now gives us 29 pack burros of ingots and dust. Finally, we have the west desert location near the Tubutama Mission. Again, if the Spaniard records are correct, they *buried* eight burro-loads of gold and silver ingots there."

I frowned. "Hell, that gives us a total of 37 burro-loads of treasure, over 2000 kilos, we need to dig up and haul out. Like you said, that's enough to sink Beltrán's poor old ship, if we sneeze! And that's to say nothing about the men, burros and pack saddles we will need," I laughed harshly.

"So?" asked Marco as we trotted across the desert.

"So, maybe we had better start making some decisions. For instance, what if we leave one of the treasures for us to pick up later–in the future?"

Marco was silent for a few moments, then said,

"Which one?"

This time I was silent. I listened to the creaking of our saddles as I thought about it.

"Well, if we get to the first one–Coscospera–and there is nothing there, we must go on and check the next location, La Escondida in the Chihuahuita Mountains."

I reflected again before I went on.

"Marco, it seems like the quicker we find something to take back to your uncle, the quicker we can make a decision, whether we can leave anything for ourselves and how much."

"I really wasn't planning on coming back here. Why can't we take everything back with us and decide what we want to keep before we get to Mexico City?"

"Well I guess that's an option. A dangerous option, but an option."

"Why is it dangerous?' Marco asked.

"We are going to have to trust or pay some people to help us get it to Mexico City. Captain Beltrán, for instance. Somewhere between here and Mexico City we are going to have to divide the treasure and hide our part. That's going to be hard to do, especially with other people knowing about it."

Marco was silent for several minutes, thinking.

"So you think we should leave our part here?"

"Yes I do, for several reasons. First, we need to confirm that the treasure is actually there. We need to do it by ourselves–you and me–and secretly. If the treasure is still in place, it would probably be safe to leave it for a few more years, or at least until we come back and retrieve it. But most importantly, we don't have to haul it to Mexico City, and don't risk losing it along the way or have your uncle hang us for stealing his money!"

Marco studied the horizon. Finally, he responded. "Chu Chu, are you saying, if we find the treasure in Cocospera, we can skip the one hidden the Chihuahuita Mountains–leave it for ourselves? Then we can go to Tubutama and get that one, if it is there, and take both to my Uncle?"

"Well, not exactly. Let's say that all three of the treasures remain, or at least most of it. First we go to Cocospera and dig that one up. Then we go to La Escondida and see if we can find where that one is hidden. If we find it, we leave it and go on to Tubutama and find that one. If we do, we take the Cocospera and Tubutama treasures back to your Uncle. We save the El Escondida treasure in the Chihuahuitas for our *retirement,* so we can join your uncle later, in Cuba," I joked.

Marco didn't laugh. "So you say we keep going until we find enough for my uncle–and hopefully leave some hidden so we can come back and get it?"

"Yes, that's about the size of it," I responded.

It was the middle of the day and we stopped at a little sad *finca* (farm) with three adobe huts, a garden, orchard and well. There were several brown, naked kids running around. A farmer was pulling water from the well with a windlass and pouring it into a trough to water his vegetables, fruit trees and animals.

We asked if we could rest and water our animals, and the farmer agreed. Marco paid him two pesos, so he was very happy. We ate some of his *membrillo* (quince) fruit, resting in the shade as we continued our conversation.

"Well, there's a part of your idea I don't like," Marco told me.

"What's that?"

"If we find something at Cocospera, I think one of us should escort it directly on to Tubutama and not risk losing it in the Apache country. That means we need to split up, and one of us must go alone to find the La Escondida treasure," he replied soberly.

"I see your point. *A bird in hand,* so to speak. I hope your friend Colonel Trujillo can help us out. I'm sure he knows the country well. Do you think we can trust him with our plan? And what will he cost us?"

"I hope we can trust him. But if we bring him in, we need to tell him only part of the plan. He must never know we are leaving something back for ourselves," Marco wisely observed.

"Absolutely!"

Marco said nothing as he got on his horse and I mounted my mule. We headed north again, toward Hermosillo. Later, as we rode north Marco made another comment that stuck in my mind.

"Chu Chu, we still have a problem. This assignment is changing us. We are striking deals with the devil to get the job done. Either Colonel Trujillo or our friend Administrator Moreno and Governor Maytorena, may hold the next key to our success. What worries me now is, *who's going to be our next devil*?" he asked rhetorically.

And that was how our conversations concluded about dividing up the treasure–a treasure we had never seen or might never see.

Our new talents for treachery and greed were developing well. And we didn't even have Santa Ana there to guide us.

Figure 4 Spanish Map of the Pimeria Alta

Chapter 16

Colonel Trujillo–Our next Devil?

We arrived at Hermosillo, in the state of Sonora, late in the evening and found a *posada* for the night. The people at the posada were friendly and took care of our animals while we secured our supplies and had a pleasant supper accompanied by beer, tequila and wine.

We decided to meet Colonel Trujillo early the next morning, taking him the Toluca wine from his friend Colonel Martinez in Guadalajara. But we needed an excuse for the missing bottle we had *broken*. With the help of the *posada* owner, Marco replaced the missing wine with a bottle of tequila. Delivery of the wine should be a good way to open our visit with the colonel, who could be critical to the success of our mission.

Later at Cantina Chato, we learned that Colonel Trujillo was out in the field with some of his troops. Early the next morning, Captain Vásquez and I rode out to the little garrison by the river to verify this information.

A single tired guard with an ancient, Spanish flintlock musket was on duty at the entrance gate to the military garrison. The garrison appeared to have been recently built and was situated near the Río de Sonora. The river had a good stream of water in it and looked pleasant as it flowed through the desert country. The architecture and construction of the modest military facility was a far cry from those in Mexico City and Guadalajara.

The garrison had an outer perimeter wall of sharpened mesquite posts interwoven with ocotillo cactus branches. It was about three meters high and looked like it would be difficult to breach. We were told that there was little threat of an Indian attack here, but the fence did provide some perimeter security and looked well made.

We found that our information about Colonel Trujillo picked up at the posada was accurate. The old guard told us Colonel Trujillo was still in the field with a detachment of his men. They were scheduled to return in two days.

As Marco and I were finishing our conversation with the guard, a boy about 12 or 13 riding a young burro bareback, came toward us from the direction of the corrals inside the garrison. The young man wore an old military cap and a ragged tan canvas cavalry jacket. He had a carved toy rifle with a leather strap slung over his shoulder and smiled broadly as he approached.

The boy saluted Captain Vásquez smartly as he rode though the garrison gate in front of us on his trotting burro. Marco hesitantly returned the boy's salute. The young boy looked back at us, beaming, happy because his salute was returned by a *real* captain.

"Who is that?" The captain asked puzzled.

"Oh he's Chico, *El Soldadito* (The Little Soldier). He's the colonel's kid," the guard responded.

The guard then made a circular movement with his fingers pointing to his head, indicating the boy was *not quite right.*

"What's he doing here?" I asked.

"He comes here every morning before dawn and helps the workers feed the horses. It's his way of being a soldier."

"Where is he going?" The captain asked the guard.

"He's going home. The colonel has a farm up the river. Chico lives there part of the time, with the family the colonel has taking care of the farm."

Marco and I glanced at each other. "I'm glad you returned his salute. I think you made his whole day," I told Marco.

He nodded in agreement.

After returning to our *posada, Noche de Paz* (Peaceful Night), we discussed the possibility of meeting with Governor Maytorena and Administrator Moreno when they returned without his fine horses from Guaymas. We decided against it since we had heard the Governor was a very emotional man. Also, Marco preferred to deal only with the military and have fewer people know about our mission. So we decided to wait for the colonel to return from his desert patrol.

Marco and I spent the next several days resting from our journey and visiting with the people around the village of Hermosillo. We talked to whomever we could–local merchants, wagon freighters, miners, *vaqueros* (cowboys), and even the priest, learning all we could about the country to the north. Most agreed that the untamed Indians, especially the Apaches, needed to be Christianized by the Church–*or killed. Not many options,* I thought.

We learned Colonel Trujillo was a tough, no nonsense soldier. His headquarters was the new garrison at Hermosillo built after the American War. It was near the abandoned Spanish presidio of *El Trampito.* He had approximately 120 soldiers garrisoned here. The colonel was under the operational control of General Ramón Pacheco in the city of Chihuahua, almost 400 kilometers to the east. Colonel Trujillo controlled this part of the Pimeria Alta and the State of Sonora–where the Spanish treasures were hidden.

According to my journal, Marco and I met with Colonel Alejandro Trujillo early Friday morning on December 3, 1852. We had to wait three days, instead of two, for him to return from his patrol north to Tucson in the Papago Indian territory, where 42 soldiers were stationed at a presidio under Trujillo's command.

At the Hermosillo garrison gate, we met the same tired guard we had spoken to several days before. He saluted Captain Vásquez, then sent us to the adobe building with a frayed Mexican flag atop a crooked mesquite pole in front of it.

A young guard in a tattered uniform and without a weapon snapped to attention as we arrived at the door of the building. Marco asked for

Colonel Trujillo. The guard responded by stepping to the open door and announcing us. He then pointed at the door for us to enter. The discipline of these young soldiers impressed me, especially considering their being so poorly equipped and paid.

Colonel Alejandro Trujillo stood inside the single roomed adobe office. He was a large, rugged man in his late thirties and was wearing an old cavalry uniform. He looked up from papers on a large table with a questioning look on his face. He had dark gray, penetrating eyes.

Captain Vásquez saluted the colonel and started the conversation.

"Good morning, Colonel Trujillo. My name is Captain Marco Vásquez and I'm from the Presidential Guard Division at the Presidio of Chapultepec in Mexico City. We are here on a *special mission* for the government."

After the colonel returned his salute, Marco continued. "We came through Guadalajara. Colonel Ricardo Martinez sent you a little gift. He also said to give you his *saludos* (greetings)."

The colonel's gray eyes brightened when he heard Colonel Martinez's name. "Good. How is my friend Colonel Martinez?"

"Just fine, sir. He said he hopes to be back up here in several years, if he doesn't retire first," Marco replied.

"That old *cabron* (bastard) should retire. He has cheated death too many times. He was my commander here and taught me how to stay alive. He is a good man," the colonel said with a chuckle.

So far so good. With that, I quickly stepped outside and asked the corporal at the door to help me unload the two cases of wine from one of the pack burros we brought with us. The corporal and I carried the two cases of wine into the colonel's office and set them on the floor. The colonel and Captain Vásquez were talking about some of the colonel's old military friends stationed around Mexico City. Marco knew some of them and was giving him an update on their status.

Marcos indicated the cases with a wave of his hand. "There, colonel. Two cases, less one bottle, of the best Toluca wine Colonel Martinez could find. He said he owed you his life, but that's *not* why he was sending you the wine. He said it was because you were his friend and a good soldier. Colonel Martinez also said the wine would be an overpayment for his life anyway," Captain Vásquez explained.

The tough colonel's eyes actually watered. Embarrassed, he quickly wiped them with the back of his large, rough hand.

"Well, that's another story. I may tell you sometime," the colonel replied.

"Who is your friend?" The colonel asked, finally taking notice of me.

"Excuse me,Colonel, I failed to introduce *Ingeniero* (Engineer) Mack. He is an explosives expert and works for an English mining company."

"What are you going to do, use explosives to uncover *some old Spanish treasures*?" The colonel asked flippantly.

Marco and I glanced at each other as the colonel motioned for us to sit down at the hand-hewn ironwood table. The keen colonel caught our glances and smiled.

"Sit down, Captain Vásquez and Ingeniero Mack. It's a little early, but let's open a bottle of Martinez's Toluca wine and talk," the colonel said.

The colonel had a strong, confident manner about him and used a probing style as he chatted. He quickly found some tin coffee cups for the wine. While he opened a bottle of Toluca wine with his knife, Marco and I again exchanged glances and nodded, this time without the colonel catching us. *This man looked like our next devil.*

As the colonel poured us each a healthy serving of wine he spoke directly.

"Gentlemen, you say you are here on a special mission for the government. What is it and how can I help?"

The colonel sat at the head of the table and looked directly at Captain Vásquez with his penetrating eyes.

"Colonel, we have been sent here to gather information on the Americans. Do they have any civilian or military forces in or near Sonora?" Marco asked rather awkwardly, trying to disguise the real reason for our visit.

"Captain, I have a simple answer for you. The Americans are not setting up anything–no military operation, garrisons, or forts–in my area. I know what is going on in the State of Sonora. The American military are not here, otherwise, I would be fighting them. There have been a few Americans passing through to California, looking for gold.

However, that's nothing for me or Mexico City to worry about," the colonel replied rather sternly.

Captain Vásquez attempted to keep control of the conversation for a little longer before we exposed our hand, "Colonel, do you know how close the Americans have their military forts to Sonora?"

"Yes, I have a pretty good idea. They are setting up a string of military posts from California across what they now call *Nuevo Mexico* and Texas," the colonel again answered, this time with less specific information.

Then taking control of the conversation, the colonel continued. "Captain, let me ask you–you say you are here on a government mission, who in the government sent you?"

Captain Vásquez hesitated a moment, then responded.

"Colonel, we are here under the direct orders of General Santa Ana. He sent us."

The colonel lurched forward, surprised, and started to laugh before catching himself.

"*That old thief?* I thought he was hiding in Cuba. Is he back?"

"Yes, he is back. And I think he's going to become president again. Anyway, we are here under his orders," the captain replied, still a bit off of his stride.

The colonel took a gulp of his wine and was quiet for a few moments. He tipped his head to one side, studying us, then he responded. "Captain, you have your orders and I have mine. What do you need?"

This time the colonel's attitude had shifted toward one of anger. He was obviously not happy. But he seemed resolved to the hopelessness of fighting Mexico City. He leaned back in his chair and clasped his hands behind his head, waiting for Captain Vásquez to speak.

Marco stood up and walked over to a map of Sonora hanging on the whitewashed adobe wall. "Colonel, what you report about the Americans is good news. This simplifies our mission very much. Are you aware of any incursions the American military have made into Sonora since the war?"

"Since the war? Hell, it's been five years! Colonel Martinez was first in charge here after the war, and I worked for him. Yes, just after the war there were a number of American troop detachments crossing Sonora, moving to the north. Most of those were remnants of a cavalry regiment in Mexico which broke up after the war and were heading to the captured territory. Since that time, the only American soldiers that have been in Sonora were after Apaches who were killing Americanos in the captured territory. The American soldiers at Fort Whipple know me. They sent word about what they are doing when they come into Mexico," the frustrated colonel explained.

He tipped his chair forward. "Except for the detachment that went through Tucson last month…."

"What happened last month?" asked the captain, standing near the map on the whitewashed wall.

"Well, besides the Americans going to California looking for gold over the last two years, there has been nothing to catch my attention. But when I was up there last week, my captain in charge of the Tucson Presidio told me a small group of gringos had gone through two weeks before. Captain Fontes said there were two gringo engineers and an officer with six soldiers to protect them from the Apaches."

"Do you know what they were doing? Where they were going?" Captain Vásquez asked.

"They came from the east, from Guadalupe on the Río Grande. Captain Fontes thought they were headed to California," the colonel explained.

This information got my attention. It tied in nicely with the conversations in Georgia at the Fields of Shannon Plantation about the proposed railroad. Senator Anderson and Congressman Fields both mentioned a strong United States interest in a new southern railroad route to California. They said that the acquisition of land for this route was going to be negotiated with Santa Ana. I said nothing.

"Did Captain Fontes know their mission, or why they were there?" Marco asked.

"No. They just said they were taking the short route to California. Captain Fontes didn't believe them, because they had engineering equipment and maps, like you." Colonel Trujillo raised an eye brow and waited.

Marco glanced at me, but I did not react.

"So there was no other American military activity in Sonora in the last six months?" Captain Vásquez asked the colonel.

"No. None. Just a few miners going to California as I said," the colonel responded, appearing impatient with the line of questioning.

Finally, the colonel stood and asked coldly.

"*Captain, now tell me why you are really here.* What does that old criminal want?"

Captain Vásquez looked at his cup and took the last gulp of his wine then replied steadily, "Colonel, there are two things we were sent here to do. One was to find out about the Americans. The second deals with the recovery of some bullion the Spanish hid during the Revolution."

"*I knew it! I knew it!* That old bastard is trying to rob our country again!" The angry colonel shouted.

He slung his coffee cup to the floor, splashing wine on the white-washed wall.

Concerned, I adjusted my chair back slightly, out of the line of fire. Perhaps this man was not our next devil. But he now knew part of our plan–and that would not be good.

The colonel quickly regained his composure and apologized to Marco for his unprofessional behavior.

"Captain Vásquez, you and I are both soldiers, and we both have our orders. But I'm damned upset. I've been out here for three years without proper support from Mexico City. But that's not your fault. So let's get on with it."

Marco said nothing, but his face was red with anger.

The colonel, trying to make up for his outburst, poured the remaining wine into Marco's cup and said, "I apologize, Captain. You came a long way out here to follow your orders and not to hear my problems. Let me know how I can help you."

The colonel's eyes narrowed. "Now tell me about your treasure. Where is it? What are you going to do with it? What do you want from me?"

Marco was silent for a few moments as his normal color returned. Then he turned toward the map.

"Colonel, I am not going to beg for your help. I'll go over to General Pacheco in Chihuahua and get his help if this bothers you. But if I do, it would end your military career, do you understand?" Captain Vásquez said in a low, deliberate voice.

The colonel, obviously not used to this type of talk from a subordinate, was silent as his face darkened. Finally he replied.

"Yes, I understand."

Marco nodded.

"And all our conversations here must remain confidential, do you understand?"

"Yes, yes–I understand. What do you need? How can I help?"

"And it ties to the questions I was asking you, do you understand?"

The colonel took a deep breath, "No, I don't understand. How does the reason the Spanish hid their gold during the Revolution tie to the Americans?"

I thought I had the perfect answer to his question. *Santa Ana wants to remove the Spanish gold from Sonora before he sells the land to the gringos. Then he's going to take the Spanish gold and the gringo money to Cuba with him.* But again, I said nothing.

Marco smiled stiffly. "Colonel, as I understand the plan, General Santa Ana wants us to gather information about the American activity, intentions, and military posts here in Sonora and in the captured Mexican land above. Also, he wants us to retrieve the hidden treasure the Spanish buried and take it to Mexico City. This he will use to finance a military expedition north to recapture some of the land Mexico lost," the captain explained trying, to make it sound creditable.

"*Que se va a la chingada* (He can go to Hell)! You don't believe that do you,Captain?" The inflammable colonel shouted.

Fighting for control, Marco nodded. "Colonel, those are my orders."

Marco studied the man confronting him, then continued. "Colonel, we need your help. Are we going to get it?"

The angry colonel stood up, strode over to Marco and glared at the map.

"Sometimes I wonder why I put my life at risk–and the lives of my men–for this? Our friend General Santa Ana was successful at giving away Texas, Nuevo Mexico, and California. *Nuevo Mexico*, can you believe it? The gringo government certainly couldn't do worse at managing the territory than we did," the colonel stated bitterly."

He took a deep breath. "Captain, what I just said was *sedition.* I could get myself shot for it in Mexico City. But it's how I feel. I was wounded twice in the American War, so I am loyal to Mexico. I'm angry with those people, the politicians, that steal from our country to make themselves rich. Santa Ana is one of the worst," the colonel stated bitterly, still looking at the map.

After a few more moments he seemed to shake off some of his rage. "Captain Vásquez, like I said, you have your orders and I have mine. Just tell me what you want to do."

"Colonel, you can help us with two things. First, I need to write a report for General Santa Ana on the information you gave me about what the Americans are doing in Sonora and north of Sonora. I will need more details from you on that."

"Fine. I will give you the information you need," the still angry colonel replied, "What else?"

"We have reason to believe the Spanish hid a load of gold and silver ingots they were hauling down from the Pimeria Alta to Mexico City when the Revolution caught them. We understand it is buried near Imuris."

"Only *one* load? I understood there were several loads, three or four. You know you aren't the first one to look for this?" Colonel Trujillo replied.

"We only have information on one load," Marco replied lying smoothly while ignoring part of the colonel's response.

The colonel put his left fist up to his lip and thoughtfully took a closer look at Imuris on the map. Then he responded, trying to control his emotions.

"Captain, if you have information on where the loads are buried, you might be able to answer a question for me. My great uncle was a guard on one of those expeditions–hauling gold and silver from the Spanish mines. During the time of the Revolution, he disappeared. It was in the Imuris area. Maybe what you find could give us a little more information about what happened to him."

The guard outside interrupted us and the colonel went out to tend to some business with several of his men. It was mid-morning.

Marco and I talked while he was gone.

"Chu Chu, what do you think? Our colonel is no friend to Santa Ana, is he?" Marco asked.

"No. At least we know where he stands. Are you going to tell him about the other two treasures?" I asked.

"No. I hope we find something at Cocospera. If not, he's going to have to know, at least about one of them. Do you think he should go with us?"

"Good question. Maybe it would be good if he did. He could control his men. But what if he wants it all for himself? Not much we could do about it, is there?" I responded.

Marco agreed.

There seemed to be nothing more to say on the matter as Marco and I waited for the colonel, who was talking to several of his men. I began to look around Colonel Trujillo's stark, dirt floored adobe office. It was about 12 feet by 16 feet with a nine-foot ceiling of layered ocotillo strips and dried mud held up with hewn mesquite *vigas* (beams). With its whitewashed walls, it smelled like desert earth sterilized with lime and was very rustic and attractive. The room was cool, with a little December breeze coming through the two open windows. The windows had no glass, only thick solid mesquite shutters soaked with cactus oil. They hung in an iron frame from hinges allowing them to be tightly closed from the inside. The shutters helped to control air circulation, keeping heat out during summer and in during the winter.

The colonel's desk and table matched. They were both made from hand hewn squared ironwood logs and held up by wooden legs buried in the dirt floor. His chairs were made from oiled ironwood limbs and leather. The rugged chairs were also comfortable. He had a simple bookcase against the wall next to his map.

I strolled about, running a hand along the bookcase that was made from three squared hand hewn mesquite logs held up by empty black powder cans. At least I hoped they were empty, as they were next to his cast-iron heating stove. Leaning over, I could see that the bottom shelf had two books, a Bible and an old Spanish military manual. It also contained an ancient pair of engraved iron, Jesuit priest stirrups shaped like a cross. *A hell of an impractical heavy thing for a priest to haul around in the desert on a poor horse or burro, I thought!*

On his top shelf, the colonel had his Spanish flintlock musket in a leather saddle scabbard, along with a powder horn with an attached charge-measuring ladle hanging by a leather thong. It looked well-used and was casually laid there, as if he was ready to grab it and walk out the door.

I told Marco I would hate to fight a flock of Indians with a flintlock musket. Just one shot! Better make it good!

The middle shelf of the bookcase was the most interesting. It held a deer hide pouch with six Indian arrows. Each arrow shaft had a blue flint arrowhead attached with a thin rawhide thong. The other end had red feathers attached to the shaft with a fine-spun cactus fiber string and glue. I wondered how long it took for an Apache buck to make each arrow and what he visualized killing with it–probably Mexicans and gringos. However, since it was sitting on Trujillo's shelf, I was sure the Apache warrior who made it no longer fought.

Marco smiled and nudged me, pointing to what looked like a string of six or seven dried apricots hanging from a nail on the shelf above the warrior's gear. They were human ears! I rubbed the notch in my left ear as I looked at it.

Also, there was an unstrung bow, a pair of simple leather *huaraches* (sandals) with straps and several other items I couldn't identify. The shelf also held a serrated gray flint knife and a pouch with seeds, *tuna* (cactus fruit) and dried jerky. The dried meat made me think of the poor horses on our sea voyage with Captain Beltrán.

Fascinated, Marco also studied everything, commenting that we might soon be seeing more of these things up north.

I had been in many offices in my travels, including that of my boss' boss, Sir Edward Chadwick, in London, also President Arista's and General Santa Ana's, both in Mexico City. Colonel Trujillo's simple adobe office was easily the most memorable. I liked the feeling and the clean, fresh, earthen smell of the room. If I ever had my own office, I thought

I would keep this one in mind.

Marco and I were looking at the map and discussing the route to Imuris and Cocospera when the colonel came back into his office.

"Captain Vásquez, you were saying you were going to prepare a report for General Santa Ana. Let me know what information you want by tomorrow. I'm going back into the field for three weeks on Tuesday.

"You mentioned the treasure. Let's talk about it," he continued in a level tone.

"Yes sir, let's talk about it. I need 12 soldiers, shovels, pack burros, plus supplies to last us for 30 days," Marco said.

The colonel smiled. "Captain, before you tell me what you need, I'm going to tell you what I need."

"Yes sir?"

"Captain, you see our situation here. We don't have any modern firearms for our soldiers. The boots and uniforms we have are a sad joke. We don't have any decent equipment or food. We need horses, saddles, feed for our animals, money to buy food for my men, and to pay them.

"We get orders from Mexico City on what they want us to do–protect Sonora, fight the Apaches and keep the gringos out. They don't bother to send us money or equipment to do it. Our corporal's pay is 50 *reales* a month. Our sergeant's is 75. I am paid 400 reales a month and sometimes I have to pay my men with it and wait for them to repay me. Those above me expect me to use the *mordida*, but these are my people. I don't do that–unless it's a gringo or foreigner passing through.

"So Captain, let me tell you what I want. If I help you find that treasure, I want one third of it before it goes to Mexico City. At least the money will stay here, where it will be put to good use. Do you understand, Captain?"

Captain Vásquez started to answer, but the colonel interrupted him. "And, Captain, before you tell me anymore about the hidden Spanish treasure, one more thing. I don't want to know anything about it or where it is, if my conditions are not acceptable to you. You and your friend can find it yourselves. I will not risk my men or waste my time. Do you understand?"

Marco was silent for a few moments. Finally he answered.

"Colonel, I understand. I agree to your conditions. When can we proceed?"

The darken-face colonel seemed surprised then relaxed a bit. "Good! I am going out into the field again. I'll be back before Christmas. Whatever I do for you must be done after Christmas. Is that acceptable?"

"It will have to be! Yes, Colonel, it is acceptable," Captain Vásquez responded, disappointment clear on his face.

"Where are you going? Can we go along?" I asked, speaking for the first time to the colonel.

Both the colonel and captain looked at me in surprise.

"You want to go with us? We are going north into Apache country. It is dangerous, and I am not going to put my men in danger to protect you," the colonel stated emphatically.

"Where are you going?" Marco asked.

The colonel studied the young officer. "We are going up the Río Sonora then over to San Lázaro. There we will decide if we are going to kill Apaches. If we don't find them, then we will go on to Quiburi, on the Río San José de Terrenate, and patrol the area for a couple of days. We will be in the middle of Apache country. If we find nothing, we will go to Río Gila and check the boundary with the gringos. We will come back through Río Santa Maria, then to Cocospera, then back here."

Marco looked at me and I nodded. We should go. We would get a hell of a lot of exposure to the new fascinating country and maybe even get a look at *two* of the Spanish hiding sites.

Marco said. "Colonel, we would like to go. This would be an excellent opportunity for us to see the country."

The colonel looked at us, still a bit surprised. Then he shrugged. "I see you are carrying the new repeating pistols. Can you use them?"

"Yes," I replied quietly.

The colonel asked if he could inspect my Colt Dragoon. I showed it to him. He carefully inspected it, turning it over and over carefully.

"I have seen only one other of these pistols. It was broken and we took it from a dead gringo officer during the war. But it was not nearly as nice as this one. This is what we need here. Look at what we have," he said, pulling his flintlock musket from the top of his bookshelf and handing it to me. He also took his flintlock pistol from the holster lying on his desk and handed it to Marco.

"When I am out in the field, I carry an extra pistol in my belt–when we are in Apache country. That gives me three shots, well, two really. I'm not going to stop and get off my horse to take out my rifle and shoot. I'd get my balls cut off if I did that!" he explained with a frustrated chuckle.

Relaxing now, he continued, "If we are attacked, I have two shots. Each of my men has one shot from his rifle, then they must use a knife or throw rocks if they don't have time to reload. When we are riding into a dangerous location, I have my men take out their rifles and carry them in their hands, ready to shoot. Sometimes I have them walk and lead their horses.

"The Apaches are very careful about when and where they attack. Like us, they don't like to take any losses, so they hide and are deadly at using surprise. They also try to scare our horses. That works well, because if our men are busy trying to control their horses, they can't get off a good shot. Or worse yet, they waste their shots. That's when the devils really attack."

"Colonel, how often do the Apaches attack your troops?" I asked.

"Not very often. They know my troops are well-trained and armed. And my men don't run. Unless the Apache bucks can get close to us and disrupt our horses, they never attack directly. They would rather steal our horses or supplies at night, or attack the last soldier in our detail, then run," he explained.

"If we have more than six troops and are careful where we go, we are seldom attacked. It's too costly for the Apaches. They would rather attack travelers and farmers."

I pointed to his second shelf and asked, "Colonel, did those things belong to the Apaches?"

The colonel turned and walked to the shelf and replied. "Yes. Take a look at these. A damned Apache with these items can travel on foot in rough country faster than we can on horseback. Out in the open, we can beat him. He usually doesn't carry water, because he knows where all the springs and watering places are. Also, he can eat cactus and get enough water to sustain himself in the desert for several days as he travels.

"If he has a horse, then we can't catch him unless he does something very stupid, and usually he doesn't."

The colonel's voice showed eagerness. "And look at this. Most Apaches don't have guns–yet. But he usually has six to eight arrows with him at all times. He can shoot all of these arrows at us in the time it takes us to fire and reload our rifles. If he is close, within 10 to 15 meters, he can hit us with his arrows, unless we are lucky enough to dodge. So we must hit him with our first shot.

"And, gentlemen, our next mission is not a routine visit up north. The Apaches are now making raids out of the Sierra de Las Chihuahuitas. I have some Opata Indians secretly tracking them right now. I want you to know what you are getting into. It's going to be a dangerous mission. And I hope you will go with us because we need your help and your new weapons," Colonel Trujillo finished, almost out of breath.

Las Chihuahuitas rang a bell! I had seen that name on the Spanish map. It was where one of the Spanish treasures was hidden!

Both Marco and I agreed we must go.

It was late morning by the time Colonel Trujillo called in Sergeant Juan Campos to work with us, making sure we were properly prepared for the trip. The colonel said he would be available if we had any questions or needed anything.

"We will be leaving before first light on Tuesday," the colonel told us, now in a friendlier mood as we finished our meeting.

We thanked the colonel then left his office.

Yes, we had found our new devil. *But this one had horns!*

During the afternoon, Marco and I discussed what maps and equipment we needed for our trip. I told him we absolutely needed the two white vellum maps and the three paper maps with their diagrams and explanations on where the treasures were located. I selected one extra map which Colonel Martinez in Guadalajara had given us. It showed good detail of most of Sonora, including mountains, roads and settlements, in case we got separated from Trujillo's group.

I suggested we make arrangements with Colonel Trujillo to store our ship's lode stone compass, sextant and extra supplies at his military post while we were gone. This would cut down greatly on what we would need to pack and take with us.

Also, I regretfully suggested we fold the beautiful rolled vellum maps so we could easily carry them in our saddlebags. Marco agreed.

Firearms, powder, lead shot, maps and emergency food. We each arranged these so we could carry what we needed on our own horses. Marco said he had never fired a revolver before and wanted to practice shooting before we left for Apache country.

The Colt revolver was not new to me. I had practiced with it extensively, alone and with Howard and JK in Georgia. I quickly got the feel for this impressive weapon and became very good with it, thanks to the training my friend Captain Will Springer had given me.

Marco had the new pair of Colt Dragoon pistols I had given General Santa Ana. I had brought three .44 caliber Colt revolvers with me. One, I was wearing and the other two were in my saddlebags. I had intended to keep the revolver I was wearing and give the other two as gifts to people who could help me in Mexico. When I found out we were headed north into Indian country, looking for treasure, I decided to hang on to them until after our trip. Eighteen shots seemed much better to me than six if Apaches were after my arse.

We ate, then loaded up our pack burros and rode over to the garrison to make arrangements with the colonel to store our excess equipment and turn in our two borrowed burros to the garrison *remuda* (herd of horses). Afterwards, we planned to go up the river and do some target practice. Marco was excited. As we rode to the garrison, I made a suggestion.

"Marco, Colonel Trujillo seems to be the man we need to make our plan work. I have three Colt revolvers and could use all three if we got into a pickle with the Apaches. You have two."

I continued. "If you don't have a problem with the idea, why don't we invite the colonel to go shoot the revolvers with us? If things go well, I might even give him my third Colt. What do you think?" I asked.

"Chu Chu, I wasn't too happy with the way he burned my ass this morning about Santa Ana and insisted on a third of the treasure. But what he said was true. My good uncle will probably take the treasure with him to Cuba. Trujillo certainly could use some of the money here.

And sure, if you want to give him your third gun, do it. We need his help, even if we have to buy it," Marco replied pragmatically.

It was early afternoon when we got back to the garrison again. Sergeant Campos met us and took us over to the colonel's office. He had just come back from lunch with his wife and children at his home in Hermosillo. He seemed to be in a decent mood.

Marco made arrangements with Trujillo to store our compass and sextant along with our excess powder, lead, lead balls, casting dies and other supplies. When we were finished, I spoke to him.

"Colonel, you seemed interested in our Colt Dragoons. Captain Vásquez and I are going up the river to practice with them. Would you like to come along and try them out?" I asked.

I knew that to a military man like the colonel, this opportunity would be even *better* than sex. He quickly accepted my offer and directed Sergeant Campos to change his schedule for the afternoon. We borrowed a canvas from Sergeant Campos so we could use it to lay out our weapons. Campos found us some rusted tin cans and wood blocks for targets. We rode up the river and stopped at a grove of cottonwood trees still with some unshed leaves and tied our horses. We walked to the other end of the cottonwood grove, so as not to spook our horses when we shot, and laid out our weapons on the canvas in a shady spot.

The river was flowing with a stream of water about a foot deep. We stood up six tin cans and some wood blocks as targets below a dirt bank next to the river. Colonel Trujillo brought along his flintlock pistol. I suggested he take a shot at one of the cans with his pistol. He shot and came close, kicking some dirt up onto one of the cans. I joked, saying I hoped he was shooting at that can.

Slightly embarrassed, the colonel smiled and asked me to try it with my Colt Dragoon. I was hoping he would.

With a Colt revolver in each hand, I slowly raised the first weapon with my right hand and fired. I hit all six of the cans, most of them close to the center. Lowering the weapon in my right hand, I raised the revolver in my left hand and fired again. Each of the scattered cans jumped again. My feel for the weapon and my nerves were still good.

I had taken 12 shots in less than a minute and hit the target with each shot. The colonel and Marco were amazed. There was a slight breeze, and the white gun smoke cleared quickly. They both asked me to teach them to shoot the pistol properly. I agreed and went into the *Captain Will Springer instructor mode.* Captain Vásquez and Colonel Trujillo were good students.

After an hour of instruction and shooting, both men's shooting improved. They were hitting the cans about half of the time. They were delighted. Marco may have been a little better shot than the colonel, but they both quickly learned. I impressed on them to load their own guns and keep them clean from dirt, moisture and foreign materials.

When we were about to finish, I told the colonel to load and shoot my third Colt Dragoon, which we had not yet fired. He did and hit four out of the six shredded cans. He was delighted with his shooting and grinned as he handed the weapon back to me.

"Keep it. It's yours," I told him.

In disbelief, he blinked first at me, then the gun. He held it up and gazed at it again.

"Mine? I can have it?"

"Yes. It's yours."

The colonel said nothing more as he smiled down at the gun, running an admiring finger tip over the cylinder that allowed all those shots in succession. He slowly turned it over and over in his hand. The gift turned out to be a good move on my part.

When we got back to the garrison of Hermosillo, Colonel Trujillo seemed to have turned a corner in his relationship with us. Inviting us over to his home in Hermosillo for dinner, he described where he lived and asked us to be there before sundown. He said he would be honored to have us enjoy *carne asada* and Toluca wine with him and his family. Marco and I gladly accepted.

Chapter 17

La Bruja (The Witch)

Marco and I returned to our *posada*, where we rested a bit, then cleaned up for our dinner engagement at Colonel Trujillo's hacienda. So far, it had been a very interesting day.

Later, we walked from our *posada* to Colonel Trujillo's hacienda at the edge of the dusty village of Hermosillo. As we arrived at the simple, adobe-walled hacienda, the sun was setting in the west and we smelled smoke from meat being barbequed on an open fire. It smelled great!

We walked through an iron patio gate and into a private courtyard with several large, old mesquite trees. Inside the walled courtyard, the colonel had many cactus and other desert plants. He also had some newly-planted fruit trees.

I was impressed with the random and artistic way the small courtyard was arranged. Apparently the colonel, or someone in his family, had a natural talent for that sort of thing. There was also an unfinished rock fountain in the middle of the small courtyard, but no water was flowing. It looked like a work in progress.

The main building was a simple L-shaped structure with thick walls and barred windows facing the patio. It had a long open porch and at the end of it a stone pathway to a well with a wooden water storage barrel next to it.

Two tables were set out on the porch, where three Indian women were busy cutting up fruit and arranging food for the meal. Even though the December evening was cold, the man cooking the meat was perspiring over the large, open fire pit also built out of rock. It had a huge iron *parrilla* (grill) on which a man was cooking the meat. It was a pleasant scene, enhanced by the smells of the roasting meat.

The colonel dressed in a comfortable Spanish jacket, was talking to two workmen near an unfinished stone walkway in the patio. He looked up, smiled, and came over to greet us.

"*Bienvenidos* gentlemen, thank you for joining me in my humble home. It is late in the season and we had a limited pick of fruit in the market. But Paco found some good beef and pork, which he is cooking. I hope you're not Jewish or *Morro* (Moorish)," the colonel said, winking at me.

He then led us over to the tables where the three smiling Indian women were busy cutting fresh fruit and preparing the meal. The colonel introduced us to the youngest, who was arranging the food on the tables.

"Gentlemen, this is my wife–*Zonia*."

Covering our surprise, Marco and I nodded and spoke to the shy but interesting looking young Indian woman. She was dressed in a simple white dress and blouse with a dark red shawl over her shoulders. She was pregnant.

Then the colonel called his children, who were shyly watching us from the far end of the open porch. There was a girl about nine and a boy about seven. Then there was Chico, the little soldier boy *(El Soldadito)* Marco and I had seen riding his burro through the garrison gate several days before. He was short and squat and looked to be about thirteen.

"Gentlemen, these are my children. Juan is the youngest. Isabella, *my princess*, is the next. And Chico is my oldest. Chico's name is Alejandro, the same as mine," the colonel said lining up his children and standing behind them.

He placed his hand on the shoulders of the youngest and oldest, displaying them proudly.

Little Chico was obviously *simple,* but he also seemed happy and smiled at us excitedly. He quickly came to attention and saluted the captain. Embarrassed, Marco glanced at the colonel then smiled and quietly returned the boy's salute.

"Chico is my oldest. His mother died when he was born. Chico doesn't speak much, but he's a good soldier. He helps us every day at the garrison. He gets up before anyone and rides his burro, Gruillo, from our farm down to the garrison and helps the men feed and saddle the horses. He's a good little soldier," the colonel explained, obviously brokenhearted, as he looked at his proud little man.

The colonel dispatched his children in a firm but loving manner, then focused on his guests, Marco and me.

Marco brought some *dulce de membrillo* (quince candy) he bought at the market and I brought two bottles of unlabeled local wine, the only thing I could find. We presented these to Señora Trujillo. She smiled when she saw my bottles of wine and placed our gifts on the table.

The colonel excused himself for a moment, then went over to Paco, the man cooking the meat, and the two other ladies. He instructed them to give the workmen finishing their work for the day some meat and fruit to take home. He then returned and invited Marco and me to join him and his family at the table on the open porch. The sun was going down and the evening was quickly getting colder.

Paco brought us a large wooden platter filled with hot *carne asada* (roasted beef) and strips of *carnitas* (pork) fresh off the parrilla. The colonel explained that Paco also cooked some with *cebollas* (onions) sprinkled with *cilantro* (coreander)and other diced Indian herbs to eat with the barbequed meat. One of the ladies brought out a fresh batch of hot flour tortillas nicely wrapped in a cotton towel. My mouth watered.

Next, the two ladies brought us sliced peaches with goat's cream and coffee. There was also a small tin can with crushed *panocha* (brown sugar) as a sweetener for the meal. The children had hot milk with *pinole* to drink, which they sweetened with the *panocha* sugar.

Little Isabella brought a little spoonful of her prepared *pinole* for me to taste. I tasted it and made a face like it was too sweet, causing her to giggle.

Zonia quietly finished working with her two helpers to get us settled with food at the table, then joined us. The two women disappeared into the house to eat separately.

Colonel Alejandro Trujillo brought out two bottles of his Toluca wine and a bottle of the unlabeled wine I'd bought in the local market. He opened my wine first and, with an unusually sober expression, handed it to Zonia. I could tell something was coming.

Smiling, she poured me a small taste of my wine into my glazed clay cup for me to sample and approve. I did and it was terrible. Its strong acidic flavor tasted so bad that I thought it dissolved some of the glaze off of my cup!

This time I made genuine sour face and quickly tossed my remaining wine into a nearby shrub. Continuing with the charade, the colonel acted like he was afraid my actions might kill his precious shrub. Then Trujillo explained that my wine was only used by the locals as trading material with the remote Yaqui Indians up in the hills when they brought their wares to town. The whole group, including Marco and I got a hearty laugh out of the little episode. Alejandro Trujillo said he would save the Toluca wine for us to enjoy after our meal.

After I apologized for my unworthy gift, Alejandro said a short prayer, thanking and asking a blessing for our food. The gathering, including Marco crossed themselves, then started to eat. I was respectful and made a similar motion, even though I was not a Catholic. My folks were always careful to respect both Spanish and Indian traditions in the Catholic dominated countries of the Americas. My father reminded us that we were guests in their countries. He also half joked that it had not been very many years since the *Inquisition*. My parents' practices and advice always proved sage.

The evening got colder, so Alejandro asked Paco to remove the iron cooking grill and stoke up his barbeque pit fire to throw off more heat. We then moved the tables down the porch, closer to the open barbeque pit where we could be warm as we ate. The fire felt good, and it made the food taste even better.

Our meal with Colonel Trujillo and his family at his simple but pleasant hacienda was enjoyable, even for Marco. This turn of events was welcomed, especially after the rocky start we had gotten off to with the colonel in the morning.

We were seeing another side to the hard colonel when he was at home with his family. Also, his unlikely young Indian wife, Zonia, seemed relaxed and pleasant. The children were mostly quiet, but giggled happily during the meal when something was done or said that pleased them. The youngest two, Juan and Isabella, seemed fascinated with me, and little Chico couldn't take his eyes off of Marco and his uniform.

I capitalized on the situation a bit by entertaining the children as we ate. I would quietly make strange faces when Trujillo was not looking, examined utensils or tasting different foods. This delighted the children to the point Alejandro Trujillo started to scold them, until he caught Zonia's glance. After noting my fake innocent look and realizing what was happening, he ignored my little antics with the children and went on with his conversation.

During the meal, Trujillo spoke kindly to and about his wife, Zonia, saying they had been married for only two years. I surmised Zonia must have been his third wife. He then went on to tell how they met.

He said while on a military excursion north with his cavalry soldiers, he became ill, then his horse fell with him, further aggravating his condition. They had reached the abandoned Spanish and Indian settlement of Quiburi along Río San José de Terrenate, when his condition suddenly became worse. It was wintertime, and they were entering Apache territory. The colonel said he and his captain made the decision for him to break away with two men and go home to recover.

Trujillo said he directed his captain to continue with the cavalry troop north to the new border with the United States along the Gila and check for both Apache and American activity. Mentally still in control, he directed the captain to return along the Río de Santa Maria and rotate some of his men out with the commander at the Presidio of *Tucson*, then return to Hermosillo. He was to deal with the Apaches as he saw fit.

Feeling terrible, Trujillo said he and two junior enlisted men headed south toward home. His condition got worse. He had a high fever and could not keep his food down. He remembered only the first several hours of their trip south. Luckily, they encountered no Apaches, and by the time they reached Mototicachi in the upper Río Sonora valley, he could no longer travel.

At Mototicachi, his worried two young soldiers found a farmer who agreed to take care of him while they went on to Hermosillo to get a wagon and return for him. That's where Zonia first met him. He laughed, saying that Zonia met him nine days before he met her–meaning he was in a coma near death during that time. He said Zonia saved his life.

The colonel continued with the story, and Zonia quietly smiled as we continued our meal in the patio, enjoying both the food and the heat and light from the large fire.

Trujillo did all of the talking and explained that Zonia was staying with the farmer and his family. She was an *Opata* Indian from the unsettled tribes in the mountains to the east toward Fronteras. The Indians of her tribe said she was a *"bruja"* (witch) and put her out of their tribe to die. But she refused to die and wandered over to the Río Sonora Valley and was taken in by the kindly farmer, Francisco Salazar, and his family. They were *mestizos* themselves.

The colonel explained that Zonia had been living with the Salazar family for about four months when he was carried unconscious and shivering through the door of their small adobe hut and laid on the dirt floor.

Trujillo said that Salazar told him that when the normally shy and reserved Zonia saw him wrapped in a blanket on the dirt floor and dying, she came over immediately and carefully examined him. She then took charge.

The colonel smiled while eating his *carne asada* and continued his interesting story. He said the farmer, Pancho Salazar, laughed and told him that Zonia's countenance suddenly changed. They saw a different person emerge, perhaps that of *La Bruja*, who so frightened the Indians.

For the next week, Zonia fiercely took over, nursing and doctoring him back to life. She went into the hills, gathering herbs known to the Indians, and prepared strange hot soups, forcing him to eat and stay alive.

"She refused to let me die."

The colonel gazed at his wife with undisguised affection. "Her people call her *La Bruja*, but I call her *Mi Ángel* (My Angel). God sent her to me when I was dying and she saved my life," he leaned forward and lovingly touched her hand.

Now, in a quieter voice, the colonel continued.

"Yet, my dear wife does have strange powers. I have seen her pick up scorpions from the floor and remove them from our home. I also saw her control a coiled rattlesnake ready to strike Isabella just by looking at it. It uncoiled and slithered away. Also, a coyote was attacking our chickens at our farm up the river. She called out and got its attention. She then stared at the animal with a snake-like look in her eyes, and the coyote stopped like it was hypnotized. She walked over to the animal and took the frightened chicken from his jaws. The confused coyote then trotted away with feathers still in his mouth. And other things too."

Zonia stopped smiling, and the colonel glancing at her said no more. Maybe she was also controlling him. It was quite a story.

After dinner, Colonel Trujillo took Marco and me inside the hacienda. Beside a roaring fire in the fireplace, we smoked a cheap cigar and drank some of his Toluca wine. He then spoke of our upcoming trip into Apache country and told us how we should pack.

Opening up, we told him we should be going near the place where the Spanish treasure was buried. We told him it was near Imuris and in Cocospera. In fact, it was in the graveyard at the Cocospera Mission.

This got his attention, and he said he might change his plans and take a more direct route so as to look at the site when we went north. He cautioned us to make sure no one else knew the true reason for our trip. He also said he wanted to be with us when we recovered the treasure. We agreed. Not that we had much choice.

Colonel Trujillo explained what he wanted to accomplish on his military expedition north. He said the Apaches had recently concentrated their attacks on several communities in Río de Santa Maria valley. They were savagely attacking missions, visitas, ranchos and small pueblos in the area. He explained that in the previous two months, there had been a series of deadly attacks in Río San José de Terrenate to the east, which killed many people and totally burned out some settlements.

The colonel theorized that the Apaches had first concentrated their forces and operated from a base in the Sierra de las Mulas, then moved to las Peñascosas to wreak death and hell in the Río San José de Terrenate Valley. Now he surmised they had moved westward to a location in the

Chihuahuita Mountains, where they were starting new attacks on Río de Santa Maria settlements.

He said his small detachments at the Presidio of Tubac and Terrenate could not deal with the multiple attacks that were occurring and his soldiers at Tucson were too far away to act without a plan. Hence he had put together a plan to deal with the situation.

Colonel Alejandro Trujillo said he had Opata and Pima Indians scouts assigned to secretly track the movements of the Apaches. His plan on this trip north was to concentrate forces from his garrison at Hermosillo with those of Tucson, Tubac and Terrenate. Together they would attack and destroy the Apache base camp if they could find it. He admitted he needed good information and a certain amount of luck. It looked like Marco and I were headed into a major battle with the Apaches. The thoughts of treasures now seemed a bit more remote in our minds.

Finally, as Marco and I prepared to leave the colonel's hacienda, we went out onto the porch and patio for a few minutes. Paco was raking the coals of the barbeque fire, preparing to cover it for the night. A flurry of sparks flew off the agitated coals and into the night sky. It reminded me of that special evening at the Fields of Shannon Plantation banquet. It was the night my love and I had danced to the New Orleans band music in the beautiful and dimly lit plantation garden. We danced, watching the fireflies flashing in the dark August night like the sparks flying skyward from this fire. It seemed so long ago, and Melanie seemed so far away. I wondered if I would ever see her again.

Chapter 18

On Into Apache Country

The next two and a half weeks, I count as the most exciting and memorable days of my life, except for the war. I saw some of the best and worst in mankind, all mixed in with strange quirks of fate and one unexplainable event.

According to my journal, the day after our pleasant evening with Colonel Trujillo was Sunday, December 5, 1852. The weather was cold and it rained. Marco and I spent the day preparing for our trip north into Apache country with Colonel Trujillo and his cavalry detachment. We were highly excited.

During the day, we sorted out those things we were going to take with us on our trek into the wild high desert country of the Pimeria Alta. Even though I had never been there, I felt like I knew the country where we were heading and could visualize the dangers we could expect. This was because Marco and I had studied the maps so many times and talked to many people who had been there.

Our gear included firearms, powder, shot and, of course, the maps. Two Colt Navy six-shooters and my Sharps rifle were my weapons. The six-shooters were excellent for close-in fighting and intimidation. The Sharps .52 caliber rifle with its windage sights was best for precise killing at 50 to 500 meters. Although it was a single-shot rifle, it used the modern, quick breach loading cartridges. This made my weapon much faster than the flintlock or improved percussion-cap muzzleloaders. They required dumping gunpowder, patch and ball down the barrel, then ramming it tight before placing flash powder or a cap on the outside striker plate. With my new Sharps, I could easily get off ten accurate shots in a minute, whereas a soldier with the muzzleloader would be lucky to get off two.

I distributed some of my revolver supplies, .44 caliber lead balls and patches to Marco and the colonel. I also gave them a liberal supply of good quality black powder, including two powder flasks with measuring spouts and extra percussion caps, for which they thanked me.

Our maps were critically important to us, even though I had almost memorized them. Captain Vásquez turned the responsibility for those documents over to me. I was careful about what maps we left behind in the colonel's office along with the lodestone compass and sextant. I did not want to give our secrets away to prying eyes while we were in the field, or if we didn't come back. I kept the folded white vellum maps and the related hand prepared paper maps close to me at all times.

I used a polished leather side pistol holster with a button-down flap for my six-shooter. It protected my firearm from the rain and brush as I walked or rode horseback. Now that we were to enter Indian country, I needed a way to carry my extra six-shooter. Again, my friend Captain Springer had offered me the solution–an underarm, open holster that could be hidden under a jacket or coat.

Colonel Trujillo gave his leatherworker, Felipe, orders to make me whatever I needed. The man was a local tradesman who made and repaired the cavalry's gear at the garrison. Felipe made me a simple but comfortable open shoulder holster for my heavy Colt dragoon. When Trujillo and Vásquez saw it, they each ordered one–Trujillo, for his flintlock pistol. Both the colonel and Marco also had Felipe make them a covered, protected holster similar to mine for their Colt .44's.

Marco and I decided to carry all of our critical supplies in our large saddlebags, which could be quickly removed from our saddles and carried on foot. I would carry my extra pistol with its shoulder holster in my saddlebag and only wear it in Indian country. By Monday afternoon, Marco and I were prepared.

Before dawn on Tuesday morning, we were on the road with Colonel Trujillo's mounted troops, moving at a good clip northeast along the Río Sonora. It was the first time I had ridden with a mounted military detachment. The colonel had Sergeant Campos put Marco and me on good mounts. I debated about using a mule, but they didn't have a good one. Excitement built up inside me as I rode through the cold morning air alongside Marco, looking forward to what lay ahead.

In the darkness, we rode past Colonel Trujillo's farm on the opposite side of the river. He quietly pointed it out as we rode by. Then he made a decision that came back to haunt us. He decided to take a different route north with his troop, because of the information we had shared about the hidden treasure site at Cocospera.

Instead of going up Río Sonora as he and his troops normally did, he turned into the tributary, the Río San Miguel, which flowed into the Río Sonora a few kilometers above Colonel Trujillo's farm. This route, he explained, would take us more directly through Cocospera and allow us to quietly investigate the hidden treasure location.

We didn't know at the time that Colonel Trujillo's little son, Chico was going to try and follow us on his burro. Also, he would go the wrong way–up the Río Sonora. Nobody bothered to tell him that we were leaving early Tuesday morning and that we would travel north along the Río San Miguel tributary rather than along the colonel's normal route up the Río Sonora.

I was impressed with Colonel Trujillo's troops. They were a mix of young, intelligent Mexican soldiers along with some older veterans. Most were of *mestizo* blood, and some had strong signs of almost pure Indian blood. All were good riders and dealt well with their horses and the remote desert country. They seemed well-trained and carefully followed Trujillo's strict orders. He was a no-nonsense person and kept his conversations with Captain Vásquez and me low key and formal if his soldiers were around, and they were almost always around.

The first day, we made a hard ride north on the well-established roads and trails along the Río San Miguel, stopping only to rest the horses and men. The December days were short and we camped after dark at a bend in the river past San Miguel de Horcasitas, about 80 kilometers from Hermosillo.

Sergeant Dominguez selected an excellent location to camp between the river and a grassy ravine, which we used as a horse trap. At the campsite, we unsaddled and turned our horses over to Sergeant Campos and several of his men. They hobbled the animals and turned them loose to graze. He posted two guards at the upper ends of the canyon to make sure the horses did not wander far.

We set up a *wet camp* making several fires to cook and keep warm. Several of the soldiers rode to local farms and bought cooked beans, tortillas and fresh goat meat, which they brought back to warm and cook over the fires. This helped save our supplies for later use.

Marco and I set up our camp and built a fire about 50 meters from the other groups of soldiers. We were sitting on a couple of cottonwood logs, drinking coffee, when Colonel Trujillo and Sergeant Compos came over. The colonel carried an empty coffee cup and Campos had some food his men had bought from a local farmer. He placed the neatly-wrapped, stained but clean cloth with the food inside on the ground near our fire. He opened it and presented us warm bean and *carnita* burritos.

We offered both men some coffee from our small pot. The colonel accepted but Campos declined and thanked us. He said he needed to go back to the main fire, where his men were cooking and eating. Colonel Trujillo then shared our coffee and the food with us as we visited.

As we ate supper, Colonel Trujillo commented that this would be one of the few nights we would have the luxury of open campfires. After we arrived in the Río Santa Maria valley, we would be in Apache country. There, if we had fires, they must be hidden so as not to be seen from the surrounding hills and mountains. Also, during the day, all fires must be covered so smoke did not give away our location.

Then Trujillo chuckled and said the Apaches would know we were there anyway. But he wanted his men to be constantly vigilant for the cunning savages. Controlling camp fires and dust from their horses were ways to help do it.

The colonel explained that when we reached San Lázaro, we would meet up with his troops from Tubac, Terrenate and Tucson. They would have their Opata and Pima Indian scouts with them. There, Trujillo said he would consult with his commanders and decide how best to deal with the Apaches.

The talkative colonel said he and his men knew the country ahead well. Based on the frequency and locations of the most recent Apache attacks into the Río Santa Maria Valley, he and his men had a pretty good idea where the Apaches might be camping. There were three possible locations with water and grass in the nearby Chihuahuita Mountains north of San Lázaro, but he would wait to hear from the Opata and Pima Indian scouts. He hoped they would have pinpointed the Apache's camp.

We learned that the cold weather, although uncomfortable for us to operate in, worked to our advantage. The Apaches would be easier to stalk because they would stay closer to their base camp and would be less likely to post guards. They were usually the stalkers. He figured they could have a few of their women with them, but most would stay in their home camp in the mountains to the east. *I wondered if we were to kill the women too*. I said nothing.

Marco asked the colonel about his commanders. The colonel said he was fortunate to have good men commanding the mounted detachments from his northern military garrisons and presidios. They were Lieutenant Peralta with his men and Opata scouts from Terrenate, Captain Fontes with his men from Tucson, and Lieutenant Muñoz with his men and Pima scouts from Tubac. We would meet them in three days, when we camped at San Lázaro.

At the San Lázaro meeting, Colonel Trujillo said he would make the final decision on the attack if the scouts had reliable information about the Apache camp and if we had a good shot at wiping them out. If we did, we would rest our men and horses for an extra day, then launch a night attack, hitting the Apache camp at first light the following morning from two directions. It sounded reasonable.

We were tired, but felt better after a good supper. Colonel Trujillo showed Captain Vásquez and me his map of the expected battleground. *It was close to La Escondida*. I don't think Captain Vásquez realized this, since he had not studied our maps as much as I had. A chill ran down my back, but not from the cold, as I thought of the possibilities. During this trip we would be getting a close look at two of the three hidden treasure locations. This would be quite a stroke of luck for us, if we did not get killed by the Apaches.

That first night I didn't sleep well. Between the excitement and all the other distractions–howling wolves, grazing, hobbled horses and soldiers visiting and laughing during the night–my sleep was interrupted many times. Finally, about two hours before first light, the soldiers built up their campfires then began to wrangle and saddle their horses. Sergeant Campos had a young soldier bring Marco's and my horse over to where we were camped.

After we saddled and gathered our gear, we walked over to the main campfire. Sergeant Dominguez offered us coffee and some food left over from supper. We ate and visited, then were on our way before first light.

We arrived at Cocospera in the early afternoon and camped up the river from the town of Cocospera, not far from the old mission.

Colonel Trujillo gave orders to Lieutenant Camacho to set up camp and get the soldiers and horses fed and rested. He said Captain Vásquez and I would ride up the river and visit his old friend Padre Silva at the mission.

I was excited and so was Marco. We rode a few minutes up the river to the old mission. There was a graveyard on the hill behind it, but it didn't look right. It looked like there were 60 to 100 graves, some new. The penciled map showed only eight graves–Spanish graves. Either the graveyard had been expanded dramatically in 35 years, or *this was the wrong place!*

I explained the problem to Marco and Colonel Trujillo.

"Let's ask my friend Padre Silva," Colonel Trujillo said, smiling.

So we did.

Padre Silva was in his early fifties and happy to see Colonel Trujillo. The colonel introduced Marco and me to the padre and briefly explained that we were going on to Guevavi and Tumacácori to stop the Apache killings.

"Padre, I hope we don't need any more graves in your cemetery for us when we finish," Colonel Trujillo said in a joking manner.

"God forbid!" The padre responded, almost in a gasp.

"Padre, my great uncle, Armando Trujillo, was killed up here somewhere during the Revolution. We never knew where he was buried. Somebody in the family thought it was in the Spanish cemetery at Cocospera. He was with the Spanish cavalry."

"Spanish cemetery? I've been here 12 years. We have no Spanish cemetery. We are all God's children. If you are a member of the Church you can be buried here. No, no Spanish cemetery or graveyard.

"Are there any other graveyards either around here or down by the town? It would have to be old if the Spaniards were using it and I would like to tell my family something," the colonel responded.

"No. Not that I know of. Some Indian graves along the river and... wait a minute. Padre Sauceda, my predecessor, said something about a small military graveyard up the canyon behind the mission here, on Cerrito Llano. It's overgrown with brush. I was only there once. Maybe it's your graveyard!"

The friendly, padre offered to have his gardener's boy take us to the location, but Colonel Trujillo said not to bother. He said he knew where Cerrito Llano was, and if we had time we might ride by. Good!

After a few more minutes of visiting, the colonel gave the padre a bottle of his Toluca wine and we left. The colonel led us up the nearby Cocospera river, making it appear we had no immediate interest in the old graveyard. After we were out of sight of the old mission, we stopped.

"Gentlemen, I know where Cerrito Llano is. It's over this ridge in the canyon behind the mission," the colonel said.

"About 1500 meters?" I asked, guessing from information I remembered from the maps.

"Yes, that's about right. I remember it's out of sight of the mission and covered with brush. I've ridden through several times, but never realized there were graves there."

I felt relieved. What I had seen at the mission graveyard was not coming together with our maps and notes.

We made it to the top of the ridge separating us from Cerrito Llano in short order. The colonel pointed out a small, flat hill covered with brush on the edge of the canyon below, Cerrito Llano. We could see the mission from the top of the ridge, but it disappeared as we rode down toward the small flat-topped hill.

Once we were on Cerrito Llano, the colonel asked, "Gentlemen, if you were going to bury somebody here, where would you do it?"

"Where the ground is soft!" I responded immediately.

Marco nodded in agreement.

The brush was thick; we tied our horses and started poking around on foot. The hilltop was relatively flat, with some rock outcroppings near where we tied our horses, so we separated and started walking in the direction where the ground looked better.

After about five minutes, Marco called out. "Over here. I think I've found it!"

Colonel Trujillo and I crashed through the brush toward Marco from opposite directions.

Marco stood smiling amidst some thick catclaw bushes. His boot rested on a pile of volcanic-looking black rocks.

We excitedly started looking for more graves. First Colonel Trujillo found another pile of rocks, then I found two more. In a matter of several minutes we had found eight piles of rocks roughly aligned in an area of about 60 to 80 feet.

"This fits the description perfectly!" I said excitedly.

Both Vásquez and Trujillo were equally excited as we paced back and forth scanning the area.

"We had better not make too many tracks or tear down any brush until we are ready to retrieve the treasure," the colonel said wisely.

We agreed.

Our minds were leaping forward, anticipating the details of how we were going to recover the treasure we hoped was still buried in the graves hidden in the desert brush. Our hopes were high, because it was obvious that the graves had remained undisturbed for many years.

We also agreed we should come the same way, over the ridge from the Cocospera River, when we returned to recover it. We could bring in men and burros to the site without being seen. The colonel recommended we leave the site in as close to the original condition as possible and not remove the undergrowth to keep the discovery of the treasure site quiet as long as possible. Again, Marco and I agreed.

It was hard to ride away from Cerrito Llano, visualizing what may lie beneath the soil. But we did.

The next day, after a hard ride, we were in San Lázaro by mid-afternoon. There we saw some old Spanish hacienda buildings in ruins and the decaying structure of an old church. I asked the colonel about it as we rode in.

"Colonel, it seems like everything in this part of Mexico is old and in ruins. Why is that?"

"Well, Chu Chu, you're right. Between kicking the Spaniards out and the marauding Apaches, everything is going to hell," he responded.

Then he added, "Chu Chu–where did you get that nickname?"

I shook my head. The name had stuck.

"Oh, my folks called me that when I was a kid. My father had a steam engine at one of his mines and I liked the sound of it. So I would go around making a sound like the engine–chu, chu, chu."

The colonel laughed.

Wanting to get back to the point, I asked. "Colonel, I understand the marauding Apaches, but why did kicking out the Spaniards cause the buildings and churches to fall into ruins? Can't the Mexicans take care of them?"

"Chu Chu, when the Spaniards were thrown out, most of the Spanish Franciscan priests went with them. The Church owned a lot of land and got a good kickback from the King, a proportion of all the gold he took out of the country. In fact, the Church helped them get it. Anyway, with the money they received, they were able to keep the churches in Mexico in good repair. They even built new ones."

"So, since the Revolution, the churches have not been maintained?"

"Well, most of the Spanish priests were slowly replaced by Mexican priests, who had no money coming in to help them. They do the best they can and some of the churches are in pretty good repair, especially those closer to Mexico City. But most up here in Sonora will be gone in a hundred years or so. And the same goes for the old military presidios."

"Too bad," I responded.

We camped near the river, a little way from the ruins of a magnificent hacienda. Some fruit trees remained alive, but the roofs of the buildings had tumbled in and the structures could not be used.

Two of the colonel's other military detachments had arrived–Captain Fontes and his men from the presidio of Tucson and Lieutenant Muñoz with his men and Pima scouts from Tubac. The Indian scouts set up their own little camp out of sight from ours. Only Lieutenant Peralta and his Opata scouts had not yet arrived from Terrenate.

The colonel and Lieutenant Camacho immediately left to confer with his other officers, while Sergeant Campos set up camp. Marco and I found a comfortable location, unsaddled and ate as the soldiers went about their duties of settling in.

Sergeant Dominguez came over and said Colonel Trujillo wanted us over at the meeting with his officers. Marco and I immediately responded and went over to a courtyard of the abandoned hacienda.

The officers were sitting on logs and rocks around a small fire, with a steaming pot of coffee sitting on coals between some adobe bricks.

The colonel looked up as we walked over and said, "Captain, I want you to hear this and I want it to be in your report to Mexico City. Sit down and listen."

We sat and listened. The colonel's officers were giving him a report on the recent Apache attacks in this valley. He had them start over.

For the next half hour we heard reports on the most recent Apache raids in the Santa Maria Valley–from Tumacácori, Calabasas, Guevavi, down to Bacoancos and near to where we were camped at San Lázaro.

Within the last month 21 people had died–no not died, were murdered, tortured and, in some instances, butchered. Almost none of the Apache massacres were a simple or routine killing, if there was such a thing. No, they involved *cruel and barbaric acts* by a tribe of Indians which had risen to a level unseen anywhere else in the Americas. *They were unique.*

One story dealt with two white merchants traveling with their black slave to Hermosillo. The two white men were tortured and burned to death after their capture. The poor black man was tied to a cottonwood tree and butchered alive. Apparently the savages wanted to see the color of the meat under his hide.

Another incident concerned a Mexican farmer and his family near Rancho San Luis, a few kilometers north of where we were camped. The farmer had two young sons working with him in the fields. His pregnant wife, with another baby boy and young girl, were in their adobe hut. The savages first captured the pregnant women and her two children in the house. They tied her and proceeded to kill her little boy in front of her by first cutting off his ears and private parts. When he was dead, they cut the unborn baby out of the live woman's stomach and placed him on the hot stove. Needless to say, she died almost immediately.

The savages then killed one of the boys in the field, wounded the father and captured the other boy. They took the wounded father and son to the house so they could see what they had done with the mother and other boy. There, they killed the father and other boy and stacked the bodies in a bloody pile inside the house and attempted to burn it down. The little girl was never found.

I knew there were atrocities, but never imagined something so cruel. No wonder the Mexicans were terrorized by these savages.

There was a story for each of the 21 people killed, most containing an evil twist.

When the officers finished their reports, the colonel dismissed them. Then for a moment, he just looked at Captain Vásquez and me saying nothing. When he dismissed us, I went back to our campsite with a sick feeling in my stomach.

It was evening when Lieutenant Peralta and his men rode in and set up their camp. He immediately conferred with the colonel.

The weather was cold as hell, but there was excitement in the air. The word was out that Lieutenant Muñoz's Pima scouts had run into the Apaches east of Guevavi, but fell back, so as not to alarm them. The Apaches disappeared up into the Chihuahuitas. But Lieutenant Peralta's Opata scouts had gone into the mountains from the east, undetected, and had found the Apache camp! It was at one of the locations Colonel Trujillo had suspected. This meant the attack was on!

The evening was cold and the colonel directed few fires be lit–only in protected locations so they could not be seen from the mountains. Fires were to be out and covered by dawn to remove all smoke from the air.

After dark, the colonel came over to Marco's and my small fire.

"Quite a report, wasn't it?" the colonel said. "Tomorrow we start positioning ourselves for the attack."

Captain Vásquez pointed to a log where the colonel could sit. I leaned back and crossed my ankles.

Marco then asked, "Colonel, what is the plan?"

"Before dawn, Lieutenant Peralta will take his men and the Opata scouts and go up the river. They will set up a temporary camp on the east side of the mountains. They'll get as close to the Apache camp as they can without being detected. We will follow.

"Captain Fontes and Lieutenant Muñoz and their men will go down the river toward Guevavi, also before first light, so as not to kick up dust. We are lucky because of the recent rains. Dust should not be a big problem, but I have instructed all soldiers to spread out and walk their horses if the ground is dry."

"Guevavi?" I asked.

The Guevavi Mission was the mission from which the La Escondida treasure was measured on our maps.

"Yes, Guevavi. But they will turn and go up La Cañada de la Palomas toward the mountain from the west as far as their Pima scouts think they can get without being seen. They will camp there until dark. During the night, they will get into position to attack from the west side at first light," the colonel explained, rubbing his hands and holding them out to the fire.

Captain Vásquez spoke up. "I assume all of your men know where the Apache camp is, and where they are going to attack from?"

"Yes they do captain," the colonel answered, seeming a little perturbed by the question.

"So what happens next?" I asked.

"Depends where they camp. Each troop will ride after dark to their prearranged attack location. At first light, I will initiate the attack from the east. Then Fontes and Muñoz's men will attack from the west. Let's hope we are successful."

"Where are the Apaches camped?" Marco asked, trying to recover from his last question.

"In the La Escondida basin. It's on the western side of mountains. It makes sense. All of their attacks down into the valley have been on the western side of the mountain. From San Lázaro to Calabasas," the tired colonel responded.

La Escondida - that was where the second treasure was! We would be able to take a close look at that location too, assuming our attack was successful. I had to be careful what I said, since *Colonel Trujillo did not know about this site.*

"Colonel, what is La Escondida? Isn't it one of the locations where you thought the Indians might be?" I asked innocently.

"Yes it is. The Spaniards named it La Escondida because it is hidden away up in the Chihuahuitas. But during the dry time of the year, there is only one small spring–a bitter spring that has water."

Then he went on. "The reason I thought it might be one of the locations is because during the wet time of the year there is also plenty of grass for their horses and running water in the canyon bottoms. There should be water there now, enough for a good-sized bunch of Apaches and their horses. Also, the canyon closes to a narrow outlet that makes it easy to control their grazing horses."

Marco tried to pick up the slack, since he now realized what I was trying to do. "Colonel, you said the Spaniards named it. Did they camp there?"

"No. They didn't normally camp there. But it was on their trail–the shortest route between the Chihuahuita mountain mines and Magdalena. They used it when the Apaches weren't a threat. They could take a shortcut through the mountains on what they called *la pista de la peña* (the cliff trail)."

I thought that might explain why the Spaniards had chosen to hide the treasure there. The gold and silver had probably already been mined and smelted in those mountains when the Revolution broke out. Rather than risk losing it to the Mexicans at the mines or on the road south, the worried Spaniards gathered it up and hid it somewhere along *la pista de la peña,* the trail they used. Their maps clearly indicated that they intended to come back and get it someday. Now, hopefully, we would do it for them.

Trying to edge the topic of conversation away from La Escondida and the cliff trail, I asked, "Colonel, where do we go tomorrow?"

"Well, after Lieutenant Peralta leaves, we will follow in about an hour so we don't have too many soldiers traveling together. The dust, you know. We will meet him at Santa Maria. From there we will travel to the east side of the mountains, to where the Opata scouts think we can carefully approach the Apache camp after dark. The cold weather should help us."

The colonel sighed, excused himself and broke away, saying he would see us in the morning. He headed toward the ruins of the old hacienda where he and his officers were camped.

During the night the wind blew hard, kicking up dust and leaves. Then it started to rain. The rain turned to snow after about an hour. Nobody slept. It was a miserable night and most of the soldiers huddled around their small, sheltered fires till dawn. At dawn, they started to put their fires out, until the colonel belayed his order. He said the clouds and wet weather would minimize any worry of the Apaches seeing our smoke. Besides, it was cold!

Captain Fontes and his troops left a little late–about first light–and headed down the Río Santa Maria. Lieutenant Peralta and his men went earlier. The rest of us with Colonel Trujillo were so miserable and cold that we saddled up rather than wait any longer. We traveled eastward along the river, following Peralta's fresh tracks in the snow. We moved fast because the wet weather removed any concerns about dust.

Most of the men wore old *ponchos* (slickers) to protect them from the cold, wet weather. The ponchos covered them, their rifle and saddle and part of their horse. Marco and I had new ones. As the morning progressed, the snow came down harder and the ground turned white. The horses were not used to the snow and were skittish, shying at the unusual shapes and shadowy things along the trail.

Several of the soldiers cursed at their frightened animals, but I thought it was humorous. Maybe it was because my horse, although nervous, just plowed ahead without shying. One of the soldiers actually got dumped on his butt–which gave everyone else a big laugh. After the little show, the men's spirits picked up despite the cold.

This is where things got a bit strange. About mid-morning as we rode north along the river toward the town of Santa Maria, we saw a soldier coming toward us on horseback. It was one of Lieutenant Peralta's men.

Lieutenant Camacho and I rode with Colonel Trujillo and Captain Vásquez at the head of the column when the corporal approached us *fast.* Finally the corporal pulled up and spoke.

"Colonel, Lieutenant Peralta sent me back. He said to tell you that *your wife and son are at Santa Maria.*"

"My wife and son?!" The amazed colonel responded unbelievingly. "Is he sure? Are they all right?"

"Yes sir. That's why he sent me back–to make sure you came straight to Santa Maria."

The surprised colonel looked at Marco and me, saying nothing. Then he spurred his horse forward toward Santa Maria, moving at a slow lope. Marco and I gazed questioningly at each other also, hardly believing the report.

The colonel then stopped, obviously with something on his mind and waited for us to catch up. When we did, he spoke to Captain Vásquez. "Captain, take the troop and meet me in Santa Maria."

"Yes sir," the captain responded.

The colonel called out to Peralta's corporal, who was riding with the rest of the men. The corporal trotted his horse forward. The two men spoke for a few moments, then again the colonel headed toward the town of Santa Maria at a slow lope.

Captain Vásquez gave orders to Lieutenant Camacho to keep the troops moving at a fast trot. As we did, I rode with Marco. We said nothing, wondering what had transpired to bring the colonel's wife Zonia here with his son.

After another hour, we arrived in Santa Maria. It was midday, the snow had stopped falling and the clouds were breaking up, letting the sun start to shine. However, there were still several inches of melting snow in most places.

Lieutenant Peralta and Lieutenant Camacho made arrangement with the locals to feed their men. Also the saddle cinches were loosened and the horses were rested. But Trujillo was not there. Peralta said he was north of town at a little farm, visiting his wife and son.

About an hour later, Colonel Trujillo came riding his big bay back into town. With a solemn look on his face, he ordered his troops to be ready to ride in fifteen minutes. The men quickly finished their food and adjusted saddles. In short order we all had our feet in the stirrups and were moving north. The colonel rode ahead with Lieutenant Peralta and one of his Opata scouts.

We rode through several small farming communities coming up the beautiful grassy valley, then through the mining camp of San Antonio. We rested our horses while Colonel Trujillo and Lieutenant Peralta talked to the man in charge. Then we moved on.

Less than an hour later, we were up in the oaks and juniper trees on the eastern edges of the Chihuahuitas. The December shadows were getting longer. I figured we had, at the most, another two hours before it got dark. I wondered where we would stop and rest up before the night ride to get us in place for the dawn attack. The colonel stayed focused on the mission and didn't talk to us as we rode on.

It was after dark when we rode into another mining camp up in the mountains. We startled the miners and their families when their dogs started barking and they heard our horses coming through the trees.

Lieutenant Peralta called out into the darkness for them not to shoot, saying we were the Mexican military.

The colonel and Lieutenant Peralta talked to the *jefe* (boss). One of the soldiers told me the mine was called *El Patagonia*, like the region in South America. The colonel then gave orders for the men to dismount, unsaddle their horses, put them in the corrals and eat our trail food. And he gave the order–no fires. When he said this, I think everyone shivered at the thought. The ground was damp with patches of snow and it was cold!

After a short conversation, the colonel allowed the mine supervisor to have his men build a fire inside the open, adobe-walled area the miners used as protection against the Apaches. The soldiers not watching the horses crowded inside the small fortress to eat and get warm.

The colonel told his men we had three hours to rest before we saddled up and rode on to the attack site. The foreman invited the colonel, Marco and me into a small rock house containing a cot, table with a kerosene lamp and a warm stove with coffee. Lieutenant Pacheco stayed with his men. This looked and felt like heaven. The foreman left the three of us alone in the small house.

Without prompting, the colonel gave us an update.

"Zonia said little Chico tried to follow us the morning we left. He went up the Río Sonora and across the mountains on his little burro, Gruillo. Farmers along the way gave him food and told him how to get to Santa Maria."

He continued, telling the story from the beginning.

"Zonia said Antonio Leon, the man that runs my farm, went down to Hermosillo mid-morning on Tuesday and told her that Chico had not come back from feeding the horses at the garrison. Antonio said he talked to another farmer who saw Chico riding his burro up the river, away from our farm, in the direction we had gone. He took some jerky, tortillas and *panocha* (brown sugar cubes), just like the big soldiers."

Eyes cast down, Trujillo continued with his story.

"As soon as Zonia heard the news, she had Antonio hitch up our old carriage and, together they went looking for Chico. They almost caught up to him the very first day, but they broke a wheel on the carriage near Sinoquipe. It was nighttime and the people there said they had seen Chico go through only about an hour before, still headed up the river. He said he was going to help his father, a soldier, fight the Apaches."

The tired colonel coughed to clear the emotion from of his throat, then continued, "A farm family in Sinoquipe gave Chico some food and his burro some hay, then Chico left without resting.

"A couple of people managed to talk Zonia and Antonio into staying and spending the cold night. They had no choice, since they needed the wheel of the carriage fixed. These same people promised to have the wheel repaired by the time they were ready to leave the next morning. And they charged them nothing. So they spent the night in Sinoquipe.

"For the next two days, they followed Chico, finally catching up with him in Santa Maria. Zonia said Chico was waiting for me there."

Marco and I were silent as we drank our hot coffee and digested the unbelievable story.

Finally I said, "Colonel, that was amazing. Is he all right? And is Señora Trujillo all right?"

"Yes, *gracias a Dios* (Thank God). They both were tired, but all right."

"When did they get to Santa Maria?" Marco asked.

"Chico got there about midday yesterday. Zonia and Antonio finally got there yesterday evening."

"They are staying at a farm north of town?" I asked.

"Yes," the colonel said hesitantly.

"She's an Opata Indian, so the only place they could find for her was with the farmer's family north of town. She left so fast she didn't bring any money. Antonio is staying with friends in Santa Maria until we return."

"I gave her a little money and told her and Antonio to get some rest and wait at the farmer's place for me to get back. I would take them home."

What a story. A little, simple-minded 13-year-old boy on his gray burro, Gruillo, had traveled almost continuously for over three days. And he got to Santa Maria a day ahead of us–unbelievable! Trujillo said he had to talk hard to have little Chico stay at the farm with Zonia. He finally agreed when the colonel told Chico he needed him to *protect* Zonia until he got back.

About half of the soldiers got a little sleep curled up in some dry sheds by the fire. The three Opatas went off by themselves. The poor colonel seemed stressed. He laid down on the cot in the little rock house, where he finally slept for over an hour, snoring loudly. Marco and I walked around outside, checking things. A lot of soldiers were coughing from the cold. We then went back to the rock house and drank coffee and talked until it was time to go. The colonel shared some coffee with us, then left to tend to his duties.

We all were saddled and on our way by 11:30 at night, according to Marco's watch, which I did not totally trust. But I didn't argue with him.

Two of the Opata scouts led the way with Lieutenant Peralta and one of his sergeants. The cold night and tension kept everyone wide awake and quiet, except for occasional, muffled coughs.

A partial moon had risen when we left the Patagonia Mining camp. It gave us enough light to easily make our way through the night, following the scouts. Fluffy clouds occasionally blocked out the moon, but quickly passed.

We came to a mesa high in the mountains. One of the soldiers called it *La Mesa de Los Guajolotes* (Turkey Flat). We rode to the edge of the mesa on the old Spanish trail and stopped where the trail dropped down into the La Escondida basin. The colonel quietly told us to dismount, then he conferred with Lieutenant Peralta and two of his Opata scouts.

We had a total of 44 men with Colonel Trujillo and Lieutenant Peralta's troops. We made quite a bit of noise even as we tried to travel quietly through night. Sparks could occasionally be seen in the darkness coming from the shod horse's hooves as they struck rocks along the trail.

The colonel waived Marco and me over to their little huddle. "Captain Vásquez, the scouts are afraid to go any further with this large group of men. Several are coughing. They suggest we take 10 to 12 well-armed men down the trail to the attack point and have the rest follow. The second group can wait behind until the attack. One of Peralta's scouts can keep our groups spaced.

"Captain, I want you and Chu Chu to go with us in the first group. You two have the repeating weapons," the colonel ordered.

"Yes sir," the captain responded.

I said nothing, but mentally agreed to go.

"Chu Chu, how about you?"

"Yes sir,Colonel." It almost sounded like I had a choice, but I really didn't.

The colonel and Lieutenant Peralta quietly picked out seven additional men, so we had a 12-man detail for the advanced attack party. The colonel directed Lieutenant Pacheco to wait for ten minutes after they stopped hearing us ride down into the La Escondida basin before they followed us.

It was bitter cold with a touch of a breeze as we followed Peralta and his two scouts down the old trail into the deep basin. Finally, at the bottom, we rode along a wide canyon for another few minutes, then the head scout in front signaled for us to stop. The scouts came back and the head scout suggested half the men dismount and wait while the remainder of us go forward and spy on the Apache camp. He said we were within two kilometers of the Apache camp.

On our ride down the mountain trail into La Escondida the moon peeked out from the clouds, and I could see the edge of a dominant cliff formation to our right! I pointed it out to Marco. We were going along *la pista de la peña* (the cliff trail). He had seen it too and nodded. We were near the site of the *second Spanish treasure!*

During the next few minutes, things seemed to get a little screwed up. We waited on a rise overlooking the Apache camp. The cold December night was getting lighter as dawn approached. There were patches of unmelted snow about from the recent storm. Then we heard a dog start to bark in the direction of the Apache camp. That was bad.

The dawn light brightened to the point where we could see the Apache camp on the edge of the canyon bottom about 300 meters downstream from us. Several smoldering fires glowed and about eight horses grazed near the camp, but two were close to us.

One of their horses looked up in our direction and whinnied. The colonel's horse started to respond, but he slapped him on the nose and stopped him.

The colonel was about to give the orders to start the attack when we heard shots from down the canyon beyond the Apache camp. It was Captain Fontes' men! Something had happened!

We jumped on our horses with our firearms ready, then the colonel ordered us to attack. The third Opata scout behind us saw what was happening and ran back to tell the men waiting behind.

Lieutenant Camacho was directed to immediately follow us into the attack when he heard shots. Colonel Trujillo led our group toward the Apache camp at a fast gallop, firing a shot as we advanced. Then we heard more shots in the distance, down the canyon in front of us, as we galloped our horses toward the Apache camp. A skinny dog came out, barking at us. Several Apaches bucks ran from the camp up a nearby ravine. They were almost naked.

We were immediately in the middle of the empty camp. Two cooking fires were burning brightly beneath wooden tripods holding metal kettles. The yappy little dog bravely took lunges at our horses until a soldier dismounted and hit him with a rock. Four of our soldiers rode up the ravine where the three Apaches we saw running had gone. Shortly, a single shot came from that direction.

Lieutenant Pacheco came galloping into the empty camp with the rest of our troops. They were all holding their rifles and ready for action. The colonel shouted for us all to fan out and search for Apaches. We did.

Marco and I loped our horses down the canyon toward the first shots we had heard earlier. Around a bend, we saw one of Captain Fontes' men at the top of a small hill. He was dismounted holding his rifle and his horse's reins. We rode over to him.

The private told us they were waiting for the colonel's orders to attack when they heard a dog bark. Almost immediately, three bunches of Apaches came running down the canyon towards them, apparently trying to escape from Colonel Trujillo's men.

The private said Captain Fontes ordered his men to shoot, and at least a dozen shots were fired. One Apache buck was killed and one wounded, but he ran off, limping.

None of Fontes' men were hit by arrows.

Captain Vásquez quickly asked the private how many Apaches he saw. He said there were three bunches running and spreading out as they came. The bigger group he guessed to be about 10 or 12 bucks. The two smaller groups he guessed to each contain about six to eight.

He said that Fontes and his men went after them, but the Indians climbed the steep sides of the canyon where it was impossible for horses to follow. He said Fontes told him to wait there for Colonel Trujillo's men and to tell them what had happened and where they had gone.

The private was sure except for the dead one, the Apaches had escaped. Then we heard two more shots down the canyon. Captain Vásquez told the private to remain and tell Trujillo's men what had occurred. We left him and loped our horses on down the trail along the steep side of the canyon toward the last two shots coming from where

Fontes and his men had gone.

The canyon quickly narrowed and became deep as we followed the old trail, climbing out along the northern side. Around the next corner, we saw three soldiers holding about ten saddled horses. Several other soldiers were on foot, holding their rifles and looking across the steep canyon to the other side. We quickly rode to the soldiers holding the horses. We could see what was happening.

Climbing out of the canyon toward the top of the opposite side, we saw about eight Apaches. Several of Fontes' men were trying to follow them on foot, but were far behind. The other soldiers remained on our side of the canyon, so they could tell the men following the Apaches what direction to go. It was a hopeless cause.

Captain Fontes stood below us on a canyon-edge vantage point with his rifle. Marco and I dismounted and removed our rifles from our saddles, then left our horses with the three soldiers. We trotted toward the place where the captain knelt reloading his muzzleloader rifle. As we got to the red-faced captain, he took another frustration shot at the Apaches far across the canyon. The round hit at least 60 feet below the laughing savages.

The Apache bucks, now shouting, laughing and waving taunts at us, stood close to the top of the high ridge opposite us. Then we saw another Apache at the very top of the ridge, on a horse. How he got up there so fast with his animal was a mystery. He too waved taunts at us.

I was dying to use my Sharps 50. Captain Vásquez took a shot with his muzzleloader with about the same effect as Fontes. Captain Fontes again started loading his rifle.

"Do you want me to scare them?" I asked.

"Scare them, hell. *Kill them!*" shouted the frustrated Fontes.

I took my Sharps 50 and rested it on a rock outcropping, adjusted the sights and fired. The loud report echoed through the canyon, dwarfing the muzzleloader's sound. About a second later, the horse dropped out from under the surprised Indian at the top of the ridge. He jumped to the side so as not to have his horse fall on him. All the taunting stopped and the rest of the bucks got the hell out of there. It was the last shot of the engagement.

"*Qué bárbaro* (good grief), *gringo!* What in the hell type of cannon are you shooting there? That had to be almost 500 meters!" laughed the frustrated but amazed Captain Fontes.

"I'm not a gringo," I replied quietly, without responding further.

Both Fontes and Marco were impressed with the lucky shot. I tried to act like it was routine, but I was surprised myself.

Back at the sorry Apache camp, the small dog lay under some bushes, watching us. Colonel Trujillo and Lieutenant Peralta walked around, looking at the Spartan remains of stuff strewn around the camp. There was a large metal pot of beans cooking on one of the fires and some venison cooking in another pot. Trujillo's soldiers gathered the skinny, abandoned Apache horses one by one, tying them to trees at the edge of the camp. Several other soldiers were busy reloading their rifles.

Four soldiers came out of the ravine where we had seen the first Apaches trying to escape earlier. They led two women by ropes tied to their hands. One of the women was a *güera* (woman of light complexion) and had brown hair.

One of the soldiers leading the women told Trujillo that they shot an old man who tried to fight them. Another soldier in their group smiled and pointed to an arrow stuck in his saddlebag near his butt. He said the old warrior had shot at him, but thank God, had missed! This got a good laugh out of the rest of the tense but now relieved soldiers.

Trujillo told Captain Fontes to post four guards and have the remaining men eat something and rest. It was good to let emotions settle a bit and take stock of our success. However, it was not much of a success–two dead Apaches, one wounded buck who escaped, a dead horse and finally two women and a dog captured. But we did get 13 skinny horses, most with Mexican brands and two with U.S. branded on them, American cavalry horses.

The men searched through the meager Apache camp and found several broken muzzleloader rifles, a working flintlock pistol, some colorful children's dresses and some supplies, including blankets, beans, mesquite flour in an *olla* (bowl) and some venison. The colonel gave the flintlock pistol to Lieutenant Peralta. Half the horses went to Lieutenant Peralta and the rest he gave to Fontes and Muñoz to take as replacement military mounts. The useable food and the other items, the colonel let the officers divide amongst themselves and their men. Obviously, Lieutenant Peralta was in good standing with the colonel.

I quietly pulled Marco aside. "Marco, we need to spend some time around here. Those are the cliffs right in front of us where the Spanish hid their treasure. They are huge. They can be seen for miles."

"What do you suggest?" Marco asked.

"Well, the colonel is going to be anxious to get his wife and boy back home. I suggest we tell him we want to stay here with Fontes and Muñoz to learn more about this part of the country, then we'll go back to Hermosillo on our own."

"That sounds a little suspicious. Can't we think up something a little better?" Marco responded thoughtfully, then continued. "I think the colonel wants the scouts to track the Apaches. He wants to kill a few more."

"Well, let's see what he decides. At any rate, we need to separate from his group, here if possible," I responded.

The men were now laughing and building up some large fires a little below the dirty Apache camp to warm themselves. The sun was coming up over the mountain, and it looked like it was going to be a good day.

One of the soldiers handed Sergeant Campos a string with two freshly cut Apache ears on it. The same slippery looking soldier who they called *Cachorra* (lizard) laughed and pointed at my notched ear and said something like he thought they had my white ear on one of their strings back home. That got a roaring laugh from the rest of the men, including Colonel Trujillo.

I smiled and said that whoever had it–that nutless bastard didn't have much to brag about. That got a few chuckles, but mainly surprised looks from several of the men. I didn't give a damn. I just wanted to be taken off the plate of jokes the men intended to dish out. It cooled things a bit and seemed to work.

The colonel told his men they had two hours to finish eating and rest before they would be on their way. He then got his officers together and started to lay out a revised strategy while they drank coffee. Marco and I listened.

Sure enough, the colonel wanted the Opata and Pima scouts to immediately start tracking the Apaches. Lieutenant Peralta volunteered his best tracker to start from the top of the ridge where we saw the Apaches cross over and where I had killed the horse.

Several officers were concerned the Apaches would break up into smaller groups now that they were mostly on foot. This would make them harder to follow. Peralta suggested that the Apaches would immediately start marauding and looting farms and ranches along the river to get fresh mounts. They all agreed.

So the following strategy was worked out: We would again break up into our two groups and go back in the directions we came, to the Santa Maria River Valley. There, each military group would start patrolling and be ready for another encounter with the Apaches. Lieutenant Muñoz would put his best Pima tracker with Lieutenant Peralta's best Opata tracker, and together they would follow the Apaches. The trackers would follow the Apache bucks wherever they went, probably down towards the Santa Maria River Valley. The other scouts would keep the trackers in touch with the soldiers, in case another attack against the Apaches could be put together.

Captain Fontes and Lieutenant Muñoz would patrol down the river with their men in the direction of the other recent attacks. Lieutenant Peralta and Lieutenant Pacheco and their men would work up river. If nothing materialized, the officers with their two separate troops would meet at San Lázaro in three days. There they would share information and prepare a new strategy–if they had a chance of killing more Apaches–or return to their home garrisons.

Finally, the colonel stated he would take four of his men and return to Hermosillo with his wife and boy.

It sounded like a plan, but one I thought had a low chance of success. I agreed with Lieutenant Peralta. The most likely situation was that the Apaches would go directly to the river valley and start pillaging and stealing to get new mounts, then return home to their mountains to the east. I was partly right.

Then came the surprise. As the meeting of the officers broke up, Colonel Trujillo told Sergeant Dominguez to take some food and water to the captive women and tend to their needs. Most of the soldiers had eaten and were trying to keep warm or sleep in the sunlight near the fires. The two tied women were sitting on dirty blankets at the edge of the Apache camp.

Interested, I watched to see how Dominguez was going to handle the situation. He glanced my way, suggesting perhaps I should help, so I did.

Dominguez and I took some food and a can of water the Apaches were using at their camp to the unhappy women glaring at us. The dark Indian woman took a swig out of the can and set it down. The other woman didn't want anything.

Then it happened. The dark Apache woman suddenly stood up and made a fuss, as if she wanted to be untied. She spoke a few words of Spanish, but not enough for us to understand what she wanted.

I suggested to Dominguez that perhaps she wanted to relieve herself. She nodded. Dominguez untied her hands but, put the rope around her neck so she wouldn't try and run off. The *güera* sat watching us, anger in her eyes.

Now what? I thought. Immediately the dark Apache woman took hold of the rope around her neck and began firmly pulling the big sergeant toward the edge of the Apache camp. Those soldiers still awake nearby were watching us and smiling. The colonel was also watching.

At first the sergeant resisted, but when she acted like she wasn't trying to escape, he relaxed, and we followed her. This should be interesting, I thought. She led us to the outside of the Apache camp, out of view of the soldiers, then quickly squatted and relieved herself without removing any clothes. She was wearing some beads, an old coat, and a dirty dress, probably picked up during one of their raids. Dominguez and I looked at each other, embarrassed.

The woman stood up and led us by the rope to the other side of the Apache camp, where some wood was stacked, along with what looked like some dirty sacks with a filthy blanket thrown onto it. She stopped and picked up the dirty blanket.

To our amazement, we saw some dark blinking eyes looking back at us. *There was a sleepy little Mexican girl bound and gagged under the blanket.*

The Apache woman hugged the little girl, trying to warm her. I untied the knotted cloth from around the little girl's head and over her mouth. I also untied the single leather strap binding her hands and feet. The little girl had a snotty nose and was shivering terribly.

Immediately, Dominguez called the colonel.

I pulled out my handkerchief and tried to wipe the little girl's nose, but the Apache lady jerked it away from me in a scolding fashion, then did a much better job of it than I had. I had to smile at her actions.

I asked the shivering, scared child her name. I was expecting a Maria, or Rosa, but instead she answered in a tiny feminine voice. Jasmine. What a beautiful name, I told her, and she smiled. That was all the information I was able to get from her before the colonel and about half of the men came walking up to inspect our find.

The little girl wore a torn little, green dress and had no shoes. I wondered if she was the missing little girl from the San Luis ranch and farms. In addition to the 31 people killed in the Apache raids, four were missing–two little girls, a young boy and a teenage girl. I wondered if any of them could also be around here. But they weren't.

The incident pretty much disrupted the tranquility of the early siesta for the soldiers. They again carefully inspected everything in the Indian camp. Finding nothing, they started saddling their horses and preparing to leave. Now was the time for us to act.

Marco told the colonel that he and I wanted to travel with Captain Fontes and Lieutenant Muñoz and help out however we could. We would return to Hermosillo with Lieutenant Camacho after we met in San Lázaro. The colonel agreed.

The colonel first planned to have Captain Fontes take the captive women to the convent in Tucson to have them as far away as possible from the Apache's eastern mountain home ground. But after Jasmine was found, he changed his mind. He said he would take them to Santa Maria and decide there what to do.

The orders were good news to me. I did not want to be a party to killing Indian women! I also thought the colonel's wife, Zonia, might have something to do with his decision, her being a pure Opata Indian.

About mid-morning the colonel, Lieutenant Camacho and Lieutenant Peralta took their men and headed back through the mountains toward the Patagonia Mining Camp and on to Santa Maria, where Zonia and Chico were waiting. That was good, because it gave Marco and me a little more breathing room to snoop around the La Escondida basin and cliffs.

Captain Fontes and Lieutenant Muñoz and their men lounged around our campsite fires awhile longer and talked. The tracking scouts had already been dispatched.

The pressure was off, even though the attack had been mostly a failure, except for Jasmine. The colonel was gone and the Apaches were on the run. The soldiers were relaxed and joking. They were going to be riding back down the steep trail out of the La Escondida basin towards the Santa Maria river valley shortly.

Killing time while Marco was talking to Captain Fontes, I walked around the empty Apache camp. The little dog still lay under the same bush, watching me. The Apache campfires were out underneath the kettles of uneaten smelly beans and venison. I took both kettles and set them on the ground near the little dog, who seemed hungry. I dumped some of the beans and meat on the ground to get his attention. When I walked away, he came out from under the bush and started eating. I thought I had made a friend.

Marco and I needed to separate ourselves from the troops so we could search for the treasure. We had three days to do it before we needed to be at San Lázaro for the trip back to Hermosillo.

What the hell excuse could we give? And it might be dangerous–just two of us riding through the mountains alone. Also, whatever we did would get back to Colonel Trujillo, so it had better make sense.

We decided to tell Captain Fontes we were going back to the Patagonia Mining Camp to get additional information for Mexico City on mining operations here in the Chihuahuitas and this part of Sonora. Marco explained that we would be spending the night there. Additionally, we might take a look at other nearby mines to document their operations. We would meet them at San Lázaro in three days–on Friday afternoon, December 17th. Captain Vásquez made it sound pretty good. At least I would have bought it, if I didn't know better.

Captain Fontes and Lieutenant Muñoz looked at us like we were crazy.

Fontes asked, "You realize the Apaches may still be around, don't you?"

"Yes,Captain, we realize it. We are well-armed and should be spending most of our time in the mining camps. Hopefully the Apaches have gone back to the Chiricahuas after our raid today," Marco responded.

Fontes shook his head and muttered something about not being responsible for our *hides*. We smiled and agreed.

About mid-day Captain Fontes and Lieutenant Muñoz and their men rode away, heading down the steep ancient canyon trail toward the Guevavi and Tumacácori Missions. We were now alone and felt a bit naked without the protection of twenty to forty soldiers around. Now we needed to find the treasure.

After they left, we spent a few minutes reviewing the maps.

I joked and rambled on while looking at the maps. "Let's see here, Marco, a pile of rocks at the top of the cliffs marked the location *below* where the treasure was hidden. But it doesn't say if this *below* is in the cliffs or buried in the ground. I guess it could even be on the backside of the mountain away from the cliffs. Seventeen burro loads, 11 of gold in cast rods, gold dust and nuggets. Also six loads of silver in cast ingots! Could it still be here? With all the Indian problems, it should be. Nobody has said anything about finding it."

"Chu Chu, how much … what do you think it's worth?" Marco asked, dreaming a bit.

Not answering directly, I responded, "You know this one should be ours. If we find the one at Cocospera for your uncle and give some to Trujillo, we should leave this one for us. Nobody else knows about it."

Marco asked, "How about the one at Tubutama? Is that one all for my *Tío* (Uncle)? Or does the colonel get a third of that one too? Or should we keep it for ourselves?"

The possibilities gave me goose bumps. Imagine, going back to Georgia and buying a plantation next to the Kerns! That would get quite a reaction from Melanie's mother.

I think Marco's mind was off on a similar voyage. This was fun! And more than that, we could make it happen. It was within our control.

Finally Marco came down to earth. "Chu Chu, we had better get our heads on straight. The Apaches could come along and cut off our balls and feed them and our carcasses to the buzzards. Let's find the treasure first, and then we can worry about how we are going to spend it."

Marco's harsh words made me momentarily angry, since it popped my bubble. But then I laughed. Yes indeed, this could be intoxicating.

"Yes, let's find it before the Apaches find us," I agreed, trying to focus again.

The Spanish maps and notes described a person standing near the treasure as being able to see the Chi Chi Mountains to the north and the Guachucas to the east. I thought we had better get up to the top of the cliff mountain, find the pile of rocks and see if we could see those mountains.

We trotted our rested horses up toward the northern side of the mountain that contained the steep cliffs. There were no trails, and the slope got extremely steep and rugged. We cut back and forth a number of times trying to pick a path less difficult for the horses. Our mounts became winded, so we stopped and gave them air. Finally, near the top of the mountain we dismounted and led our horses for the last several hundred feet to the top edge of the cliffs. It was a much harder climb than we had anticipated. I noticed my little friend, the Apache dog, was still following us.

At the top we tied our sweaty horses to a manzanita bush, then hiked along the narrow crest of the cliffs. It looked like several million years ago an earthquake had pushed the cliffs several hundred feet straight out of the mountains and here they had stood ever since, rugged and dangerous.

About 200 feet from where we tied our horses, I spied a neat pile of red colored rocks on the crest of the mountain above the steep cliffs.

"Here it is! That was easy, almost like Cocospera," I shouted back to Marco, who was behind me.

"Yes, I hear you. I think every Apache in Chihuahuitas heard you too," he joked.

We looked around and could see a mountain range to the north and one to the east. They were both there, just as described in our maps and notes!

Then Marco, looking over my shoulder, said, "What's that?"

I turned and about a hundred feet behind me on the crest of the mountain was another neat pile of red rocks.

"What the hell does that mean?" I mumbled to myself.

We walked over and inspected them. The second stack of rocks was near a steeper part of the huge cliffs below.

The afternoon sun was lowering in the sky and a stiff, cold wind was blowing over the face of the cliffs. We decided we needed more time to investigate these mysterious cliffs. We agreed to head back to the Patagonia Mining Camp for the night and come back the next day.

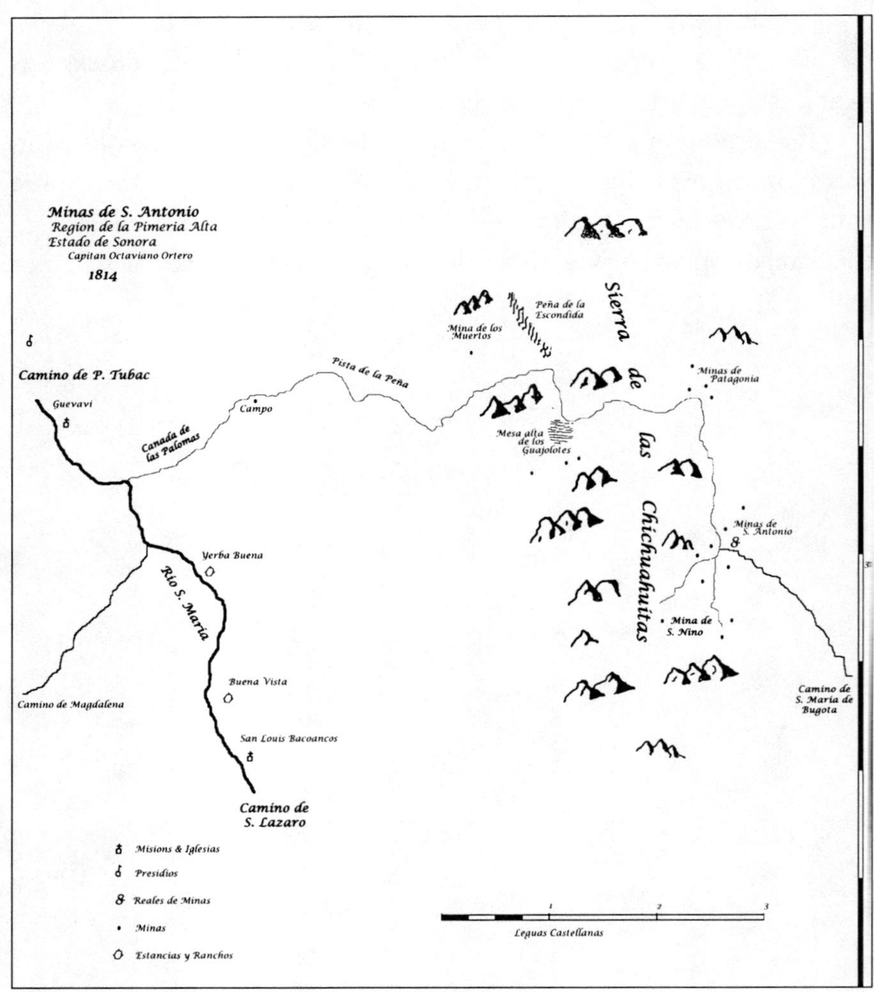

Figure 5 Spanish Map of La Escondida

Chapter 19

And then the Dog Barked

We untied our horses from the manzanita bush and led them along the narrow crest of the mountain cliffs to select a shorter way toward the Patagonia Mine camp. It was getting late in the day and we wanted to get to the camp before dark. Our horses were tired and so were we. The wind wasn't so bad once we got off the high cliffs, but it was still cold as we moved down the mountainous trail. Some decent food and rest sounded good.

The little Apache dog cautiously followed us at a safe distance. Marco tried to scare him off, but I laughed and said to leave him alone, he wasn't hurting us. Marco mumbled as he led the way along the old trail.

In an hour, we were well along our way back to the mining camp. We could see the colonel's troop horse tracks on the damp ground in front of us.

A tired Marco asked, "Chu Chu, what are we going to need when we come back tomorrow to find the treasure? Will we need ropes?"

"Yes. Definitely some ropes. But I'm still stumped about where they hid 17 burro-loads of gold and silver. They had to do it fast and stay out of sight. Coming up from the bottom of those cliffs–it's a hard, open climb. Maybe there's a cave in the cliff. But we…."

And then the dog barked!

Marco and I jerked our trotting horses to a stop, then grabbed for our pistols.

There was a loud blood curdling scream; I heard and *felt* an arrow whistle as it passed my head. *We were under attack!* Our horses shied and I damned near fell off, trying to hold my two pistols ready for action and steady my nervous animal.

From behind a tree to my left, an Apache buck came at me, screaming, with a large steel knife raised to strike. He was only about 10 feet away. I fired and hit him with my first shot, then almost fell as I jumped down from my rearing horse. Three more painted Apaches rushed me, one grabbing for my loose horse. I fired again, this time missing. When my second shot missed, the bucks gave me a leering look that said–*now we've got you–you bastard!* Then they came in for the kill. Marco was also under attack and off his horse. He had fired once.

Trying to control my rattled nerves, *I carefully placed my next shots.* The surprised bucks fell, two with mortal wounds in the middle of their bodies and the third with a serious hit to his groin. Four bucks were on the ground, one trying to crawl away.

Now on foot, Marco was in trouble in front of me. A bleeding Apache buck held the reins to his horse while two others were trying to corner my friend for the kill. He fired again, this time hitting one of his tormentors in the belly. The other buck held up for a second, surprised at the *second* shot from Marco's gun. I shot him immediately in the side. The remaining bleeding Apache dropped the reins to Marco's horse and started to run. Marco shot him in the back, and he too fell.

When the white smoke cleared from our firestorm of shooting, we had seven Apache bucks lay bleeding on the ground. Four were dead and two were dying. However, the one I shot in the groin was trying to crawl away. Frightened and angry, Marco ran over to the buck and shot him in the back of the head. It exploded, splattering blood and brains all over Marco. He puked.

Our horses had run off during the wild fracas. We stood with unsteady legs, gasping for air as we tried to recover our wits. After a few seconds, I took off running, hoping to find our horses which had disappeared down the trail toward the mining camp. I finally managed to catch Marco's horse after following him several hundred yards. I jumped on the skittish animal and caught up with my horse almost a mile further down the trail where he was trotting toward the camp with broken reins dragging.

I slipped a rope on my horse and led him back to where Marco was leaning on a tree near the dead Apaches. He had wiped some of the blood and brains off himself.

I said nothing as I handed him the reins to his horse and started to repair my own horse's broken reins. The whole event left a sick feeling deep in my stomach.

"What shall we do with them?" I asked.

"Nothing. Let the bastards rot!" Marco replied.

Then Marco pointed to my face. I was bleeding. The damned arrow had grazed my cheek. He had a torn jacket sleeve and was bleeding from where an Apache had tried to stab him in the left arm. Amazingly, neither of us was seriously wounded.

I started to get on my horse then remembered something. I returned and inspected each of the filthy-smelling dead bucks and removed some trophies. Maybe I would start my own collection for my future office, as the colonel had.

Marco watched me, then shook his head and cursed. He took his knife and cut off a large part of the ear from each of the bucks, placing them in a bloody cloth and tucking it in his saddlebag. He too had his trophies.

I got on my horse and saw the little dog standing by a tree looking at us and the dead Apache warriors. He seemed to be trying to decide if he had made the right choice.

Immediately, I jumped down from my horse, opened my saddlebag and took out three pieces of jerky. Walking over to the shy Apache dog, I threw him the jerky–a piece at a time. The little dog wagged his tail and smiled at me as he gobbled it down. Afterwards, he looked at me with increased confidence, as though he had made the right choice.

We loped our horses down the trail to the mining camp and got there after dark. Again, the miners were worried about our arrival until Marco identified us. The manager made us feel welcome and said that

Trujillo and Pacheco had passed through in the middle of the afternoon on their way to Santa Maria.

When the miners learned of our episode with the Apaches, we were heroes, especially after Marco showed them the ears. After we did our best to clean up, they fed us well and gave us the same little rock house where we had rested the night before.

After visiting all evening, Marco and I lay quietly, trying to relax on cots in the darkness of the little house. The fire in the stove was flickering as we mentally recounted our day's experiences.

Finally, Marco said, "Chu Chu, you know something?"

"What?"

"If it hadn't been for that little dog you made friends with tonight we would be laying dead up there along the trail instead of those Apaches."

I said nothing for a few moments, then answered. "Yes, I know."

Saying nothing, we both got up, gathering some excellent *carne asada* we had left from supper. The dog was resting near the horses in the corral, trying to sleep. He saw me and hurried over. I was now able to pet the skinny little animal on the head as he ate and wagged his tail.

Marco and I slept much better after we fed little *Bravo* (brave one), our new watchdog.

Chapter 20

The La Escondida Treasure Mystery

For the first part of the night after the Apaches attacked us, I slept well, but after midnight I found myself wide awake. Perhaps it was because our predawn military schedules and rides were starting to become more habitual. But no, that wasn't the reason. Instead, it was because of the hidden treasure in the La Escondida basin. It looked like the treasure was really lost.

Like Cocospera, something was wrong here also–or missing.

I got up, lit the lamp and made a fire in the stove. Thinking about the information on our maps, I made some coffee. Marco continued to snore.

Pulling out the maps from my saddlebag, I tried to make sense of them. On the maps for the other two locations, the Spaniards had given detailed descriptions. Although somewhat crude, the maps did show where the loads of treasure were buried. On the other two maps there was one point of consistency–both of the other treasures were buried.

It was as though this map lacked a piece of information. To go from the rock pile at the top crest above the cliffs, an additional piece of information was needed. Like the treasure was buried 200 meters from the bottom of the cliffs, or there was a cave or tunnel in the cliffs where the treasure was hidden, or it was buried 50 meters down the back side of the mountain away from the cliffs. Something. But the information wasn't there.

Another point of inconsistency was our maps and notes only indicated that there was a single pile of rocks at the top of the cliff mountain. In fact, there were two. Did they move the treasure? Did the two piles of rocks give a distance or a bearing sighting to where the treasure was hidden?

In the 35 years or so since the treasure was hidden and the maps made, had a piece of paper been lost or destroyed? Considering the Mexican Revolution and the number of hands the secret maps had passed through before General Santa Ana got his paws on them, the possibility of something being lost or accidentally destroyed was not unlikely.

Now came the big question–could we still find the treasure? And could we discover it before we had to meet Lieutenant Pacheco in San Lázaro? We only had that day and the next to find it before we needed to get back to San Lázaro.

By the time Marco woke up, I had reached two conclusions. First, the treasure was still up there somewhere. Otherwise we would have heard about someone finding it. That sort of a discovery was too big; people couldn't keep their mouths shut.

My second conclusion was that we were missing the final and most critical piece of information about where the Spaniards had hidden it.

After Marco had his second cup of coffee and was properly awake, I described our problem.

"Chu Chu, do you think we can find it?"

"Hell, Marco, we have to! We didn't come all the way from Mexico City and get this close to go back empty-handed. We've got to find it! It's our retirement! Without it, we can't go down to Cuba and visit your uncle!"

Marco almost choked on his coffee, laughing.

"So what are our options? How do we go about finding it?" he asked.

I didn't answer immediately, twirling my empty coffee cup from one finger.

"Marco," I said at last, "we need to look at this from several angles. You are a military man. If you were the Spanish officer instructed to hide it so your bosses or you could come back and recover it in five or ten years, where would you put it? Put yourself in his mind and come up with the answer."

"So, what's another angle?"

"Immediate action, gut instinct–get ropes, equipment–a pick and shovel, and go look for it."

Marco grinned. "That sounds more practical. But, don't you think it's going to look a little strange for us, a gringo and a military man from Mexico City, borrowing ropes and a pick and shovel from our friends here at the camp?"

"I'm not a gringo."

Marco's smile faded slightly, "Oh, sorry about that, Chu Chu. But it's still a little bit strange, no?"

"Sure it is. But you can tell them that I am a geologist and mining engineer. I'm looking for new mining locations for the British. And that's true, you know. That's why you need the equipment, because of the crazy Scotsman."

Eating breakfast at the mining kitchen, we visited with our hosts and asked if we could operate out of their location for several days. Marco explained what we were doing–or at least our official story. They agreed and even offered us fresh mounts to let our horses rest. We gladly accepted. They even lent us four 60-foot *reata* (braided rawhide) ropes, and a pick and a shovel, without asking any questions.

Before saddling up and while having our last cup of coffee, I turned to Marco.

"Say, amigo, what are the chances some of those Apaches are still up there? I assume the ones we killed yesterday were part of the same bunch we jumped down in the basin in the morning."

"Well, I guess it's possible. But Peralta thought they were going to split up and head down to the ranches and farms by the river to steal more horses. Apparently our bunch just hadn't gotten there yet."

"Too bad the trackers didn't follow those bastards, the ones who almost killed us," I commented.

"I hope you are going to bring your dog," Marco said, smiling once more.

"Oh, *Traitor*? Sure, we can't go without him. He's our insurance policy."

"Traitor? Why Traitor? I thought it was Bravo."

"Yes, that's his new name. After he warned us about those Apaches, he looked at me like a *traitor*–until I fed him some jerky. Then he was fine. He's a traitor, *but he does it only for a price,*" I joked. "He probably followed the Apaches home after one of their raids and they fed him –so this probably wasn't the first time," I continued.

Marco protested, "He's no traitor! They probably raised him from a pup."

"Well anyway, that's his name–Traitor. We should be comfortable with that name."

Smiling Marco nodded, knowing where I was coming from.

In less than two hours, we were back on top of the cliffs overlooking the La Escondida basin. The sun was bright and the day was much warmer. Things were looking up.

On our ride over from the mining camp, we had decided we were going to look at our clues in reverse. The treasure was hidden out there somewhere. The two piles of rocks at the crest of the mountain were close to the treasure, and were the key to discovering it. Somehow they were connected.

I did not look forward to climbing down the faces of all those cliffs on a thin *reata* looking for caves or hiding spots. If the ropes didn't break and kill one of us, it would still take at least a week to properly search the cliffs.

No. There had to be a better way.

Marco sat on one pile of rocks, and I walked over to the other. We carefully scanned the area, looking for clues. I pulled the maps out of my saddlebag and studied them again.

The only thing I noticed on the maps was that there had been an unusually high number of mining locations in the Chihuahuita Mountains. Two were close to where we were. That was not new information, but it might be related.

We strolled around the top of the cliff walking back and forth, trying out different theories. Finally, I sat on the first pile of rocks to rest. Then I saw it!

On the edge of the mountain about 35 feet from the rock pile was an old manzanita bush. It was different. *It had been trimmed–years ago.* One of the old, dead limbs was sticking up a few inches above the others.

"Marco, I think I've found something," I said in a matter of fact tone.

"What? What is it?" he replied as he quickly turned and headed in my direction.

I explained my theory.

"Let's assume we can see where the treasure is hidden from up here. What would be a good way to find it and not be too obvious?"

"I don't know. Tell me," Marco replied impatiently.

"Take a look at that old manzanita bush. See anything unusual?"

"No. What is it?"

We walked over to the old bush and I showed him where it had been trimmed, indicating the longer limb that protruded above the others. New branches had grown up and almost obscured it.

"I think this is a sighting point–from that pile of rocks to this branch. This line points at the hidden treasure!"

Marco quickly got the idea. "You think there is another sighting point from the other pile of rocks?"

"Yes."

Marco quickly ran over to the second pile of rocks and started looking off in the direction of the basin below. I joined him. There were a number of manzanita and juniper bushes, both dead and alive, in the general direction we thought would be correct.

We began to carefully inspect each bush along the edge of the cliff, one by one, looking for any signs of a branch having been thinned or sharpened.

One manzanita bush seemed especially suspect, but it was dead and hanging close to the edge of the cliff by some dead roots. Then Marco looked closer, saying that he saw signs of trimming on the leaning bush.

I ran to our tied horses and retrieved one of the reatas. Marco took it from me and expertly lassoed the dead bush, and together we gently pulled it into what we thought was the original position some 35 years ago, and secured the rope.

Sure enough, several of the branches were trimmed and one dominant branch stood several inches above the others. Success!

Now we knew what we were looking for. Some rocks at the top of both of the rock piles had been knocked off over the years. However, there were only a few reddish rocks lying at the bottoms of each pile to choose from.

We carefully restacked the missing rocks on each pile to establish the precise, likely sighting point. Then we stood back from each rock pile and sighted from the top rock to the trimmed manzanita bush limb, looking down into the basin far below. It was like sighting down the barrel of a rifle.

The two sighting lines converged on a point thousands of meters away, along a side ravine leading into the main canyon in the basin far below. We were excited at our apparent success.

It was late morning, so we took a break, drinking water and eating some burritos the mine manager's wife had made for us. I gave my second burrito to Traitor, who was quietly watching us from where the horses were tied. Marco gave him half of his other burrito also.

"How did they do it?" Marco asked.

"Marco, I'm lazy and I think they did it like I would."

"How's that?"

"Well, I think I would find the easiest place down there in the basin to hide or bury the treasure, and do that first."

"Fine, then what?"

"Well, using this technique, I would get far away from the treasure–on a high point where I could see it–and set up sighting markers to find it."

"How in the hell could they set up the marking points?"

"Oh, that's easy. A couple of them probably just about killed their horses, like we almost did, and scrambled up here. They knew where they hid the treasure, so they found a couple of good sighting trees, in this case, manzanita bushes and marked them. They figured the bushes should last for fifty or a hundred years."

Marco jumped ahead again. "Then they went behind their marking points and set up their piles of rock in the correct places to make the treasure location line up with their manzanita bushes."

"You got it."

We ate quickly, then spent about a half hour carefully sighting along the indicated lines down toward the treasure location. We noted the exact ravine and some dominant rock formations and trees close by, so we could find them when we rode down into the basin.

We untied the reata holding the dead manzanita bush and tried to lay it over on its side again, but the *honda* (loop) on the reata broke, and the old dead bush went crashing down the face of the cliff.

"I hope we don't need that again," Marco said, looking off the steep cliff.

An hour later, we were deep in the La Escondida basin and near our target point. We were both quietly calling out our reference points. Finding the deep, dry ravine, we rode up it.

The first time we ventured up the narrow ravine, we saw nothing suspicious, so we turned around and rode back down, slowly.

Being a mining man, and having spent much time with my father at mining camps, I noticed some signs of old man-made erosion partially hidden by some juniper trees.

"There it is," I said.

"Where? I don't see anything," responded a frustrated Marco.

We tied our horses to some bushes at the bottom of the ravine below the tell-tale trees and erosion. We climbed up into the trees and, sure enough, there were still a few signs of an ancient mining works. It looked like an old, caved-in tunnel.

I showed Marco where the mouth of the tunnel had been. It had filled in with dirt and rocks and was pretty much washed away.

"What about the tailings?" Marco asked. "Shouldn't a mine have a huge dump or pile of tailings in front of it?"

"Yes, they do. But, if the tailings are dumped into a ravine or canyon like this, they would wash away after the floods from the first rainy season. The dump was once there, but washed away."

"Shouldn't we dig into the tunnel and see if our treasure is there?"

"Yes, we should. But we need to leave the dirt so we can cover it over again, and also make sure the damned thing doesn't cave in and bury us."

Marco chuckled, but I could tell his heart wasn't in it.

For the next four hours or so we dug and dug. Several large rocks had slid down from above, and it took quite a bit of time and effort to move them.

Finally, we decided to return the next day and finish our work. We were exhausted, but certain we had found the right location.

The next morning, we were at our treasure location as the sun was peeking over the high cliffs. It was going to be another beautiful day. In an hour we had broken into the opening of the old original tunnel. Then, a surprise.

Yes we found the treasure, but we found more–human skeletons, eight of them. Probably the Mexicans hired by the Spaniards to help haul the burro-loads of gold and silver. Maybe some Mexicans in the Spanish army too. This was probably what happened to Trujillo's great uncle at one of these Spanish treasure sites.

We had brought several candles with us. We prepared to go into the partially cleared tunnel, but the air was so foul we waited about a half hour let it clear out. Finally, we ventured further into the stagnate old mine, stepping on and over piles of dirt, rocks and skeletons. The inside of the tunnel was partially caved in, but we counted twenty-five decaying canvas and rawhide bags. Inside some of the old canvas bags were silver *planchas* (pancake shaped, crude castings), many almost black with age and tarnish. Other canvas bags contained smaller gold *planchas* and beautiful rod castings!

I picked up a rotten rawhide pouch which broke in my hand, spilling out gold dust and nuggets! Marco gasped, trying to catch the spilling gold dust.

We estimated that the 17 burro-loads of treasure would have been hauled in 34 canvas or leather bags–two on each burro. It looked like they were probably all there, but some appeared to be spilled from rotten bags or still buried under a partially caved-in section of the tunnel. We had found our treasure!

For the next half hour, Marco and I were dancing on air, congratulating ourselves and taking inventory of the treasure. One bag was filled with clipped gold rods–roughly double thumbnail sized, and five crudely stamped *escudos* (gold coins). In a second bag we found more clipped rods and the handled iron stamps for striking the escudos.

Finally, coming back to earth, we decided we would each take some of the treasure with us and leave the rest. We decided to each take a pouch of gold dust and nuggets along with the five escudos. Spanish ingots or planchas would be hard to explain if anyone saw them. Also, we couldn't easily get rid of them. But we must carefully hide the rest of the treasure until we could come back and recover it. Like the Spaniards, we didn't realize then how long that would be.

We spent the rest of the morning carefully covering and hiding the entrance of the tunnel again. By a little past mid-day, we were satisfied we had properly restored everything to as close to its original, hidden condition as possible.

Then we dumped everything out of our saddle bags and carefully packed our gold dust and nuggets into them. We filled the remaining saddle bag space with our maps and some of our supplies and gear. The rest we rolled up in our coats and tied them onto the back of our saddles. Finally, with our newly found treasure, Marco led our horses down the ravine and I followed behind, covering our tracks by dusting them with dead branches.

We were back at the Patagonia Mining Camp by late afternoon. The world now had a new glow to it and was looking wonderful to us.

Chapter 21

The Santa Maria Incident

Marco and I were feeling invincible. The Apaches had tried to kill us and they hadn't. We had found the La Escondida treasure and almost certainly knew where to find the Cocospera treasure. We had *Traitor* as our Apache protector, and he was happy. And the weather was excellent, cold in the morning, but warm by mid-day. Also, we were on schedule to meet Lieutenant Pacheco and the other officers for our meeting at San Lázaro. Things couldn't be much better.

We left the Patagonia camp early on Thursday, after eating breakfast with our hosts. They laughed at our blistered hands. Marcos *lied*, saying we cleared a trail to a high place on the mountain, which I thought had some promising ore showings and could be a new mining site for my English company.

Our horses were rested and our saddlebags were a *little heavier* as we trotted out of the mountains down toward the pueblo of Santa Maria on the river. Marco was generous with our hosts, paying them for their help. He used Santa Ana's money.

We arrived at the village of Santa Maria by late morning and decided to eat lunch and rest a bit before going on to San Lázaro. We ate at a local cantina, having several beers and shots of *mezcal* (a local brew made from cactus of the same name). There we heard the two big stories that were floating around town. The first dealt with the incident of Zonia and Chico–Trujillo's wife and boy, and the second was about finding Jasmine.

According to the first story we heard several days earlier Colonel Trujillo returned from the mountains after our raid on the Apache camp, collected his family and went home to Hermosillo. But what happened before he arrived at the Figueroa farm north of town, where Zonia and Chico were staying, was what had the town folks talking.

Apparently later on the same day we raided the Apache camp in the La Escondida basin, some Apaches raided the Figueroa farm where Zonia and Chico were staying. It happened in the afternoon, and the Apaches involved were almost certainly some of the same bunch that escaped from our raid. It certainly wasn't their day, because after a rude awakening involving our gunfire in the morning, the savages were now unknowingly dealing with *la bruja*–the witch.

As the story went, during that afternoon little Chico went out riding on his burro, Gruillo, on the road north of the farm, hoping to meet his father returning from the mountains with his soldiers. Instead, he was captured by four Apaches.

The Apaches caught little Chico and tied his hands with a leather strap. One of the bucks hopped on his burro and led the frightened boy behind him with a rope tied around his neck. They then headed south to the nearby Figueroa farm.

José Figueroa was plowing with his team of old horses and saw them coming. Figueroa abandoned his team and equipment in the field, running to protect his family and Zonia.

The Apaches caught Figueroa's plow animals and removed their harnesses. They selected the better horse to ride and put a *bozal* (simple halter) on it. They *slit the other animal's throat* and left him standing there to bleed to death. Thinking they could capture more animals and raise hell, the Apaches went over to the Figueroa farm. The angry savages were on the rampage, determined to kill and plunder.

The Apache bucks first approached the farm from a safe distance and waited for a few minutes, watching for activity. When they realized there were people inside the adobe building, the buck riding Chico's little burro led the bound and frightened boy to the front of the building, where they could easily be seen by the people inside. The other three bucks cautiously followed on foot, one leading the old plow horse.

José Figueroa, his wife and Zonia watched from inside the adobe farmhouse as the drama heightened and the menacing savages approached the farmhouse with the scared, *feeble-minded* boy. José stood behind his farmhouse's cracked door, holding his old, broken shotgun and peering through the cracks.

Once the Apaches saw there were people barricaded in the farmhouse and they were not shooting at them, they became more bold. The buck with poor little Chico jumped off the burro and dragged the boy even closer to the house, putting a knife to the boy's throat. His intent was obviously to kill the frightened boy and terrorize the people inside the farm house.

Seeing what was about to happen, Zonia immediately pushed past Mr. Figueroa. She opened the door and quickly walked outside toward the savage threatening to slit the boy's throat.

At first the threatening Apache buck holding little Chico laughed at the sight of a woman coming out to challenge him. The other Apache bucks watched. Then he became angry at the idea of a woman, a pregnant Opata woman, no less, confronting him.

He pushed Chico to the ground, the point of his knife cutting the boy in the process and causing him to cry out. Zonia took several more steps forward and stopped, locking her stare with that of the angry savage.

Apparently that's when things really got interesting. Zonia raised her hand while continuing to stare at the Apache. Then she let out a whistling noise and took rapid short steps toward the savage holding down Chico with his knee. The Apache froze, as if in a trance and didn't move. With her hand raised, Zonia gave the paralyzed buck a little shove. He fell to the ground, dropping his knife and going into a spasm–shaking, kicking and coughing foam out of his mouth.

But that wasn't the end of it!

Zonia helped the shaking and bleeding Chico to his feet and started to lead him toward the house, but then she stopped and turned her *ojo de diablo* (evil eye) toward the other savages who were watching from close by. Suddenly realizing they were witnessing something unnatural, they got the hell out of there.

Two of the bucks ran for the nearby trees and the third jumped on the old plow horse and jerked him around, trying to make him run. But the old horse wouldn't cooperate, and instead tried to pitch the savage off his back. But when the old horse couldn't unseat the tough Apache warrior, he dropped to the ground and quickly rolled, catching the surprised buck under him. When the old horse completed his roll, the Apache buck lay on the ground, moaning with a broken leg. Seeing this, his two friends ran back and grabbed their injured partner, rapidly dragging him off.

The first Apache, the one who attacked Chico, finally stopped his convulsions and never moved again.

Chico was not seriously injured. His father and the rest of the soldiers arrived several hours later. When José Figueroa told the colonel the story, the colonel just looked at Zonia and smiled. They spent the night in Santa Maria and left for Hermosillo the next morning.

Somehow this story didn't surprise Marco and me as much as it delighted the local folks. We knew a little more about Zonia and her unusual powers.

We stuck around the cantina and enjoyed our food and drink. The second story we heard was about Jasmine.

As this story was told, Jasmine was a five-year-old girl from the Buena Vista settlement on the Santa Maria River. A little less than two weeks earlier, her family had been killed and the child kidnapped by the Apaches. She was not the missing girl from the San Luis Ranch.

The story went on. Colonel Trujillo's men rescued her from the savages camp in the Chihuahuitas after a fierce battle *in which eleven Apaches were killed. Jasmine was tied naked to a tree and was nearly frozen.* One of the Apache women then tried to hide her, so the soldiers wouldn't find her.

An interesting story–not quite right, but interesting nevertheless. Instead of a raging battle in which eleven Apaches were killed, only two had been killed. One was an old man trying to run away and the second a buck hit by a lucky shot fired by one of Captain Fontes' men. But we said nothing.

We got to San Lázaro about 3:30, according to Marco's borrowed gold watch which he periodically reset by looking at the midday sun.

Captain Fontes and Lieutenant Muñoz had their camp set up. Some of the men were sleeping and others visiting under the nearby cottonwood trees. The weather was wonderful–no coats needed–and the water in the river was pleasant so we washed up.

Lieutenant Peralta and Lieutenant Pacheco came to camp with their men about an hour later. Their scouts weren't with them, neither were Muñoz's.

A little later, the officers met at Captain Fontes' and Muñoz's campsite. The atmosphere was relaxed–really almost sloppy, without their commander, the tough Colonel Trujillo, being around. Fontes invited Captain Vásquez and me to join them. They had a bottle of tequila, which they shared. Each officer gave his report of happenings since we departed from the La Escondida basin.

First Lieutenant Peralta reported. He gave a close account of the Zonia incident at the Figueroa farm. Also he reported that his Opata tracker couldn't get along with Lieutenant Muñoz's Pima tracker. The Indian trackers gladly parted when the Apache tracks showed they separated into four different groups in the mountains, the two men gladly going different ways.

Apparently no one had followed the group that attacked Marco and me. Again, we said nothing.

Lieutenant Peralta's tracker and other scouts were successful at putting Peralta and his men close behind one group of Apaches. They caught up with them while they were attacking the Teyechea farm up the river. The Apaches were in the process of trying to burn down the farm house when Peralta and his men arrived. A fight ensued and one Apache was killed. The others escaped.

Lieutenant Peralta proudly held up a string with *two Apache ears*, one belonging to the old man that ran from the La Escondida camp and the other from the Teyechea farm the Apaches attacked up the river.

Lieutenant Pacheco gave no report, since he was with Lieutenant Peralta.

Next came Captain Fontes and Lieutenant Muñoz. A large part of their report was about where they had patrolled up and down the river. Also they reported that their Pima tracker lost the trail of his group of Apaches in the rocky country on the edge of the mountain near Cerro Tordillo. The good news was that the Apaches were heading toward their home ground in the mountains across the valley to the east. Fontes proudly held up his string with *a single ear* cut from the Apache killed by one of his men with a lucky shot in the basin.

Finally, Captain Fontes looked at Captain Vásquez and me with a cynical smile. "How about you two killers? See anything?"

"No. Not much," Vásquez said nonchalantly.

The other officers chuckled patronizingly and started to talk about something else, when Marco quietly held up *his string of seven ears.*

The shock on the faces of the four officers was stunning as they stared at the trophies.

"You said not much! Where did you get those?"

"Up in the Chihuahuitas, the afternoon after we separated."

"Just the two of you?"

"Yes."

The four officers glanced at each other with questioning looks, but said nothing as they passed around the string of trophies.

Peralta looked at me and casually touched his cheek in the place where mine had a fresh cut. I nodded.

And that was what took place at our San Lázaro meeting.

Back in Hermosillo, we found out about Jasmine and the two Apache women captives. Colonel Trujillo told us that Jasmine's family had been killed and that her only relatives lived in the Río Sonora. He and Zonia decided to have her stay with them until she could be reunited with family members.

The colonel said he also decided to let the Apache women go at Santa Maria. The *güera* took off immediately and disappeared. However, the older, darker Apache women wanted to stay with Jasmine rather than returning to her tribe. So Trujillo took her to Hermosillo with them. She was temporarily helping out at his hacienda and he was considering moving her to his farm until the Apache woman decided what she wanted to do.

It seemed the tough old colonel had a big heart. So did his wife.

Besides these updates, the colonel had a package waiting for me at his office when we visited two days before Christmas Eve. It was from General Santa Ana and addressed to *Ingeniero Mack in care of Captain Vásquez*. It was wrapped in heavy brown paper and was about the size of a large book, but not as heavy. I couldn't imagine what it was.

Colonel Trujillo handed it to me, then the captain and he watched. I wasn't sure I wanted to open it up in front of them, but I did.

Underneath the first paper cover was another. It was the cover of a package sent to me from James Kenny (JK) Kerns, The Fields of Shannon Plantation, Savannah, Georgia, United States of America!

Inside was a box of expensive cigars! Some of them were damaged. Additionally, there were several letters, one from Melanie.

We all laughed as I handed out an undamaged cigar to the colonel and then to Marco. I saved the letters for later. We tried to surmise how the package had caught up to me.

Marco's guess was probably the best. He thought the package must have showed up at Señora Hortencia Elías' Hacienda in Mexico City. It looked important so she got it over to her dead husband's cousin, the general. From there the general must have sent it up to Hermosillo by military courier. Quite a trip! I wondered aloud if it had travelled on Captain Beltrán's ship, *La Bruja*, as we jokingly called her.

Colonel Trujillo and Zonia invited Marco and me over for tamales and other good food and drink on Christmas Eve. I managed to buy a more appropriate gift this time for the evening meal. *And I had the money to do it.*

When we got there, Zonia looked pale and unwell. The colonel told Marco and me confidentially that Zonia had lost her baby. When we entered the room with Trujillo's children, a shy little girl with pigtails ran over and hugged me. It was Jasmine! A further surprise happened in Trujillo's visiting room when Marco, Lieutenant Pacheco and his wife Myra, and I were seated visiting and eating *botanas* (appetizers). Zonia came in with one of the ladies who helped her.

"This is *Tuti*." Zonia said, "She's helping to prepare our meal tonight."

The shy lady wore a neat, cotton dress and had her hair braided neatly and tied with red ribbons. Then I recognized her. It was the dark Apache woman who had mothered Jasmine and scolded me. I don't think Captain Vásquez or Lieutenant Pacheco realized who they had just met.

Tuti gave me a sly little smile and I responded. She then departed for the kitchen in a hurry. Zonia smiled at me, sharing the little secret. Besides her husband, I was the only one who recognized the woman. What a change. I mentally wished the little Apache woman my best, knowing she had a good start at a new life, thanks to the Trujillo's family.

We left early after a pleasant evening with the colonel and his family. It had been a success, since we avoided talking business. We also had playful chats with Chico and the children. Little Jasmine acted like she wanted to adopt me. She was a delightful and charming little girl.

Between Christmas and New Years day, Marco and I had time on our hands. We refined our strategy for our chess end-game, recover the Cocospera treasure, then the one at *Tubutama*, if it was there. After that, we would go on to the sea where we hoped Captain Beltrán would be waiting with his ship. Finally, we must get the treasure to Mexico City and General Santa Ana.

We hoped Colonel Trujillo would go with us only as far as Cocospera, where we would recover that treasure and divide it with him. After dividing it, we planned for him to return to Hermosillo with his part and send us on to the Sea of Cortez with the remaining treasure. *He must not know* about our planned stop in Tubutama, at least not until after we were safely aboard the ship, *La Doncella* and had sailed south.

If things went according to our plan, the colonel would assign some of his men to safely escort us to the sea. In Tubutama, we would stop and search for the third treasure. If we were successful, we must find extra burros with pack saddles to carry that treasure with us to the waiting ship. Our plan seemed simple enough, but the unpredictable colonel was the weak link.

Captain Vásquez was a fine fellow and my friend, but over the past many weeks we had spent a lot of time together, too much. His personality was a little different than mine. He was quieter and more formal, as that of a good military man should be, whereas I joked a lot, perhaps too much sometimes and had something of a temper. But we were good friends. We had to be, because we were also partners to the biggest hidden Spanish treasure in the Pimeria Alta, the La Escondida treasure, which awaited us in the Chihuahuita Mountains.

A new factor that weighed heavily on our friendship was that Marco was married and had a baby boy in Mexico City. However, since we had returned from our expedition to Apache country, he'd found a cute Indian girl in Hermosillo and was spending a lot of time with her. Perhaps it was my upbringing, but I didn't think it was right.

Finally, there was the captain's relationship with Colonel Trujillo and his family. It seemed that after I gave the colonel my extra Colt Dragoon six-shooter and taught him to shoot it, the ice was broken between us.

However, the colonel's relationship with Marco was not good, not since our first meeting, when Marco threatened the colonel's career to get his cooperation. Even though both men tried to be civil to each other, it seemed as though the two men never quite professionally or socially meshed. General Santa Ana sending us up here undoubtedly played into it too, even though the colonel didn't know Marco and the general were related.

New Year's Day was a Saturday, and I rode out to the garrison in the morning hoping to see the colonel if he was around. He was. He even had his children and Jasmine there.

Chico was helping feed and tend to the horses while Juanito was playing outside the colonel's office with the sentry. Isabella and Jasmine both were drawing pictures at the colonel's table. The colonel himself was working on a ledger at his desk. It was a charming picture.

I presented the colonel with a package of *jamoncillo* (milk sugar candy), which went over great with the children. The colonel smiled and told them to give a piece of the candy to the sentry before they could eat some. Isabella ran outside with the candy, giggling.

When things settled down a bit, I asked the colonel for a favor. Jasmine sat on my lap, nibbling her piece of jamoncillo. She had managed to snatch a piece of the candy before the sentry.

"Colonel, I …."

"Chu Chu, call me *Lobo* (wolf). All my men do, behind my back. Anyway, you are a friend, and you can call me Lobo."

"Yes,Colonel, I mean Lobo. Sure.Colonel, I need a favor."

The colonel laughed.

"What's your favor, Chu Chu?"

"Colonel, we have a little time on our hands. I would like to look around in Sonora for potential mining sites for my company. Maybe a couple of weeks out in the field. Any suggestions on where I might look? Also I would like to hire a reliable man to go with me. Any suggestions there?"

Little Jasmine immediately said she wanted to go with me. We laughed.

"Well, Chu Chu, first, stay out of Apache country. Even though I think our little campaign discouraged them. We haven't heard of any Apache raids since we got back, thanks to the damage you and Captain Vásquez did."

"That's good. So stay south of the Santa Maria and San José rivers?"

"Yes."

"How about someone I could hire to go with me?"

"What do you want him to do?"

"Oh, just help watch my back and maybe do a little digging for some ore specimens. Yes, and cook. I'm a terrible cook. Traitor and I want some good chow."

We laughed.

The colonel recommended a retired sergeant, Juan Sáldate. He said Sáldate was a good, reliable man familiar with the country I wanted to investigate.

Later, I told Captain Vásquez what I planned to do. I also told him

I might investigate the Tubutama area while I was out there and see if I could find the site where the Spanish had hidden the third treasure. I asked if he wanted to come along. I knew the answer. No, he trusted me.

I asked Marco if he would trade me some hard currency and hold my decaying leather pouch of gold dust and nuggets, which for protection I had wrapped in heavy paper and stuffed into a cotton flour sack. He gave me 100 pesos in silver and said he would have a new leather pouch made for my stash by the time I returned.

Two days later, on my birthday, Juan Sáldate, Traitor and I again headed north with a pack burro to do some *prospecting*, back into the Pimeria Alta country.

During the next eighteen days, we saw a lot of beautiful desert country, along with many Seri, Yaqui and Papago Indians. Most Indians were wary, but left us alone. However, some were friendly. Juan knew many of them and I never felt we were ever in a threatening situation. Traitor seemed comfortable too.

We rode almost directly to Tubutama. We spent three days in the area scratching around. I tried not to be obvious about looking for the hidden treasure, so I took mineral specimens from all around the area. But I did locate the place where the maps showed the loads of silver and gold ingots should be buried. The site appeared undisturbed, except for a little flooding and sand erosion from the rains over the years. I was sure we could easily find and recover it. I was also encouraged to encounter no reports from the people living at Tubutama suggesting anything unusual being found in the area, except for several small, abandoned Spanish mining works.

My prospecting trip through the desert was refreshing, nectar for my soul. It gave me some privacy and the needed time away from Marco and the pressures of our assigned mission by General Santa Ana. Also, Juan Sáldate was an interesting man to travel with and visit. He gave me information on everything–from what he didn't know about women, to what jaguar tracks looked like in the desert. He was a widower with two grown children, a son and a daughter. He was a retired sergeant and his son was in Trujillo's troop.

Best of all, I had time to think. Think about Melanie and me and how our first year might go together. Think about my job, working for the New Wales Equipment and Mining Company. Think about Marco and me–and how we would recover our La Escondida treasure in the future.

Life was moving in directions I had not planned. I had a good job, a beautiful woman that I loved and hoped loved me. Also, with the unexpected experience General Santa Ana handed me, I was potentially wealthy. In fact with the way the cards were falling, I might become a very wealthy man. Not bad for a mining engineer of 23 who had been almost broke two months earlier!

Yes, it seemed fate was pushing me in exciting but unexpected directions. This made me think of Melanie and her father. He said that he would be dead before we were married. In fact, the dream indicated he would die on February the 24th. That was a little over a month away. I still wouldn't be back to Mexico City by that time. I wondered if Melanie would let me know if something happened. Yes, I was sure she would.

So what did it mean if he did die? And if he didn't? Many questions and no answers. But those were again things beyond my control, so I would put them aside for awhile.

One thing I did know was that *I was changing*. My thinking and my attitudes were changing. I was getting harder and more cynical. Things were less simple, less black and white. Was this part of becoming a man? Perhaps, but that was not the cause of all of it. I hoped it would not affect my relationship with Melanie. I wondered if she was changing too. Hopefully, we were not growing apart.

There was not much I could do about any of this here in the middle of northern Mexico. I recognized I was in a game whose rules were being made up by powerful people like Senator J. P. Anderson from South Carolina and General Santa Ana in Mexico City. To make things even more interesting, not even they realized that they too were pawns in a game being played at an even higher level. *Life was an adventure and I was going to enjoy it.*

Juan Sáldate and I returned on Friday, January 21st. Besides successfully scouting out the Tubutama treasure site near the old mission, I had enjoyed the time, finally purging my mind of thoughts and worries which were beyond my control to resolve. I also had made a friend of Juan Sáldate.

During the trip, I used the maps and found three Spanish silver mining sites and one old gold mine that looked good for future examination, if my company was interested. The best site was near Imuris, at a place called Cerro Blanco.

Returning to Hermosillo, I was tempted to go by the Cocospera Cerro Llano graveyard site, but didn't. I knew Juan would be reporting back to the colonel, and I didn't want to poison his well with suspicion.

At our posada in Hermosillo, I found Marco asleep. It was noon. When he awoke and came to the door, he looked like hell. He had been drinking.

"Did you find it?" He asked, yawning.

I glanced around. "Yes, I think it's still there," I said quietly, "I didn't try to dig it up. I had Juan with me."

"So you think it's still there? Will it be hard to get?" Marco again asked, rubbing the mussed-up hair out of his eyes.

I pushed my way past him, not wanting to discuss this outside. "Yes, I think it's still there. It's like the map and notes said. And the site has not been disturbed. It should be easy to get, the ground looks soft."

"Good. Good." Marco slurred as he backed over to his bed and sat down.

"How about a drink?" he asked me as he poured a shot glass full from a half empty-bottle of tequila.

"No. No thanks. Don't you think it a little bit early to start that?"

Marco laughed and responded. "We stayed up late last night. I've got to have this to start my brain working. How about some breakfast?"

"Sure. Maybe some lunch. I'll see you out in the patio when you're ready."

I left rapidly, disgusted with his appearance and actions.

I got another room from the innkeeper and put my saddlebag, rifle and other gear from my trip in it. I also had a heavy canvas bag with leather-strap handles about half full of ore samples, I dumped those in the room too. Going to the patio, I ordered a beer and waited for Marco.

Lunch was cooking and it smelled great. My appetite suddenly came alive so I ordered a quesadilla and some guacamole while I waited. My temper had settled down by the time Marco arrived, not looking much better.

We ate a pleasant meal, and Marco had coffee instead of beer. By the time we finished, he was his old self. I jokingly told him that now that I had money, I was getting my own room. He laughed and agreed it would give him more privacy too. I knew what he meant.

After lunch, I moved the rest of my stuff from his room to my new room. He handed me a new leather pouch and asked if I wanted to weigh it. I said no, I trusted him, and we laughed.

Marco was anxious to start the last leg of our trip back to Mexico City to deliver the goods to his uncle. We were betting that the two sites would deliver the treasures documented in the Spanish maps and notes. If they didn't, we were in trouble. Not only with Santa Ana, but also with Trujillo, and he was closer. However, we were confident.

Marco said he had only talked to Colonel Trujillo once since I had been gone and that it didn't go very well. He said he was ready to get out of this God forsaken land and get back to civilization and his family. He said he wanted us to be on the sea at the mouth of *Río Conception* on February the 15th, and that Beltrán had better be waiting there with his ship. That was our original plan, and it was fine with me.

He asked me to talk to Colonel Trujillo and coordinate the details for our trip to Cocospera, then on to the sea by way of Tubutama. Marco looked away, repeating that he and the colonel weren't getting along too well and that I should deal with him. I was a little hesitant, but agreed to do it.

The next day I went to the garrison early in the morning, in hopes of seeing Trujillo. I was in luck, or maybe not. He was preparing to go out into the field for two days and was impatiently trying to get his troops ready to hit the trail. Things weren't going well for him.

He had just cussed out Sergeant Campos for not having the right men and gear ready for their short outing and was stomping back to his office when he saw me. He waved me over. I said I could meet with him when he got back, but he insisted that I come to his office. He had something he wanted to discuss with me. That didn't sound good.

Inside his office, Trujillo pointed to the chair and asked me to sit, while trying to get his temper under control. I sat.

"What do you want?" The colonel asked me directly.

"Colonel, Captain Vásquez asked me to work out the details of our trip to Cocospera, then on to the sea coast at Desemboque. But we can talk about it when you return."

Obviously, something had broken down between him and Captain Vásquez.

"No. Let's do it now. When do you want to go?"

"We were thinking the 2nd of February. That should give us enough time to go to Cocospera, then on to Desemboque."

"What do you need from me?"

"Well, I think you and Captain Vásquez agreed to split whatever we found at Cerro Llano, and you said you wanted to be there when we dug it up. I guess what we need are the men and equipment to dig it up and the burros with pack saddles to haul it out of there."

The colonel exploded. "Damn it I don't want you and your worthless captain to give me any more shit! I know there is more than one place the Spaniards buried their gold. My uncle is probably buried at one of them.

"That drunken friend of yours has been spreading *gold dust* around here since you got back from the Chihuahuitas. There's a place up there, one *you found* when you separated from my men. And your trip over to Tubutama–there's probably a treasure there too."

The colonel's fiery eyes widened. "So don't play me for a fool! I told the captain my terms, one third of whatever is buried at Cerro Llano. I said I would help you, and I will. But I want your asses out of here–and if I hear the captain or Santa Ana takes that gold to Cuba or anywhere else instead using it to help Mexico, I will follow and strangle them both."

"So tell your worthless captain to be ready on the 2nd of February and have whatever he needs ready to get his gold to the sea. I will go to Cerro Llano with him and divide it there. I will send five men to escort you to Desemboque. After that I hope I never see either of you again!"

"Yes sir."

The angry colonel jumped up from his desk and stormed out. Without a word, he mounted his horse and rode off with his troops.

Well, I had negotiated the deal with the colonel, as Marco had asked me to do. But it was a bit one-sided. I later informed Marco what had happened, and we decided we had better get prepared and stay out of the colonel's sight until we were ready to go.

On February 2nd, the weather had turned bad again. It was cold and there had been some rain. Marco and I found some sorry horses and bought them to use since we were in the bad graces of the colonel. Also, we bought a string of eighteen burros–some of them *half broke* (untrained). We had mesquite pack saddles made with tree branch hooks and heavy canvas bags. Felipe made both the pack saddles and canvas bags for us and did a competent job. We hired Juan Sáldate to help us with the burros and our extra gear and food. The official word was that I was opening up a mine near Cocospera.

Early Wednesday morning on the 2nd of February Captain Vásquez, Juan Sáldate and I rode into the garrison at Hermosillo on our pitiful horses. Each of us led a string of burros with the animals tied halter to tail. Marco led the party with his string of four burros; I came next with my burros, followed, by my embarrassed-looking, skinny little Indian dog, Traitor. Juan Sáldate brought up the rear with his string of six burros. Our strange caravan reminded me of what a lost Bedouin tribe might look like coming down the Persian Trail.

The colonel and his men were all mounted and tensely waiting in a line to depart when we came parading through the garrison front gates. The grumpy, tired soldiers were in need of a break in tension and we gave it to them.

There were some smirks and mumbling amongst the mounted soldiers even before a couple of Captain Vásquez's green-broke burros started bucking. They jerked away from him and ran back toward the entrance gate, dumping their pack saddles. In the rear, Juan Sáldate quickly dropped the line to his burros and headed Captain Vásquez's renegade asses off before they escaped back through the front gate.

There was a whoop of laughter from the soldiers. The colonel laughed the loudest of them all. I had to laugh too. We looked like a troop of clowns that had escaped from a circus–skinny horses, bucking burros and one shame-faced dog. Captain Vásquez, dressed in his clean and proper Mexico City military uniform, didn't think it was so very funny.

The colonel assigned several of his soldiers to help us with the burros, and we were on our way.

On our way back out the gate, I saw Chico watching us from down by the corrals. I dropped to the back of the troop, and then rode over to where the sad boy was standing. I got off my scrawny horse.

"Chico, we are leaving. I'm glad I saw you. I didn't have a chance to tell you and your brother and sister good-bye. Will you tell them for me?"

"Sure, Chu Chu. Will we ever see you again?"

"Well, I sure hope so, Chico. Will you do me another favor?"

The boy grinned. "Sure, Chu Chu, what is it?"

"Will you take care of my dog, Traitor?"

The excited little soldier in his special military jacket replied, "Sure, Chu Chu, does that mean I can have him?"

"It sure does, if you will take care of him. Do you want him?"

"Yes, I do. Yes–yes, I do," little Chico said, dancing around with joy.

I quickly got a piece of a rope hanging on the corral fence and looped it around Traitor's neck. After petting my little mongrel dog for a moment, I handed the rope to Chico.

"Chico, I have one other favor. Could you do it for me?"

The boy looked up at me eagerly. "Sure, what is it Chu Chu?"

Reaching into my pocket, I pulled out four small gold nuggets with a thread strung though a hole in them. Each was stamped with a tiny initial.

"One of these is for you. Please give one to Isabella and one to your brother Juanito. And give Jasmine one too. Will you do that for me, Chico?"

Little Chico clutched them like he was holding a treasure–and he was.

"*Ay Chihuahua* (wow), Chu Chu, and you put our initial on each one?"

"Yes, Chico. Will you do that favor for me, Chico?"

"Sure, Chu Chu–and thank you." Then, with tears in his eyes he whispered. "Chu Chu, *vaya con Dios.*"

"You're welcome, Chico. Gracias and adios, my little soldier friend."

I mounted my scrawny steed and looked down at the little boy who would never grow up. He stiffened and with a trembling lip, gave me his proud military salute.

I smiled and returned Chico's salute, then turned my horse and rode away with a lump in my throat.

Riding out through the Hermosillo garrison gates, I wondered if I would ever see little Chico again. I had a feeling I would not. And I was right. A year later I heard that Chico was accidently trampled and killed in the darkness early one morning while trying to help the soldiers tend to their *remuda*.

Chapter 22

Cocospera, Tubutama and on to the Sea

It was evening and we had just ended our second day on the old Spanish road to Cocospera, heading up the Río San Miguel. I was putting hobbles on my horse so he could graze for the night when Sergeant Campos came over and said the colonel wanted to talk to me after we ate supper. I agreed.

The weather had been cold and rainy, the results of another storm passing through. However, the soldiers had an open field mess with big, hot fires and good food, much of which Marco and I had packed on the burros for the trip. It was a good move on our part and did much to cheer the men up and take the dreariness out of the evening.

After supper, I walked over to the colonel's separate fire near a *cumero* (hackberry) tree. He sat alone, leaning against his saddle and drinking coffee.

"Good evening, Colonel. Sergeant Campos said you wanted to talk to me."

The colonel acknowledged my greeting and offered me coffee, which I accepted.

"Colonel, what can I do for you?"

"I need a favor."

"A favor?" I said, surprised. "I thought you were angry and never wanted to see me again."

"I am and I don't, but I still need a favor," the colonel responded staring at his coffee cup but now with an affable look on his face.

I lightened up. "You did me several favors, so what can I do for you?"

"Chu Chu, do you think we will find the gold at Cerro Llano?"

"Gold and silver? Yes,Colonel, I do."

"If we do, I want *to place an order*. An order for some things my men desperately need out here."

He waited for a response, but I said nothing.

With a deep breath, he continued.

"I demanded a third of the Cerro Llano treasure if we found it. When I did that, I was taking it away from General Santa Ana. That was a dangerous thing to do."

Again I did not respond, just listened.

"The captain has my career, really my life in his hands, depending on what he tells General Santa Ana."

"Yes, I suppose he does," I responded, and then asked. "So what's your favor?"

"If we are successful at finding the Cerro Llano gold, I want to place an order for some things we need. I want you to get them for us."

"What do you need,Colonel?"

"Chu Chu, we need a lot of things. First of all, I want 10 more six-shooters like the one you gave me. And maybe it's silly, but I want a new Mexican flag for each of my garrisons. I want good ones! Four of them."

He continued, staring into the fire.

"We are Mexicans, and I want my men to be proud to stand in formation and salute a nice new flag, not one of the old rags we have now. It will do a lot for morale."

"Certainly."

"And there's more. Uniforms, rifles, powder, lead, casting dies, slickers, a lot of things. I had my clerk Faustino make a list for me. Here it is."

Colonel Trujillo handed me a folded piece of paper. I opened it and saw a long list of items neatly written in ink. I was impressed with his sense of patriotism and loyalty to his men. He was making good on his reason for demanding a third of the treasure from Marco.

"Colonel, this is quite a list. How do you propose I pay for it? And how do I get these things to you?"

"I've thought about that. Can I give you part of the treasure we recover?" he asked innocently.

"No. I don't think so. Santa Ana is going to be all over the treasure when we get it to Mexico City. We cannot have a separate stash nearby that he could find out about. No, that won't work."

"I'm not smart about those things. How can we do it? Can I send one of my men down later with the money? And have him bring back the supplies?" The colonel asked.

My conversations with Salvador Villarreal, the second in command at the Bank of Mexico, crossed my mind.

"Colonel, you have a small bank in Hermosillo. What are you going to do with the gold and silver ingots when you get them? Where are you going to keep them?"

"Chu Chu, we're in Mexico, not England. I can't put them in the bank. Ours gets robbed about twice a year. Usually, me and my men catch and hang the thieves. But not always. No, it can't go into the bank. I need to keep it."

I had to smile.

I was touched by this man's loyalty to his job and troops and his simplistic view of the world. He was putting his career on the line, and maybe his life, to improve the conditions for his men. He was using part of Santa Ana's treasure to buy things his government wouldn't or couldn't provide him. I wondered if this man could be corrupted as Santa Ana, Marco and I had been. Perhaps, but for now I must take him at his word.

"Colonel, I suggest you talk to your banker and see if he has any dealings with the Bank of Mexico in Mexico City. I know an important man there. If you put enough money in the Hermosillo bank to pay for your supplies, perhaps your banker could work out a letter of credit I could use with the Bank of Mexico to pay for it."

"I don't know what you are saying, Chu Chu. Me give the money to my bank and you buy my supplies in Mexico City?"

"Yes, something like that. Talk to your banker and see what he says. I'll give you the address where you can send me a letter in Mexico City.

I know how to get mail to you, but the military courier would work better. I'll ask Captain Vásquez if we can use it."

The colonel stiffened. "I would prefer it if Captain Vásquez doesn't know about this. He's too close to General Santa Ana. Can we keep it between you and me?"

"Yes we can," I said slowly. "But we need to work out the money question before I can buy anything. Also, I think Captain Vásquez could be a good friend to you in Mexico City, if you let him."

"I don't know. Maybe. We will see."

We were about to end our interesting conversation when I decided our relations were improved enough for me to give him the two strung nuggets I had been carrying in my pocket–one for Zonia and a smaller one for Tuti. I was taking a chance, since having these nuggets strongly suggested Marco and I had found another treasure site. I did it anyway.

"Colonel, you and your wife have been very gracious to me. Here is a little gift I wish you would present to her. And it was wonderful what you and your wife did for Tuti. I have one for her too."

I pulled out the two gold nuggets with a thread strung through a hole in them. I showed him where I had stamped a small initial in each: a Z for Zonia and a T for Tuti.

The colonel took the gifts and held them up to examine in the campfire light. He said nothing, but his lips tightened emotionally for a moment. Then he thanked me and I left.

The colonel's strategy for digging up the Cerro Llano treasure was different from what Captain Vásquez and I had in mind. Our strategy was to come in *like thieves in the dead of the night*, dig it up, cover our tracks and steal away. Not Colonel Trujillo.

I thought we were in concert with the colonel until we got to Cocospera and set up camp the next evening. Trujillo sent Sergeant Campos and two of his men to go round up six or eight local farmers and have them report to our camp the first thing in the morning with digging tools–picks and shovels. This action didn't seem to be very subtle, Marco and I thought, but the colonel didn't ask us.

The next morning, seven farmers reported to our camp. The weather was cold but clear and there were signs of snow on the distant mountaintops to the north. The colonel was very friendly to the farmers and offered them coffee. Then he gave a little speech.

"Gentlemen, thank you for joining us this morning. Today we are going to correct a wrong committed by the Spaniards over thirty years ago. They were stealing gold and silver taken out of the hills and mountains of Mexico, by Mexicans, and they were taking it to Spain.

"For years, the Spanish had been robbing Mexico of her birthright, her wealth. Finally, *El Grito*–the Revolution, stopped them. Some of the last gold and silver they were trying to steal did not leave Mexico. The Spaniards hid some of it close by, so they could come back and steal it later.

The colonel's voice rang out in the morning air. "Today, we are going to recover that gold and silver for Mexico. You all will be working for your country–Mexico. You'll be helping to right this terrible wrong. Thank you for your help."

He raised his hand. "Viva Mexico!"

The surprised farmers and soldiers responded with a halfhearted *"Viva Mexico."* It was an inspiring speech, but it also was entirely too early, too cold and the men too sober to get easily excited.

Marco and I looked at each other during the colonel's little speech. We certainly had not counted on this! The colonel had tried to pump everyone up, making it sound like it was their patriotic duty to go recover the gold and silver for Mexico. Perhaps it was.

The colonel then got on his horse and led our group directly to Cerro Llano, which was about half a mile away. We went by the old mission, where Padre Silva stood at the door looking out and wondering what was happening. The colonel and about half of our group waved to him as we rode by. A few minutes later, we arrived at Cerro Llano.

The colonel directed everyone to clean out the brush from around the Spanish military graves. That took about 20 minutes. When completed, there they were–eight sets of carelessly stacked stones marking the unknown contents below. We were about to find out what was buried there.

The colonel, in true military fashion, assigned diggers to four of the eight graves, the farmers on one end and the soldiers on the other. Juan and I helped the farmers on the second grave from the end. The soldiers started to dig up the two graves at the opposite end. The colonel and Captain Vásquez watched.

Almost immediately, one of the farmers working on the grave next to us called out "Bones!" and crossed himself. The colonel and Marcos came over to investigate. About that time, the farmer digging in our hole knelt down and carefully uncovered some old clothes and bones. This was not a good start.

Everyone else stopped digging and came over to our two holes to watch. After a few minutes of careful digging, the remains of two clothed bodies were pulled out of the first grave and laid on top of the ground. They were soldiers! It looked like they had been killed, then carelessly thrown into the grave one on top of the other. Both still had their boots and spurs on.

This angered the colonel. He ordered one of his soldiers to go and fetch Padre Silva. He then assigned six soldiers to continue digging in the first two graves and to carefully extract any remaining bodies and lay them out side-by-side. The superstitious farmers didn't want anything to do with it.

The colonel then ordered me and Marco to take the farmers and extra soldiers and supervise the cleaning out of the remaining six graves. We did.

At about two feet deep, the soldiers hit something. They carefully uncovered it as Marco and I watched. It was an old canvas bag filled with something heavy, like rocks or bricks. It tore open as the soldiers were lifting it out of the hole and black ingots fell out of it. *We knew then that we had found the second treasure site.* All work stopped again, as everyone came over to inspect the find.

The colonel pulled Marcos and me aside. "Captain Vásquez, I want you and Chu Chu to inventory everything that comes out of the ground. Make sure nothing goes into any pockets. Do you understand?"

"Yes sir." We responded almost in unison.

"I will supervise removing the bodies. Father Silva is coming and we will see what he thinks we should do with them," the stressed colonel said.

"So get to it!" he ordered.

Everyone, including the farmers, went back to work. One by one, the remaining graves were beginning to reveal their hidden canvas bags. I had the farmers and soldiers carefully carry each decomposing bag and lay them before us. After cutting the binding leather cord which held them closed, and a quick inspection, Captain Vásquez laid them out in two adjacent rows, one for gold ingots and one for silver.

Both the silver and gold were in ingots, the gold not being rod casting like the treasure from La Escondida. Most of the silver ingots were tarnished and almost black from the time and moisture. However, the gold casting retained their recognizable color.

Many of the rotten bags tore, and some of their contents spilled out. Marco tried to keep a close eye on the activities, even stopping work at times so one bag could be removed from the hole at a time. He caught one farmer trying to hide a silver ingot in his trousers, but it fell through his pant leg and hit his toe, causing him to cry out. The man was sent home in shame. Work went better after that.

The men became quiet as they worked. Gold and silver ingots were being removed from the remaining six graves and decaying bodies removed from the first two graves. It was an exciting, but also a sobering sight. It became obvious what had transpired years ago. As at the La Escondida treasure, the Spaniards had slaughtered those Mexicans or Indians who were helping to haul the treasure.

The padre arrived on a mule with five or six young boys following. Sergeant Campos chided the boys and told them to go home. Instead, they went to the nearby ridge overlooking the work and watched.

The padre and the colonel, along with another soldier, carefully inspected the bodies being removed from the two graves. It was a sobering and smelly job–sometimes required putting the bones of decayed legs and arms together with what appeared to be the rest of the body. Although rotten, the shirts, jackets and trousers of the dead victims helped keep most of the bodies together. After sorting out the bodies as best they could, the padre gave them the last rites and sprinkled a dash of holy water on them, even though it was about thirty years too late.

The padre sent for some blankets to rewrap each of the seven rotten bodies into its own separate bundle. The colonel was totally focused on respectfully handling the murdered victims, and didn't interfere with what was happening at our end of the graveyard.

Finally, by late morning, we were finished. At least Marco and I thought we were. There were seven bodies carefully laid out, four of them soldiers according to their clothes, and the others, either workers or burro tenders.

On our side of the graveyard, we had 12 neat piles of the treasure–seven of silver ingots and five of gold. Exactly what our maps and notes had indicated.

As the day wore on, a crowd of women, children and farmers grew. They watched the unusual sight from the opposite hill.

Finally, the colonel conversed with the padre, and the work stopped. Then he came over to Marco and me.

"Padre Silva decided that this would be an easier place to bury these men. The graves are already here and mostly opened. We decided to clean out seven of the graves, dig them to the proper depth and rebury these men today.

"I'm having some of the men go down, get lunch and bring it back in a wagon. We will continue working here until the seven men are properly buried. Padre Silva plans to hold a short mass here and another memorial mass tomorrow morning at the church. I want *all of us* to attend both services. These men gave their lives for Mexico. And, by the way, *I found my uncle*."

"Your uncle? Are you sure it was your uncle?" I asked.

"Yes. I'm sure," he grimly muttered, holding a rusted Spanish spur with a large, sharp rowel.

"See this? Take a look at the silver rattlesnake head design on it. My grandfather made two sets of spurs with that design. One he gave to his brother Ángel, and the other he gave to his son Francisco, my father. This one is Ángel's. The other pair is on the fireplace mantel at my hacienda. Yes, I'm sure this is my Uncle Ángel."

Marco and I said nothing as the colonel slowly examined the rusty spur.

Then Trujillo asked, "Have you found all the gold and silver?"

"Yes, Colonel," answered Captain Vásquez.

"How much is there?"

Marco looked at me, so I answered. "Colonel, there were twelve loads buried in the six graves."

"Loads?" he asked.

"Yes. When I say *loads*, I mean *burro loads*. The Spaniards hauled and buried each burro-load of ingots in the canvas bags they hauled it in. That's how we have it separated. Seven loads of silver ingots, and five loads of gold ingots."

"Can we separate it? I mean, what is it worth?" The colonel answered, now shifting his mind from murdered men and his uncle to gold.

The sudden change was disconcerting. "Can we separate it?" I replied. "Sure. What is it worth? Well that's a little more complicated. I have to inventory it to get an exact count on the ingots. The silver ingots are tarnished, but still good. They are each stamped with their mining foundry markings. The gold ingots are perfect. They also have their foundry casting markings. I have to inventory and weigh them before I can give you an estimate of what they are worth."

The tired colonel responded. "Give me a rough idea–40,000 *reales*? 60,000 reales?"

"No,Colonel. I think there's going to be over 80,000 *escudos* in gold alone. Maybe over 120 thousand *reales* in silver," I responded.

The colonel seemed stunned. He blinked twice before finding his voice. "Over 80,000 in gold escudos?"

"Yes sir. I will know after I inventory the piles we've laid out there."

Marco broke in. "Colonel, Chu Chu and I have been trying to keep tight control on the ingots. We need to keep everyone away, except for the one or two men we need to inventory it. Then we need to separate a third of it out for you."

"Yes,Captain. Yes, do what you need to do," the colonel replied hoarsely.

He then walked over with us and I opened several rotten bags full of ingots. Some had already broken open and ingots were lying next to them on the ground. The colonel seemed overwhelmed at the sight.

He shook his head. "I didn't think there was this much money in the whole world! Look at it! The damned Spaniards took that much out of Mexico every week. Can you imagine that?"

We did not respond, just nodded. I wondered if the colonel's conscience was starting to bother him. He didn't want Santa Ana to have it all, but perhaps he also was feeling guilty or worried about taking some of what the general had ordered be delivered to Mexico City.

The colonel walked over to a pile of freshly dug dirt and sat down. We followed but remained standing.

Taking off his hat and rubbing his head, the colonel said, "Over 80,000 escudos? That would buy half of Sonora. All I wanted was enough to properly outfit my soldiers. Is that unreasonable?"

Again, neither Marco nor I answered.

The colonel took a deep breath and looked up at us."Captain, what should I do? You know our situation here in Sonora.

I thought, *this ought to be interesting!*

Looking into the captain's eyes, I tried to read Marco's mind. I guessed Marco should be thinking something like–*Okay, you old bastard, you wouldn't cooperate with me when I asked for your help. You hate Santa Ana, like a lot of people do. But you played tough with me and made me pay one third of this treasure as mordida for your help. Now reality has set in. You see the treasure and realize that Santa Ana will soon know about all of this. Now you're frightened the old general will throw you out of the military or kill you. Finally, I've got you by the balls where I want you!*

But I read Marco wrong.

Marco studied the colonel slumped on the pile of dirt and said nothing. He then turned and took several steps toward the rows of ingots on the ground.

Finally Marco turned and replied. "Colonel Trujillo, you said you were going to use the money to help your men and garrisons here in Sonora. What do you need, and how much will it cost?"

I was surprised at Marco's un-vindictive response. I thought he was going to thrust it into the tough colonel. I think the colonel had expected it too.

The surprised colonel uncharacteristically stumbled over his words. "Well, Captain, err, I ah .... Captain, I gave Chu Chu a list of what I want for my garrisons and men. He has the list. I don't know what it will cost."

The response surprised Marco. He looked at me and I nodded. That action by the tough old colonel probably saved his life.

"You gave Chu Chu a list of what you need? When?"

"Yes. Two nights ago."

I again nodded, then reached into my pocket for the list and handed it to Captain Vásquez. He carefully read through it and handed it back to me.

"*Flags?* You need flags, Colonel?"

"Yes. Only two of my men have been to Mexico City. I've never been there myself. They, err....*we* are dedicated Mexican soldiers. I was wounded for Mexico, twice during the American war. The flag is something my men can see and be proud of. There's not much more–low pay, dangerous conditions, poor food and equipment. They ...we are dedicated to Mexico City and bosses we have never seen. No, it's better to say we are dedicated to the Mexico we have seen."

The colonel went on with a theme we had heard before, his voice gaining strength. "They expect us to take *mordidas* from the people to make up for what we don't get from Mexico City. I can't do that. Yes, we get food and other things from our people, but we also help them, and most are our friends and family. They know how poorly we are supplied. But our people are poor and I can't take money or property from them."

I think Marco was impressed with the tough old colonel's actions and answers. I sure as hell was. *He was genuine.*

Marco turned to me and asked, "Chu Chu what will the things on the colonel's list cost?"

"Captain, I haven't figured it out. The guns will be expensive, and the flags. The other thing shouldn't be too bad," I responded.

"The flags, expensive?" Marco responded with a half-smile.

"Yes. The good flags are made in France. They will cost almost as much as a six-shooter. The colonel wants *good flags*."

Captain Vásquez turned to the contrite colonel sitting on the pile of dirt. "Colonel, are you asking me to take out the money you need for your supplies from that?" He pointed to the stacks of ingots.

"Yes,Captain, I am."

The captain was quiet again as he rubbed the back of his neck. Finally he replied. "I will,Colonel. What are you going to do about helping us get to Desemboque and our ship?"

Colonel Trujillo stood, dusting off the seat of his uniform. "I'll do what I said I would do. I plan to send Sergeant Campos and five men to escort you there."

"Make it Campos and eight men."

"Done."

Captain Vásquez swelled visibly, back in control again.

The colonel then spoke up respectfully. "Captain, we need to properly bury these men murdered by the Spaniards. I would consider it a favor if you and the nine men I just assigned to you could help us finish the graves and stay to attend the services by Padre Silva. There will be a service this afternoon here and the one in the morning at the church."

"We will. We will be happy to. These men were heroes and loyal Mexicans. Yes, Colonel, we will be happy to," the captain responded.

With that, *the hatchet was buried* between the colonel and the captain. And the colonel undoubtedly saved his career, and probably his life.

The colonel told Marco to do anything we needed to do with the ingots. He would take care of the bodies. He said his men were available as we needed them. Then he gave orders to Sergeant Campos to feed his men, then have the farmers and soldiers clean out seven of the graves to rebury the dead men. He also told the sergeant to assign four soldiers to help Marco and me with the ingots, saying to assign more if we needed them.

After Captain Vásquez posted Campos and a second soldier to watch the treasure, we climbed down off Cerro Llano to where two wagons were waiting with lunch. After we washed up and ate, we got back to work. The day had warmed up and was pleasant.

Later, we returned to the site. The farmers and most of the soldiers cleaned out and deepened seven graves, while separately Marco and I, along with four soldiers, tended to the ingots.

We had Juan Sáldate and three soldiers bring the burros over and unload the new canvas bags. Then we inventoried each pile of the old

Spanish ingots and repacked them into the new bags.

The Spaniards had methodically made even loads for the burros. Each burro carried two bags, each with approximately 30 kilos of ingots in it. The bags were draped over the burros and tied onto the packsaddles with leather straps, so as to counterbalance the load. We were going to do the same thing, remembering what we had seen in the La Escondida hidden tunnel.

We had brought a string of eighteen burros and forty bags from Hermosillo, anticipating success at both Cerro Llano and Tubutama. However, the existence of the Tubutama site was still a secret. We would pack the burros lightly here–and deal with the Tubutama site when we got there. If we found everything shown on the Spanish maps, we would need more burros. We figured we could easily find more burros there.

We repacked the ingots into 36 bags for our eighteen burros, ready for our trip to Tubutama. Then Marco started to separate what he was going to give to the colonel. I watched him.

"Chu Chu, what do you think the colonel needs to buy his supplies? Would it be better to give him silver ingots or gold?" Marco asked.

"Well, silver would probably be easier for him to convert to cash here in Sonora. And gold would be easier for us to haul to Mexico City," I responded pragmatically.

"So, what should we give him, 10,000 reales? 20,000 reales?"

"It's probably going to take him over 10,000 reales to buy what he has on his list. Seems like we should give him a little more than that. One burro-load of the silver ingots is worth more than 18,000 reales. It seems like we should give him at least that," I responded.

Marco agreed, so we loaded two bags with 15 silver ingots in each. Marco looked at it for a moment then put two more gold ingots in, one in each bag.

"What's that for?" I asked.

"That's for his retirement."

I nodded, and then put in three more gold ingots.

"What's that for?" Marco asked incredulously.

"That's so he can retire a little earlier," I responded.

We both laughed.

Everyone worked hard. By late afternoon, all the bodies were wrapped in blankets and reburied in the seven graves. The rocks were restacked and all the weeds and brush were cleared from around the neat graves. The men had done a nice job.

The men rested for a few minutes while the padre rode his mule back to the mission, gathering a proper vestment, some incense and holy water for a short graveside mass. When he returned, we all removed our hats and stood while he conducted his service. It seemed proper for these murdered men to finally have a Christian burial.

That evening, we returned to our previous night's camping ground along the Cocospera River, close to the mission. Marco, Juan, three other soldiers and I unloaded the burros and set the sacks of ingots in squared off rows next to where Marco and I were to sleep. People continued to walk by, trying to get a look at the treasure. Sergeant Campos tried to be polite, but did keep them at a distance.

The colonel directed Campos to have two of his men trade horses with Marco and me. He realized we needed better animals to ride to Desemboque.

Early the next morning, the mission bells rang. The colonel and most of the men including Captain Vásquez, rode off to the early mass for the dead men we reburied. Juan and I, along with three other soldiers, didn't attend the mass but stayed to saddle and load the burros.

As soon as the mass was finished, the colonel and Marcos came riding over to where I was standing with the loaded burros. They dismounted and came over to talk. I handed Marco the halter rope to one of the loaded burros.

Marco in turn handed the rope to the colonel. "Colonel, this should be more than enough for you to purchase the supplies for your men."

The colonel took hold of the rope nodding, but silent.

Then the captain awkwardly tried to joke with the colonel.

"Colonel, Chu Chu said we needed to put something in there extra for your retirement, so we did."

The colonel looked at me, then the captain, and smiled. "I must say you two are the most unusual men I've ever met coming from Mexico City."

He thanked Marco and shook his hand. He turned to me. "And Chu Chu, you are the most unusual living gringo I have ever met."

I started to say something, but he interrupted with a chuckle. "Yes, Chu Chu, I know. You are not a gringo."

Then he took something wrapped in a paper from his saddlebag and handed it to me. "Chu Chu, I thought you might like to have these. They're very special to me."

I opened the paper. Inside were two rusty old Spanish spurs, each with a small silver rattlesnake head on them–*his dead uncle's spurs.*

"I can't take these, Colonel. These are too special to you," I insisted.

The colonel, a little emotional, said nothing and pushed them back to me.

I thanked him and shook his hand. We then left.

Traveling with the loaded burros slowed us down. The burros did well after the green-broke ones settled down with their loads. Several of the packsaddles came apart, but we fixed them with leather straps.

It took us almost two days to get to Tubutama. We camped away from the mission and almost on top of the place the maps showed where the treasure was buried. Juan Sáldate realized what we were doing, since he and I had been there several weeks before.

Not being as altruistic and patriotic as Colonel Trujillo, Marco and I kept a low profile in the Tubutama area. As soon as we set up camp in the late afternoon and had the animals tended to, we started to dig. In less than two feet, we struck the first wooden box. It was made of bark-stripped mesquite branches with the ends tied with rawhide straps. Inside, wrapped in burlap, were silver ingots. Success! *We had found the last of the hidden Pimeria Alta treasures.*

The weather was good, so we ate and continued digging using candle light after dark. By midnight we had found all the boxes, with the exception of one–one containing silver. There were supposed to be two loads with silver ingots, but we could only find one. We quit a little after midnight and finally got some rest.

Early the next morning the soldiers and Juan continued to dig while Marco and I inspected the boxes. They were in remarkably good shape, except for the burlap material inside. We decided to transfer the ingots to our extra new bags, which would be easier for us to carry on our pack saddles.

The single load of silver ingots was different from those from the La Escondida and Cocospera sites. They were also stamped with mine foundry markings, but the ingots were shaped differently. The six boxes with gold ingots were also cast differently. Four of the six boxes of gold ingots were cast in a longer, square bar shape. The other two boxes contained ingots cast into small square blocks. They obviously came from a different part of the Pimeria Alta or perhaps from California.

Periodically Marco and I went over to where the men were digging and suggested new locations to look. Two soldiers helped us repack all seven boxes of ingots into the new bags. We would need to overload our seventeen burros to start with and see if we could pick up some additional burros on our way down the Río Concepción to Desemboque, where the small desert river flowed into the sea.

It was late morning and we were about to give up finding the lost box of silver ingots when Marco took a break to relieve himself. When he came back, he was limping. I asked him what happened, and he said he stepped on a thorn that went through his boot. He said he would be all right.

Still not finding the last mesquite box with its silver ingots, we had the men cover the holes we had dug and attempt to restore the area to its original looking condition. We ate a quick lunch, then loaded the burros.

According to my journal, it was midday on Friday, February 11, 1853, when we headed west toward Pitiquito. We were slightly ahead of schedule for meeting Captain Beltrán and the weather was good again. We traveled slowly with our caravan of pack burros, overloaded with the treasures of the Pimeria Alta, or at least some of them. Fixing sprung or broken packsaddles and shifting loads on the burros so they wouldn't rub the animals and cause sores, became a never-ending task. Also, Marco's foot was bothering him.

That evening, we bought three more burros from a local farmer. Marco said most of Santa Ana's money was now gone. I still had a little money with me, but that also would soon be gone. We would need to use care cashing in some of the treasure to pay our expenses to get back.

Marco and I paced ourselves so we would arrive at the sea on the 15th. We didn't want to have idle time on our hands with Juan, Sergeant Campos and his eight men thinking about our treasure. We also discussed how we were going to dismiss the men and leave on good terms. The solution was simple–*pay them and pay them well!*

We arrived on the coast near Desemboque late morning on Tuesday the 15th of February. It was a poor little fishing village of about twenty simple adobe homes where Mexican fishermen lived near the mouth of the river and the bay. Up the beach from the Mexican village, we could see a few Seri Indian open huts with desert bear-grass roofs held up with mesquite and ironwood poles. Some naked Seri children played on the beach nearby along with three emaciated pups. A few pelicans and sea birds flew around, keeping a cautious eye on us.

Marco rode over to a Mexican fisherman's house and asked the lady if she had seen a ship recently. She replied yes, but it had sailed up the coast the evening before. At least Captain Beltrán was in the area.

We set up a temporary camp near a well at the mouth of the Río Conception, which flowed into the sea within sight of the village of Desemboque. The location was picturesque, having a small stream flowing from the desert through the trees. We watered the horses and burros, ate, then waited for Beltrán.

In the afternoon, Beltrán's dilapidated old ship, *La Doncella Pechisima*, came slowly sailing down the coast. The old girl looked better to me that day than the most majestic three mast sailing ship I had ever seen leaving from the Liverpool Harbor. I guess it was a matter of perspective and desperation, since we had no back-up plan.

Sergeant Campos sent a man on horseback loping up the beach to hail Beltrán's ship. We saw the anchor splash into the water and the old ship come to a stop near the beach. A few minutes later, Beltrán and two of his crew rowed over in their old rowboat to meet us.

Marco and I were anxious to get the gold and silver loaded and be on our way. But then we encountered a little problem we hadn't anticipated. How would we get the ingots from the pack burros to the ship and still maintain our vigilance over it? It would be easy for an ingot to disappear here or there during the transfer.

After a quick discussion, we decided that Marco would go over with the first load of ingots, along with Beltrán and his two crewmen. I would remain and get the rowboat loaded with a counted number of ingots for each trip. He would watch the unloading of ingots on the ship and I would watch them loaded on shore. I would tie the canvas bags shut and we would both watch the sailors transporting them to the ship.

Everyone worked hard, and in two hours we had the ingots loaded. I kept back one partial bag of silver ingots.

After finishing our task, I thanked Sergeant Campos and his men. I also thanked Juan Sáldate. I told Juan to take back the burros with their packs and sell them, splitting the money with Colonel Trujillo. I paid him, then gave him two ingots of silver. He was delighted.

A few minutes later, I pulled Sergeant Campos to one side. I again thanked him and gave him two ingots of silver. After he put them out of sight, we went to each of his eight men, and I gave them each a single ingot. We all left on great terms.

Finally, with a sense of both relief and sadness, I climbed into the rowboat and rode back to the ship. At my feet was the remaining canvas bag. Only one silver ingot remained inside. The sailors eyed the bag and touched it curiously as we boarded the old ship.

We pulled anchor and set sail, heading south as the evening sun dropped into the Sea of Cortez in the west. Beltrán said it would be safe for us to sail at night as long as the weather was good and we traveled slowly. If there were any problems, he said we would drop anchor. Marco and I slept outside the locked room with our treasure inside. *We were now on the last leg of our adventure.*

Chapter 23

The Pirate

That evening as I stood alone at the railing of the old ship watching the winter sun go down over the Sea of Cortez, I wondered if Melanie had watched the same sunset at the Fields of Shannon Plantation in Georgia. I also wondered how Mother was doing. I missed them both, and someday soon hoped to bring Melanie *home* to Mexico with me as my new bride.

Mother's biblical quotation came to mind: *For where your treasure is, there will your heart be also.*

Smiling, I reasoned that General Santa Ana's image of treasures were vastly different than mine. Packed away on our ship were some of Santa Ana's physical treasures. If he knew of them, I was sure *part of his heart* would be here with us. And yes, Marco and I still had some phenomenal Spanish treasures hidden away in the distant Chihuahuita Mountains, *but my heart and treasure was with Melanie and always would be*. I would be happy when we were together again.

Captain Beltrán's men quickly raised the ship's anchor and trimmed the sails. The canvas caught a soft breeze, and we began moving south along the nearby rocky and arid coastline.

My mind again wandered. Watching the desert plants along the shore move silently by as the ship sailed south, it seemed like we were living a life out of the pages of a storybook. Georgia was a foreign land far, far away.

Marco and I had done well in finding all three of the hidden Spanish treasures in the Pimeria Alta. The old general knew he had stumbled onto something when he laid his hands on the old Spanish maps. That must have been an interesting story in itself. And we were making a few more of his dreams come true with our little venture. I hoped he would make good on his promise to me and let The New Wales Equipment and Mining Company do business in Mexico.

Having gone through this experience, I now had a better feel for how fluid and tenuous national and international politics could be. It was possible Marco and I could have done all of this while Santa Ana negotiated with the Americans for a new railroad route, only to then find himself thrown out of power. Then I would have harvested nothing, at least as far as my company was concerned. Right now I had nothing except the general's word. According to Marco, that too was questionable, depending on how the wind was blowing and the general's whims on a particular day. We would see.

Getting the treasure to Mexico City could be the hardest part of our assignment. The existence of the treasure was now public knowledge, and we were traveling in another world, *the water*. At least on land I could pick our trails and the times we would travel–and have a dog like Traitor along to warn us of an impending attack. Here on this little ship, I felt we were available for the taking, so to speak.

The most likely threat Marco and I had discussed was for word of the treasure to travel southward by land as we traveled by sea. An attack could await us almost anywhere before we got to Mexico City. Colonel Trujillo's unexpected actions in Cocospera had disrupted our plans by letting everyone know he was digging up the hidden Spanish treasure at Cerro Llano. He had publicly exposed our plans sooner than we expected.

According to our original plans, we expected the unpredictable Colonel Trujillo to secretly take his part of the Cocospera treasure, then quietly steal back to Hermosillo with his men. Only then would word get out about our finding the treasure. By that time, Marco and I would have also recovered the Tubutama treasure and would have been halfway to the sea. Instead, the colonel made a big public display of the whole affair–and now we could solidly be in someone's sights, someone who meant us no good.

As it happened, not only did we have an external threat, we also found we had a potential internal threat on board the ship.

After darkness set in, Captain Beltrán invited Marco and me to his cabin for supper. Knowing our concerns about the treasure, he suggested we leave his door open so we could watch the small, locked cabin with our goods. We gladly agreed.

At supper, Captain Beltrán was very cordial and brought us up to date on his activities since we had last seen him. He had done some repairs on *La Doncella* in Mazatlán with part of the money Marco gave him and had also changed several crew members. He laughed about a new man he had hired, the one the other crewmen called *El Pirata* (The Pirate).

During dinner, the captain also brought up the subject about the ship's balance. He was concerned about the weight of our goods in his ship. He said we needed to redistribute the weight in the small ship, otherwise it could capsize in the wind or a turn. He said it was so noticeable, he might even drop anchor for the night to reduce the danger of the ship toppling. Marco was against redistributing our goods throughout the ship and so was I.

But I knew Beltrán's concerns had merit and suggested several other methods to deal with it. I suggested he redistribute some of the other supplies and equipment to compensate for the weight and location of our goods located high on the ship. Also, I suggested he could take on some ballast. Although not happy, he agreed. About an hour later, we dropped anchor for the night. Marco and I slept on mats and blankets outside our locked storage room.

The next morning, Beltrán had the crew move some of the equipment and limited cargo on board before we set sail. This temporarily helped to better distribute the weight in the ship. We sailed down the coast for several hours, then dropped anchor again along a rocky shore.

Captain Beltrán had the crew go ashore and pick up four rowboat-loads of smooth beach stones. These, he had the men place on pallets above the keel of the ship to help stabilize the vessel. When we pulled anchor and started moving again, Captain Beltrán was much more confident with his control of the ship, even though it sat lower in the water.

Marco's infected foot continued to bother him. Captain Beltrán and I asked him to let us take a look at it. It was seriously infected, and the thorn was still in it. Beltrán had the cook heat some salt water for Marco to soak his foot. Afterwards, I performed an operation with a needle. After removing a large broken thorn from his foot, some pent up puss drained from the wound. I hoped this would help.

The logistics of acquiring food and other supplies for the ship became a problem. We didn't want unwanted conversations about our cargo to take place between our crewmen and people on the shore. This would further open the door for a possible attack.

Marco reached an agreement with Beltrán that the ship would be dedicated to us alone for the duration of the trip south, and no unnecessary stops would be made or cargo carried. We thought we could trust Captain Beltrán, but decided I would be the only person to go ashore to buy supplies because of Marco's bad leg. We agreed that two crewmen would row me to the dock, leave me, then return to the ship. Two hours later, I would meet them at the dock with the supplies, and we would load up and return to the ship.

This arrangement was not going to be very popular with the crew, but I knew how to handle it from our trip north with them. I would buy good food, sweets and a little wine. Too bad I couldn't throw in a woman now and then. We figured the crew should be able to endure a trip south confined to the ship if they had plenty of good food and drink. At least it would help.

Two days later, we made our first stop at Guaymas. We arrived in the afternoon, dropped anchor, and I was rowed to the docks as planned. I hired a buckboard and immediately went around to the shops, picking up ham, beef, *pan dulce*, bottles of wine and other things the cook needed.

At the second shop, someone tapped me on the shoulder from behind. I turned, and there stood a tired–looking Sergeant Dominguez smiling at me.

"Manuel, what are you doing here?!" I asked, astonished.

"Chu Chu, the colonel sent me. You are in danger."

I pulled Sergeant Dominguez outside, where we could have a little more privacy.

"Danger? What kind of danger? What did the colonel say?"

Sergeant Dominguez explained that Lieutenant Pacheco, who worked under Colonel Trujillo, was the nephew of General Pacheco, in Chihuahua–Trujillo's boss. That was news to me. Second, he said General Pacheco was a close friend to General Escalante in Guadalajara.

Now this was getting interesting, since I had met General Escalante on our trip north.

Finally, Colonel Trujillo said to tell us that the day we left Cocospera, Lieutenant Pacheco wrote a message to his uncle, General Pacheco, and hired a local man from Cocospera to deliver it directly to the general *post haste*. The colonel was sure Lieutenant Pacheco told his uncle about the treasure and our plans to take it to Desemboque. There we would catch a ship south, and finally deliver it to General Santa Ana in Mexico City.

A conspiracy had been hatched, and we had some big players involved.

I thanked Sergeant Dominguez after asking him if there was anything else the colonel wanted to pass on to us. He said no. Dominguez and I had developed a friendship during our military outing into the Pimeria Alta territory. After bidding him goodbye, I gave the big sergeant 200 *realés* and a small nugget I carried in my vest pocket. We shook hands as friends, knowing most likely we would never meet again.

That evening, back on board ship, I told Marco about Sergeant Dominguez's warning from Colonel Trujillo. We decided we must share the information with Captain Beltrán. We did–at supper.

After hearing of the potential threat, Captain Beltrán became quiet and a bit pensive, trying to digest what he had heard. Then he spoke.

"Gentlemen, if those men are involved we have a serious problem. Too bad we can't get General Santa Ana to deal with them before they bother us. But I guess that's not an option–yet."

We discussed the problem further but arrived at no different strategy. We would keep moving south as quickly as possible, making minimal stops at unusual places and times. That was difficult, because few ports had the supplies we needed.

Our previously relaxed and joking relationship with the crew had changed. There was now a tension in the air between us because of our cargo. The crewmembers also sensed that we could be in danger from an attack and grumbled about it, saying that they weren't being paid to be guards.

And we met *El Pirata*. His nickname was fitting. He was a large, stout man, a little taller than Marco and me, but also outweighing us each by about a third. He had a large scar which crossed a bad eye to his brow. He also wore a gold ring in his ear and kept his long hair tied in a knot at the back of his head. He didn't have a sword or a limp, but he did have a knife and a deep, gravelly voice.

The man's appearance and presence on the ship would have almost been humorous, except we knew little about this unusual character. Also, he seemed to have a natural leadership ability and was fast becoming popular amongst the crewmembers. Marco and I anticipated we could have problems with this fellow.

The next evening at supper, Captain Beltrán suggested a new strategy to deal with the problem of a possible attack. Marco and I were impressed with his interest in helping us. First, he suggested that if General Escalante was involved, most likely there would be an attempt to take the treasure near Guadalajara. San Blas or Puerto Vallarta would be likely ports, or on the road to Mexico City. He then asked how we were going to get the ingots to Mexico City.

Other than getting several military wagons and a military escort, we had nothing more planned.

He also asked us to which port we planned to return. Again, San Blas–where we first met him on our departure was our answer. This too was within General Escalante's jurisdiction, and our idea now seemed faulty.

The captain went on to explain that his plan was to stock up with extra food and supplies at Mazatlán, then, with favorable weather, move to open seas and bypass the likely locations where we would be in peril.

Instead of hugging the coast as we usually did and making port at San Blas, we would sail directly to Acapulco, where I could be dropped off and go directly to Mexico City to get help from General Santa Ana.

At Acapulco, Beltrán explained that they could get additional water, food and supplies for the ship and sail south for a week, then return. The plan was to have me waiting with help from General Santa Ana. It sounded like a bold and workable strategy. Bold in the sense I hoped Beltrán's old ship wouldn't sink out in the open sea. We liked the idea, so I proposed a toast to Captain Beltrán's idea, and we drank to it.

It was Sunday night, the 20th of February, 1854 when we dropped anchor near Topolobampo, outside the bay near Río Fuerte. We were two days out of Mazatlán, our next supply stop.

The weather was good, but with the extra weight on the ship, Captain Beltrán considered it prudent to drop anchor at night while we were traveling within sight of land. The idea of later moving to open seas still concerned me a bit, because of the extra weight of the treasure and ballast on the small ship. But the captain assured us his repairs of the vessel had fixed most of the leaks, and he had a new bilge pump. Also, moving away from the dangers of rocks near the shore, sailing at night, should pose no danger, unless we had bad weather.

That night after midnight I awoke and heard some unusual bumping against the ship. I cocked my Colt Dragoon and went to investigate. I came face to face with a man coming over the side onto the ship. I loudly ordered him to halt and called out to Marco and anyone else I could awake.

Sleepily, Marco lit a lamp and came limping over with his six-shooter. The man I had apprehended was El Pirata–Lino Quintero, our crew-man! He was stark naked, dripping with water and shivering. He had a wooden 10-liter bucket slung over his arm with his clothes and boots inside. A few moments later Captain Beltrán came out of his cabin in his nightshirt with a lamp and shotgun.

Shivering, Quintero smiled broadly as he pulled his clothes out of the bucket and started to get dressed. He explained that he was worried about Captain Vásquez's infected foot and had gone ashore to find some medicine. Still smiling, he handed Marco a little paper package tied with a string, then finished putting on his clothes and boots.

The big man explained that he had gone into Los Mochis and found a herbalist and bought some medicine for Marco. Even though I did not trust this dangerous man he did have a package.

Marco, Captain Beltrán and I inspected the contents of Lino Quintero's package by lantern light. It did contain a small quantity of two desert herbs, *yerba de pasmo* and *marijuana.* He laughed, telling Marco that by smoking one and soaking with the other–he would feel better in no time. *His leg might fall off, but he would feel happy about it.*

I almost laughed at the man's comments, but the circumstances dictated that I remain somber. Also both Marco and I were familiar with *yerba de pasmo,* because the Patagonia Mine manager's wife, Elena, had brewed up some of the same desert herb to tend to our wounds after the attack by the Apaches in the Chihuahuita Mountains. And it had worked well, for awhile.

So part of *El Pirata's* story rang true. After some grumbling and further questioning, Captain Beltrán dismissed Lino and we tried to get back to sleep.

The next morning, after we pulled anchor and were having breakfast, Captain Beltrán discussed the incident with Marco and me. He was going to dismiss Lino when we got to Mazatlán. He hoped this would take care of the situation.

During the day, things were tense between us and the crew as we sailed south. The weather looked like there could be a change coming. Marco and I wondered what El Pirata was brewing up.

That night, after midnight, I awoke with a start. I listened and at first heard nothing. Then I heard a muffled splash and noise like someone trying to walk quietly on deck. I again grabbed my revolver and investigated.

The night was dark, but there was a quarter moon and a few clouds low in the sky. After my eyes adjusted to the dark, I could find my way around the ship without a lamp. Barefooted, I tiptoed with my cocked revolver around to the other side of the ship, trying not to pick up splinters from the rough wooden deck. Something was happening, so I hollered out in the darkness.

There was a flurry of activity as a man tossed something down on to what looked like a raft floating in the water below. It made a thunk metallic sound when it hit the raft below. It also made the distinctive clear, ringing sound of *gold* when it hit the raft! They were stealing our treasure!

The thief who had tossed the canvas bag of ingots jumped off the ship into the water alongside the raft. I could see another man on the raft. I fired a shot into the water next to them and shouted for at them to stop. Marco came alongside me with his revolver and a lamp. The men started frantically rowing the raft toward the shore.

"Marco, they've got some of the ingot bags!" I yelled.

Marco started firing at them in earnest, and so did I. Captain Beltrán came out of his cabin in his nightshirt, carrying a lamp and shotgun. Marco quickly told him what was going on, then Beltrán took an explosive shot with his shotgun at the fleeing men on the raft. Even with the ringing in our ears from the shotgun blast, we heard a yelp from one of the thieves out in the darkness on the water.

The captain ordered a couple of sleepy crewmen watching the action to quickly drop the rowboat into the water while we reloaded our weapons. The rowboat's oars were missing, so the men fumbled around for a few seconds and found other oars. Marco wanted to go with us, but I told him to stay on board to take care of his infected foot and our cargo. He reluctantly agreed.

From the rowboat in the water, we could see the outline of the raft nearing the small waves breaking along the shore. The two crewmen rowed our boat like mad, while Beltrán sat in his nightshirt with a shotgun resting across his lap, I was barefoot and without a shirt. We anxiously watched the fleeing thieves trying to escape.

The thieves reached shore a minute or so in front of us and one of the men appeared to be trying to unload two canvas bags. I took a carefully aimed shot, which caused the frightened man to drop a bag into the shallow surf. He started to run with the other bag when I took another shot. Despite the motion of the boat, the second shot must have hit the thief, because he suddenly fell forward into the water. Almost immediately, he pulled something out of the bag, jumped up and continued to run from the beach toward some trees and bushes. The first man remained on the raft, which was caught in the surf.

Our eyes were now much better adjusted to the night. As soon as we hit the beach I jumped out of the rowboat and took a couple more shots in the direction of the man who was running away. Beltrán trotted over to the raft and I followed.

A crewman lay bleeding on the raft, apparently hit by several of Beltrán's shotgun pellets. Two canvas bags were still on the raft with the injured man. After wading through the nearby surf, I found the bag the fleeing thief dropped into the water. I picked it up and waded to the beach, then over to the second bag dropped by thief who had fled. It contained gold ingots! A shining gold ingot lay on the wet sand next to the bag.

After catching my breath for a few moments, I walked back to where Captain Beltrán and our two crewmen were examining the injured man on the raft. It was one of the new men Beltrán had hired.

The two crewmen, José and Moses, helped me gather up the four bags of ingots and load them into our rowboat. I tied the leather handle straps tightly together so a free hand couldn't drop into the bag in the darkness and pull out a souvenir. Luckily, three of the four bags had silver ingots. However, the fourth bag, and the one the thief had pillaged, contained gold ingots. I was sure he grabbed a few gold bars before he ran off. We were certain the thief was Lino Quintero, the Pirate.

I marked the sand on the shore where the activity took place so I could come back in the daylight for a closer look, hoping to see what we missed. We then returned to the ship.

Everyone was awake. The crewmen on board helped to load the injured man onto the ship. He was bleeding seriously and began dropping into unconsciousness while being hauled onboard. Captain Beltrán tended to the injured man while another crewman and I got the stolen canvas bags onboard and into our locked storeroom. Also, Quintero was *missing*.

A few minutes later, Marco showed the captain and me where Quintero had cut a neat hole in the wooden wall between the galley storage room and our storage room. He had used this new entry to take the bags of ingots without our knowledge. Marco thought five bags were missing, but was not positive. He thought four bags contained silver ingots and the fifth, gold. If he was right, we were still missing a bag of silver ingots.

Not being able to sleep, Marco and I immediately started to inventory our cargo. The way we had stacked the canvas bags of ingots inside the storage room made it easy to know what was missing. Captain Beltrán brought us some coffee and another lamp. In a few minutes, we had determined a full bag of silver ingots was missing as well as six gold ingots were gone from the bag Quintero dropped on the beach. I figured they should keep him in beer money for a good while.

As we were finishing our inventory, the captain stuck his head in the storage room and said the injured man had died. Beltrán again confirmed that the dead man was one of the new crewmen he hired at the same time as Quintero.

At sunrise I went back to the beach with our two crewmen, José and Moses, to look for the missing bag and anything else we could find. We tried to follow a line between the ship and the shore, looking for the missing bag we thought was under the water, probably near where the ship was anchored.

The water was fairly clear near the shore, but too deep to see or recover anything near the ship, where we thought the canvas bag was lost. I was sure the splash I first heard during the dark of night was the bag hitting the water instead of the raft. We found nothing.

On the shore, José and Moses helped me look around. Moses followed Lino Quintero's tracks away from the beach. We were about to return to the ship when Moses came back and handed me a gold bar that Quintero had dropped. That meant that El Pirata had stolen four, not five gold ingots. I was impressed with Moses' honesty.

Before we pulled anchor, Captain Beltrán had four crewmen get shovels and load the dead thief's body wrapped in a bloody blanket into the rowboat. I accompanied the captain and crewmen back to shore in the rowboat with the dead man.

On shore, the crewmen laid out a simple, makeshift stretcher and placed the body on it. The captain ordered his men to follow him with the body.

We followed the captain a short distance from the beach to some nearby trees where the ground was soft. Beltrán pointed to the ground, and there the four crewmen quickly dug a shallow grave and rolled the body into it.

Captain Beltrán removed his cap and soberly uttered the following words:

"We reap what we sow. You chose thievery and *you reaped its rewards.* May God have mercy on your soul."

Twenty minutes later, we were on board *La Doncella Pechisima*, where the crew pulled anchor and set the sails. Once again, we were headed south.

Chapter 24

Getting Our Stories Straight

After we buried the thief on the beach, Captain Beltrán was still confident we could reach Mazatlán by evening. However, the weather was changing, with the wind picking up and the clouds gathering. Another winter storm was approaching. This would affect Beltrán's suggested strategy of bypassing San Blas and the other nearby ports where we could expect problems from our adversaries, Generals Pacheco and Escalante. We were approaching Escalante's stomping grounds.

As we sailed toward Mazatlán, Beltrán, Marco and I discussed our situation. For better or worse, Beltrán was now in the middle of our plans and was key to their success. We didn't have much choice since we were in Beltrán's world–the sea.

Captain Beltrán had the cook prepare a list of supplies that would allow us to sail directly from Mazatlán to Acapulco without an intermediate stop. That would take about 10 to 15 days sailing in this slow, old ship, depending on the prevailing winds and whether we traveled on the open sea or along the coast and dropped anchor at night. We wanted the option to go either way, but the weather seemed to be dictating that we must initially travel along the coast.

We arrived at Mazatlán in the evening, and I prepared to go ashore and buy supplies again. Marco and I were running out of spending money, so we traded some silver with Captain Beltrán for the additional money we needed. Beltrán drew it from the nice little stash under his bed.

Both Marco and Beltrán warned me to exercise care on shore because, according to our estimates, our adversaries now had enough time to start positioning themselves for an attack. We weren't sure if it would be on the water or on land.

We agreed that José and Moses would take me to the docks and wait until I returned. Captain Beltrán gave José an old, Spanish flintlock pistol and Moses, his shotgun–in case we ran into problems on shore. For a naval vessel, Beltrán certainly didn't have much firepower, just five or six flintlock rifles, two pistols and a small blunderbuss canon mounted on a broken swivel attached to the ship's railing.

Things went well on shore, and I found most of the supplies we needed. I even found some more *yerba de pasmo* for Marco's leg. I also got some extra cheese, wine and sweets. But, I was being watched. There was always one of three boys who took turns following me to the different markets and stores. I saw one of the boys run down the street and talk to two soldiers sitting drinking and smoking outside a cantina. They occasionally cast an interested glance in my direction.

A little later I met José and Moses at the dock, and we returned to the ship. Captain Beltrán set up a night guard to warn us of any approaching boats or other unusual activity. Marco and I were happy with his cautious actions and slept much better because of it.

The next day, the weather turned worse and it rained, but Beltrán pulled anchor anyway, and we slowly sailed south. During the day, Captain Beltrán debated whether to drop anchor and wait for the weather to improve, but he chose to slowly move on. The men were in a decent mood, because they had good food and little work. They visited and played games. Beltrán usually did not knowingly allow alcohol on board with his crew, but for this trip allowed limited drink with the meals.

Two days later the weather improved, so we headed out to open waters beyond sight of land. Captain Beltrán estimated we would be at Acapulco in eight days.

The first full day we were in open waters things went well. The wind was right, the food was good and the crew was back to their old, joking selves. Removing *El Pirata* and his buddy had dramatically changed the crew members' attitudes and eliminated the tension between us. And according to my journal, it was *February the 24th, 1853,* a date indelibly locked in my mind.

Sitting on a frayed wicker mat and leaning against the ship's storage cabin wall, I updated my journal while nibbling on some cheese and sipping red wine from an old metal cup. *I thought of Melanie.* This was the day her father was to die, according to what he had told us. In his strange dream he had seen a new headstone in the graveyard on the Fields of Shannon Plantation. Mr. Kerns said he saw his name engraved on the headstone and the date– *February 24, 1853.*

What could his premonition mean? Certainly the dream forecast a terrible war. But many people thought that secession could result in a war, a war that the South could quickly win, then sue for peace. Afterwards, they would move on with their own independent nation, the *Southern States of America.*

But why would God reveal this to Mr. Kern, or was he going crazy? What was he supposed to do with this knowledge? How did Melanie and I play into it? Again, many questions and no answers. I was sure Melanie would write me, either way, on what happened back home in Georgia, but I really didn't have a home–not yet.

The next few days were pleasant as we sailed toward Acapulco. Marco and I had plenty of time to further assess our situation. Colonel Trujillo had warned us of the threat from the two generals–Pacheco and Escalante–and we were taking Santa Ana only *part* of the Spanish treasure he sent us after.

General Escalante was in control of much of central Mexico from his headquarters in Guadalajara, and we were headed in his direction. Would he dare challenge General Santa Ana?

We concluded our best strategy was to go along with Captain Beltrán's recommendation to get General Santa Ana's help and let the military deal with the military. Our plan using Beltrán's suggested strategy called for me to get off the ship at Acapulco and quickly travel to Mexico City to get General Santa Ana's help. That trip would be over

400 kilometers and would take three to four days of hard riding.

Marco's foot and leg were better, but we agreed he would stay with the ship and treasure. Marco and Beltrán would sail south to kill time, then return and meet me and Santa Ana's men at an agreed upon location near Acapulco. That should reduce the chance of losing the treasure on land. If later the treasure was lost on land, after turning it over to General Santa Ana, at least it would be his responsibility–not ours.

Captain Beltrán said he knew all the regular ships between Punta Bórica and Desemboque. He said none of them posed a significant threat of an attack by sea. Beltrán was also concerned about Admiral Serrano–his commander in Acapulco. He didn't want the old admiral to know about this venture, otherwise he would want a cut of the action–a *mordida*.

According to Marco's earlier deal with Captain Beltrán, he paid for total use of Beltrán's ship until the treasure was unloaded for delivery to General Santa Ana in Mexico City. Sixty kilos of silver ingots–two canvas bags full was what it took. The captain secretly stored the bags of silver in his cabin with the rest of his goods.

I joked with Beltrán, suggesting he get a floating bed in case his ship sank. I think my idea hit a responsive chord.

A day before we arrived at Acapulco, Marco, using his cane, limped over to where I sat writing in my journal. He tapped my open saddlebags with his cane.

"Chu Chu, what do we do with that?"

"That? What do you mean, Marco?"

"The general's maps. What do we do with them? We found all *three* of the Spanish treasures, but we are bringing back the gold and silver from only *two* of them. If we give him back his maps, he could send someone else out to look for the La Escondida treasure, our retirement stash."

"The answer is easy. *We lose the maps*."

"Yes, I think we should. Better yet, destroy them."

I agreed.

So I removed the folded maps and notes bound together with a string from my saddlebags, left them on the deck with Marco and went to the galley to borrow an empty lard can from the cook. After returning, I pulled out a couple of JK's broken cigars from my saddlebag and handed one to Marco. We set fire to the beautiful old vellum maps and paper notes, then threw them into the empty can. As the flames flared up out of the can, we used them to light our cigars. It seemed an odd tribute, celebrating the destruction of the maps which were key to our newly-found wealth. But for practical reasons, we had to do it.

My mind wandered back to our recent experiences in the Pimeria Alta as we silently watched the flames slowly turn the maps into ashes. Beltrán came over and asked what we were doing?

"Having an expensive smoke," I quipped.

Marco laughed at our private joke.

I gave Beltrán my last broken cigar, and he joined us. After visiting for a few minutes and finishing our smoke, he left. Then I brought up the big question on my mind.

"Marco, what are we going to tell the general about the third treasure site–our *retirement* site? We had better have a good story on that too, one we agree on."

"Yes, Chu Chu. I've thought about it. We *lost* the maps, so it would be hard for somebody to go back and find La Escondida, *unless there's another map*, and I doubt that. It seems like we would be better off if we said the treasure wasn't there. We looked for it and *it was gone*."

"If the general bought our story, he wouldn't send somebody back to try and find it."

"Yes. That's the idea."

"So let's use that as our position. We followed the maps and found where someone had already removed the treasure. It was gone."

"Fine. That's our position," Marco replied.

"So how did we lose the maps?" I asked.

"Any suggestions?"

"Well, we had our little incident with *El Pirata*. What if the maps were in the silver ingot bag that got lost? And it sank to the bottom of the ocean in that bag?"

"Good. I like it. El Pirata tried to steal some of the bags of ingots. The maps happened to be in the bag that sunk to the bottom of the ocean. There was no longer any useful information on the maps, so it was not a big loss."

I agreed, but also felt a tinge of regret. The maps would have been a beautiful memento to have hanging on my future office wall, along with Colonel Trujillo's uncle's Spanish spurs. But I said nothing.

The next afternoon, as we approached the coast near Acapulco, Marco, Beltrán and I had our last meeting. The plan was for me to take the rowboat to shore with José and Moses. There I would buy provisions for 12 days for the ship. Moses and José would bring the supplies back to the ship. Captain Beltrán and Marco would depart at first light the next morning, take the ship south, then return in ten days.

Our plan required me to get a good horse and burn up the road to Mexico City. They recommended I rest on the road and avoid posadas and inns as much as possible. I was also to avoid all military garrisons and presidios. We estimated it would take me three to four days to get to Mexico City and about a week to get back with help from the general.

Captain Beltrán said he would sail south for a few days. Afterwards, they would return and keep the ship anchored about 40 kilometers south of Acapulco at a location where they could watch Cerro San Miguel. When I arrived back in Acapulco, I was to go to the high hill south of town and signal them, using a mirror during the day or building two fires about 500 meters apart at night. That would be the signal for them to return and meet me at *Tres Palos* Beach. There we could secretly transfer the ingots to General Santa Ana's military wagons.

Beltrán laughed and said he had used the beach many times before for smuggling activities.

By midnight that night, I was traveling east from Acapulco. I had been riding for several hours, and it was dark and foggy. I was having trouble finding the right roads, so I stopped, unsaddled and secured my horse, then tried to rest for awhile.

But rest did not come, I was uneasy. Weighing on my mind was not just General Escalante but also the damage failure would cause to my plans for my company's mining business in Mexico. I was only able to sleep for about an hour before again hitting the road at first light.

The first day traveling to Mexico City I was nervous and felt people were spying on me, watching my every move. To further aggravate the situation, my saddle was ill fitting and made my legs sore. Also, the extra weight from my saddle bags loaded with over 50 kilos of the gold dust and nuggets I carried from the La Escondida treasure was hurting my horse's back.

In the pueblo of El Ocotito, I traded my horse and saddle, this time getting a much more comfortable saddle and a rested and much stronger animal. The man at the stables suspiciously watched me change my heavy saddle bags and said little. I could visualize him sending word to the nearest military garrison, reporting my strange and hurried activities, and this information getting back to General Escalante's spies.

Determined not to let my imagination get ahead of my good sense, I recalled another of my Mother's Bible quotations: *the guilty flee when no man pursuith, but the righteous are as bold as a lion.*

Smiling at the thought, I decided several things were working in our favor. General Escalante's spies would be targeting *La Doncella*, because it carried the treasure. So perhaps our little move where I quietly left our ship at night and slipped away on horseback from Acapulco would be successful. Also, a single traveler travelling light and fast could carry little treasure, so that should not draw too much attention. But the most important thing working in our favor–we were getting closer to General Santa Ana's flagpole, the center of his power.

The rest of my trip to Mexico City was uneventful except for the long, hard ride. By the time I reached Cuernavaca, I had some annoying sores on my legs and arse because of my first badly fitting rented saddle. In Cuernavaca, I got some lard to grease my aching legs and bottom. That helped some.

By the time I rode into Mexico City after midnight, I had been on the road for three-and-a-half days and had traded out eight horses and two saddles. I pounded on La Doña Elías' hacienda gate until a sleepy Pepe answered and let me in. I removed my heavy saddlebags and slicker, then handed him the reins to my horse and asked him to tend to the tired animal. I staggered to my rented casita in the rear of the hacienda and fell onto the bed. A few minutes later, there was a knock at the door.

It was Xinata, the pretty Aztec girl, with some soup, corn tortillas and a big glass of red wine. I thanked her, scarffed it down and was asleep in about ten minutes.

The sun was coming through my window the next morning when I awoke. Someone was knocking on my door. It was Xinata, this time with some breakfast and a small pot of coffee on a heavy tray. After thanking her, I enjoyed my meal while sitting on my sore butt, staring out the window at the sadly-cared-for grounds of the magnificent old hacienda. La Doña knocked on my door next.

I limped to the door and let her in. Señora Elías carried her own cup of coffee, along with a cloth bag with my mail! After visiting a few minutes, the gracious lady left. Then I sorted through my months of mail.

There were six letters from Melanie, two from my company and one from my cousin Howard Taylor at the Taylor Plantation in Georgia. Also there was a letter from Mother.

Next Pepe knocked at my casita door and told me that he had built a fire and heated the water in the Roman-styled bathhouse. After thanking him, I put on a robe, grabbed Melanie's letters and hobbled to the bathhouse. There I soaked in the delightful warm water and almost went to sleep.

My plans were to rest and get caught up on my mail for a few hours before I went looking for General Santa Ana. Also, I wanted to remove the heavy leather pouches of gold dust and nuggets from my saddle bags and carefully tuck them away.

Although still sore, a good rest, food in my belly and knowing my adventurous assignment to northern Mexico was coming to an end pumped excited energy into my being. Best of all, six of Melanie's unopened letters lay before me.

With a shaking hand, I laid out Melanie's letters by the dates she wrote them. I opened the last letter first, to make sure there were no big surprises. I didn't like surprises. There was a little one in it, one that I had to think about.

Basically most of Melanie's letters were dear and personal, similar to the one I received along with JK's package of cigars at Colonel Trujillo's office in Hermosillo. Her first three letters told about her projects, working to improve the conditions of their slaves, or *workers,* as she called them. She also told me she was learning to cook and sew, to do practical things like prepare meals and mend clothes. She also acknowledged that she knew I was away on my trip and her letters would probably stack up until I returned, but she still needed to write to me. She seemed to be the same sweet Melanie, although I noted a gradual change in tone in her letters, perhaps a little more maturity and an appreciation of broader issues.

Her later letters spoke of my cousin Howard's projects and his engagement to Virginia Anne Davis of Atlanta. Their wedding was to be after ours in October. She wondered if we could alter our departure schedule so we could attend their wedding before we left for Mexico.

Her fifth letter spoke of some tension building between her brother, JK, and her regarding her projects to improve conditions for their workers.

Then there was her sixth and last letter. It predated February the 24th, and it said nothing about Mr. Kerns' premonition. She only said her father and mother were well. In this letter, she opened a door I had not expected. *She wanted to come to Mexico to be with me as soon as I arrived from my trip to northern Mexico.* She said she didn't even care if we were not married, but also wrote that a short civil ceremony in Mexico might be proper after she arrived. She said she no longer wanted the big formal Georgia wedding in October.

Obviously something had happened and was troubling her. I hoped nothing too serious had prompted her strong desire to join me in Mexico, nothing other than wanting us to be together.

I kept thinking about Melanie's last letter. In a way, it simplified my life, especially if she could get to Mexico on her own. Since her brother, JK Kerns, owned an interest in a shipping company and had connections, I was sure he could and would help his sister, even if he had to send her directly to Veracruz on one of his own ships.

My trip north had changed me and I liked the idea of Melanie's unexpected change in plans. Regardless of my company's policy about initially not having employee wives and families join them, I now felt more in control of my destiny. I went back to the casita and read my other letters.

Mother's letter was sweet. She was very complimentary of Melanie and said how she enjoyed their visits. She also wrote about people and projects around the plantation and Savannah. She spoke of her work to expand her textile factory in Savannah. She said the simple little brooch I made for her was a constant reminder of Father, and she wore it often. And in her normal endearing fashion, she both chided and instructed me "*not to dally and lose Melanie, because she was a gift to me from God. She was a gem of a woman who loved me dearly and would be the best thing that could happen to me.*" I had tears in my eyes when I finished her letter.

My cousin Howard Taylor's letter was friendly. He said the offer from him and JK was still open, giving me a partnership in some of their operations. He also mentioned his betrothal to Miss Davis. He invited Melanie and me to their wedding.

Finally, I read the two letters from my boss, Mr. Walter M. Kearny, of The New Wales Equipment and Mining Company, Ltd. The first letter said that the company had sent a draft for £2500 (pounds) to the Bank of Mexico City which I could draw against, anticipating my success in getting approval for our new Querétaro mining operation. The second letter, sent a month later, wanted to know the status of the project. Obviously they were anxious to get a new mining operation going in Mexico.

Before my recent travels north to the Pimeria Alta, I would have been thrilled at the added responsibility my company was giving me and would have been impressed with the company's money in my budget and under my control. But now, well, I had much more money in those saddlebags sitting on the chair in front of me. My perspective had changed.

I dropped off to sleep again until there was another knock on the door. It was La Doña; this time she carried a tray with lunch. I dumped my heavy saddlebags to the floor and offered her the extra chair. She waited at the table as I went and changed from my robe into some fresh clothes in the bedroom. I came out, and we visited as I ate.

She noticed the new scar on my cheek and asked me about it. I told her. She also asked about the package she forwarded to General Santa

Ana for me. We laughed when she found out it was only a box of *cigars* with the letters.

Then I asked her about Melanie coming to Mexico. She smiled and said Xinata would be disappointed, but she would be happy to make Melanie welcome and comfortable there at the hacienda until I had things ready in Querétaro. I thanked her for her graciousness.

Two hours later, I was talking to the guards at General Santa Ana's fortress type hacienda on the edge of Mexico City. The guards gave me the *normal bullshit and run around* until they sent a man to inform the general that I was there. A few minutes later, the military guard came running out of the hacienda grounds and grabbed me by the arm, almost dragging me toward one of the interior buildings. Inside, I was taken directly to the general, who sat alone, eating a late lunch with a large black dog lying on the floor by his side.

Smiling, the general greeted me and shook my hand while pointing toward an empty chair at the table. I sat down. He casually asked if I would like some lunch and described several food options. I thanked him, saying I had already eaten, but a glass of wine sounded good. After the servant poured me a glass, the tough old general again spoke.

"Ingeniero Mack, can I call you *Chu Chu*?"

"Yes, of course, General."

"Tell me, Chu Chu, *success or failure*?"

"General, mostly success. We found the sites where the Spaniards hid their gold and silver ingots."

The general's eyebrow arched as he corrected me.

"*Our,* gold and silver ingots."

"Yes, of course, General. *Mexico's* gold and silver ingots," I replied, immediately thinking I had made another *faux pas*.

The general smiled as he took a bite of his shrimp and sipped some obviously expensive bubbly wine.

"What is it worth–the gold and silver?"

"Over *200,000 escudos* in gold and over *130,000 reales* in silver.

This time both eyebrows rose as the general set down his fork and looked directly at me. He asked incredulously. "Over 200,000 *escudos* in gold and over 130,000 *reales* in silver? Are you sure, Chu Chu?"

"Yes, General, if we don't lose it."

"Lose it? Where is it?"

"That's the problem, General. It's floating on a ship on the Pacific Ocean somewhere south of Acapulco."

"Why is it there?"

"We were warned that there would be an attempt by two generals to steal it before we could deliver it to you here in Mexico City."

"What threat? Who told you about the threat? Who are the generals? "

"Sir, we were told that two generals–Pacheco from Chihuahua and Escalante from Guadalajara might try to abscond with it before we could get it here."

"Who told you?"

"Colonel Trujillo from Hermosillo. He sent a man down to catch us at Guaymas and warn us. He said Lieutenant Pacheco sent word to his uncle, the general in Chihuahua, about the ingots we found and were taking to Mexico City. He also understood there was a close connection between Pacheco and Escalante."

"Trujillo? I remember him. He was wounded twice during the *Gringo* War. He's a good man."

I didn't reply, just nodded–knowing that the feeling was *not* mutual.

"Yes, I know about Pacheco, Escalante told me about him. I think Pacheco and his nephew, if they are still alive, are headed to California about now," the general said with a wink.

"So there is no threat? Nobody is going to try and take away the treasure when Captain Vásquez and I bring it to shore?"

"No, but I want to be there anyway. When will you be ready to leave?"

"Anytime, General."

"When did you get in?"

"Last night after midnight."

"How long did it take you?"

"Three-and-a-half days."

"Three-and-a-half days from Acapulco?"

"Yes."

He seemed impressed.

The general took a bite of his dessert and another sip of wine. He set his fork down and leaned back, resting his stub of a leg on a pillow tied to a stool. With a pleased smile, the sly old general clasped his hands behind his head and stared at the ceiling.

"Over 200,000 escudos in gold and 130,000 reales in silver, huh?"

"Yes sir."

"Chu Chu, be ready to leave at first light tomorrow. Are you still staying at Señora Elías' place?"

"Yes sir."

"I'll send my carriage over to pick you up," the general said, speaking in a manner clearly indicating that our conversation was over.

"Yes sir," I replied, taking a final gulp of my wine.

As I stood, the old general, still seated, extended his hand to me.

"*Bien hecho!* (Well done!)"

"Thank you, sir."

I left, relieved that it had gone well. It should have. Over 200,000 escudos in gold and over 130,000 in silver reales should impress anyone. It certainly impressed General Santa Ana.

At first light the next morning, I stood in front of the gate to La Doña Elías' hacienda. Xinata had packed the general and me a nice basket lunch with burritos and some fruit. La Doña added two bottles of wine.

A large carriage drawn by two matched gray horses arrived with a military driver and an armed guard sitting together on top. I hopped in. We returned to the general's hacienda, where we waited for about an hour before the old man came out using his crutch. An aid carried a carpetbag and a strange, narrow leather case.

The general climbed aboard, bidding me good morning, and we were off. The carriage rode very smoothly, which was a welcome change from my torture on horseback.

The general carefully placed his queer-looking box on the seat next to me. I debated about asking what it contained, and finally did.

"*Mocho's* in there. That's Mocho's house," he replied seriously.

"Mocho?" I asked.

He smiled and directed me to remove the leather belts and open the case. It contained a skin colored wooden leg with a shiny black military boot on it!

"That's Mocho," he chuckled.

Then he asked me to hand it to him.

Inside the hollow leg, there was a built-in holster with a small double-barreled cap and ball pistol and a jewel-handled dagger. Also, he had some paper money folded inside. "Gold was too heavy," he said, smiling.

"I have to dump all that stuff out when I dance with the ladies," he added still smiling.

I was seeing a totally different side of the general. The man actually had a sharp sense of humor and could be pleasant when he so chose.

It took us six days of hard travel to get to Acapulco. Twice a day we would swap out his two-horse team, usually at military garrisons. In the evenings, we would normally stop at a magnificent hacienda and leave the general. The carriage driver would take me to a nearby posada and leave me there until the next morning. I tried to pay for my stay but the owners would insist–I pay no money. However, I usually left a generous gift on the table after breakfast.

Santa Ana's carriage driver picked me up early, then we would wait for the general anywhere from a half-hour to an hour before he would come out with a servant carrying his carpetbag and Mocho's house.

The general and I had plenty of time to visit on our trip to Acapulco. I was careful not to become too informal or familiar with the general and it worked well.

The second day on the road, he talked about some of his battles with the *gringos* and his glorious military victories. Finally, after finishing a one-sided conversation describing the Texas campaign he said, "You do what you have to do."

The next day, he went into some of the politics and history of the *Gringo* War with General Zachary Taylor and General Winfield Scott. He respected General Taylor as a military man and president, but despised Scott. I didn't bother to tell him I was related to Taylor. Also, by the way he made it sound, he won the war. Again Santa Ana finished with a sigh and the same phrase.

"You do what you have to do."

The third day on the road, he started to probe me about our trip north to the Pimeria Alta. "Chu Chu, tell me about Captain Beltrán. Did he help you get the treasure down from Desemboque?"

I went on to truthfully tell him about Beltrán's help.

"Is he taken care of?"

"Yes, Captain Vásquez has everything taken care of."

Then, again, he uttered his familiar phrase. "Well, you do what you have to do," he said, nodding.

"Yes sir, that's right," I acknowledged, also nodding.

The general continued with his line of questioning. He got into almost every detail of our trip. A lot of questions were about Colonel Trujillo and his competency and the operation of his command. I tried to give a glowing report of Trujillo's help. I certainly didn't mention a word about Trujillo's demand for a part of the treasure to help equip his men.

Then he asked his key question.

"Is Trujillo satisfied? Did you take care of him?"

"Yes, General, I believe he is. He and his men were critical to our finding and recovering the treasure."

The general gave a sharp nod. "You do what you have to do."

I was beginning to understand what he meant.

He asked about the Apaches. I told him of their intense savagery when attacking helpless farmers and travelers. Also I described the military custom of collecting Apache warrior's ears to keep count of the number of savages killed.

Again, he gave his normal response.

Casually, he then asked about the hidden La Escondida treasure site. With a straight face, I described in detail how we used the Spanish maps and notes to find the place, but it was empty, the treasure was gone. It had been removed some time in the past.

The general hesitated for a moment *then*, almost glaring at me, said, *"Well, Chu Chu, I assume you and Captain Vásquez did what you had to do–huh?"*

A shiver ran up my back and I said nothing. *We had not fooled the shrewd old general one farthing by our clever actions.*

That was the end of our conversations for the day.

When we arrived at Acapulco, the general arranged for three military supply wagons with four-horse teams and a mounted military escort of 14 men. I sent the signal from Cerro San Miguel, and we met *La Doncella* at the Tres Palos Beach.

The transfer of the bags of ingots went well, and in less than three hours we were finished. It was a little past midday.

The general seemed a little cool to Captain Vásquez and especially distant towards Captain Beltrán. After the wagons were loaded, the general called Captain Vásquez and me over to his carriage, where he sat watching.

"Captain, you did a good job. Keep the Colt revolver I lent you. But I need the gold watch. Do you have it?"

"Yes sir," Marco replied as he removed the watch and handed it to the general. The general asked nothing about Marco's use of a cane and his limp.

Then the general looked at me and handed me a large envelope. "Ingeniero Mack, this should open the doors you need to get your company's Querétaro operation going. Remember, sixty percent before expenses," he said with a straight face.

"Thank you, General. Yes sir, forty percent after expenses," I replied with a wink.

The old general laughed. "Chu Chu, I expect we will be seeing more of you in the future."

"Yes, General, I hope so. And thank you again for this," I replied holding up the envelope he gave me.

He turned back to Captain Vásquez and extended a weathered hand.

"Captain, I knew you would do a good job. That's why I sent you. I'll be seeing you back in Mexico City?"

"Yes sir," Captain Vásquez replied as he shook the general's hand.

With that, the general hollered to his driver and the carriage took off with a lurch, tossing the general back in his seat. The freight wagons and mounted soldiers followed.

We watched silently as the treasures of the Pimeria Alta rumbled slowly eastward on wagons toward Mexico City. *Well, at least part of it.*

Chapter 25

Interesting Times in Mexico City

After unloading our cargo at Tres Palos Beach, General Santa Ana left us stranded on foot, so Marco and I rode the captain's ship up to Acapulco that evening. Captain Beltrán paid his excited crew well and warned them to keep their mouths shut, but to no avail. They talked, but only secretly. That added *spice* to their stories, making them better and more exciting.

When the crew left the ship, only Captain Vásquez, Captain Beltrán and I remained on board. Beltrán went to his cabin and brought back two canvas bags and handed them to Vásquez. Marco turned and handed one to me. I looked inside. It contained gold ingots!

"What's this?" I asked Vásquez, my breath taken away.

"Gold," he replied.

I moved a little distance away from Captain Beltrán and asked Marco again, "Yes, I know it's gold, but I thought we were not going to take any more of the general's gold?"

"The general's gold? I thought this was *Mexico's* gold."

"Yes, you're right. You know what I mean."

"I hope you didn't tell the general exactly how much he had."

"No, just that he had over 200,000 escudos in gold."

"Good. Well, now he doesn't have much over 200,000 escudos in gold. Do you want me to give it back?"

"No! Hell no! Well, anyway, I'm surprised. It feels like a full bag."

"It is. And Beltrán knows about it. For what he's done, I think we each should give him a couple of bars out of our bags. Are you game?" Marco asked.

"Sure."

I pulled out and handed Vásquez a bar from my bag. Marco pulled another out of his bag and handed the two ingots to Beltrán.

"Gentlemen, in my eighteen years on this old girl, this is certainly the most interesting and profitable trip I've ever made. I have enjoyed doing business with you gentlemen. *When is our next trip?*"

We all laughed.

Marco asked if we could spend the night on the ship.

"Certainly! Before the cook left, I had him prepare a special final, meal for us. I also have several bottles of Toluca wine under my bed I planned to open. I was counting on both of you joining me for dinner."

"Captain, I would like to see what else you have under that bed," I joked.

With the pressure off, we stayed and enjoyed our last evening meal with Captain Beltrán. It ended the most exciting and profitable adventure of my life, at least up to that point.

The next morning, Captain Beltrán, Marco and I rowed ourselves to the docks at Acapulco and bid our *saludos* and goodbyes. I rented a horse and simple open carriage with a pop-up canvas roof for our trip to Mexico City. We loaded our sparse traveling gear, firearms and *other stuff,* then we were off.

Marco was still having problems with his swollen foot and leg. He said he was going to see a doctor when he got home. A week later we were in Mexico City.

My mind turned to Melanie's request to join me, and also to the company business, in that order. I wrote her a letter. After my trip to the Pimeria Alta, I felt no longer *beholden* to so many other people about my future. If I wanted Melanie here with me, I wasn't going to let Mr. Walter M. Kearny or Sir Edward Chadwick dictate my future. I would do my job for them and do it well. If they didn't think I should have a wife with me, then they could go to hell. I would take up Howard and JK in their offer and make more money, or do something else. Yes, my trip north had changed me.

In my letter to Melanie, I told her how much I loved and missed her. I told her to make arrangements with JK to get her safely to Veracruz, where I would pick her up. I told her I would pay JK for her passage, even though I knew that would never happen. I wrote little of my trip north, except to say that it was successful and I had returned safely.

The second day after returning to Mexico City, I was working inside my rented casita, with the table covered with papers for our company's Querétaro mining operation. It was about noon when there came a knock at the door. It was Doña Elías.

Señora Elías said she had a nice lunch set up in the large back patio and asked if I would join her. I gladly agreed.

After we were seated in the beautiful but neglected patio grounds, I handed La Doña a folded piece of paper. Curiously, she carefully opened it. Two of my little trademarks nuggets were inside, each strung with a thread. The larger nugget I explained was for her and the smaller one, for Xinata. I showed her the small stamped initials on them, an H for Hortencia and an X for Xinata. The dear lady was obviously touched by the gesture. She thanked me, folding the little gifts back into the paper and setting it by her plate.

As we started eating, La Doña asked me about my plans and about Melanie. I told her I had just sent Melanie a letter asking her to make arrangements to join me as soon as she could.

"Well, Chu Chu, I am happy for you. You and she can use my hacienda as your headquarters until you get established in Querétaro. I will be looking forward to meeting your Melanie and teaching her Spanish," she joked.

"Doña, I would like to make arrangements with you to use your hacienda as my office in Mexico City. Could we work something out?"

Tears glistened in the woman's eyes. She looked down at her food.

Sensing something was wrong, I quickly tried to recover and restate my question. "Of course, if that's not practical, I can make other arrangements."

Finally, she looked up at me. "Chu Chu, since my husband died, things have not gone well for us. My daughter is, well, not able to take care of herself, and I no longer have money coming in to take care of our expenses. My husband had several farms, which I have sold to pay for our expenses here. *Being a woman*, I was taken advantage of, and didn't get much money for the farms."

"Chu Chu, *I'm broke*. I can't afford to pay the expenses to keep this hacienda or even to take care of my own daughter. And I don't want to ask for help from my husband's family. My own family has nothing."

Momentarily shocked, I didn't know what to say. Finally I asked, "Doña, I am sorry. Is there anything I can do?"

She hesitated for a moment, then looked at me. "Chu Chu, do you want to buy this hacienda?"

Again, I was almost speechless.

"No. Well, what do you mean? Would it help you?"

She went on to explain her situation.

"Chu Chu, I don't even have the money to pay Xinata or Pepe. Pepe has been working for two months without pay. Xinata, well, I haven't paid her for three months. She's just staying here to help me with Carmen. What little money I have, we have been using for food. That was the money you paid me for rent. I am terribly embarrassed, Chu Chu. I don't know what to do."

I was shocked. I had no idea this gracious and, I had assumed, wealthy woman was in such a desperate situation. And here we were, eating a lovely lunch in her patio. It was probably paid for by her few remaining reales. I had to help her.

"Doña, how can I help? What can I do? I can pay you in advance the rent for my casita if that would help? Tell me."

She reached out and gratefully touched my hand.

"Thank you, Chu Chu. When you arrived in October, I had been praying that God would help me with my problem. Several of my husband's relatives have offered me almost nothing for this place. My husband made a special paper to give me title to it. Normally women don't own the property here, but my husband wanted to take care of me and Carmen. He knew he was dying."

"When I saw you, I wondered if God had answered my prayers. Then you paid me in advance for the use of the casita. That was a small miracle. It gave us money to live on for a few more months. Now I am broke. More than broke. I owe money to Pepe and Xinata. I've already let go of our cook and two other servants during the last year."

"Doña, if it would help, I could pay you in advance for a year, or for two years for the casita. Tell me what you want. I would be happy to give you the money to pay Pepe and Xinata."

"That's another problem. I'm probably going to send Xinata away."

"Don't do that. You need her to help with Carmen. Besides she's too pretty." I joked.

"Yes, she is." La Doña replied looking me squarely in the eyes. "That's the problem."

"Why is that a problem?" I asked, half-innocently.

"Chu Chu, she likes you. I told her about your new wife, that she may be coming to Mexico soon, but she doesn't care. She's just turned seventeen and is very strong-willed. She wants you."

Embarrassed, I looked down at my plate and said nothing.

"That's why I need to send her away," she continued.

Finally, I replied. "Well, let's deal with that later. What can I do now to help you?"

"Chu Chu, do you want this hacienda?" she insisted.

"Well, it's beautiful. But I don't want to take advantage of you like those men who bought your farms, or your relatives who want this place," I replied, motioning toward the estate.

I thought for a moment. "How can we work it out for all of us?"

"Chu Chu, I'll give it to you if you help us. Carmen and I don't need that big, empty house, the main house. There are four buildings where people can live. There's the guest casita, where you stay, the main building, where we are, the workers' casita, where Pepe and his wife live. Then there is the other big guest casa or posadita that's in bad repair on the other side. It's not being used," she explained.

"I see. How do you see us proceeding?" I asked.

We had stopped eating, the delicious food forgotten.

"Chu Chu, if we could fix up the large *posadita* (guest house) for me and Carmen and Xinata, that would be more than adequate for us. Some servants could also live there with us. You could have the rest."

I was still taken aback by what I was hearing.

"Are you saying that if we could fix up the old guest house on the other side of the grounds for you and Carmen, you would give me the whole hacienda?"

"Yes, Chu Chu, that's what I am saying. I know it's not fair to ask you to take care of us for life, but perhaps only for as long as you own the property. Maybe we could find something else after that. Also, we would work and we don't need much. My family was poor, so I know what it means to work and live with little. We are doing that now. We could help watch and take care of the *La Hacienda Hermosa*. I know all about that," she said with a sad little laugh.

La Hacienda Hermosa. I hadn't heard that name since I was a child, when we would stay here. I liked the sound of it, *La Hacienda Hermosa*.

I was quiet for a while as I sipped some tea. Finally I replied. "Doña, let's not make any decisions now. I will give you 40 escudos now to take care of your bills. Consider it an advance on my rent. After we both have time to think about it more, we can talk. And don't worry. I plan to be here in Mexico for a quite a while, so we can work something out. I won't let you lose your place."

"No, Chu Chu, I want to do something now. Yes, certainly you can think about it, but I prayed about it and here you are. I know what is best for us. I hope it can be good for you and your wife. The hacienda and all the grounds are yours if you can help us. Yes, you think about it, but I want to transfer the papers over to you immediately, if you agree."

The sad and embarrassed lady stood and gave me a little *abrazo* (hug) and kiss on the cheek, then left. She hadn't touched a bit of her food. This lady had taken care of me for my folks when I was a child. I played here as a boy, when the hacienda was in its prime. I viewed

Hortencia Elías as family, like an aunt. I sat there for several minutes, staring at the food on my plate, thinking of the sacrifice she had made just to fill that plate. Then I carefully finished eating the food, which now tasted different.

That afternoon, I walked over and knocked on the door of the main house. Smiling sweetly, Xinata answered the door and invited me in. Embarrassed I asked for La Doña.

When Señora Elías came into the room, smiling, I thanked her for the nice lunch and pressed a cloth bag containing a hundred escudos into her hand.

"Doña, you are my family. Thanks for talking to me. This should take care of things for a while. Let me know if you need anything else."

Tears swelled in her eyes as she grasped the cloth bag. I kissed the dear lady's cheek, then left.

It was Tuesday evening, March the 29th 1853. I had spent the day ordering materials for our Querétaro mining operation and had had lunch with my banker, Salvador Villarreal. Someone knocked on my door and I answered. Xinata came in with my supper and a bottle of wine on a tray. We exchanged pleasantries as she set the tray on the table. Then she said I had received a letter. I went to the tray immediately. There lay a letter from Melanie! I was sure it had news about her father.

I thanked Xinata, hurried her out of the room, and opened the letter.

March 2, 1853

My Dearest Jack,

I am sorry to inform you that yesterday we buried Father. He died just as he predicted on February the 24th. He killed himself with a pistol on a hill overlooking the Fields of Shannon Plantation headquarters. Philip, one of our field workers found him and told JK. It happened at sunrise, and no one even knew he was out of the house.

Inside Father's journal in his study was a folded letter to the family. It said:

February 24, 1853

Dearest Constance Grace, James Kenny, Mary Helen and Melanie Ellen,

I love you all very much and regret bringing this pain into your lives. However, I have known for several months I was dying from the cancer. Doctor Gentry informed me I had but a few months to live. He said the last days on this earth would be painful and dreadful for me.

Connie, please forgive me for leaving you. Know that you and your love have been the greatest blessing that God has bestowed on me during my time on this earth.

JK, you have the operation of the plantation well in hand. Take care of the family and do what is right–as God directs you. Also, continue to take care of the businesses, the Fields of Shannon Plantation, and our dear workers.

Mary Helen, may God bless you and your family. You have always been a comfort to me. Take care of your dear family.

Melanie Ellen, my dear little rebel. I say that with no malice and only love in my heart. You were right to help our dear workers and I thank you. Take care of Jack and may God grant you both a wonderful life.

I have always been a coward in regard to pain and suffering, so I chose the easy way out. May God have mercy on my soul.

Your loving Husband and Father (unsigned)

Jack, Mother was furious with me when she learned of Father's dream and premonition. JK explained to her that nothing could have been gained by me telling her of it. Also, he said that in the last several months Mother herself knew something was wrong with Father.

In my last letter, I said I wanted to join you in Mexico as soon as possible. I still do and also would like Lilly to come with me. I would release her to a freeperson's status if she came and if we could not afford her, I would like to find her a safe Christian, family to employ her. She is the only person on the plantation I have the authority to release. It is important to me. Please write and tell me how we can make all this happen.

I am fine and I love and miss you greatly.

Always Yours and with Love,

Melanie

Unsettled by Melanie's letter, I asked Pepe to stoke up a fire for me in the bathhouse so I could enjoy a relaxing evening. The evening was cool, so I put on a robe and took a book, thinking to read by the lamp in the bathhouse, if I chose. I needed to think about Melanie's letter.

The expansive but run-down Roman style bathhouse was private and pleasant. After a quick dip, I was relaxing on a lounge chair, trying to decide whether to read my book or nap when Xinata walked in. She carried a tray with a bottle of wine and wedge of cheese. I thanked her. She smiled and turned as if she was going to leave. Instead, she nimbly unbuttoned her dress *and let it drop*.

There stood a nude, beautiful, bronze maiden with long black hair and a body like a Greek goddess. A *nude* bronze Greek goddess with a gold nugget hanging about her neck! She walked over and daintily dipped her toe into the water. Then she came back smiling and took me by the hand, leading me to the warm pool. I said nothing and did not resist. My life had suddenly become more *complicated.*

I soon decided it was time to spend more time out of town, preparing to get the Querétaro mining operation launched. It was an exciting project, my first as a mining engineer. I spent a week down at Veracruz, where I hired José Delgado, my friend who drove me to Mexico City when I first arrived. He was delighted.

I put José in charge of our still nonexistent Veracruz company operations. The operations office would include all aspects of equipment and mineral storage, warehousing and transportation to and from Querétaro.

Since we were starting from nothing, I rented a small piece of land near the harbor with a dilapidated building on it. This I decided to repair and use as our temporary warehouse and office in Veracruz. Delgado's first job was to build a security fence around the property and to expand and improve the building so it would be useable.

Upon arriving this time in Veracruz, I checked with the municipal customs chief at the docks. They processed all mail coming in on the ships. He remembered no recent mail coming in for me, so I wrote to Melanie.

In my letter I expressed my condolences to her and her family over the passing of her father, Mr. Kerns. I said to certainly bring Lilly. We would make sure she was properly cared for. I also told Melanie I wanted her here with me as soon as she could safely arrange it and apologized that I could not go and fetch her in proper style. I also emphasized for her to work closely with JK, since he had the connections to get her to Veracruz safely. I suggested she try to get to Veracruz during the first ten days of June, and I would be waiting for her. I hoped it would allow her to travel ahead of the hurricane season.

The next morning, I posted the letter with the municipal customs office and put it into the hand of the departing captain of a clipper freighter heading for Havana. He promised he would put the letter into the hands of one of JK's new steamer ship captains heading to Savanna. I gave him a generous gratuity, for which he thanked me.

Back in Mexico City, Pepe brought me my breakfast the next morning, after Xinata had slipped in and visited me during the night. I told her that this could not continue, but found I did not have the strength to resist her visit.

She gave me a charming smile. "Chu Chu, I love you. I know you will have a wife, but I will be your número dos (number two). My people can have multiple wives. I will be happy to be número dos."

I thought that that sounded pretty good, but knew it wouldn't work. I tried to explain, but she smiled and held up two fingers, as if I were simpleminded.

As I was eating breakfast, La Doña came to my casita with her cup of coffee in hand and joined me.

"Chu Chu, what have you decided?"

My mind was on Xinata's visit during night and I amusingly wondered, *does she mean, have I decided to have two wives?* I discarded my wayward thoughts.

"Decided? Do you mean about *La Hacienda Hermosa*?"

"Yes, what did you think I meant?" she replied with a skeptical look.

"Oh, I was thinking about something else."

"I certainly imagine you were! Yes, I meant about the hacienda," she replied with a coy smile, then she continued. "So tell me, do you want the hacienda?"

"Doña, can I ask you something?"

"Yes, Chu Chu, what is it?"

"Doña, I've always thought of you as family. Can I call you *Tía* (Aunt)? *Tía Tencia*?"

She smiled broadly.

"*Tía*? You want to call me *Tía Tencia*?"

"Yes, I would like that if it's all right with you."

She clapped her hands together. "Chu Chu, I would be proud if you call me *Tía*."

"Well *Tía*, I would like to work out something with you, something that is fair to you about your hacienda. After all, you are family and my *Tía,*" I responded, winking at her.

She laughed and gave my hand a little squeeze.

"Good. How do we work out the details about Carmen and me living here, living in the old guesthouse, *La Posadita*? Can we stay there and help you take care of the property?"

"Yes, *Tía*. If that's what you want, that's what we will do."

"When can we start?" she asked, excitedly.

"Whenever you want. I will get workmen in here tomorrow and

start to get *La Posadita* back in shape for you and Carmen to live in it. As soon as it is repaired, you can move in."

"Wonderful! Chu Chu, I want to get the papers signed so the property is yours. I don't want there to be any question about who owns it if I die. Can you help me with that?"

"Certainly, *Tía*. I can take care of that if you like. But I still don't feel right about taking your beautiful property."

"Chu Chu, I can't afford to own or maintain it properly. You are an answer to my prayers. I can now relax and enjoy taking care of Carmen and the rest of my family, you and your wife," she said sweetly.

So it was done. I was now the owner of a magnificent, run-down sprawling old hacienda hidden in the foothills on the edge of Mexico City. It had enormous potential, and I was just the one who could bring it back to its glory days. I certainly had the money, and now had family here to help me take care of it. It seemed like a wonderful arrangement. And best of all, both my Tía and I were elated. Finally, I had a home.

Tía stood and was ready to go. I had hardly taken a bite of my cold breakfast.

"Chu Chu, I almost forgot. Captain Vásquez came over yesterday and said they wanted to have lunch with you today."

"*They*, who is they?" I asked as I took my second bite of breakfast.

"Oh, he said he and General Santa Ana, at the general's hacienda. He said they would send a carriage over to pick you up before noon, if you had returned."

I nodded, a little surprised. I was hoping the general had not changed his mind about any of his promises.

"Also, Chu Chu, did you know that the doctors took off part of Marco's foot? He developed a terrible infection on your trip."

Suddenly, I had lost my appetite. "No, I didn't know that. Is he all right?"

"Well, apparently he's better. He came over in a carriage and was walking on crutches. He said he thinks the bad part of the infection was removed. I hope so."

I stood and gave *Tía* a little *abrazo* and kiss on the cheek. She seemed very relieved as she left the room.

The next day, I had a crew of workmen come in and put them to work under the direction of my *Tía*. She was delighted.

At about two o'clock, I was sitting at lunch with General Santa Ana and Captain Vásquez. The general had a huge, dumb-looking dog sitting at his side that caught scraps the general threw to him. I generally got along with dogs, but this ugly monster growled at me, to the general's delight, when I entered the room. Marco was seated at the table with the general. He looked thin and pale.

As we went through the normal pleasantries, I became a little tense, wondering what the general was going to drop on me. He knew about Melanie coming and asked about her.

"Yes, General, my future wife is coming soon. We plan to be married here in Mexico when she arrives."

"Will you be married in St. Mary of the Holy Cross Church?"

"No, General, we plan on a small civil ceremony."

"Why?"

"Well, she's not Catholic. She's Christian."

"What the hell do you think we are–*pagans*?" The general asked gruffly.

Embarrassed at my gaffe, I responded, "No. I mean she's Protestant. I guess we all are Christians, both Protestant and Catholic. I've never understood what the problem was."

"It is lucky you are my friend, or I would report you to Bishop Valdez. He would *barbeque* you before his next mass."

I tried to chuckle politely, but it was difficult.

Finally, the general turned to a more pleasant topic, my project.

"Chu Chu, how is your operation going at Querétaro? Are you set up yet, and did my letters help?"

"General, I am making excellent progress at getting the operation up and going. And yes, your letters have made it much easier. Thank you," I responded, wondering if this was why I had been invited to lunch.

"When do you think you will have your first shipment ready?" Marco asked.

"My company is expecting it sometime in October, but with the way things are going, I think July seems more likely. We will be operating initially with old equipment and ore reduction methods, but we will soon improve on that," I responded proudly.

Then the general asked the key questions. "Chu Chu, do you think your company will do well and make money on the operation?"

"Yes, General, I think–with our arrangement– both our company and the Mexican government will make money."

"Is there any reason you can't set up two companies?"

"Two companies? What do you mean, General?"

Marco answered. "If your company does well, is there any reason you can't set up another company and do the same thing, so long as your company is doing well?"

"Two companies, well I hadn't thought about it. Why would I want to set up two companies?"

"Simple, you would run one operation for your company, and a second for us," the general answered directly.

"Us?"

Marco answered stiffly smiling. "Yes, for us. You would be a partner with the general and me. We would make sure your company did well, but ours did *better*. Could you do it?"

I squirmed a little bit, thinking about the question.

The general continued. "Before you answer, Chu Chu, let me explain. We want your company to do well. Even better than well. But Mexico needs more industry and mining. Our national resources are important to us, and we need the ability to do something with them. Yes, Captain Vásquez and I would be partners with you, but also Mexico. We would want Mexico to benefit from anything we set up. And we are talking about more than silver. We are talking about a national mining company that processes all types of metals. What do you think, could you do it?"

"Well, gentlemen, I work for The New Wales Equipment and Mining Company, but you are saying we could make sure they do *well*? Maybe even better than well if we set up a separate Mexican operation that bought equipment from my company?"

"Yes, that's exactly what we are saying," Marco answered.

I was relieved. This was not what I had expected. I was afraid something had gone wrong, or the general had changed his mind or something. This option was *fascinating*.

"Well, gentlemen, I like the idea. To answer your question, yes. Yes, I could easily set up a separate Querétaro operation, but I would want to be fair to my company. They employ me, and I would want to make sure they came out well."

"Of course. We would make sure of that, even if we had to reduce Mexico's cut, but I hope we wouldn't have to do that," the old general said, smiling.

"So tell me, what did you have in mind?"

Marco went on to describe the details of their plan as we ate. The more I heard, the more excited I became. I seemed to have stepped into the land of golden opportunities when I came back to Mexico, and what I was hearing could easily be the biggest opportunity of them all.

Basically, their idea was for us to set up a parallel company to the one I was already establishing. Marco would be my active partner, managing the second Mexican company under my direction and control as a full partner. The general would remain a silent partner and be responsible for expediting approvals and removing obstacles and impediments. Initially, my company did not have to know anything except that things were going well with me in Mexico. It sounded great.

There was no reason I could see not to jump at the opportunity. If I didn't, they could easily shut my whole operation down, and my company would gain nothing. I agreed, and we shook hands on our new partnership. General Santa Ana was now my silent partner. I liked the idea.

Before I left the general's hacienda, I thanked him for the excellent meal. I then invited him and Captain Vásquez to Melanie's and my civil wedding ceremony, even though I didn't know exactly when and where it would be. They both accepted. The old general even laughed and said *Juez* (Judge) Lucero would be happy to perform the ceremony for us whenever I knew the details. We all laughed, but I knew he was serious and that I was probably going to take him up on it.

For the next few weeks, I was torn between spending less time in Mexico City and the excitement of renovating the magnificent La Hacienda Hermosa *and other things*. I hired six additional men and put them under the control of José Delgado, who I brought from Veracruz to expedite the renovation effort. The progress was dramatic. The magnificent old place was coming back to life. In fact, I was using ideas I had seen at plantations in the South and on estates in England to enhance the beauty of the old hacienda.

The workers found an old water spring buried in the side of the hill. It was mostly flowing down a ravine and being wasted. I directed them to clear out a small lake in the middle of the back patio grounds and have the spring water fill it, then let the overflow water the gardens. It came together wonderfully. Tía was so impressed that she asked me if she could get some goldfish, ducks and swans for the small lake. I told her that they were already ordered.

During April and May, Xinata slipped in and visited me when I was back at my casita at La Hacienda Hermosa. I feebly tried to discourage her, but always she would tease me, insisting she was my *Ńumero Dos*. Then she was gone.

One morning in late May, at breakfast time, there came a knock at my casita door. There stood a pleasant *fat little Indian lady about 40 years old*. She said her name was Conchita, and that La Doña had hired her to help with her daughter Carmen and to do work at the hacienda.

I had mixed emotions–feeling both disappointed and relieved. Later that day, I saw Tía Tencia pruning some freshly-planted rose bushes on the renovated grounds of La Hacienda Hermosa.

She stopped her work and asked, "Chu Chu, how was your breakfast this morning?"

"It was good, but not exciting," I answered, my expression a bit sour.

She laughed.

"Tía, thank you for taking care of the situation. Do you know what happened to Xinata? Where did she go?"

"Yes, I sent her to the convent and orphanage so she could help them with their children. She didn't want to go. I explained the situation again to her. She said she would *always be your Ńumero Dos*."

I stared at Tía Tencia for a moment, then said. "Thank you. Melanie should be here in June. I hope this doesn't blow up in my face."

"It won't. Xinata gave me her promise," Tía Tencia responded. And that was the last I heard of Xinata, at least for awhile.

Chapter 26

Melanie Steps Into a New World

The first day of June, I returned to Veracruz from Mexico City and started helping José Delgado work on our new office and storage facility, which was located within sight of the harbor. I was anxiously waiting for Melanie's ship to arrive. When I suggested to Melanie that she try to get to Veracruz within the first ten days of June, I knew her brother JK would make it happen, even if he had to use one of his own company's steamers to transport her directly from Savannah to Mexico. He was that sort of a fellow.

Our work at La Hacienda Hermosa was going well. Before leaving, I let several work crews go who were being supervised by Ernesto Garcia at the hacienda. They had finished the cobblestone paving of the carriage and walking paths inside the walls of the magnificent old hacienda. Also, they had finished planting the new trees, shrubs and flowering bushes, and had repaired the main aqueduct bringing water into the estate for the buildings, two fountains and bathhouse.

They had also finished my favorite project, developing the flowing spring on the property and rerouting it over a small waterfall into the new, large pond. It worked well, and the pond was filling rapidly. I even had the men build a Moorish version of the gazebo similar to the one hidden in the back garden on the Kerns' plantation. It had been a favorite place for Melanie and me to visit during my last visit to Georgia.

I also had Ernesto Garcia, a new man I hired in Mexico City, managing other work crews constructing, painting and repairing roofs on the buildings and doing other projects around the hacienda. Tía Tencia and Felipe, or Pepe, as we called him, were helping Ernesto by overseeing this work. I was hoping to have the magnificent old hacienda back in shape by the time Melanie and Lilly arrived. In fact, I wanted it to be better than new.

I was not going to tell Melanie immediately of my recent good fortune or that I was now the new owner of the La Hacienda Hermosa–not until having some fun with my dear young lady. We both had expected to live under Spartan conditions when she came to Mexico, and perhaps for the rest of our lives. Also, I knew my good fortunes could evaporate as quickly as they had come.

Bringing the stately old hacienda back to life had been an exciting project for me. I had admired English estates, with their magnificent gardens and grounds, and the almost royal plantations in the South. I never imagined I would have the opportunity or money to try my hand at renovating one myself, especially with such a wonderful estate as La Hacienda Hermosa. Tía Tencia was amazed and almost as excited as I was when she saw our plans quickly being transformed into reality.

Finally, on Friday afternoon, the 3rd of June, an animated José walked into the first adobe and stone office building we were finishing for our Veracruz operations. He said a converted clipper-steamer freighter was coming into the harbor. I was just hanging a framed certificate of export-import authorization from the Mexican government that Santa Ana's letter, plus 200 reales, had magically arranged for us.

Heart in my throat, I jumped into our rented one-horse wagon and whipped the old horse into a lope down to the docks. There, I anxiously waited for the captain to deliver his manifest ashore to the municipal harbor office. The ship came in under a Portuguese flag. Shortly after the ship dropped anchor and lowered the sails, I could make out a rowboat headed toward the dock with what appeared to be the first mate and two crewmen.

Waiting inside the municipal harbor office, I watched as the arriving mariner gave his papers to the clerk at the desk. When the Portuguese sailor finished his business with the Mexican officials, I asked him about passengers. He replied they had a businessman, a military officer and two women, a white lady and a fat black girl.

Finally, they had arrived!

The first mate said the passengers would be disembarking from the ship as soon as he could get several more rowboats to help unload the ship. He complained that the white lady had quite a load of stuff with her–trunks, boxes, some plants, a dog and a bird.

I had to smile to myself, thinking this was going to be an interesting transition for Melanie. Perhaps not so hard for her now, because of my good fortune and being the new owner of La Hacienda Hermosa, but I was going to let her worry for a while. I wanted to see what she would do.

At my urging, the first mate quickly found three additional rowboats with men and returned to the ship. The first boat returned with Melanie and Lilly sitting on some of the bags. I stood on the dock and waved as they approached in the boat. Both of them happily waved back.

After the boat bumped into the dock and the men tied it fast, I helped Melanie and Lilly out. Poor Melanie was excited to see me, but seemed a little dazed and disoriented. It was the first time she had traveled by sea, much less to a totally different country. I think she had been to Charleston, South Carolina, but only twice before in her life. This was a new experience for her and I was going to make it memorable.

On the other hand, young Lilly was all wide-eyed and full of smiles, taking everything in. She gave me a little curtsy and giggled. She carried all her worldly possessions. Under her left arm, she held a tattered wooden box with a leather strap and with her other hand she held a new carpetbag, which was about half full, but she was happy.

After a warm embrace and kiss, Melanie started to nervously chatter about her luggage.

"Jack, honey, I brought *a few things*, I hope you don't mind. If we can't take them, maybe we could give them to somebody that needs them. Perhaps some little Mexican family?"

I stood there listening and smiling. Then I slowly lost my smile when

I saw the men come in with a second rowboat with more of her stuff. They began to unload it on the dock. I had planned to take Melanie and Lilly with their things to Mexico City in my one-horse carriage. Foolish me.

José rolled onto the dock with the freight wagon to receive two company equipment crates that came in on the same ship, things for our mining operation. He looked at Melanie's stack of trunks, carpetbags, boxes and the cage on top with the parakeet. A dog was inside one of the boxes, barking. José broke out laughing.

He called to me, "Chu Chu, what should I do? Take the mining equipment or Miss Melanie's clothes?"

Not answering, I tipped the grumbling dock workers, then walked around the pile of luggage and critters, trying to decide what to do.

Embarrassed, poor Melanie melted. "I'm sorry, Jack. What should I do? Mother and my friends all gave things to bring with me, and JK said he would transport anything I wanted to take."

Then she gave her little mischievous smile. "But when JK saw it, he said, 'What in the hell is Jack going to say when he see's all of this shit?'"

Melanie's comment broke me up. "Yes, Melanie, JK was right. I'm wondering if he would take it back."

Melanie stood there, trying not to laugh. "Shall we send it back to the ship?" she said very sweetly.

She already knew exactly how to handle me, and she had not been on Mexican soil for more than fifteen minutes.

I smiled, scratching my head, and told Melanie we would sort it out when we got to Mexico City. Then I helped José place her treasures into the loaded freight wagon along with the two crates of mining equipment. The wagon was overflowing, and we had to use ropes to tie it down. I told José to buy some canvas covers to protect it from rain while he transported it to Mexico City.

It was late afternoon by the time we got everything sorted out. José then left the dock and headed his spotted mule team pulling the freight wagon toward Mexico City. I had to laugh when we saw the dog barking as it stood tied on top of the pile of luggage and crates as José disappeared around a curve in the road. We took the parakeet with us.

We went to the local posada where I was staying, and I got two more rooms. After an early dinner, Lilly went to her room to rest. Melanie and I visited a little longer before she too went to her room.

The next morning, we ate early and left for Mexico City in the rented one-horse carriage. Melanie sat in the front seat with me as I drove. She was excited by all the new sights, burro carts, naked children playing in the streets, women in colorful dresses, roadside vendors and volcanoes. She asked dozens of questions. It was wonderful having my excited Melanie with me–permanently.

It took the usual three days to get to Mexico City, traveling steadily and trading out our horse each day. Lilly enjoyed the ride and sights while Melanie and I got caught up on all the news.

We decided it would not be practical for us to try to go back to Savannah for Howard's and Miss Virginia Anne Davis' formal wedding in October. Also, Melanie agreed that a civil marriage ceremony in Mexico City would be fine for us. She did ask me if I minded not cohabitating until we were married. I joked with her saying I did mind, and I didn't think I could wait. She laughed and I could see the quick, fun-loving girl that I fell in love with in Georgia was just as I remembered.

She asked me the first evening about the new scar on my cheek, and I briefly told her about the Apache attack on Marco and me. I didn't go into much detail about either the attack or the purpose for our trip north. There were plenty of other things to talk about.

She asked me about my projects. I went into quite a bit of detail on what was happening and told her I was very happy with the progress we were making on my company's project. She wanted to know if I had found a place in Querétaro for us to stay. I told her no and that we would be using Mexico City as our main headquarters for a while.

"Oh, are you still staying at Mrs. Elías' place?"

I responded with a simple yes, and left it there.

Then we talked about her father's death and premonition.

"Jack, that was strange. I knew he was not well, but never expected him to take his own life. Mother was furious with me when I told her that Father shared his premonition with us when you were there. Thank goodness JK stepped in and calmed her down."

"Why was she so upset? She knew he was sick."

"Yes she did, and that's what JK explained to her. JK told her that it didn't make a feather's bit of difference whether I had told her or not. It would only have worried and upset her more. I appreciated JK stepping in for me like that."

"Did you tell her that he foresaw our wedding later at the Fields of Shannon Plantation?"

"No. I upset her so much with what I told her, I didn't say anything else. Besides, that was a good reason why I didn't want to be married there. I didn't want his dream to come true–with the war and all."

"So what did JK say when you asked him to help you get to Veracruz, to come down to meet me?"

"Jack, that was almost funny. I never have seen him so relieved in my life. My little projects were scaring him to death. He was afraid that if I didn't start a revolt with our darkies, I'm sorry, our workers, the neighbors would burn our place down or string me up."

"So he helped you?"

"Helped me, my goodness, yes! He delayed one of his steamers and rerouted it through Havana just so he could put Lilly and me on a safe clipper to Veracruz. I'll declare, he was going to send one of his senior captains on the clipper with us if he didn't think we were safe. Captain Rivera insisted we would be fine and he would take total responsibility for us. JK paid Captain Rivera well and seemed satisfied. Why I think my older brother would gladly have personally sailed one of his steamers down to Veracruz just to get rid of me," she laughed.

"So JK rode with you to Havana?"

"Yes, he was on his way to Liverpool."

"So, what do we owe him?"

"Jack, I told him what you wrote about paying him. He cursed a little and said not to bring it up. He reminded me that if it had not been for you, he would not be around to do you the favor. Jack, he respects you greatly. Maybe he doesn't like you, but he does respect you," she joked.

"Well I respect him too. Don't much like him, but respect him," I responded in kind, also joking. "I've always been impressed with JK's tenacity. He will move mountains to achieve his goals. We've always seemed to be on different pages, but I do like the guy. And I do appreciate him getting you down here safely."

"Jack, I know he likes you too. He and Howard have mentioned you and they always ask me how you are doing."

My life was feeling more complete. Mexico seemed more like home now that Melanie was with me. I remembered my thoughts while sailing south on Beltrán's ship about *where your treasure is.* Well *now my heart and treasure were both together,* and I was happy. Silently, I gave Melanie a little hug and she giggled.

The next morning, I knocked on Melanie's door at the inn and she came out with tears in her eyes. She had just found her parakeet dead in his cage. I tried to console her, but was secretly relieved we didn't have to deal with the little pest any more.

We drove through the gates of La Hacienda Hermosa late in the afternoon. It was Lilly who delighted me with her comment.

"My Lordie me, Miss Melanie! It looks like we is back in Georgia!"

Melanie commented too.

"My goodness Jack, Lilly's right! Is this Mrs. Elías' plantation?"

"Yes Melanie, this is the old Elías place. But here they call them haciendas, not plantations."

"Jack, the place is beautiful. For some reason, I didn't expect a place like this in Mexico. Huts and hovels, you know."

"Yes, Melanie, there are plenty of huts and hovels. But there are also many places like this too. Mexico is a large and wealthy country. Mexico has been settled for longer than you have been in the States."

"Well, Jack, I am impressed. Will we be staying here? Did you rent a place here?"

I pointed out La Casita in the back and drove our carriage over to it. So far Melanie had asked good questions, at least the kind I didn't have to *fib* about to give an answer.

As we stepped down from the carriage, both Tía Tencia and Felipe came over. I introduced them to Melanie and Lilly. Tía looked tired, but enthusiastically greeted both of my guests. She gave Melanie an abrazo and spoke to Lilly caringly.

Melanie looked at me, a little startled when Tía hugged her, but then laughed and responded appropriately.

"That's the way they do things here in Mexico," I said in English.

"It's different, but I like it," Melanie said with a laugh.

Pepe took our horse and carriage to the stables in the back part of the hacienda. Tía said she would have supper ready for us in the garden after we rested. She also said that José had delivered Melanie's things earlier in the day and that he put them in La Casita. I thanked her, then she left.

"She seems like a nice lady. When did her husband die?"

I explained that he had died a few years before as we stood at the entrance of La Casita. La Casita was a good-sized adobe and stone building with a large central room, two bedrooms and a little cooking and eating room, but not exactly a kitchen. It also had a porch on the front, side and on the back. Sitting anywhere on the porch, you could see the stately hacienda wall behind the trees, the beautiful grounds and part of *La Casa Grande*.

Melanie stood on the porch several moments, taking in the view of the magnificent grounds and beautiful pond with its flowing fountain and tiny waterfall before we stepped inside. Stacked in the middle of the main room were all of Melanie's necessities, trunks, bags and all the rest of it. It almost filled half of the room and rose nearly to the high ceiling. I could hear the dog barking out back on the porch.

"Well Melanie, this is our new home. Which bedroom do you want?"

Melanie looked bewildered for a moment, and then giggled as she touched the giant pile of luggage. Next she quickly walked through the casita, checking each room.

"Jack, this is nice. A bit small, but nice. Where is Lilly going to sleep?"

"With you, I guess. Unless she wants to sleep with me."

Lilly giggled. "Oh, Mr. Jack!"

Melanie also laughed, but not quite as loudly.

"Well, I guess she can sleep with me. Can you sleep out here with my things?" she asked sweetly.

"No, I don't think so. Let me ask Tía. She may have another room for Lilly."

So we got through our first little test.

We gathered Lilly's two pieces of travel gear, the small wooden box with a cord wrapped around it and new red carpet bag. I carried the carpet bag and Lilly *insisted* on carrying the old box. Curious about both, I asked the chubby 15-year old Miss Lilly what treasures she carried inside each.

Excitedly, little Miss Lilly responded. She called back over her shoulder, "Oh, Miss Melanie, can I show Mr. Jack what you bought for me?"

"Certainly, Lilly, show Jack," Melanie replied.

We stopped on the cobblestone pathway to the newly refurbished *posadita* (small inn) part of the hacienda. Lilly carefully set down the old wooden box she carried, grabbed the carpet bag I was carrying and held it high for me to see.

"Look, Mr. Jack. Miss Melanie bought this specially for me. And wait and see what else is inside that she bought me," the chubby girl exclaimed.

She set the carpet bag on the walkway, quickly unbuttoned it and drew out a Bible and two calico dresses, one red and one yellow, both with large polka dots on them.

"Look, Mr. Jack, Melanie gave me a Bible and she's teaching me how to read out of it. And look, Mr. Jack–store-bought dresses–just for me. Aren't they beautiful?"

Lilly quickly handed a dress to Melanie, held the other dress up against her and did a little jig, showing it off. Then she quickly exchanged dresses with Melanie and did the same with the second dress.

"My goodness, Lilly–they are beautiful. Maybe you could wear one for dinner tonight. Would you do that?" I responded admiringly.

Lilly looked at Melanie. "Could I do that, Miss Melanie? Could I do that?"

"Certainly, Lilly. That sounds like a good time to wear it."

The little black girl was elated.

Then I asked about her wooden box.

"Lilly, what treasures do you have in your little box?"

Lilly's expression quickly changed to one of embarrassment. Melanie glanced at me, then to Lilly waiting to see what she would do. I knew I had touched on a sensitive subject.

"Oh, it's nothing Mr. Jack. It's just something I brought with me," Lilly said, embarrassed and looking down.

After an awkward pause, Melanie responded. "Go ahead, Lilly. Show Jack what you brought with you. He would like to know."

Still embarrassed, Lilly looked first at Melanie, then at me. She dropped to her knees and carefully untied the cord from around the old box and removed its lid. Inside, she slowly pulled out a ragged cloth and stick doll with its face painted black and a red ribbon around its stick hair. She partially held it up so I could see.

Knowing there was a story there, I carefully asked, "Lilly, that's very nice. Tell me about her."

With tears in her eyes, poor Lilly was quiet for a moment then replied. "Mr. Jack, this was from my Mama. She gave it to me. See, there's a string around her neck with a paper. It says *Matilda*."

"Matilda, that's very nice. Is Matilda you doll's name? When did your mother give it to you?" I asked.

I noticed Melanie's attention was riveted as the girl answered.

"No sir, Mr. Jack. Matilda was my Mama's name. She gave the doll to me when I was two years old–when they took her away to another farm. *She wanted me to remember her name. I don't remember my Mama,*" Lilly replied, hanging her head in shame.

Melanie had tears streaming down her cheek as she reached down and lifted Lilly up. Melanie looked at me over the girl's shoulder.

Her reasons for wanting to leave the South were again abundantly clear to me.

After our sobering little episode, I showed Melanie around part of the hacienda grounds as we walked Lilly over to *La Posadita*. Still with tears in her eyes, Lilly walked along behind us, carefully hugging her little wooden box.

When we got to the La Posadita, Tía was there, giving directions to the new cook and two new servants who were preparing our meal. Yes, she had another bedroom for Lilly. She told me she would assign me a bedroom in La Casa Grande.

On our walk back to the *Casita*, I showed her the bathhouse building.

I now humorously called it *Caesar's bathroom*, because it was a Moorish miniature version of a grand Roman bathhouse. Pepe was inside checking the temperature of the water and said no fire was necessary, because the water was perfect.

Inside the bathhouse was a tiled pool about four feet deep, which could easily accommodate up to eight people. Tía had the new maid lay out clean robes, towels and several scented soaps for us. The tile was now cleaned and the place looked new.

"My goodness, Jack, what is this?"

"This is the hacienda's bathhouse."

"Bathhouse? Do people take public baths here?"

"Yes, some of them do, or you can keep it private and take a bath by yourself."

"Do they take their clothes off?"

"No, Melanie, what you are wearing would be just fine!" I laughed. "Of course they take their clothes off!"

"Oh my, Jack. *How wicked*," she giggled, embarrassed.

"Are you going to join me in a bath this evening?"

"Oh Jack, don't tease me. Should we?"

I had to laugh, but didn't push her. She was fascinated with these new heathen ways, and I didn't think it would have taken much to convince her to join me. But instead I suggested she should take her bath first, I would follow later. Teasing, I also warned her that if she didn't hurry, I might accidentally come in before she was finished. She thought the idea was devilishly delicious.

At supper, La Doña, or Tía, had a beautiful table set with fresh-baked bread, fruits, roasted goat meat and wine. Her daughter Carmen and Lilly joined us. Poor Lilly was uncomfortable, but bravely enjoyed the new experience. Melanie urged her to relax and enjoy the evening and the meal.

Melanie asked Tía many questions about her family and the beautiful old hacienda. I served as the interpreter and filtered her questions, but Tía knew what I was up to and went along with the charade about her still being the owner of the elegant estate. However, Tia did suggest I turn the casita over to Melanie and Lilly, and she would find an extra guest room in the large hacienda for me to use. So we did as Tía suggested.

The next day I drove Melanie around Mexico City in the hacienda's carriage, which was a little better than the one I rented in Veracruz. She was amazed that the city was built on a lake in the middle of an ancient volcano and sat at 7000 feet above sea level. She was delighted with the cool June weather and scarce mosquitoes!

I suggested to Melanie that we get married soon and she, joking asked, "tomorrow?" I explained we needed to get the necessary approvals and paper work, before we could be married. The ceremony could be held possibly the following Friday, if she approved. I also explained I had to go out of town for several days on a business trip to set up a relay location for my company's Querétaro mining operation. She was a little disappointed, but said nothing.

That evening, before supper, I asked Melanie if she wanted to take her turn in Caesar's *Bathroom* first. She suggested we call it Caesar's *Bathhouse,* because it would sound more proper. Then she told me to take my bath first; and she would go later.

But before I had finished, things got interesting. I was in my robe, reading a newspaper and enjoying a glass of wine when who should walk in with an embarrassed smile on her face but my sweet, innocent and proper Melanie. She went into the small changing room and came out with her robe *almost on.*

We were late for supper.

On Tuesday, I returned from my business trip and checked with Tía. She said all was arranged for a Friday night civil wedding ceremony at the hacienda. She said she would make sure all went well. I thanked her and gave her 25 escudos.

That evening, in the bathhouse, I told Melanie about how La Doña was desperate for money to run the beautiful old hacienda and take care of her daughter Carmen. I explained that she didn't want to ask her dead husband's family for help, so we had worked out an arrangement where I would own the estate and she would help take care of it. I told her that the gracious lady was delighted with the arrangement.

"Jack, that was a lovely thing for both of you to do. I certainly did not expect to come to Mexico and live in a place like this! Now that you finally told me, maybe I should invite mother down," she said with a sly smile.

"Please, don't ruin the moment," I responded with a visible shiver.

She laughed as we sat in the pool enjoying our wine. She was beginning to be less embarrassed being around her husband-to-be.

At suppertime, Tía and I were going over our guest list for the civil wedding ceremony and dinner afterwards. They included Captain Marco Vásquez and his wife; Salvador Villarreal and his wife; Tía Elías and Carmen; Lilly; General Santa Ana and maybe a friend.

"Who is General Santa Ana?" Melanie asked.

Tía could not believe Melanie had never heard of the general.

"Oh, he's an important man here in Mexico. He used to be president, several times," I replied.

"You know him?"

"Yes, and Tía's husband was related to him. He's an interesting man."

"Oh."

The next several days Melanie jumped in and helped Tía work out the details to prepare *La Casa Grande* for our wedding and dinner. We continued to stay in separate rooms on the hacienda, at least part of the time. Melanie again mentioned that her mother would enjoy being there and helping to decorate La Casa Grande for our *post boda* (after wedding party). To my relief, Melanie, also joking, acknowledged that her mother could not do it without breaking the Bank of Mexico in the process.

Perhaps so I thought, but maybe not Marco's and my hidden bank account at La Escondida in the mountains of the Pimeria Alta.

Melanie casually observed that The Fields of Shannon Plantation mansion were much larger than La Casa Grande, but the walled grounds of La Hacienda Hermosa were larger than those of their plantation grounds, and more beautiful. And we had no slaves here, which amazed Melanie.

The civil wedding ceremony and *post boda* went beautifully, but *Juez* (Judge) Lucero was not available to conduct the civil ceremony. He was away at his hacienda in Guadalajara for a month and could not be reached. So General Santa Ana found a substitute judge to do the honors. The young judge was named *Juez Benito Juárez.* The general said he was trying to cultivate Juárez, even though he was a Zapotec Indian from Oaxaca. It was a fateful decision for Santa Ana and for me–negative for the general, but positive for me.

Afterwards, Tía oversaw the serving of a fine post boda banquet meal in La Casa Grande.

Our guests brought nice little gifts for Melanie and me. Juez Juárez attended alone and brought a box of cigars for me and a bouquet of flowers for Melanie. Marco and his wife bought us a set of crystal wine glasses. Tía gave us an antique setting of *olla* pottery storage pots her grandmother had given her. But for me, the general's gift was the most interesting of all.

When the old general first arrived, he hobbled through the door with his lady friend. He carelessly used a long, tubular box as his cane, while his lady carried his usual silver-handled cane.

Once inside, he tossed the tubular box to me. "Here, Chu Chu, here's your wedding present," the old general said with a sly smile.

I'm sure my eyebrows rose when he did it, because I had seen such a tubular box before. I noticed Marco's reaction was similar to mine.

I thanked the general for the gift and wondered if the sly old Fox was again a step in front of us, and he was.

The wedding ceremony was short and formal. However, the small banquet dinner with our guests was grand. Even though Melanie understood little of what was being said, she made a big hit with her beauty and grace. She was going to fit in admirably with my friends. She made me very proud.

After our guests were gone, I opened the tubular container and pulled out two neatly rolled *white vellum maps.* I unrolled them. They were a *second* original hand-inked copy of the maps Marco and I had taken with us on our exciting trek to Sonora, then burned when we returned on La Doncella. They showed the locations for the Treasures of the Pimeria Alta! I now had the perfect place to hang them, on the wall in my new office in La Casita.

The gift again confirmed that Captain Marco Vásquez and I had not fooled the crafty old general about keeping part of the Spanish treasures of the Pimeria Alta for ourselves. In keeping with the old general's saying–*we did what we had to do–and he knew it.*

Chapter 27

Golden Times in Mexico and a Prelude to War

Between 1854 and 1860, our life in Mexico was full of wonderful experiences and some heartaches. Melanie learned Spanish, but spoke it with a southern accent, I joked. She took well to her new experience of living outside of the South. Our lives were much different than even I could have imagined, starting with my unexpected and successful trip to the Pimeria Alta looking for General Santa Ana's lost Spanish treasures. The success of that adventure opened doors in Mexico beyond my wildest expectations, including those of my bosses in England.

However, I was under no false illusions on the reasons behind my successes in Mexico. It had less to do with my talents and more to do with my blind luck and accidentally falling under the shade of the right political forces in the country. I knew that could change.

A personal disappointment for Melanie and me was that we were not able to have children. Melanie lost a baby prematurely and, with the second loss, she almost died. However, late in 1854 something happened. We were living in La Casa Grande on La Hacienda Hermosa and I was immersed in running our dual companies, one for my English bosses and one for a Mexican company in which I was a partner.

Melanie knew about Xinata and me, because I had told her before we were married. I wanted nothing between us to be disruptive to our marriage. She cried a little when I told her, but then asked if I would be faithful to her during our marriage. I said I would, but also knew I must keep away from the Aztec girl because I still couldn't help having feelings for her. I thought that was the end of it.

It was November of 1854, just after Melanie and I had prematurely lost our first child, a little boy, when Tía Tencia joined me. I was smoking a cigar and reading the paper in the gazebo one morning between business trips.

"Buenos días, Chu Chu. *Cómo amaneciste?* (How are you this morning?)," she said in a friendly mood, carrying her usual *empty coffee cup*.

I filled her cup from the fresh pot on the table and visited with my favorite aunt.

After the normal niceties, she said. "Chu Chu, I've debated about telling you something, but I must."

"What, Tía? What haven't you told me?"

"Chu Chu, it's about Xinata. She's in trouble."

"Xinata, in trouble. What do you mean?" I asked, quickly putting the paper down.

"She has a baby. A handsome little Indian boy, with blue eyes," she said, watching me for my reaction.

Her comment shook me. "A baby boy? With blue eyes?"

Tía was silent as I hesitated for a moment. I cleared my throat. "Tía, when was he born?"

"He was born on *February the 24th*."

That date rang a bell with me. A year earlier, Melanie's father had shot himself on that date.

"Does she have a husband, or boy friend?"

"No, Chu Chu. You remember what she said about you. She said she would always be your Number Two."

Her comment made me shiver. "Are you saying the baby is mine, Tía?"

"Yes, Chu Chu, it is."

"Is that the problem, she has a baby?"

"Well, part of it. She's still at the convent and orphanage. But she wants to leave. She wants to see you. She wants to give you the baby."

That really shook me. I shook my head. "Give me the baby? *Why*? Can't I help her some other way? I can't take the baby," I responded.

"I don't know, but she is coming today. She said if you wouldn't see her, she would disappear forever."

This was going from bad to worse. I was too upset to stay seated.

Beginning to pace, I said, "Disappear forever, with the baby? What did she mean, Tía? She's not going to kill herself and the baby, is she?"

"Chu Chu, I don't know. She's a strange girl with a very strong will. I don't know what she meant."

"When did you see her?"

"Yesterday, at the convent. I have been going down and visiting her weekly when I go shopping."

"You have? So you *knew* about the baby?"

"Yes, I learned she was pregnant shortly after I sent her to the convent. The Sisters didn't want to keep her, but I convinced them to let her stay and help them. Then she did such a good job, she worked herself into their hearts. She's a good girl, Chu Chu."

"Yes, yes, I know," I replied, trying to think.

"Chu Chu, I had to let you know. I have been helping her with a little bit of the house money you've been giving me and keeping her up to date on you and Melanie. Maybe that was a mistake."

I turned with a jerk. "Why? Why was that a mistake?"

"Well, Chu Chu, I told her about you and Miss Melanie losing your little baby. I told her it was a boy."

With a groan, I asked."What time is she coming? Is she going to your place?"

"Yes, she's coming to *La Posadita*. She's going to ask me if you will see her. She's coming this morning."

I was almost in a panic. I couldn't turn her away. I had to help her. But first of all, I had to tell Melanie, who was still recovering from our recent sad loss.

What happened next has tugged at my heart forever.

Melanie insisted we meet with Xinata and help her. Melanie quickly dressed herself for our meeting. She also prepared a little basket of presents for Xinata and the baby. About ten in the morning, Melanie and I were having tea on the porch of La Casa Grande when up the cobblestone walkway from the other building came Tía Hortencia and Xinata. Xinata was carrying a little bundle wrapped in a colorful Aztec blanket.

Politely and a little embarrassed, I introduced Xinata to Melanie. Melanie smiled and asked to see the baby. With damp eyes, Xinata proudly folded back the top of the blanket and handed Melanie the child to hold. Carefully, Melanie took the baby and began tickling his nose, admiring the good looking little fellow. A few moments later, when all of us were focused on the smiling and cooing little baby, Xinata quickly turned and left. Shaken, I called out to Xinata, but she did not stop. *I never saw her again.*

So that's how little *Juanito* came to be a permanent part of our family.

Shortly after that the general, Marco and I formed the partnership in our new Mexican company. I showed General Santa Ana the list of equipment and supplies from Colonel Trujillo. Trujillo had not yet tried to make contact with me about funding his order.

The general was quiet for a few minutes as he read through the list.

"So Trujillo says he needs these things, huh, Chu Chu?"

"Yes, General, he did."

"How does he plan to pay for them?"

"I don't know," I lied.

"Does he need them? And the flags?"

"Yes, General. He is desperately short of everything."

Then I told the general Trujillo's story about why he wanted a good flag–a good flag for each of his garrisons. I explained that it was important to Colonel Trujillo to have a good flag so that his young soldiers could salute it and be proud to be Mexican soldiers–soldiers who had never been to Mexico City. Despite everything he had seen, this seemed to touch the tough old man.

The general was quiet for a few moments as he looked at the list then said. "You know Trujillo was wounded twice during the Gringo War, don't you?"

"Yes sir."

"Can you get these supplies, Chu Chu?"

"Yes, General. I might need a little help on some of the items, but yes, I can get them."

"Get them and double the order. Colonel Trujillo is a good soldier. And send the invoice to my office. I will pay for it with Mexico's gold."

The order was filled and sent two months later. And Santa Ana paid for it. I sent a note with the supplies to Colonel Trujillo, carefully explaining this order had been doubled and paid for by General Santa Ana. I also sent my warm regards to him and his family and Tuti. I told Colonel Trujillo that he or any of his family or friends were always welcome to visit and stay with us at La Hacienda Hermosa in Mexico City, emphasizing the Mexican philosophy of *mi casa es su casa* (My home is your home).

Captain Marco Vásquez, or *El Matador* (The Killer), as I sometimes jokingly called him because of our Apache incident, and I did not soon return to reclaim the La Escondida treasure because, first of all, we didn't need it. Second, we viewed it as our old age money, even though we were accumulating more than we could ever spend operating *La Compañia de Minas y Manufactureras de Mexico* (The Mining and Manufacturing Company of Mexico), with our silent partner, General Santa Ana. Third, and possibly a technicality, we discovered the treasure was now on land General Santa Ana had sold to the United States in the Gadsden Purchase for the southern railroad route to California. This was the deal I heard Senator Anderson and Congressmen Shields talking about that night at the banquet at the Fields of Shannon in 1852. Finally, and probably the most important reason for us not to try to retrieve the treasure, was that we understood the Apaches were still in control of the land and continued to terrorize the territory. We figured that as long as the Apaches were wandering free, there was less probability that the hidden site would be discovered.

Every time Marco Vásquez would visit my office at La Hacienda Hermosa and look at the white vellum maps in their gold frames on my wall, he would bring up the subject about going and recovering our treasure. Poor Marco was in no shape to make the strenuous trip with his bad leg, which had never healed properly. He had gained weight and couldn't easily get on a horse, and so he was mostly limited to traveling in a carriage.

In April of 1855, my two bosses came from England to visit me and our company's operation in Mexico. They were amazed at the silver production I was able to get out of Mexico. The Querétaro silver mining operation was the second most productive foreign mining operation in the world for the company. A group of South African gold and diamond mines were at the top, but I was catching up.

I met my boss, Mr. Walter M. Kearny, and his boss, Sir Edward Chadwick, in Veracruz. They had contracted with JK's company to have one of their ships in Liverpool alter their schedule to drop the two men off in Veracruz. The ship was to return in two weeks, after making its normal stops in Charleston, Savannah and Havana, and take the two important men back to England. My bosses had no idea my brother-in-law, JK, was a major owner in the shipping line they had used to cross the Atlantic. It turned out to be an interesting visit.

I was alone on the dock when the two men disembarked directly from the steamer. One of the docks had been expanded to receive steamers and my Mexican company had done the work.

I strode forward. "Gentlemen, *bienvenidos* to Mexico. How was your voyage?" I asked.

The two men looked haggard, but wore their formal clothes and tried to be pleasant. It was mid-morning, so I suggested showing them around our new shipping and receiving facilities at Veracruz.

"Jack, we would be pleased to see the facilities. Is this where all of our products are received and shipped from?" Sir Chadwick asked.

"Yes sir. We also use it for the products shipped by The Mining and Manufacturing Company of Mexico," I explained.

A year prior, I had explained the arrangement I had made with the Mexican company about dual use of facilities, an arrangement which basically competed with our English company. However, I failed to mention that I was an owner and General Santa Ana was a silent partner in the Mexican company.

"Yes, Jack, I understand that. I want to talk to you about that arrangement later," Sir Chadwick commented a bit curtly, stroking his beard.

"Yes sir, whenever you want."

I spent several hours showing them around and introducing them to José Delgado, my manager for the Veracruz operations. They were impressed, but it was clear something was bothering them.

That evening, I put them up in the best hotel in Veracruz and provided them a good Mexican dinner. It all was very humble compared to their standards in England, but they were seasoned travelers and had traveled about the world, so they didn't complain.

I hired a coach in Mexico City and had it brought down to Veracruz especially to give my important employers a comfortable trip back to the capital of the country. The English gentlemen were friendly, but more than a little patronizing. Me being only 26 and them, the age of my father probably had something to do with it. However, they were very complimentary about the *amazing* production coming out of Mexico under my management.

Several days later, we rode through the open gates of La Hacienda Hermosa and up to *La Casa Grande*. Melanie and I had moved into the La Posadita building with Tía Elías to give our guests total use of the main building.

"My goodness, what a beautiful place. I had no idea the Mexicans had anything like this here. It's better than my estate," commented Sir Chadwick, amazed.

"Yes sir, it is nice," I responded.

"Jack, are we going to stay here?" asked Mr. Kearny.

I nodded. "Yes sir. I made arrangements with the owner to use it for a week while you gentlemen visit Mexico. You are very important visitors, and we want you to have a pleasant stay."

"Good show. Good show, *old chap*. This will be *adequate,*" Sir Chadwick responded with a wink.

"Gentlemen, there is a cook and four servants at La Casa Grande, all at your beck and call. There is also a good supply of liquor available. Also, I understand the bathhouse will be ready for you to use after five," I explained.

"*Bathhouse?* What is that?" Mr. Kearny asked.

"Well, the Spaniards brought some excellent Roman and Moorish ideas to the new world. The bathhouse is a small version of a Roman bath."

"Do they bathe in the nude?" Sir Chadwick asked.

I kept a straight face. "Yes sir, that's usually how they bathe."

"How beastly. How uncivilized. But I like it. I can't wait to try it."

Sir Chadwick laughed, but Mr. Kearny had an embarrassed smile on his face.

That evening, after their baths, we had a pleasant dinner by the pond on the hacienda grounds. Tía Tencia, her daughter Carmen and Melanie joined us at the meal. Lilly had married a Mexican soldier and had moved in with his large, accepting family. I asked Melanie and Tía not to say anything about the ownership of the hacienda.

Mr. Kearny leaned back. "Jack, this is very pleasant. You have gone out of your way to make these arrangements for us. Are we paying for this?" Mr. Kearny asked.

"Are we paying for it? Yes sir, we are paying for it," I responded truthfully.

Sir Chadwick studied the water cascading in the nearby fountain. "Jack, I know things are going well for you here in Mexico, but we owe a responsibility to our stockholders to be *frugal.* Walt and I enjoy being taken care of, but this is a bit extreme. Do you understand?"

"Yes sir, I do," I replied, and then in the same breath continued. "Mr. Salvador Villarreal, our banker, wants to visit with you while you are here. I took the liberty of inviting him and several other people over here for dinner tomorrow. We will have a formal dinner in the big house. Does that meet with your approval?"

"We would like to see Salvador. It would be here, tomorrow night, and a formal dinner?" Mr. Kearny asked.

"Yes."

"That sounds exquisite," Sir Chadwick responded, overriding Mr. Kearny's obvious concerns.

Mr. Kearny looked at Sir Chadwick and then me. "Well, I suppose if you have already arranged it, it would be satisfactory. But, Jack, remember what we said about company resources. We must be careful and give our owners a good and proper return on their investment."

Sir Chadwick smiled. "Walt, that's fine. But let's enjoy our visit here with Jack. He's trying to give us a pleasant experience."

I could tell Sir Chadwick was a bit annoyed with Kearny's obvious attempt to get on his good side by espousing proper fiscal management and restraint. Mr. Kearny did not pursue the topic any further, and we finished the evening with wine and Georgian cigars.

The following evening, Sir Chadwick and Mr. Kearny came to the massive, carved front doors of La Casa Grande in formal dress after their servant announced our arrival. Melanie and I had dressed and walked over with Tía Tencia from *La Posadita,* where we were staying. Sir Chadwick offered us a drink and had a second uniformed servant pour wine for all of us. Then he proudly walked us into the huge dining room.

"Can you believe this?" Sir Chadwick said, pointing his wine glass at the room.

Tía Tencia smiled and told me in Spanish that it never looked so good. The large dining room table was set with silver, fine china and multiple crystal glasses for each of the place settings. Wrought-iron chandeliers hung above, with candles burning within glass cases. The huge table and chairs were carved from Mexican mahogany.

"Mother would even be impressed if she were here," Melanie whispered to me in her broken Spanish.

Mr. Kearny slipped up behind me, a bit irked. "Jack, we're paying for all of this? And all of this is *just for Villarreal*?"

"Yes, Walt, we're paying for this. And yes, it is for Mr. Villarreal and several other guests."

My familiarity in calling him by his first name, Walt, bothered him.

The manservant dressed in his formal Mexican server uniform announced that several carriages were arriving.

The ladies remained inside as Walt, Sir Chadwick and I strolled to the entrance to greet our arriving guests. The first carriage was plain and carried Marco Vásquez and his wife. Marco was no longer in the Mexican Army, because of his injury. Both he and his pleasant and attractive wife wore formal Mexican attire.

We chatted for a few minutes, then Melanie came out and spoke to Marco's wife and took her inside. I was busy doing introductions and translating for our guests. Next to arrive was Salvador Villarreal, in a little better carriage. We had Pepe and another yardman park the carriages and tend to the horses.

Salvador spoke good English, so he helped me with the translations for our English guests.

"Finally, our guest of honor has arrived. It's a hoot to see you, Salvador," Walt Kearny said, slapping Villarreal on the back.

"Guest of honor? Who, me?" Villarreal said, glancing at me.

I winked at him.

The banker caught on to the game. "Oh yes, I'm honored. May I have a glass of wine?"

Sir Chadwick, playing the host, signaled for the servant to bring wine, and quickly Salvador had a full glass in his hand.

We were standing at the porch entrance talking when another carriage came through the gate. This was a fancy black carriage with windows in the doors and sides. It had a team of two matched black horses with two small Mexican flags flying above the horses' harnesses.

"Bloody me, who can that be?" asked Sir Chadwick.

Nobody answered as the fancy carriage pulled up in front of us and a uniformed military officer jumped down from the seat next to the driver, then quickly opened the door to the coach.

Salvador leaned closer.

"Gentlemen, prepare to meet the President of Mexico, President José Manuel de la Peña and his wife," he quietly whispered to our British guests.

They were shocked.

"The President of Mexico?!" Walt said, spilling a little of his wine.

"Yes," replied Salvador.

Before the President and his wife were out of there carriage, a large, ornate coach drew up in behind, this one with a team of four matching gray horses.

"Who in the hell is that–*God*?" asked a flabbergasted Sir Chadwick.

"*Almost. It is General Santa Ana!*" Villarreal whispered as he stepped forward to receive, then introduce the President and his wife.

"By God, it *is* God!" the thunder-struck Sir Edward blurted out.

I had to hold back my laugh.

I had prearranged with Salvador for him to do the honors of introducing and seating our guests. We had Mexican *mariachis* playing in the patio and four formal musicians in the dining room to entertain us with European music as we ate. The reaction of our English guests was everything I could have hoped for!

Mr. Villarreal did an excellent job of getting everyone introduced and followed proper protocol in speaking. I remained quiet, to one side, watching the whole show.

General Santa Ana winked at me as he entered. He knew what the show was all about and also wanted to impress our English guests. He had an elegant woman on his arm as he limped through the massive doors with his cane.

As we stood around visiting, Villarreal busily trying to keep up with the translations, Walt slipped behind me again.

"We are paying for all of this, Jack?' he asked in a more than annoyed tone.

General Santa Ana heard Walt and asked Villarreal to translate Walt's question for him.

Embarrassed, Villarreal tried to tactfully avoid directly translating Walt's question, but the gruff, grandly-uniformed general demanded that he do it.

After hearing Villarreal's translation, the tough old general turned to our two English guests and responded brusquely.

"Villarreal, tell them this. We are all guests tonight on the estate of Ingeniero Mack and his lovely wife, Melanie. Chu Chu is paying for everything, not their company. Tell them we are proud to have them visiting as our guests in Mexico. And also tell them that, if it had not been for my friend, Chu Chu here, *their* company would not be doing business in Mexico."

Santa Ana smiled broadly during the translation. President de la Peña nodded in agreement.

Walt and Sir Chadwick looked at each other, then at me, saying nothing. I raised my half-full wine glass towards them and smiled to myself. Melanie stood by my side and heard everything.

We all had a wonderful evening, visiting, eating and drinking too much. My silent partner, the general, was not so silent. His words worked like a miracle. Sir Chadwick totally enjoyed the rest of his visit to Mexico, and Walt occasionally called me *Mr. McIntyre* after that.

As icing on the cake, I casually mentioned on the coach ride back to Veracruz with my English bosses, that they were fortunate to have one of my brother-in-law's ships take them back to England. All I ever received from my company in the future were accolades and generous raises in my salary.

Money always fascinated me, but I did not live for it. My father talked about saving for a rainy day when I was growing up. He tried to save, but his rainy day came before he expected it. He also philosophized about Joseph's prediction to the Pharaoh that said after Egypt's seven years of plenty–there would come seven years of famine. He would tell me–"*Son, always save when you can, because Joseph's not around to tell you when the famine is coming.*" That turned out to be good advice.

First of all, Marco and I theoretically still had the hidden La Escondida Spanish treasure, but a lot could go wrong before we could get our hands on it. Someone else might find it, *or we might die*. My salary was good, and I was able to negotiate for a percent of the net profit my company received–after Walt's and Sir Chadwick's visit. That was a nice chunk of change. However, *the most profitable venture* was my partnership in our Mexican company with Marco Vásquez and our silent partner, the general. Also, I had one of the nicer haciendas in Mexico City, thanks to Tía Hortencia Elías.

The period between 1856 and 1859 were big money-making years for me in Mexico. During that time, I had my banker friend Salvador Villarreal set me up through his famous letters of credit with savings at three foreign banks. One was in Edinburgh, Scotland; another in Manchester, England; another in New York. I also placed funds in the Bank of Mexico. Additionally, I had money in another small local bank, the Hermosillo Bank in Hermosillo in the Mexican state of Sonora. Melanie asked if I didn't want to send some money to the Charleston Bank in South Carolina. I didn't.

Salvador said the money in the different major banks was safe unless there was a war or the banks failed. The only one he was worried about was the Bank of Hermosillo. I laughed and told him that Colonel Trujillo said it was usually robbed twice a year and half the time the robbers got away. Anyway, it wasn't much money, just 10,000 *escudos*.

With some of the money I sent to Scotland, I asked Uncle Angus to purchase and operate the beautiful farm I had visited. It was located near Dundee, overlooking the Firth of Tay.

During those years, I made three trips to England. The third was in 1859 and I took Melanie and little Juanito with me. I showed her Liverpool, Manchester and London. We also visited Sir Chadwick in his office and on his estate, the Chadwick Manor. He gave us first-class treatment in London, including a room at one of the finest hotels and including exquisite dining every evening and a private carriage at our disposal–*all at the company's expense*. Even Walt was pleasant.

Then I took Melanie and Juanito to Scotland to meet Uncle Angus and Aunt Rachael. She fell in love with my aunt and uncle, and with Scotland. The farm was as beautiful as I had remembered, and Melanie loved it. Uncle Angus had a capable friend running it on shares. I made arrangements with Uncle Angus to have a new stone-and-brick home built on a high spot overlooking the fields, with the lakes and bay beyond.

But by 1859 and 1860, the words of secession and war were growing strong in the South. Reports Melanie and I were receiving from Georgia were sobering. I recommended to both Howard and JK that they get some of their money into banks in England and other countries.

Although many high-ranking and powerful people in Mexico could see no connection between a war in the States and the well-being of Mexico, I knew better. Howard, the politician in the family, carefully explained to me before I returned to Mexico that the United States had adopted what was known as the Monroe Doctrine, instituted by President Monroe. Although seemingly innocuous, he explained that the doctrine warned European powers not to again attempt colonization in the Americas, under threat of military intervention by the United States. And the United States was becoming a power player on the world stage. A war between the northern states and the South would open the door to European expansion and colonization again in the Americas and this was something that would not be tolerated.

Chapter 28

Back in Harshaw – Still a Mission to Accomplish

"Jack. Jack. *Jack*, can you hear me?"

It sounded like Preacher Mike's voice. I opened my eyes. It was Preacher Mike Sullivan looking down at me, so I nodded.

"Finally, Jack! We were worried you weren't going to come back to us. Can you drink something?"

My poor head was throbbing and I couldn't focus my eyes. I was cold and lying in a bed. Finally I asked, "Do you have some coffee?"

"Sure," Mike responded.

The big man gave me a cup, holding me up so I wouldn't choke or spill it.

"It's Christmas day! Merry Christmas, Jack," Mike said happily, obviously trying to boost my spirits.

What the hell had happened? Why was I here?

Pieces of my memory started coming back. *It was my old nemesis, Jenkins, again.* I realized that I had fallen off the wagon again and gotten drunk.

"What happened? How did I get here?" I meekly asked Preacher Mike.

"Oh, three days ago you were down at the Durazno Bar. When you went out back to take a leak, someone hit you over the head and robbed you. Too bad I wasn't there to help you this time. You have been lying here unconscious ever since."

He patted my hand. "Molly Henderson and Padre de la Riva have been by several times a day to visit you. Molly brought some food over, but you were out cold, so I ate most of it. But there is still some soup. Here, I'll fix it for you."

I started to get out from under the covers and discovered that I was *naked.* More than that, I realized I was a *wrinkled, weak old man* with a terrible rolling headache.

"Mike, do you have my clothes?"

"Sure, Jack. Molly washed them. They are hanging on the back of the chair."

Mike set a bowl of hot soup on the table while I fumbled around getting dressed.

"What time is it?"

"Oh, it's about 10:30–10:30 in the morning." Mike chuckled.

It wasn't very funny. Barefooted, I took several steps on the cold dirt floor over to the table, spilling some hot coffee on my foot in the process. It burned. I sat on the chair and stared at the bowl of hot soup.

"Three days, huh? My damned head sure hurts."

Picking up the spoon, I tried to sip some hot chicken soup while Mike poured me some more coffee.

Smiling, Mike worked around the stove, then casually commented, "Molly said to get word to her when you woke up. She would bring over some Christmas dinner for you."

"That was nice of her," I said hoarsely.

"And, let's see, what else should you know? Everything has been pretty quiet here in town since you got whacked on the head. Oh yes, there was *a rich, old Mexican* who came into town looking for you. He came the day after you were hurt. He came over here to the shop to see you."

My head came up. "Who was he? Rich, you say. What did he look like?"

"The guy had a gimpy leg. He walked with a cane and, yes, he looked rich. He had an expensive rented wagon, picked it up in Nogales, he said. And no, I don't know his name. He said to give you this when you woke up. He said you would know who he was."

My head throbbed. Mike handed me a folded paper with something in it. I opened it up, and a small gold nugget fell onto the table. I fumbled for my glasses and examined it. There was a hole through the nugget and a small initial stamped on it. *The initial was X!* It was the nugget I had given to Xinata, my little Aztec princess and my Number Two–many, many years ago.

A shiver ran down my back.

Mike continued our one-sided conversation. "Oh, Jack, you talked quite a bit when you were unconscious. *By the way, who is Melanie? And who is Xinata?* And while I'm at it, who was the *traitor* you called out to?"

Another chill ran down my back as I stared at the little gold nugget. I said nothing, as memories poured through my mind.

My work here in the *Patagonia Mountains* was not finished.

Book II

THE PROSPECTOR'S SECRET –

At The Sabre's Edge

(to be published fall, 2010)

List of Characters

1. Anderson, Senator J. P. Anderson–powerful senator from South Carolina, involved with acquiring the southern railroad route to California
2. Arista, President Mariano Arista–President of Mexico, but under the political power of General Santa Ana
3. Ashburn, Pete Ashburn–owner of Ashburn's livery stable in Harshaw, wife, Nancy
4. Bartholomew–Jack's faithful mule
5. Becker, Mr. & Mrs. Becker–ranchers in San Rafael Valley murdered along with their six year old daughter by "Indians," really Texas bandits
6. Beltrán, Captain Jesus Beltrán–captain of *La Doncella Pechisima* (The well endowed Maiden), the old Mexican navy ship Captain Marco Vásquez and Jack take north to the port of Guaymas
7. Best, Dr. Best–dentist and man who witnessed Jack's father's death in Boston, a good man
8. Brickwood, John Brickwood–Durazno Bar owner
9. Camacho, Lieutenant Camacho–military man reporting to Colonel Trujillo at the Hermosillo Garrison
10. Campos, Sergeant Juan Campos–one of Colonel Trujillo's men in Sonora, Mexico
11. Chadwick, Sir Edward Chadwick–President of The New Wales Equipment and Mining Company, Ltd. Jack's big boss.

12. Chapman, Bolton Chapman–bully and base man in Boston who killed Jack's father in an unfair duel
13. Chapman, Jack Chapman–owner of the Humboldt Mine
14. Contreras, Corporal Tiburcio Contreras from Pachuca–27 year-old carriage driver for Marco and Jack between Mexico City and Tepic on their trip north
15. Davis, Governor Davis–powerful and wealthy plantation owner from Atlanta, Georgia, Howard's father-in-law, cousin to President Jeff Davis
16. Davis, Virginia Anne Davis–lady friend and later wife of Howard Taylor, daughter of a wealthy banker and ex-Governor of Georgia, niece of the Mexican War hero and Senator from Mississippi, a certain *Colonel Jeff Davis*
17. De la Riva, Padre Lorenzo de la Riva–good friend of Jack's in Harshaw
18. Del, Tom & Sam–three Texas killers who murdered the Becker rancher family, captured in Harshaw by Molly's Maulers
19. Delgado, José Delgado–carriage driver from Veracruz to Mexico City, later manager of Jack's warehouse facilities in Veracruz
20. Dominguez, Sergeant Dominguez–one of Trujullo's men out of the Hermosillo Garrison; a good man and soldier who saved Chico's life
21. Elías, Carmen Elías–Doña Hortencia Elías' crippled daughter.
22. Elías, Señora Hortencia Elías (Doña Hortencia or Tencia)–widow of Señor Juan Alberto Elías de Salazar and owner of the Elías Hacienda in Mexico City, where Jack and his parents stayed when he was a child; a nice lady and dear friend, also relative to General Santa Ana through her dead husband
23. Farrell, Mr. James Farrell–Harshaw merchant and businessman
24. Felipe–leather tradesman in Hermosillo, did work for Jack, Captain Vásquez and the military garrison
25. Fontes, Captain Fontes–Commander of the Tucson Presidio
26. Franklin, Brigadier General George C. Franklin–West Point graduate and visitor to the Fields of Shannon Plantation banquet in fall of 1852, also fought with General Zachary Taylor in Mexican War

27. Gallagher, Donald Gallagher–eldest son of family owning the Stratford Plantation, married Mary Helen Kerns
28. Garcia, Ernesto Garcia–foreman Jack hired to do work at *La Hacienda Hermosa* in Mexico City
29. Gentry, Dr. Gentry–Kerns family doctor in Savannah
30. Hammond, Mr. & Mrs. Hammond–rich plantation owners from South Carolina
31. Harrison, Dorsey Harrison–a broken-down doctor in Harshaw, also a veteran of the Civil War on both sides and an unexpected man out of Jack's past
32. Henderson, Molly Henderson–a widow and café owner in Harshaw, major person in story
33. Herrera, President José Herrera–previous president of Mexico, headed the Mexican government during the *War with the U.S.*
34. Jenkins, Randolph P. Jenkins–*Dolpho*, a slave trader Jack met in Savannah and disliked immediately; Jack's nemesis
35. Johnson–Sheriff Johnson of Pima County
36. Juanito, Juan or Johnny–Jack's son out of wedlock with Xinata (Zeenata), a beautiful Aztec girl
37. Juárez, Juez Juárez–judge, conducted marriage for Jack & Melanie; later President of Mexico
38. Kearny, Walter M. Kearny–Jack's immediate boss in The New Wales Equipment and Mining Company Ltd., was General Manager of the New Exploration and Business Division of the company in Manchester, England
39. Kerns, Constance Grace Kerns–Melanie's materialistic mother
40. Kerns, JK (James Kenny) Kerns–neighbor to Howard, heir to The Fields of Shannon plantation, brother to Jack's wife, Melanie Ellen
41. Kerns, Mary Helen Kerns–Melanie Ellen Kerns' older sister, married to a rich neighbor plantation owner's son, Donald Gallagher
42. Kruger, Deputy B. K. Kruger–big German hooligan in Harshaw
43. Lilly–Kerns family slave girl and chaperone to Melanie and Jack, later released to Melanie and went with her to Mexico
44. Lucero, Juez Lucero–high court judge in Mexico City

45. Maria de la Cruz–Doña Elías' attractive relative
46. Martinez, Colonel Ricardo Martinez–one of the commanders at the large Presidio in Guadalajara; gave advice to Captain Vásquez and Jack about the dangerous Pimeria Alta (Sonora) region of Mexico, curious about their mission
47. Martinez, Juan Martinez–miner who worked for Jack Chapman in Harshaw, Arizona Territory (A.T.)
48. Maytorena, Governor Maytorena–Governor of Sonora; owner of the fine horses that were killed by *sharks* in the bay at Guaymas
49. McIntyre, Alice McIntyre–Jack's baby sister who died in Venezuela of snakebite
50. McIntyre, Alice McIntyre–Jack's father's sister who died as a child in Scotland
51. McIntyre, Elizabeth (Lizzie) May Taylor McIntyre–Jack's mother and daughter of a plantation owner
52. McIntyre, John Kenneth McIntyre–Jack' father, a Scottish mining engineer who worked for The New Wales Equipment and Mining Company Ltd., married Lizzie May Taylor, daughter of a Georgia plantation owner, traveled in Mexico, Central and South America; killed in Boston duel with ruffian Bolton Chapman
53. McIntyre, John Taylor McIntyre–central character of the story, called Jack, Mack and Chu Chu in Mexico, and Jack McAllister in Harshaw, A.T.
54. McIntyre, Juanito–Jack's son by his Aztec lover–Xinata, born February 24, 1854
55. McIntyre, Melanie Ellen Kerns McIntyre–Jack's wife and love of his life
56. McIntyre, Uncle Angus and Aunt Rachael McIntyre–Jack's aunt and uncle in Scotland
57. McKinney, Mary McKinney–fickle girlfriend of Jack's while at the University in Scotland
58. Montigo–Howard's spirited, sorrel carriage horse
59. Moreno, Administrator Moreno–nervous head staff man to Governor Maytorena, Governor of Sonora

60. Pacheco, General Ramón Pacheco–chief military commander of northern Mexico, out of Chihuahua, Chihuahua
61. Pacheco, Lieutenant Pacheco–nephew to General Pacheco and one of Col. Trujillo's traitorous officers
62. Paco–a soldier, also Col. Trujillo's private cook
63. Pepe–Felipe, a gardener and loyal worker at the Elías Hacienda and later at La Hacienda Hermosa
64. Perkins, Franklin J. Perkins–engineer working for the American Steam Engine Company in Allentown Pennsylvania; an inventor and good friend of Jack's
65. Quintero, Lino, *El Pirata* (The Pirate)–a bad crewmember on Captain Beltrán's ship
66. Ribeiro, Rafael Ribeiro–a Portuguese ship captain who sailed the ship taking Jack back to Veracruz in 1852
67. Riva, Padre Lorenzo de la Riva–ostensibly a Mexican priest in Harshaw, Arizona Territory, new friend of Jack's, a major character in story
68. Salazar, Francisco Salazar–kindly farmer who took in Col. Trujillo when he was sick
69. Sáldate Juan Sáldate–retired sergeant, prospector guide for Chu Chu into the Pimeria Alta
70. Santa Ana, General Antonio Lopez de Santa Ana–ex-president of Mexico; for years the most powerful man in Mexico, very interesting and dangerous man, Jack's friend and partner in a large, national business
71. Sauceda, Padre Sauceda–Padre Silva's predecessor at Cocospera Mission in Sonora
72. Serrano, Admiral Serrano–Captain Beltrán's boss in Acapulco
73. Shields, Congressman Colonel Charles D. Shields–visitor to the Taylor Plantation and attendee at the Field of Shannon Plantation banquet in September of 1852
74. Silva, Padre Silva–Priest at Cocospera Mission
75. Sorrells, Ty Sorrells–deputy sheriff in Harshaw

76. Springer, Captain William Springer–Will Springer, captain in U.S. Army, 1844 graduate from West Point, general during Civil War; a good friend of Jack's
77. Styles, Brigadier General Humphrey Styles–in U.S. Army, boss of Captain William Springer, had connections in Mexico resulting from Mexican War
78. Sullivan, Preacher Michael Sullivan–friend of Jack's in Harshaw, major person in story
79. Swartz, Benjamin Swartz–#1 man at the Bank of Mexico
80. Sykes, Vice Admiral Sir Geoffrey Sykes–British Admiralty, friend of Brigadier General Humphrey Styles; also had connection with something going on in Mexico
81. Taylor, Matilda May & Constance Grace–Taylor cousins visiting the Taylor Plantation in 1852
82. Taylor, Uncle Will–William Howard Taylor II, Jack's mother's brother, owner of the Taylor Plantation in Savannah
83. Taylor, William Howard Taylor III–cousin and close friend of Jack McIntyre, son of William Howard Taylor II; second cousin to the famous Zachary Taylor of Mexican War fame and later short time president of the U.S. (died in office)
84. Trujillo, Chico–Colonel Trujillo's retarded son, called *El Soldadito* (The Little Soldier)
85. Trujillo, Colonel Alejandro Trujillo–tough, powerful military commander of Hermosillo Garrison and Sonora military commander
86. Trujillo, Isabella and Juan–Colonel Trujillo's children from his second wife
87. Trujillo, Señora Zonia Trujillo–Trujillo's wife; Indian girl, known as *La Bruja* (The Witch) by the Opata Indians, who kicked her out of their tribe because of her *supernatural* powers
88. Tuti–captive Apache woman
89. Valdez, Bishop Valdez–Catholic Bishop of Mexico City
90. Vásquez, Captain Marco Vásquez–ambitious officer in Mexican army; nephew to General Santa Ana and related to the Elías family; major character in the story

91. Villarreal, Salvador Villarreal–company contact in Mexico City, #2 man at the Bank of Mexico in Mexico City, became a good and loyal friend to Jack
92. Von Koffland, Mr. Von Koffland–an owner and partner in the Dutch shipping company, (Rotterdam International Transport Company), which JK Kerns and his family bought into
93. Von Voorberg, Captain Clouse Von Voorberg, (Captain Vo Vo)–Dutch captain of the *Flying Duchess* clipper ship working for the Rotterdam International Transport Company
94. Walters, Mr. Walters–another Boston man who witnessed Jack's father's death
95. Watkins, Samuel Paul Watkins–assayer in Harshaw who bought Jack's *color* (gold pannings)
96. Xinata (Zeenata)–beautiful young Aztec girl working at the Elías Hacienda in Mexico City, Jack's short-time lover and mother of his son, Juanito

LaVergne, TN USA
12 January 2011
212115LV00005B/15/P